W9-BYS-809

DISCARD

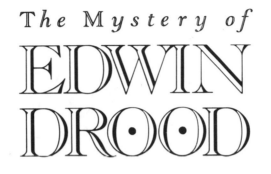

The Mystery of
EDWIN
DROOD

Sedate and Clerical

The Mystery of

EDWIN DROOD

CHARLES DICKENS

concluded by

LEON GARFIELD

introduced by

EDWARD BLISHEN

illustrated by

ANTONY MAITLAND

PANTHEON BOOKS, NEW YORK

The Mystery of Edwin Drood by Charles Dickens
First published 1870

A completion of *The Mystery of Edwin Drood*
First published 1980 by André Deutsch Limited,
105 Great Russell Street London W.C.1.
Copyright © 1980 by Leon Garfield
Illustrations Copyright © 1980 by Antony Maitland
Introduction Copyright © 1980 by Edward Blishen

Library of Congress Cataloging in Publication Data

Dickens, Charles, 1812–1870.
The mystery of Edwin Drood.

I. Garfield, Leon.   II. Title.
PR4564.A2G3   1981   823'.8   80-8850
ISBN 0-394-51918-3

Manufactured in the United States of America
First American Edition

I am greatly indebted to Grace Hogarth whose idea this was and who gave constant encouragement; to André Deutsch for his patience; and most of all to Russell Hoban who, with characteristic generosity provided me with a most shrewd and penetrating essay that was of the utmost value.

Contents

Introduction

I

WHEN Dickens died on June 9, 1870 — of an explosion of infirmities that would long before have killed a man of less remarkable spirit — he had completed six of the twelve monthly parts of *The Mystery of Edwin Drood*. He left behind, therefore, a half-novel: a matter apparently of murder, and so apparently of a murderer. But he failed to leave any statement of his intentions for the second half of the story. Strong hints had been given to this person or that (chiefly his friend and biographer, John Forster, and his illustrator, Luke Fildes): but there were no notes to be found, no forward plans. (He had offered Queen Victoria rather more than hints, to be imparted at the slightest show of impatient royal interest: but she was obviously, and exasperatingly, content to wait for the monthly parts as they came out). As a consequence, this great stump of a novel, Dickens' fifteenth, has been for more than a century the subject of fascinated and sometimes irritable discussion. There have been several hundred studies of the puzzle, from works expressing utter confidence ('The Great Mystery Solved', by Gillian Vase, 1878) to works expressing utter despair ('The Drood Mystery Insoluble', by Sir J. C. Squire, 1919). There have also been a fair number of attempts to supply the missing half of the story.

The problem lies partly in the fact that, as most agree, the mystery is less than totally mysterious. That's to say, the element of the whodunnit is very small, if it exists at all. Every clue points to the murderer of Edwin Drood. If it is not Jasper, the respectable Choir Master who is also the disreputable opium addict (and surely one of the most improbable youngsters in fiction — it is always astonishing to remind oneself that he is only six-and-twenty), then we must say that Dickens was in a fix: and that to get out of that fix in the remaining half dozen instalments would have required startling narrative acrobatics.

One of the few who have found Jasper innocent was the actor, Felix Aylmer, an indefatigable inquirer into the corners of Dickens' life and work, who proposed (in *The Drood Case*, 1964) that Jasper was truly Edwin Drood's friend and champion, but that a mysterious Egyptian appeared on the scene who, having threatened the lives of both men, then actually made an attempt on them: and that this was misunderstood by Edwin, who thought himself under attack from Jasper, and so disappeared. Behind the whole farrago (though to be fair, it's a keenly argued farrago) lay an old feud, and the code that governs such feuds in Islamic families.

Felix Aylmer was clearly moved by the feeling expressed by one student of the story (William Bleifuss, 'The Re-examination of Edwin Drood', 1954) that if the climax showed that the murder had been carried out exactly as Dickens had hinted, then it would have become an anti-climax. Perhaps:

11 *Edwin Drood* was the usual novel about murder. But, as Una Pope-Hennessy has said: 'If this were an ordinary murder story we should think the number of clues offered absurd. There is almost nothing for us to find out.'

The other area in which a very small minority have supposed that all is not as it seems to be, in Dickens' apparently very careful disposition of clues, is the actual, essential matter of there being, or not being, any murder at all. Again there has been anxiety, in some quarters, to extract the fullest possible value from the title. 'If Edwin Drood is dead,' as G. K. Chesterton observed, 'there is not much mystery about him.' So perhaps he isn't dead, after all. It happened, come to that, in the novel before this one: John Harmon, in *Our Mutual Friend*, is confidently believed to be dead, but turns out to be very much alive. Philip Hobsbaum, who has perhaps read more of what he calls Droodiana than anyone else, says the view that Edwin Drood is alive after all is found most often in adaptations and completions of the story for stage or screen. It provides an obvious *coup de théâtre*.

Some have attempted to satisfy at a blow two of the questions left unanswered by Dickens, with the supposal that the mysterious Datchery (about whom Dickens seems either to be indicating that he is disguised or strongly suggesting that he is not) is really Edwin Drood. In one solution Drood is not only alive but, in the end, is married to Rosa. The absence of seriousness towards her, on his part, and absence of a suitable degree of love towards him, on hers, have been tested by the whole appalling affair, and they have become aware of their true feeling for each other. But the fact is that Dickens could have contrived such a climax only by making emotional nonsense of the passages in which, in his tenderest and most irreversible fashion, he has made obvious the love of Tartar for Rosa, and hers for him.

As we have seen, most of the Droodists (again, this word is a useful invention of Philip Hobsbaum's) agree that Jasper is the murderer. They are left with the question of his motive. Some are straightforward about this: he loved Rosa, and that was enough. (Imagine a novel by Dickens as simple as this!) There are the sentimentalists, as I think they must be called, who believe the motive was a desire to save Rosa from a miserable match (which might be, but oh so feebly, an alternative explanation to the obvious one of Jasper's horror on learning that the engagement had been broken off). It has been supposed, at a low level of supposition, that Jasper was after the Drood fortune. In a peculiarly complex suggestion, he is not Jasper at all, but his own half-brother, who is altogether a half-creature, being a Eurasian: he has taken Jasper's place, a substitution made possible because . . . Mind and imagination boggle together. Perhaps the limpest suggestion as to motive was the most horribly obvious: that Jasper committed the murder whilst temporarily insane, as a result of drug-taking.

The most cogent, perhaps, of all these views of Jasper sees him as a Thug — a member of the Indian religious organisation of murderers and robbers that had been put down more than a quarter of a century before *Edwin Drood* was written. Dickens had serialised an account of this sect in his magazine, *All the Year Round*: where he had also serialised his friend Wilkie Collins' *The Moonstone* – largely a matter of Indians, drugs and violence, with religious roots. Dickens had made it clear that he thought he could improve on his friend's narrative method, given similar materials. Murder as carried out by a Thug involved the use of a scarf . . . and it is abundantly clear from hints in the text, and even larger hints outside it, that Edwin Drood was slain by strangling, and that the strangler used a scarf — Jasper's.

The outstanding mystery, these others aside, lies in the identity of Dick Datchery. He has been taken to be, quite obviously, Drood himself: and by many, Helena Landless — the grounds for this supposal lying in her having been described as running away from home, during her desperate childhood in Ceylon, dressed as a boy. The folklorist Andrew Lang thought Datchery might have been Helena's brother, Neville. A strong case has been made for his being Grewgious, Rosa's guardian, who has the distinction of being the only lawyer in Dickens' fiction with a clean bill of moral health: just as Crisparkle is the only clergyman, excepting one, ever to command the author's respect.

Kate Perugini, Dickens' daughter, believed that Datchery was Bazzard, Grewgious's clerk, on the grounds that he was interested in dramatics, and so might have been at home in a wig (though it must be said that Datchery seemed curiously not at home in his). Others have seen in Datchery some floating member of the Drood family: a brother-in-law (this is most elaborate) of Crisparkle's mother: and, most inventively, Edwin Drood's real guardian, Jasper being only an unsatisfactory understudy in that role.

II

Essays discussing the way the story of *Edwin Drood* might have developed, and actual attempts at completing the tale, cover an even wider range of surmises than has been glanced at here. It is interesting, against such a background of often very free guesswork, to remind ourselves of what is known of Dickens' intentions. We return to those strong hints referred to earlier. The fullest of them were confided to Forster, who was told of the germ of the tale in a letter written by Dickens eleven months before his death. 'What should you think,' he was asked, 'of a story beginning in this way? — Two people, boy and girl, or very young, going apart from one another, pledged to be married after many years — at the end of the book. The interest to arise out of the tracing of their separate ways, and the impossibility of telling what will be done with that impending fate.' A few weeks later he had moved on: 'I laid aside that fancy I told you of, and have a very curious and new idea for my new story. Not a communicable idea (or the interest of the book would be gone), but a very strong one, though difficult to work.' But if not communicated by letter, and never entirely revealed, the story was still made known to Forster in not altogether cloudy outline: it 'was to be that of the murder of a nephew by his uncle; the originality of which was to consist in the review of the murderer's career by himself at the close, when its temptations were to be dwelt upon as if, not the culprit, but some other man, were the tempted. The last chapters were to be written in the condemned cell, to which his wickedness, all elaborately elicited from him as if told of another, had brought him. Discovery by the

murderer of the utter needlessness of the murder for its object, was to
follow hard upon the commission of the deed; but all discovery of the
murderer was to be baffled till towards the close, when, by means of a gold
ring which had resisted the corrosive effects of the lime into which he had
thrown the body, not only the person murdered was to be identified but the
locality of the crime and the man who committed it. So much was told to
me before any of the book was written; and it will be recollected that the
ring, taken by Drood to be given to his betrothed only if their engagement
went on, was brought away with him from their last interview. Rosa was to
marry Tartar, and Crisparkle the sister of Landless, who was himself, I
think, to have perished in assisting Tartar finally to unmask and seize the
murderer.'

Other evidence comes from the cover of the monthly parts, which carried
the usual design — much like the opening credits in a certain kind of film,
giving promise of the character and drift of the tale to come. What Luke
Fildes drew for *Edwin Drood*, acting on Dickens' instructions, cannot be
taken as hard-and-fast evidence of anything, since Dickens had to give these
instructions at a time when the writing had barely begun. Other cover
designs of his had turned out to be, forgivably, inconsistent with the
finished story. What is shown in the case of *Edwin Drood* is a double
movement of events, one on each side of the title, with symbolic figures
half-hidden in curtains at the top that indicate that one line of ascent is that
of Good, the other that of Evil. The first leads clearly to Rosa's marriage in
the cathedral, though we can't make out who the bridegroom is: the ascent,
by way of a hand being passionately kissed and a woman peering at a poster
headed LOST, owes its source to the fumes from Princess Puffer's pipe —
oddly, since she belongs plainly to the strand of evil in the story. On the
other side Jasper seems to be looking across bitterly at the bridal pair, while
up a spiral staircase pursuers come, pointing accusingly towards him (in a
draft version of the design the pursuers were actually policemen): the source
of the whole movement here being the fumes from a pipe being smoked by
a Chinaman — presumably the opium-seller who is the Princess's rival. At
bottom centre is a tableau that remains a puzzle: a young man, much like the
bridegroom and wearing light clothes expressive of his being of the Good,
is confronted by a man, holding a lantern, in the dark clothes of the Evil.

To these clues, two others may be added: that when out walking with his
elder son Charles, Dickens said very clearly that Jasper had killed Drood;
and that he had already proposed taking Luke Fildes to see the inside of
Maidstone jail — which suggests that Forster was not mistaken in
understanding that the novel would have its climax in the condemned cell.

III

That, then, is a brief history of the attempts to guess the direction *Edwin
Drood* might have taken, and a resumé of the fairly meagre — but, it could
be argued, also fairly suggestive — evidence which such conjecture ought to
take into account.

Between all this, sometimes rather silly, detective work and the actual attempt to complete the novel there is an obvious gulf. There are two problems for the *Drood*-completer. The first is simply one of style. Most of these attempts have tripped at the very start over that huge obstacle which is Dickens' manner . . . a fabulously rich complexity of language and spirit. Perhaps never more than in *Edwin Drood* did Dickens demonstrate that, when it comes to great writing, narrative and voice are inextricable. Here is narrative at its most carefully organised: here is the voice at its most splendid, in one sense at least, since it had to be what it *freely* was, given any object whatever to contemplate, together with what it *fixedly* must be, or what it must be within strict limits, in relation to obligatory details of intricate story-telling.

A characteristic example of the downfall of one continuator (George Sampson's curious word): someone who made his attempt in 1914 and whose best stroke was to mask himself with initials: W.E.C. In his version, Datchery, without his wig and walking 'with the elastic step of a man on the right side of thirty years of age,' has 'sauntered forth into the fresh air of a lovely summer's day', turning the mystery over in what emerges as a mind rather like that of an average late-Victorian contributor to *Punch*. He encounters a 'ruddy-faced plough boy' and asks him if there is an inn nearby.

> The boy, whose mouth was full to its utmost capacity, attempted to thrust the contents to one side and immediately something resembling half of a small, red apple appeared on the outside of his cheek.
>
> 'Huck, wuck, wuck,' he answered, jerking his thumb over his left shoulder.
>
> Mr Datchery regretted that Chinese was a language of which he had not the smallest knowledge. The boy let a portion of the contents of his cheek back into the working machinery of his mouth and recommenced chewing.
>
> Mr Datchery, watching the contour of the red-apple-like cheek grow perceptibly flatter, repeated his question.
>
> 'Huck, wuck, arn rooad,' began the boy, but becoming sensible after a gulp that a partial vacancy had occurred in his mouth he again raised the pork to his lips . . .

And so on. It reminds us that if Dickens is facetious, he is never feebly facetious: and that his jocosity always rests on an original vision of the thing he's joking about. It is the nature of the man's greatness: the constant originality of his viewpoint. He is barely capable of seeing things in a stale manner. He is always ready to bounce, as W.E.C. is bouncing: but it is never bouncing on the spot. When he lingers, he has the supreme gift of making his lingering seem like forward movement. He has in mind, always, the effect he wishes to have on the reader at this moment, part of the effect he wishes to have over the whole sweep of the story: and, if you detach yourself, you feel Dickens' concern for such things at work on you as the reader. Anyone who is to convince us that he is, with any sort of plausibility, completing *Edwin Drood* must give us this sensation to which Dickens has accustomed us, of being, as it were, adventurously safe in his storyteller's hands. It is, indeed, a sensation, and it must be there.

So we need a 'continuator' with an original gift for language and storytelling not hopelessly unlike that of Dickens himself. But he must also be able to put himself — or to make the most sensitive attempt possible to put himself — into Dickens' shoes, c.1869–70. 'All too few of these mystery solvers,' Angus Wilson has justly thundered, 'are concerned with the fact that the mystery was invented by Dickens and not by themselves.' All too many of them, I think it might be added, have been concerned with the book as a puzzle, as 'an ordinary murder story'. This it quite plainly is not. It would be foolish to argue that the mysterious detail of the story is quite unimportant. Dickens wasn't perhaps the best plot-maker in the world: but of course it mattered that he offered his readers the exquisite pleasure of mystification with his enigmatic Datchery, his teasing keys and gold rings and ambiguous heaps of lime. Nevertheless, it must be true that, as his daughter Kate Perugini wrote thirty-six years after his death: 'Greatly as he was interested in the intricacies of that tangled skein, the information that he gave to Mr. Forster, from whom he had withheld nothing for thirty years, certainly points to the fact that he was quite as deeply fascinated and absorbed in the study of the criminal Jasper, as in the dark and sinister crime that has given the book its title.'

It's that second problem that I believe the *Drood*-completer is faced with: that of thinking himself, and especially in relation to the fascination exerted on Dickens by Jasper, into the mind of that great dying man, a century ago. It is so important, this *thinking* as the background to the writing of a continuation, that I believe it may be worthwhile for me to say, briefly, what I know was in Leon Garfield's own mind as he set to work. We talked a great deal about *Edwin Drood*, and about Jasper in particular. Was he really in his twenties? That curious unconvincingness of his being so young made one look hard at him, in terms of what one knew about Dickens' own condition at the time. Since 1858 he'd been in the position of having a mistress, the young actress Ellen Lawless Ternan, but being unable even to hint publicly at this plain central fact of his existence. It's difficult enough to calculate the effect on an ordinary Victorian of the refusal of the age to acknowledge the full truth of what it is to be human: what can have been the effect on a Victorian as deeply sensitive and aware as Dickens, and as professionally given to the exploration of human nature? The strain between public image and private reality must have been intolerable to him. Add to this that he was an ageing man — much older, physically, than his fifty-eight years: a shattered person, who needed a stick to walk with, whose hand went black during his last public readings from his work, who could not read the left-hand side of the names on shop fronts. He was an old, broken man, one of the most public men in England whose private life had to be a terrible secret. He was the broken, elderly lover of a very much younger woman . . .

If he was 'deeply fascinated and absorbed in the study of the criminal Jasper', a man appallingly divided, whose dreadful final relief must come from having one half of himself condemned by the other half — and if he created a Jasper who, six-and-twenty according to the text, seems an infinitely older creature — are these facts of his fiction, so to speak, not most likely linked to his own condition, in real life?

'The divided man,' I remember Leon Garfield saying often in our discussions, 'must betray himself.'

Jasper, clearly, has problems — of passion, appetite, balked desire — that he cannot confess to because the society in which he lives (which is the society in which his creator lives, and the more intensely so because Cloisterham is the Rochester of his youth, of *Pickwick Papers*: the early jovial, laced with Gothic, having become the late sinister, Gothic triumphant) will not acknowledge the existence of those problems. He is subject to the Dean, as Dickens was subject to the British public — and for the Dean there can be only one response when human reality breaks through the smoothness of appearances and pretences: the evidence must be moved outside the sacred edifice.

In his notes for the first monthly number of *Edwin Drood* Dickens wrote: 'Touch the key note: "When the wicked man — ".' The phrase is from Ezekiel 18:27: 'Again, when the wicked man turneth away from his wickedness that he hath committed and doeth that which is lawful and right, he shall save his soul alive.'

I have three more memories of my discussions of *Edwin Drood* with Leon Garfield. The first was his interest in those curtains which frame the design for the cover of the monthly parts. Definitely a theatrical frontispiece, he thought: they seemed quite certainly to be proscenium curtains. The second was a remark at once light-hearted and deeply felt. 'I wish Dickens had finished *Drood*,' said this latest *Drood*-completer, 'and left others to begin it.' And the last memory is of his saying that, *had* Dickens finished the novel, it might have been impossible as well as unnecessary for Robert Louis Stevenson to write, sixteen years after Dickens' death, another great story reflecting the increasingly unbearable nature of Victorian dividedness: *Dr. Jekyll and Mr. Hyde.*

— *Edward Blishen*

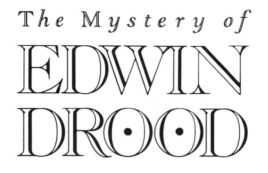

The Mystery of

EDWIN DROOD

The Dawn

AN ancient English Cathedral Tower? How can the ancient English Cathedral tower be here! The well-known massive gray square tower of its old Cathedral? How can that be here! There is no spike of rusty iron in the air, between the eye and it, from any point of the real prospect. What is the spike that intervenes, and who has set it up? Maybe it is set up by the Sultan's orders for the impaling of a horde of Turkish robbers, one by one. It is so, for cymbals clash, and the Sultan goes by to his palace in long procession. Ten thousand scimitars flash in the sunlight, and thrice ten thousand dancing-girls strew flowers. Then, follow white elephants caparisoned in countless gorgeous colours, and infinite in number and attendants. Still the Cathedral Tower rises in the background, where it cannot be, and still no writhing figure is on the grim spike. Stay! Is the spike so low a thing as the rusty spike on the top of a post of an old bedstead that has tumbled all awry? Some vague period of drowsy laughter must be devoted to the consideration of this possibility.

Shaking from head to foot, the man whose scattered consciousness has thus fantastically pieced itself together, at length rises, supports his trembling frame upon his arms, and looks around. He is in the meanest and closest of small rooms. Through the ragged window-curtain, the light of early day steals in from a miserable court. He lies, dressed, across a large unseemly bed, upon a bedstead that has indeed given way under the weight upon it. Lying, also dressed and also across the bed, not longwise, are a Chinaman, a Lascar, and a haggard woman. The two first are in a sleep or stupor; the last is blowing at a kind of pipe, to kindle it. And as she blows, and shading it with her lean hand, concentrates its red spark of light, it serves in the dim morning as a lamp to show him what he sees of her.

'Another?' says this woman, in a querulous, rattling whisper. 'Have another?'

He looks about him, with his hand to his forehead.

'Ye've smoked as many as five since ye come in at midnight,' the woman goes on, as she chronically complains. 'Poor me, poor me, my head is so bad. Them two come in after ye. Ah, poor me, the business is slack, is slack! Few Chinamen about the Docks, and fewer Lascars, and no ships coming in, these say! Here's another ready for ye, deary. Ye'll remember like a good soul, won't ye, that the market price is dreffle high just now? More nor three shillings and sixpence for a thimbleful! And ye'll remember that nobody but me (and Jack Chinaman t'other side the court; but he can't do it as well as me) has the true secret of mixing it? Ye'll pay up accordingly, deary, won't ye?'

She blows at the pipe as she speaks, and, occasionally bubbling at it, inhales much of its contents.

"Unintelligible!"

'O me, O me, my lungs is weak, my lungs is bad! It's nearly ready for ye, deary. Ah, poor me, poor me, my poor hand shakes like to drop off! I see ye coming-to, and I ses to my poor self, "I'll have another ready for him, and he'll bear in mind the market price of opium, and pay according." O my poor head! I makes my pipes of old penny ink-bottles, ye see, deary — this is one — and I fits-in a mouthpiece, this way, and I takes my mixter out of this thimble with this little horn spoon; and so I fills, deary. Ah, my poor nerves! I got Heavens-hard drunk for sixteen year afore I took to this; but this don't hurt me, not to speak of. And it takes away the hunger as well as wittles, deary.'

She hands him the nearly-emptied pipe, and sinks back, turning over on her face.

He rises unsteadily from the bed, lays the pipe upon the hearthstone, draws back the ragged curtain, and looks with repugnance at his three companions. He notices that the woman has opium-smoked herself into a strange likeness of the Chinaman. His form of cheek, eye, and temple, and his colour, are repeated in her. Said Chinaman convulsively wrestles with one of his many Gods or Devils, perhaps, and snarls horribly. The Lascar laughs and dribbles at the mouth. The hostess is still.

'What visions can *she* have?' the waking man muses, as he turns her face towards him, and stands looking down at it. 'Visions of many butchers' shops, and public-houses, and much credit? Of an increase of hideous customers, and this horrible bedstead set upright again, and this horrible court swept clean? What can she rise to, under any quantity of opium, higher than that! — Eh?'

He bends down his ear, to listen to her mutterings.

'Unintelligible!'

As he watches the spasmodic shoots and darts that break out of her face and limbs, like fitful lightning out of a dark sky, some contagion in them seizes upon him: insomuch that he has to withdraw himself to a lean arm-chair by the hearth — placed there, perhaps, for such emergencies — and to sit in it, holding tight, until he has got the better of this unclean spirit of imitation.

Then he comes back, pounces on the Chinaman, and seizing him with both hands by the throat, turns him violently on the bed. The Chinaman clutches the aggressive hands, resists, gasps, and protests.

'What do you say?'

A watchful pause.

'Unintelligible!'

Slowly loosening his grasp as he listens to the incoherent jargon with an attentive frown, he turns to the Lascar and fairly drags him forth upon the floor. As he falls, the Lascar starts into a half-risen attitude, glares with his eyes, lashes about him fiercely with his arms, and draws a phantom knife. It then becomes apparent that the woman has taken possession of this knife, for safety's sake; for, she too starting up, and restraining and expostulating with him, the knife is visible in her dress, not in his, when they drowsily drop back, side by side.

There has been chattering and clattering enough between them, but to no purpose. When any distinct word has been flung into the air, it has had no sense or sequence. Wherefore 'unintelligible!' is again the comment of the watcher, made with some reassured nodding of his head, and a gloomy smile. He then lays certain silver money on the table, finds his hat, gropes his way down the broken stairs, gives a good morning to some rat-ridden doorkeeper, in bed in a black hutch beneath the stairs, and passes out.

That same afternoon, the massive gray square tower of an old Cathedral rises before the sight of a jaded traveller. The bells are going for daily vesper service, and he must needs attend it, one would say, from his haste to reach the open Cathedral door. The choir are getting on their sullied white robes, in a hurry, when he arrives among them, gets on his own robe, and falls into the procession filing in to service. Then, the Sacristan locks the iron-barred gates that divide the sanctuary from the chancel, and all of the procession having scuttled into their places, hide their faces; and then the intoned words, 'WHEN THE WICKED MAN — ' rise among groins of arches and beams of roof, awakening muttered thunder.

A Dean, and a Chapter Also

WHOSOEVER has observed that sedate and clerical bird, the rook, may perhaps have noticed that when he wings his way homeward towards nightfall, in a sedate and clerical company, two rooks will suddenly detach themselves from the rest, will retrace their flight for some distance, and will there poise and linger; conveying to mere men the fancy that it is of some occult importance to the body politic, that this artful couple should pretend to have renounced connection with it.

Similarly, service being over in the old Cathedral with the square tower, and the choir scuffling out again, and divers venerable persons of rook-like aspect dispersing, two of these latter retrace their steps, and walk together in the echoing Close.

Not only is the day waning, but the year. The low sun is fiery and yet cold behind the monastery ruin, and the Virginia creeper on the Cathedral wall has showered half its deep-red leaves down on the pavement. There has been rain this afternoon, and a wintry shudder goes among the little pools on the cracked, uneven flag-stones, and through the giant elm-trees as they shed a gust of tears. Their fallen leaves lie strewn thickly about. Some of these leaves, in a timid rush, seek sanctuary within the low arched Cathedral door; but two men coming out resist them, and cast them forth again with their feet; this done, one of the two locks the door with a goodly key, and the other flits away with a folio music-book.

'Mr. Jasper was that, Tope?'

'Yes, Mr. Dean.'

'He has stayed late.'

'Yes, Mr. Dean. I have stayed for him, your Reverence. He has been took a little poorly.'

'Say "taken," Tope — to the Dean,' the younger rook interposes in a low tone with this touch of correction, as who should say: 'You may offer bad grammar to the laity, or the humbler clergy, not to the Dean.'

Mr. Tope, Chief Verger and Showman, and accustomed to be high with excursion parties, declines with a silent loftiness to perceive that any suggestion has been tendered to him.

'And when and how has Mr. Jasper been taken—for, as Mr. Crisparkle has remarked, it is better to say taken — taken —' repeats the Dean; 'when and how has Mr. Jasper been Taken ——'

'Taken, sir,' Tope deferentially murmurs.

'— Poorly, Tope?'

'Why, sir, Mr. Jasper was that breathed ——'

'I wouldn't say "That breathed," Tope,' Mr. Crisparkle interposes with the same touch as before. 'Not English — to the Dean.'

'Breathed to that extent,' the Dean (not unflattered by this indirect homage) condescendingly remarks, 'would be preferable.'

'Mr. Jasper's breathing was so remarkably short' — thus discreetly does Mr. Tope work his way round the sunken rock — 'when he came in, that it distressed him mightily to get his notes out: which was perhaps the cause of his having a kind of fit on him after a little. His memory grew DAZED.' Mr. Tope, with his eyes on the Reverend Mr. Crisparkle, shoots this word out, as defying him to improve upon it: 'and a dimness and giddiness crept over him as strange as ever I saw: though he didn't seem to mind it particularly, himself. However, a little time and a little water brought him out of his DAZE.' Mr. Tope repeats the word and its emphasis, with the air of saying: 'As I *have* made a success, I'll make it again.'

'And Mr. Jasper has gone home quite himself, has he?' asked the Dean.

'Your Reverence, he has gone home quite himself. And I'm glad to see he's having his fire kindled up, for it's chilly after the wet, and the Cathedral had both a damp feel and a damp touch this afternoon, and he was very shivery.'

They all three look towards an old stone gatehouse crossing the Close, with an arched thoroughfare passing beneath it. Through its latticed window, a fire shines out upon the fast-darkening scene, involving in shadow the pendant masses of ivy and creeper covering the building's front. As the deep Cathedral-bell strikes the hour, a ripple of wind goes through these at their distance, like a ripple of the solemn sound that hums through tomb and tower, broken niche and defaced statue, in the pile close at hand.

'Is Mr. Jasper's nephew with him?' the Dean asks.

'No, sir,' replied the Verger, 'but expected. There's his own solitary shadow betwixt his two windows — the one looking this way, and the one looking down into the High Street — drawing his own curtains now.'

'Well, well,' says the Dean, with a sprightly air of breaking up the little conference, 'I hope Mr. Jasper's heart may not be too much set upon his nephew. Our affections, however laudable, in this transitory world, should never master us; we should guide them, guide them. I find I am not disagreeably reminded of my dinner, by hearing my dinner-bell. Perhaps, Mr. Crisparkle, you will, before going home, look in on Jasper?'

'Certainly, Mr. Dean. And tell him that you had the kindness to desire to know how he was?'

'Ay; do so, do so. Certainly. Wished to know how he was. By all means. Wished to know how he was.'

With a pleasant air of patronage, the Dean as nearly cocks his quaint hat as a Dean in good spirits may, and directs his comely gaiters towards the ruddy dining-room of the snug old red-brick house where he is at present, 'in residence' with Mrs. Dean and Miss Dean.

Mr. Crisparkle, Minor Canon, fair and rosy, and perpetually pitching himself head-foremost into all the deep running water in the surrounding country; Mr. Crisparkle, Minor Canon, early riser, musical, classical, cheerful, kind, good-natured, social, contented, and boy-like; Mr. Crisparkle, Minor Canon and good man, lately 'Coach' upon the chief Pagan high roads, but since promoted by a patron (grateful for a well-taught son) to his present Christian beat; betakes himself to the gatehouse, on his way home to his early tea.

'Sorry to hear from Tope that you have not been well, Jasper.'

'O, it was nothing, nothing!'

'You look a little worn.'

'Do I? O, I don't think so. What is better, I don't feel so. Tope has made too much of it, I suspect. It's his trade to make the most of everything appertaining to the Cathedral, you know.'

'I may tell the Dean — I call expressly from the Dean — that you are all right again?'

The reply, with a slight smile, is: 'Certainly; with my respects and thanks to the Dean.'

'I'm glad to hear that you expect young Drood.'

'I expect the dear fellow every moment.'

'Ah! He will do you more good than a doctor, Jasper.'

'More good than a dozen doctors. For I love him dearly, and I don't love doctors, or doctors' stuff.'

Mr. Jasper is a dark man of some six-and-twenty, with thick, lustrous, well-arranged black hair and whiskers. He looks older than he is, as dark men often do. His voice is deep and good, his face and figure are good, his manner is a little sombre. His room is a little sombre, and may have had its influence in forming his manner. It is mostly in shadow. Even when the sun shines brilliantly, it seldom touches the grand piano in the recess, or the folio music-books on the stand, or the book-shelves on the wall, or the unfinished picture of a blooming schoolgirl hanging over the chimneypiece; her flowing brown hair tied with a blue riband, and her beauty remarkable for a quite childish, almost babyish, touch of saucy discontent, comically conscious of itself. (There is not the least artistic merit in this picture, which is a mere daub; but it is clear that the painter has made it humorously — one might almost say, revengefully — like the original.)

'We shall miss you, Jasper, at the "Alternate Musical Wednesdays" to-night; but no doubt you are best at home. Good-night. God bless you! "Tell me, shep-herds, te-e-ell me; tell me-e-e, have you seen (have you seen, have you seen, have you seen) my-y-y Flo-o-ora-a pass this way!"' Melodiously good Minor Canon the Reverend Septimus Crisparkle thus delivers himself, in musical rhythm, as he withdraws his amiable face from the doorway and conveys it down-stairs.

Sounds of recognition and greeting pass between the Reverend Septimus and somebody else, at the stair-foot. Mr. Jasper listens, starts from his chair, and catches a young fellow in his arms, exclaiming:

'My dear Edwin!'

'My dear Jack! So glad to see you!'

'Get off your greatcoat, bright boy, and sit down here in your own corner. Your feet are not wet? Pull your boots off. Do pull your boots off.'

'My dear Jack, I am as dry as a bone. Don't moddley-coddley, there's a good fellow. I like anything better than being moddley-coddleyed.'

With the check upon him of being unsympathetically restrained in a genial outburst of enthusiasm, Mr. Jasper stands still, and looks on intently at the young fellow, divesting himself of his outward coat, hat, gloves, and so forth. Once for all, a look of intentness and intensity — a look of hungry, exacting, watchful, and yet devoted affection — is always, now and ever afterwards, on the Jasper face whenever the Jasper face is addressed in this direction. And whenever it is so addressed, it is never, on this occasion or on any other, dividedly addressed; it is always concentrated.

'Now I am right, and now I'll take my corner, Jack. Any dinner, Jack?'

Mr. Jasper opens a door at the upper end of the room, and discloses a small inner room pleasantly lighted and prepared, wherein a comely dame is in the act of setting dishes on table.

'What a jolly old Jack it is!' cries the young fellow, with a clap of his hands. 'Look here, Jack; tell me; whose birthday is it?'

'Not yours, I know,' Mr. Jasper answers, pausing to consider.

'Not mine, you know? No; not mine, *I* know! Pussy's!'

Fixed as the look the young fellow meets, is, there is yet in it some strange power of suddenly including the sketch over the chimneypiece.

'Pussy's, Jack! We must drink Many happy returns to her. Come, uncle; take your dutiful and sharp-set nephew in to dinner.'

As the boy (for he is little more) lays a hand on Jasper's shoulder, Jasper cordially and gaily lays a hand on *his* shoulder, and so Marseillaise-wise they go in to dinner.

'And, Lord! here's Mrs. Tope!' cries the boy. 'Lovelier than ever!'

'Never you mind me, Master Edwin,' retorts the Verger's wife; 'I can take care of myself.'

'You can't. You're much too handsome. Give me a kiss because it's Pussy's birthday.'

'I'd Pussy you, young man, if I was Pussy, as you call her,' Mrs. Tope blushingly retorts, after being saluted. 'Your uncle's too much wrapt up in you that's where it is. He makes so much of you, that it's my opinion you think you've only to call your Pussys by the dozen, to make 'em come.'

'You forget, Mrs. Tope,' Mr. Jasper interposes, taking his place at the table with a genial smile, 'and so do you, Ned, that Uncle and Nephew are words prohibited here by common consent and express agreement. For what we are going to receive His holy name be praised!'

'Done like the Dean! Witness, Edwin Drood! Please to carve, Jack, for I can't.'

This sally ushers in the dinner. Little to the present purpose, or to any purpose, is said, while it is in course of being disposed of. At length the cloth is drawn, and a dish of walnuts and a decanter of rich-coloured sherry are placed upon the table.

'I say! Tell me, Jack,' the young fellow then flows on: 'do you really and truly feel as if the mention of our relationship divided us at all? *I* don't.'

'Uncles as a rule, Ned, are so much older than their nephews,' is the reply, 'that I have that feeling instinctively.'

'As a rule! Ah, may-be! But what is a difference in age of half-a-dozen years or so? And some uncles, in large families, are even younger than their nephews. By George, I wish it was the case with us!'

'Why?'

'Because if it was, I'd take the lead with you, Jack, and be as wise as Begone, dull Care! that turned a young man gray, and Begone, dull Care! that turned an old man to clay. — Halloa, Jack! Don't drink.'

'Why not?'

'Asks why not, on Pussy's birthday, and no Happy returns proposed! Pussy, Jack, and many of 'em! Happy returns, I mean.'

Laying an affectionate and laughing touch on the boy's extended hand, as if it were at once his giddy head and his light heart, Mr. Jasper drinks the toast in silence.

'Hip, hip, hip, and nine times nine, and one to finish with, and all that, understood. Hooray, hooray, hooray! — And now, Jack, let's have a little talk about Pussy. Two pairs of nut-crackers? Pass me one, and take the other.' Crack. 'How's Pussy getting on, Jack?'

'With her music? Fairly.'

'What a dreadfully conscientious fellow you are, Jack! But *I* know, Lord bless you! Inattentive, isn't she?'

'She can learn anything, if she will.'

'*If* she will! Egad, that's it. But if she won't?'

Crack! — on Mr. Jasper's part.

'How's she looking, Jack?'

Mr. Jasper's concentrated face again includes the portrait as he returns: 'Very like your sketch indeed.'

'I *am* a little proud of it,' says the young fellow, glancing up at the sketch with complacency, and then shutting one eye, and taking a corrected prospect of it over a level bridge of nut-crackers in the air: 'Not badly hit off from memory. But I ought to have caught that expression pretty well, for I have seen it often enough.'

Crack! — on Edwin Drood's part.

Crack! — on Mr. Jasper's part.

'In point of fact,' the former resumes, after some silent dipping among his fragments of walnut with an air of pique, 'I see it whenever I go to see Pussy. If I don't find it on her face, I leave it there. — You know I do, Miss Scornful Pert. Booh!' With a twirl of the nut-crackers at the portrait.

Crack! crack! crack. Slowly, on Mr. Jasper's part.

Crack. Sharply on the part of Edwin Drood.

Silence on both sides.

'Have you lost your tongue, Jack?'

'Have you found yours, Ned?'

'No, but really; — isn't it, you know, after all ——'

Mr. Jasper lifts his dark eyebrows inquiringly.

'Isn't it unsatisfactory to be cut off from choice in such a matter? There, Jack! I tell you! If I could choose, I would choose Pussy from all the pretty girls in the world.'

'But you have not got to choose.'

'That's what I complain of. My dead and gone father and Pussy's dead and gone father must needs marry us together by anticipation. Why the — Devil, I was going to say, if it had been respectful to their memory — couldn't they leave us alone?'

'Tut, tut, dear boy,' Mr. Jasper remonstrates, in a tone of gentle deprecation.

'Tut, tut? Yes, Jack, it's all very well for *you*. *You* can take it easily. *Your* life is not laid down to scale, and lined and dotted out for you, like a surveyor's plan. *You* have no uncomfortable suspicion that you are forced upon anybody, nor has anybody an uncomfortable suspicion that she is forced upon you, or that you are forced upon her. *You* can choose for yourself. Life, for *you,* is a plum with the natural bloom on; it hasn't been over-carefully wiped off for *you* ——'

'Don't stop, dear fellow. Go on.'

'Can I anyhow have hurt your feelings, Jack?'

'How can you have hurt my feelings?'

'Good Heaven, Jack, you look frightfully ill! There's a strange film come over your eyes.'

Mr. Jasper, with a forced smile, stretches out his right hand, as if at once to disarm apprehension and gain time to get better. After a while he says faintly:

'I have been taking opium for a pain — an agony — that sometimes overcomes me. The effects of the medicine steal over me like a blight or a cloud, and pass. You see them in the act of passing; they will be gone directly. Look away from me. They will go all the sooner.'

With a scared face the younger man complies by casting his eyes downward at the ashes on the hearth. Not relaxing his own gaze on the fire, but rather strengthening it with a fierce, firm grip upon his elbow-chair, the elder sits for a few moments rigid, and then, with thick drops standing on his forehead, and a sharp catch of his breath, becomes as he was before. On his so subsiding in his chair, his nephew gently and assiduously tends him while he quite recovers. When Jasper is restored, he lays a tender hand upon his nephew's shoulder, and, in a tone of voice less troubled than the purport of his words — indeed with something of raillery or banter in it — thus addresses him:

'There is said to be a hidden skeleton in every house; but you thought there was none in mine, dear Ned.'

'Upon my life, Jack, I did think so. However, when I come to consider that even in Pussy's house — if she had one — and in mine — if I had one ——'

'You were going to say (but that I interrupted you in spite of myself) what a quiet life mine is. No whirl and uproar around me, no distracting commerce or calculation, no risk, no change of place, myself devoted to the art I pursue, my business my pleasure.'

'I really was going to say something of the kind, Jack; but you see, you, speaking of yourself, almost necessarily leave out much that I should have put in. For instance: I should have put in the foreground your being so much respected as Lay Precentor, or Lay Clerk, or whatever you call it, of this Cathedral; your enjoying the reputation of having done such wonders with the choir; your choosing your society, and holding such an independent position in this queer old place; your gift of teaching (why, even Pussy, who don't like being taught, says there never was such a Master as you are!), and your connexion.'

'Yes; I saw what you were tending to. I hate it.'

'Hate it, Jack?' (Much bewildered.)

'I hate it. The cramped monotony of my existence grinds me away by the grain. How does our service sound to you?'

'Beautiful! Quite celestial!'

'It often sounds to me quite devilish. I am so weary of it. The echoes of my own voice among the arches seem to mock me with my daily drudging round. No wretched monk who droned his life away in that gloomy place, before me, can have been more tired of it than I am. He could take for relief (and did take) to carving demons out of the stalls and seats and desks. What shall I do? Must I take to carving them out of my heart?'

'I thought you had so exactly found your niche in life, Jack,' Edwin Drood returns, astonished, bending forward in his chair to lay a sympathetic hand on Jasper's knee, and looking at him with an anxious face.

'I know you thought so. They all think so.'

'Well, I suppose they do,' says Edwin, meditating aloud. 'Pussy thinks so.'

'When did she tell you that?'

'The last time I was here. You remember when. Three months ago.'

'How did she phrase it?'

'O, she only said that she had become your pupil, and that you were made for your vocation.'

The younger man glances at the portrait. The elder sees it in him.

'Anyhow, my dear Ned,' Jasper resumes, as he shakes his head with a grave cheerfulness, 'I must subdue myself to my vocation: which is much the same thing outwardly. It's too late to find another now. This is a confidence between us.'

'It shall be sacredly preserved, Jack.'

'I have reposed it in you, because ——'

'I feel it, I assure you. Because we are fast friends, and because you love and trust me, as I love and trust you. Both hands, Jack.'

As each stands looking into the other's eyes, and as the uncle holds the nephew's hands, the uncle thus proceeds:

'You know now, don't you, that even a poor monotonous chorister and grinder of music — in his niche — may be troubled with some stray sort of ambition, aspiration, restlessness, dissatisfaction, what shall we call it?'

'Yes, dear Jack.'

'And you will remember?'

'My dear Jack, I only ask you, am I likely to forget what you have said with so much feeling?'

'Take it as a warning, then.'

In the act of having his hands released, and of moving a step back, Edwin pauses for an instant to consider the application of these last words. The instant over, he says, sensibly touched:

'I am afraid I am but a shallow, surface kind of fellow, Jack, and that my headpiece is none of the best. But I needn't say I am young; and perhaps I shall not grow worse as I grow older. At all events, I hope I have something impressible within me, which feels — deeply feels — the disinterestedness of your painfully laying your inner self bare, as a warning to me.'

Mr. Jasper's steadiness of face and figure becomes so marvellous that his breathing seems to have stopped.

'I couldn't fail to notice, Jack, that it cost you a great effort, and that you were very much moved, and very unlike your usual self. Of course I knew that you were extremely fond of me, but I really was not prepared for your, as I may say, sacrificing yourself to me in that way.'

Mr. Jasper, becoming a breathing man again without the smallest stage of transition between the two extreme states, lifts his shoulders, laughs, and waves his right arm.

'No; don't put the sentiment away, Jack; please don't; for I am very much in earnest. I have no doubt that that unhealthy state of mind which you have so powerfully described is attended with some real suffering, and is hard to bear. But let me reassure you, Jack, as to the chances of its overcoming me. I don't think I am in the way of it. In some few months less than another year, you know, I shall carry Pussy off from school as Mrs. Edwin Drood. I shall then go engineering into the East, and Pussy with me. And although we have our little tiffs now, arising out of a certain unavoidable flatness that attends our love-making, owing to its end being all settled beforehand, still I have no doubt of our getting on capitally then, when it's done and can't be helped. In short, Jack, to go back to the old song I was freely quoting at dinner (and who knows old songs better than you?), my wife shall dance, and I will sing, so merrily pass the day. Of Pussy's being beautiful there cannot be a doubt; — and when you are good besides, Little Miss Impudence,' once more apostrophising the portrait, 'I'll burn your comic likeness, and paint your music-master another.'

Mr. Jasper, with his hand to his chin, and with an expression of musing benevolence on his face, has attentively watched every animated look and gesture attending the delivery of these words. He remains in that attitude after they are spoken, as if in a kind of fascination attendant on his strong interest in the youthful spirit that he loves so well. Then he says with a quiet smile:

'You won't be warned, then?'

'No, Jack.'

'You can't be warned, then?'

'No, Jack, not by you. Besides that I don't really consider myself in danger, I don't like your putting yourself in that position.'

'Shall we go and walk in the churchyard?'

'By all means. You won't mind my slipping out of it for half a moment to the Nuns' House, and leaving a parcel there? Only gloves for Pussy; as many pairs of gloves as she is years old to-day. Rather poetical, Jack?'

Mr. Jasper, still in the same attitude, murmurs: '"Nothing half so sweet in life," Ned!'

'Here's the parcel in my greatcoat-pocket. They must be presented to-night, or the poetry is gone. It's against regulations for me to call at night, but not to leave a packet. I am ready, Jack!'

Mr. Jasper dissolves his attitude, and they go out together.

The Nuns' House

FOR sufficient reasons, which this narrative will itself unfold as it advances, a fictitious name must be bestowed upon the old Cathedral town. Let it stand in these pages as Cloisterham. It was once possibly known to the Druids by another name, and certainly to the Romans by another, and to the Saxons by another, and to the Normans by another; and a name more or less in the course of many centuries can be of little moment to its dusty chronicles.

An ancient city, Cloisterham, and no meet dwelling-place for any one with hankerings after the noisy world. A monotonous, silent city, deriving an earthy flavour throughout from its Cathedral crypt, and so abounding in vestiges of monastic graves, that the Cloisterham children grow small salad in the dust of abbots and abbesses, and make dirt-pies of nuns and friars; while every ploughman in its outlying fields renders to once puissant Lord Treasurers, Archbishops, Bishops, and such-like, the attention which the Ogre in the story-book desired to render to his unbidden visitor, and grinds their bones to make his bread.

A drowsy city, Cloisterham, whose inhabitants seem to suppose, with an inconsistency more strange than rare, that all its changes lie behind it, and that there are no more to come. A queer moral to derive from antiquity, yet older than any traceable antiquity. So silent are the streets of Cloisterham (though prone to echo on the smallest provocation), that of a summer-day the sunblinds of its shops scarce dare to flap in the south wind; while the sun-browned tramps, who pass along and stare, quicken their limp a little, that they may the sooner get beyond the confines of its oppressive respectability. This is a feat not difficult of achievement, seeing that the streets of Cloisterham city are little more than one narrow street by which you get into it and get out of it: the rest being mostly disappointing yards with pumps in them and no thoroughfare — exception made of the

Cathedral-close, and a paved Quaker settlement, in colour and general confirmation very like a Quakeress's bonnet, up in a shady corner.

In a word, a city of another and a bygone time is Cloisterham, with its hoarse Cathedral-bell, its hoarse rooks hovering about the Cathedral tower, its hoarser and less distinct rooks in the stalls far beneath. Fragments of old wall, saint's chapel, chapter-house, convent and monastery, have got incongruously or obstructively built into many of its houses and gardens, much as kindred jumbled notions have become incorporated into many of its citizens' minds. All things in it are of the past. Even its single pawnbroker takes in no pledges, nor has he for a long time, but offers vainly an unredeemed stock for sale, of which the costlier articles are dim and pale old watches apparently in a slow perspiration, tarnished sugar-tongs with ineffectual legs, and odd volumes of dismal books. The most abundant and the most agreeable evidences of progressing life in Cloisterham are the evidences of vegetable life in many gardens; even its drooping and despondent little theatre has its poor strip of garden, receiving the foul fiend, when he ducks from its stage into the infernal regions, among scarlet-beans or oyster-shells, according to the season of the year.

In the midst of Cloisterham stands the Nuns' House: a venerable brick edifice, whose present appellation is doubtless derived from the legend of its conventual uses. On the trim gate enclosing its old courtyard is a resplendent brass plate flashing forth the legend: 'Seminary for Young Ladies. Miss Twinkleton.' The house-front is so old and worn, and the brass plate is so shining and staring, that the general result has reminded imaginative strangers of a battered old beau with a large modern eye-glass stuck in his blind eye.

Whether the nuns of yore, being of a submissive rather than a stiff-necked generation, habitually bent their contemplative heads to avoid collision with the beams in the low ceilings of the many chambers of their House; whether they sat in its long low windows telling their beads for their mortification, instead of making necklaces of them for their adornment; whether they were ever walled up alive in odd angles and jutting gables of the building for having some ineradicable leaven of busy mother Nature in them which has kept the fermenting world alive ever since; these may be matters of interest to its haunting ghosts (if any), but constitute no item in Miss Twinkleton's half-yearly accounts. They are neither of Miss Twinkleton's inclusive regulars, nor of her extras. The lady who undertakes the poetical department of the establishment at so much (or so little) a quarter has no pieces in her list of recitals bearing on such unprofitable questions.

As, in some cases of drunkenness, and in others of animal magnetism, there are two states of consciousness which never clash, but each of which pursues its separate course as though it were continuous instead of broken (thus, if I hide my watch when I am drunk, I must be drunk again before I can remember where), so Miss Twinkleton has two distinct and separate phases of being. Every night, the moment the young ladies have retired to rest, does Miss Twinkleton smarten up her curls a little, brighten up her eyes a little, and become a sprightlier Miss Twinkleton than the young ladies have ever seen. Every night, at the same hour, does Miss Twinkleton resume the topics of the previous night, comprehending the tenderer scandal of Cloisterham, of which she has no knowledge whatever by day, and references to a certain season at Tunbridge Wells (airily called by Miss Twinkleton in this state of her existence 'The Wells'), notably the season wherein a certain finished gentleman (compassionately called by Miss Twinkleton, in this stage of her existence, 'Foolish Mr. Porters') revealed a homage of the heart, whereof Miss Twinkleton, in her scholastic state of existence, is as ignorant as a granite pillar. Miss Twinkleton's companion in both states of existence, and equally adaptable to either, is one Mrs. Tisher: a deferential widow with a weak back, a chronic sigh, and a suppressed voice, who looks after the young ladies' wardrobes, and leads them to infer that she has seen better days. Perhaps this is the reason why it is an article of faith with the servants, handed down from race to race, that the departed Tisher was a hairdresser.

The pet pupil of the Nuns' House is Miss Rosa Bud, of course called Rosebud; wonderfully pretty, wonderfully childish, wonderfully whimsical. An awkward interest (awkward because romantic) attaches to Miss Bud in the minds of the young ladies, on account of its being known to them that a husband has been chosen for her by will and bequest, and that her guardian is bound down to bestow her on that husband when he comes of age. Miss Twinkleton, in her seminarial state of existence, has combated the romantic aspect of this destiny by affecting to shake her head over it behind Miss Bud's dimpled shoulders, and to brood on the unhappy lot of that doomed little victim. But with no better effect — possibly some unfelt touch of foolish Mr. Porters has undermined the endeavour — than to evoke from the young ladies an unanimous bedchamber cry of 'O, what a pretending old thing Miss Twinkleton is, my dear!'

The Nuns' House is never in such a state of flutter as when this allotted husband calls to see little Rosebud. (It is unanimously understood by the young ladies that he is lawfully entitled to this privilege, and that if Miss Twinkleton disputed it, she would be instantly taken up and transported.) When his ring at the gate-bell is expected, or takes place, every young lady who can, under any pretence, look out of window, looks out of window; while every young lady who is 'practising,' practises out of time; and the French class becomes so demoralised that the mark goes round as briskly as the bottle at a convivial party in the last century.

On the afternoon of the day next after the dinner of two at the gatehouse, the bell is rung with the usual fluttering results.

'Mr. Edwin Drood to see Miss Rosa.'

This is the announcement of the parlour-maid in chief. Miss Twinkleton, with an exemplary air of melancholy on her, turns to the sacrifice, and says, 'You may go down, my dear.' Miss Bud goes down, followed by all eyes.

Mr. Edwin Drood is waiting in Miss Twinkleton's own parlour: a dainty room, with nothing more directly scholastic in it than a terrestrial and a celestial globe. These expressive machines imply (to parents and guardians) that even when Miss Twinkleton retires into the bosom of privacy, duty may at any moment compel her to become a sort of Wandering Jewess, scouring the earth and soaring through the skies in search of knowledge for her pupils.

The last new maid, who has never seen the young gentleman Miss Rosa is engaged to, and who is making his acquaintance between the hinges of the open door, left open for the purpose, stumbles guiltily down the kitchen stairs, as a charming little apparition, with its face concealed by a little silk apron thrown over its head, glides into the parlour.

'O! it *is* so ridiculous!' says the apparition, stopping and shrinking. 'Don't, Eddy!'

'Don't what, Rosa?'

'Don't come any nearer, please. It *is* so absurd.'

'What is absurd, Rosa?'

'The whole thing is. It *is* so absurd to be an engaged orphan; and it *is* so absurd to have the girls and the servants scuttling about after one, like mice in the wainscot; and it *is* so absurd to be called upon!'

The apparition appears to have a thumb in the corner of its mouth while making this complaint.

'You give me an affectionate reception, Pussy, I must say.'

'Well, I will in a minute, Eddy, but I can't just yet. How are you?' (very shortly.)

'I am unable to reply that I am much the better for seeing you, Pussy, inasmuch as I see nothing of you.'

This second remonstrance brings a dark, bright pouting eye out from a corner of the apron; but it swiftly becomes invisible again, as the apparition exclaims: 'O good gracious! you have had half your hair cut off!'

'I should have done better to have had my head cut off, I think,' says Edwin, rumpling the hair in question, with a fierce glance at the looking-glass, and giving an impatient stamp. 'Shall I go?'

'No; you needn't go just yet, Eddy. The girls would all be asking questions why you went.'

'Once for all, Rosa, will you uncover that ridiculous little head of yours and give me a welcome?'

The apron is pulled off the childish head, as its wearer replies: 'You're very welcome, Eddy. There! I'm sure that's nice. Shake hands. No, I can't kiss you, because I've got an acidulated drop in my mouth.'

'Are you at all glad to see me, Pussy?'

'O, yes, I'm dreadfully glad. — Go and sit down. — Miss Twinkleton.'

It is the custom of that excellent lady when these visits occur, to appear every three minutes, either in her own person or in that of Mrs. Tisher, and lay an offering on the shrine of Propriety by affecting to look for some desiderated article. On the present occasion Miss Twinkleton, gracefully gliding in and out, says in passing: 'How do you do, Mr. Drood? Very glad indeed to have the pleasure. Pray excuse me. Tweezers. Thank you!'

'I got the gloves last evening, Eddy, and I like them very much. They are beauties.'

'Well, that's something,' the affianced replies, half grumbling. 'The smallest encouragement thankfully received. And how did you pass your birthday, Pussy?'

'Delightfully! Everybody gave me a present. And we had a feast. And we had a ball at night.'

'A feast and a ball, eh? These occasions seem to go off tolerably well without me, Pussy.'

'De-lightfully!' cries Rosa, in a quite spontaneous manner, and without the least pretence of reserve.

'Hah! And what was the feast?'

'Tarts, oranges, jellies, and shrimps.'

'Any partners at the ball?'

'We danced with one another, of course, sir. But some of the girls made game to be their brothers. It *was* so droll!'

'Did anybody make game to be ——'

'To be you? O dear yes!' cries Rosa, laughing with great enjoyment. 'That was the first thing done.'

'I hope she did it pretty well,' says Edwin rather doubtfully.

'O, it was excellent! — I wouldn't dance with you, you know.'

Edwin scarcely seems to see the force of this; begs to know if he may take the liberty to ask why?

'Because I was so tired of you,' returns Rosa. But she quickly adds, and pleadingly too, seeing displeasure in his face: 'Dear Eddy, you were just as tired of me, you know.'

'Did I say so, Rosa?'

'Say so! Do you ever say so? No, you only showed it. O, she did it so well!' cries Rosa, in a sudden ecstasy with her counterfeit betrothed.

'It strikes me that she must be a devilish impudent girl,' says Edwin Drood. 'And so, Pussy, you have passed your last birthday in this old house.'

'Ah, yes!' Rosa clasps her hands, looks down with a sigh, and shakes her head.

'You seem to be sorry, Rosa.'

'I am sorry for the poor old place. Somehow, I feel as if it would miss me, when I am gone so far away, so young.'

'Perhaps we had better stop short, Rosa?'

She looks up at him with a swift bright look; next moment shakes her head, sighs, and looks down again.

'That is to say, is it, Pussy, that we are both resigned?'

She nods her head again, and after a short silence, quaintly bursts out with: 'You know we must be married, and married from here, Eddy, or the poor girls will be so dreadfully disappointed!'

For the moment there is more of compassion, both for her and for himself, in her affianced husband's face, than there is of love. He checks the look, and asks: 'Shall I take you out for a walk, Rosa dear?'

Rosa dear does not seem at all clear on this point, until her face, which has been comically reflective brightens. 'O, yes, Eddy; let us go for a walk! And I tell you what we'll do. You shall pretend that you are engaged to somebody else, and I'll pretend that I am not engaged to anybody, and then we shan't quarrel.'

'Do you think that will prevent our falling out, Rosa?'

'I know it will. Hush! Pretend to look out of window — Mrs. Tisher!'

Through a fortuitous concourse of accidents, the matronly Tisher heaves in sight, says, in rustling through the room like the legendary ghost of a dowager in silken skirts: 'I hope I see Mr. Drood well; though I needn't ask, if I may judge from his complexion. I trust I disturb no one; but there *was* a paper-knife — O, thank you, I am sure!' and disappears with her prize.

'One other thing you must do, Eddy, to oblige me,' says Rosebud. 'The moment we get into the street, you must put me outside, and keep close to the house yourself — squeeze and graze yourself against it.'

'By all means, Rosa, if you wish it. Might I ask why?'

'O! because I don't want the girls to see you.'

'It's a fine day; but would you like me to carry an umbrella up?'

'Don't be foolish, sir. You haven't got polished leather boots on,' pouting, with one shoulder raised.

'Perhaps that might escape the notice of the girls, even if they did see me,' remarks Edwin, looking down at his boots with a sudden distaste for them.

'Nothing escapes their notice, sir. And then I know what would happen. Some of them would begin reflecting on me by saying (for *they* are free) that they never will on any account engage themselves to lovers without polished leather boots. Hark! Miss Twinkleton. I'll ask for leave.'

That discreet lady being indeed heard without, inquiring of nobody in a blandly conversational tone as she advances: 'Eh? Indeed! Are you quite sure you saw my mother-of-pearl button-holder on the work-table in my room?' is at once solicited for walking leave, and graciously accords it. And soon the young couple go out of the Nuns' House, taking all precautions against the discovery of the so vitally defective boots of Mr. Edwin Drood: precautions, let us hope, effective for the peace of Mrs. Edwin Drood that is to be.

'Which way shall we take, Rosa?'

Rosa replies: 'I want to go to the Lumps-of-Delight shop.'

'To the ——?'

'A Turkish sweetmeat, sir. My gracious me, don't you understand anything? Call yourself an Engineer, and not know *that*?'

'Why, how should I know it, Rosa?'

'Because I am very fond of them. But O! I forgot what we are to pretend. No, you needn't know anything about them; never mind.'

So he is gloomily borne off to the Lumps-of-Delight shop, where Rosa makes her purchase, and, after offering some to him (which he rather indignantly declines), begins to partake of it with great zest: previously taking off and rolling up a pair of little pink gloves, like rose-leaves, and occasionally putting her little pink fingers to her rosy lips, to cleanse them from the Dust of Delight that comes off the Lumps.

'Now, be a good-tempered Eddy, and pretend. And so you are engaged?'

'And so I am engaged.'

'Is she nice?'

'Charming.'

'Tall?'

'Immensely tall!' Rosa being short.

'Must be gawky, I should think,' is Rosa's quiet commentary.

'I beg your pardon; not at all,' contradiction rising in him. 'What is termed a fine woman; a splendid woman.'

'Big nose, no doubt,' is the quiet commentary again.

'Not a little one, certainly,' is the quick reply. (Rosa's being a little one.)

'Long pale nose, with a red knob in the middle. *I* know the sort of nose,' says Rosa, with a satisfied nod, and tranquilly enjoying the Lumps.

'You *don't* know the sort of nose, Rosa,' with some warmth; 'because it's nothing of the kind.'

'Not a pale nose, Eddy?'

'No.' Determined not to assent.

'A red nose? O! I don't like red noses. However; to be sure she can always powder it.'

'She would scorn to powder it,' says Edwin, becoming heated.

'Would she? What a stupid thing she must be! Is she stupid in everything?'

'No; in nothing.'

After a pause, in which the whimsically wicked face has not been unobservant of him, Rosa says:

A happy walk

'And this most sensible of creatures likes the idea of being carried off to Egypt; does she, Eddy?'

'Yes. She takes a sensible interest in triumphs of engineering skill: especially when they are to change the whole condition of an undeveloped country.'

'Lor!' says Rosa, shrugging her shoulders, with a little laugh of wonder.

'Do you object,' Edwin inquires, with a majestic turn of his eyes downward upon the fairy figure: 'do you object, Rosa, to her feeling that interest?'

'Object? my dear Eddy! But really, doesn't she hate boilers and things?'

'I can answer for her not being so idiotic as to hate Boilers,' he returns with angry emphasis; 'though I cannot answer for her views about Things; really not understanding what Things are meant.'

'But don't she hate Arabs, and Turks, and Fellahs, and people?'

'Certainly not.' Very firmly.

'At least she *must* hate the Pyramids? Come, Eddy?'

'Why should she be such a little — tall, I mean — goose, as to hate the Pyramids, Rosa?'

'Ah! you should hear Miss Twinkleton,' often nodding her head, and much enjoying the Lumps, 'bore about them, and then you wouldn't ask. Tiresome old burying-grounds! Isises, and Ibises, and Cheopses, and Pharaohses; who cares about them? And then there was Belzoni, or somebody, dragged out by the legs, half-choked with bats and dust. All the girls say: Serve him right, and hope it hurt him and wish he had been quite choked.'

The two youthful figures, side by side, but not now arm-in-arm, wander discontentedly about the old Close; and each sometimes stops and slowly imprints a deeper footstep in the fallen leaves.

'Well!' says Edwin, after a lengthy silence. 'According to custom. We can't get on, Rosa.'

Rosa tosses her head, and says she don't want to get on.

'That's a pretty sentiment, Rosa, considering.'

'Considering what?'

'If I say what, you'll go wrong again.'

'*You*'ll go wrong, you mean, Eddy. Don't be ungenerous.'

'Ungenerous! I like that!'

'Then I *don't* like that, and so I tell you plainly,' Rosa pouts.

'Now, Rosa, I put it to you. Who disparaged my profession, my destination ——'

'You are not going to be buried in the Pyramids, I hope?' she interrupts, arching her delicate eyebrows. 'You never said you were. If you are, why haven't you mentioned it to me? I can't find out your plans by instinct.'

'Now, Rosa, you know very well what I mean, my dear.'

'Well then, why did you begin with your detestable red-nosed giantesses? And she would, she would, she would, she would, she WOULD powder it!' cries Rosa, in a little burst of comical contradictory spleen.

'Somehow or other, I never can come right in these discussions,' says Edwin, sighing and becoming resigned.

'How is it possible, sir, that you ever can come right when you're always wrong? And as to Belzoni, I suppose he's dead; — I'm sure I hope he is — and how can his legs or his chokes concern you?'

'It is nearly time for your return, Rosa. We have not had a very happy walk, have we?'

'A happy walk? A detestably unhappy walk, sir. If I go up-stairs the moment I get in and cry till I can't take my dancing lesson, you are responsible, mind!'

'Let us be friends, Rosa.'

'Ah!' cries Rosa, shaking her head and bursting into real tears, 'I wish we *could* be friends! It's because we can't be friends, that we try one another so. I am a young little thing, Eddy, to have an old heartache; but I really, really have, sometimes. Don't be angry. I know you have one yourself too often. We should both of us have done better, if What is to be had been left What might have been. I am quite a little serious thing now, and not teasing you. Let each of us forbear, this one time, on our own account, and on the other's!'

Disarmed by this glimpse of a woman's nature in the spoilt child, though for an instant disposed to resent it as seeming to involve the enforced infliction of himself upon her, Edwin Drood stands watching her as she childishly cries and sobs, with both hands to the handkerchief at her eyes, and then — she becoming more composed, and indeed beginning in her young inconstancy to laugh at herself for having been so moved — leads to a seat hard by, under the elm-trees.

'One clear word of understanding, Pussy dear. I am not clever out of my own line — now I come to think of it, I don't know that I am particularly clever in it — but I want to do right. There is not — there may be — I really don't see my way to what I want to say, but I must say it before we part — there is not any other young ——'

'O no, Eddy! It's generous of you to ask me; but no, no, no!'

They have come very near to the Cathedral windows, and at this moment the organ and the choir sound out sublimely. As they sit listening to the solemn swell, the confidence of last night rises in young Edwin Drood's mind, and he thinks how unlike this music is to that discordance.

'I fancy I can distinguish Jack's voice,' is his remark in a low tone in connection with the train of thought.

'Take me back at once, please,' urges his Affianced, quickly laying her light hand upon his wrist. 'They will all be coming out directly; let us get away. O, what a resounding chord! But don't let us stop to listen to it; let us get away!'

Her hurry is over as soon as they have passed out of the Close. They go arm-in-arm now, gravely and deliberately enough, along the old High-street, to the Nuns' House. At the gate, the street being within sight empty, Edwin bends down his face to Rosebud's.

She remonstrates, laughing, and is a childish schoolgirl again.

'Eddy, no! I'm too sticky to be kissed. But give me your hand, and I'll blow a kiss into that.'

He does so. She breathes a light breath into it and asks, retaining it and looking into it:—

'Now say, what do you see?'

'See Rosa?'

'Why, I thought you Egyptian boys could look into a hand and see all sorts of phantoms. Can't you see a happy Future?'

For certain, neither of them sees a happy Present, as the gate opens and closes, and one goes in, and the other goes away.

Mr. Sapsea

ACCEPTING the Jackass as the type of self-sufficient stupidity and conceit — a custom, perhaps, like some few other customs, more conventional than fair — then the purest Jackass in Cloisterham is Mr. Thomas Sapsea, Auctioneer.

Mr. Sapsea 'dresses at' the Dean; has been bowed to for the Dean, in mistake; has even been spoken to in the street as My Lord, under the impression that he was the Bishop come down unexpectedly, without his chaplain. Mr. Sapsea is very proud of this, and of his voice, and of his style. He has even (in selling landed property) tried the experiment of slightly intoning in his pulpit, to make himself more like what he takes to be the genuine ecclesiastical article. So, in ending a Sale by Public Auction, Mr. Sapsea finishes off with an air of bestowing a benediction on the assembled brokers, which leaves the real Dean — a modest and worthy gentleman — far behind.

Mr. Sapsea has many admirers; indeed, the proposition is carried by a large local majority, even including non-believers in his wisdom, that he is a credit to Cloisterham. He possesses the great qualities of being portentous and dull, and of having a roll in his speech, and another roll in his gait; not to mention a certain gravely flowing action with his hands, as if he were presently going to Confirm the individual with whom he holds discourse. Much nearer sixty years of age than fifty, with a flowing outline of stomach, and horizontal creases in his waistcoat; reputed to be rich; voting at elections in the strictly respectable interest; morally satisfied that nothing but he himself has grown since he was a baby; how can dunder-headed Mr. Sapsea be otherwise than a credit to Cloisterham, and society?

Mr. Sapsea's premises are in the High-street, over against the Nuns' House. They are of about the period of the Nuns' House, irregularly modernised here and there, as steadily deteriorating generations found, more and more, that they preferred air and light to Fever and the Plague.

Over the doorway is a wooden effigy, about half life-size, representing Mr. Sapsea's father, in a curly wig and toga, in the act of selling. The chastity of the idea, and the natural appearance of the little finger, hammer, and pulpit, have been much admired.

Mr. Sapsea sits in his dull ground-floor sitting-room, giving first on his paved back yard; and then on his railed-off garden. Mr. Sapsea has a bottle of port wine on a table before the fire — the fire is an early luxury, but pleasant on the cool, chilly autumn evening — and is characteristically attended by his portrait, his eight-day clock, and his weather-glass. Characteristically, because he would uphold himself against mankind, his weather-glass against weather, and his clock against time.

By Mr. Sapsea's side on the table are a writing-desk and writing materials. Glancing at a scrap of manuscript, Mr. Sapsea reads it to himself with a lofty air, and then, slowly pacing the room with his thumbs in the arm-holes of his waistcoat, repeats it from memory: so internally, though with much dignity, that the word 'Ethelinda' is alone audible.

There are three clean wineglasses in a tray on the table. His serving-maid entering, and announcing 'Mr. Jasper is come, sir,' Mr. Sapsea waves 'Admit him,' and draws two wineglasses from the rank, as being claimed.

'Glad to see you, sir. I congratulate myself on having the honour of receiving you here for the first time.' Mr. Sapsea does the honours of his house in this wise.

'You are very good. The honour is mine and the self-congratulation is mine.'

'You are pleased to say so, sir. But I do assure you that it is a satisfaction to me to receive you in my humble home. And that is what I would not say to everybody.' Ineffable loftiness on Mr. Sapsea's part accompanies these words, as leaving the sentence to be understood: 'You will not easily believe that your society can be a satisfaction to a man like myself; nevertheless, it is.'

'I have for some time desired to know you, Mr. Sapsea.'

'And I, sir, have long known you by reputation as a man of taste. Let me fill your glass. I will give you, sir,' says Mr. Sapsea, filling his own:

> 'When the French come over,
> May we meet them at Dover!'

This was a patriotic toast in Mr. Sapsea's infancy, and he is therefore fully convinced of its being appropriate to any subsequent era.

'You can scarcely be ignorant, Mr. Sapsea,' observes Jasper, watching the auctioneer with a smile as the latter stretches out his legs before the fire, 'that you know the world.'

'Well, sir,' is the chuckling reply, 'I think I know something of it; something of it.'

'Your reputation for that knowledge has always interested and surprised me, and made me wish to know you. For Cloisterham is a little place. Cooped up in it myself, I know nothing beyond it, and feel it to be a very little place.'

'If I have not gone to foreign countries, young man,' Mr. Sapsea begins, and then stops: — 'You will excuse me calling you young man, Mr. Jasper? You are much my junior.'

'By all means.'

'If I have not gone to foreign countries, young man, foreign countries have come to me. They have come to me in the way of business, and I have improved upon my opportunities. Put it that I take an inventory, or make a catalogue. I see a French clock. I never saw him before, in my life, but I instantly lay my finger on him and say "Paris!" I see some cups and saucers of Chinese make, equally strangers to me personally: I put my finger on them, then and there, and I say "Pekin, Nankin, and Canton." It is the same with Japan, with Egypt, and with bamboo and sandalwood from the East Indies; I put my finger on them all. I have put my finger on the North Pole before now, and said "Spear of Esquimaux make, for half a pint of pale sherry!"'

'Really? A very remarkable way, Mr. Sapsea, of acquiring a knowledge of men and things.'

'I mention it, sir,' Mr. Sapsea rejoins, with unspeakable complacency, 'because, as I say, it don't do to boast of what you are; but show how you came to be it, and then you prove it.'

'Most interesting. We were to speak of the late Mrs. Sapsea.'

'We were, sir.' Mr. Sapsea fills both glasses, and takes the decanter into safe keeping again. 'Before I consult your opinion as a man of taste on this little trifle' — holding it up — 'which is *but* a trifle, and still has required some thought, sir, some little fever of the brow, I ought perhaps to describe the character of the late Mrs. Sapsea, now dead three quarters of a year.'

Mr. Jasper, in the act of yawning behind his wineglass, puts down that screen and calls up a look of interest. It is a little impaired in its expressiveness by his having a shut-up gape still to dispose of, with watering eyes.

'Half a dozen years ago, or so,' Mr. Sapsea proceeds, 'when I had enlarged my mind up to — I will not say to what it now is, for that might seem to aim at too much, but up to the pitch of wanting another mind to be absorbed in it — I cast my eye about me for a nuptial partner. Because, as I say, it is not good for man to be alone.'

Mr. Jasper appears to commit this original idea to memory.

'Miss Brobity at that time kept, I will not call it the rival establishment to the establishment at the Nuns' House opposite, but I will call it the other parallel establishment down town. The world did have it that she showed a passion for attending my sales, when they took place on half holidays, or in vacation time. The world did put it about, that she admired my style. The world did notice that as time flowed by, my style became traceable in the dictation-exercises of Miss Brobity's pupils. Young man, a whisper even sprang up in obscure malignity, that one ignorant and besotted Churl (a parent) so committed himself as to object to it by name. But I do not believe this. For is it likely that any human creature in his right senses would so lay himself open to be pointed at, by what I call the finger of scorn?'

Mr. Jasper shakes his head. Not in the least likely. Mr. Sapsea, in a grandiloquent state of absence of mind, seems to refill his visitor's glass, which is full already; and does really refill his own, which is empty.

'Miss Brobity's Being, young man, was deeply imbued with homage to Mind. She revered Mind, when launched, or, as I say, precipitated, on an extensive knowledge of the world. When I made my proposal, she did me the honour to be so overshadowed with a species of Awe, as to be able to articulate only the two words, "O Thou!" meaning myself. Her limpid blue eyes were fixed upon me, her semi-transparent hands were clasped together, pallor overspread her aquiline features, and, though encouraged to proceed, she never did proceed a word further. I disposed of the parallel establishment by private contract, and we became as nearly one as could be expected under the circumstances. But she never could, and she never did, find a phrase satisfactory to her perhaps-too-favourable estimate of my intellect. To the very last (feeble action of liver), she addressed me in the same unfinished terms.'

Mr. Jasper has closed his eyes as the auctioneer has deepened his voice. He now abruptly opens them, and says, in unison with the deepened voice 'Ah!' — rather as if stopping himself on the extreme verge of adding — 'men!'

'I have been since,' says Mr. Sapsea, with his legs stretched out, and solemnly enjoying himself with the wine and the fire, 'what you behold me; I have been since a solitary mourner; I have been since, as I say, wasting my evening conversation on the desert air. I will not say that I have reproached myself; but there have been times when I have asked myself the question: What if her husband had been nearer on a level with her? If she had not had to look up quite so high, what might the stimulating action have been upon the liver?'

Mr. Jasper says, with an appearance of having fallen into dreadfully low spirits, that he 'supposes it was to be.'

'We can only suppose so, sir,' Mr. Sapsea coincides. 'As I say, Man proposes, Heaven disposes. It may or may not be putting the same thought in another form; but that is the way I put it.'

Mr. Jasper murmurs assent.

'And now, Mr. Jasper,' resumes the auctioneer, producing his scrap of manuscript, 'Mrs. Sapsea's monument having had full time to settle and dry, let me take your opinion, as a man of taste, on the inscription I have (as I before remarked, not without some little fever of the brow) drawn out for it. Take it in your own hand. The setting out of the lines requires to be followed with the eye, as well as the contents with the mind.'

Mr. Jasper complying, sees and reads as follows:

ETHELINDA,

Reverential Wife of

MR. THOMAS SAPSEA,

AUCTIONEER, VALUER, ESTATE AGENT, &c.,

OF THIS CITY.

Whose Knowledge of the World,

Though somewhat extensive,

Never brought him acquainted with

A SPIRIT

More capable of

LOOKING UP TO HIM.

STRANGER, PAUSE

And ask thyself the Question,

CANST THOU DO LIKEWISE?

If Not,

WITH A BLUSH RETIRE.

Mr. Sapsea having risen and stationed himself with his back to the fire, for the purpose of observing the effect of these lines on the countenance of a man of taste, consequently has his face towards the door, when his serving-maid, again appearing, announces, 'Durdles is come, sir!' He promptly draws forth and fills the third wineglass, as being now claimed, and replies, 'Show Durdles in.'

'Admirable!' quoth Mr. Jasper, handing back the paper.

'You approve, sir?'

'Impossible not to approve. Striking, characteristic, and complete.'

The auctioneer inclines his head, as one accepting his due and giving a receipt; and invites the entering Durdles to take off that glass of wine (handing the same), for it will warm him.

Durdles is a stonemason; chiefly in the gravestone, tomb, and monument way, and wholly of their colour from head to foot. No man is better known in Cloisterham. He is the chartered libertine of the place. Fame trumpets him a wonderful workman — which, for aught that anybody knows, he may be (as he never works); and a wonderful sot — which everybody knows he is. With the Cathedral crypt he is better acquainted than any living authority; it may even be than any dead one. It is said that the intimacy of this acquaintance began in his habitually resorting to that secret place, to lock-out the Cloisterham boy-populace, and sleep off the fumes of liquor: he having ready access to the Cathedral, as contractor for rough repairs. Be this as it may, he does know much about it, and, in the demolition of impedimental fragments of wall, buttress, and pavement, has seen strange sights. He often speaks of himself in the third person; perhaps, being a little misty as to his own identity, when he narrates; perhaps impartially adopting the Cloisterham nomenclature in reference to a character of acknowledged distinction. Thus he will say, touching his strange sights: 'Durdles come upon the old chap,' in reference to a buried magnate of ancient time and high degree, 'by striking right into the coffin with his pick. The old chap gave Durdles a look with his open eyes, as much as to say, "Is your name Durdles? Why, my man, I've been waiting for you a devil of a time!" And then he turned to powder.' With a two-foot rule always in his pocket, and a mason's hammer all but always in his hand, Durdles goes continually sounding and tapping all about and about the Cathedral; and whenever he says to Tope: 'Tope, here's another old 'un in here!' Tope announces it to the Dean as an established discovery.

In a suit of coarse flannel with horn buttons, a yellow neckerchief with draggled ends, an old hat more russet-coloured than black, and laced boots of the hue of his stony calling, Durdles leads a hazy, gipsy sort of life, carrying his dinner about with him in a small bundle, and sitting on all manner of tombstones to dine. This dinner of Durdles's has become quite a Cloisterham institution: not only because of his never appearing in public without it, but because of its having been, on certain renowned occasions, taken into custody along with Durdles (as drunk and incapable), and exhibited before the Bench of Justices at the townhall. These occasions, however, have been few and far apart: Durdles being as seldom drunk as sober. For the rest, he is an old bachelor, and he lives in a little antiquated hole of a house that was never finished: supposed to be built, so far, of stones stolen from the city wall. To this abode there is an approach, ankle-deep in stone chips, resembling a petrified grove of tombstones, urns, draperies, and broken columns, in all stages of sculpture. Herein two journeymen incessantly chip, while two other journeymen, who face each other, incessantly saw stone; dipping as regularly in and out of their sheltering sentry-boxes, as if they were mechanical figures emblematical of Time and Death.

To Durdles, when he had consumed his glass of port, Mr. Sapsea intrusts that precious effort of his Muse. Durdles unfeelingly takes out his two-foot rule, and measures the lines calmly, alloying them with stone-grit.

'This is for the monument, is it, Mr. Sapsea?'

'The Inscription. Yes.' Mr. Sapsea waits for its effect on a common mind.

'It'll come in to a eighth of a inch,' says Durdles. 'Your servant, Mr. Jasper. Hope I see you well.'

'How are you, Durdles?'

'I've got a touch of the Tombatism on me, Mr. Jasper, but that I must expect.'

'You mean the Rheumatism,' says Sapsea, in a sharp tone. (He is nettled by having his composition so mechanically received.)

'No, I don't. I mean, Mr. Sapsea, the Tombatism. It's another sort from Rheumatism. Mr. Jasper knows what Durdles means. You get among them Tombs afore it's well light on a winter morning, and keep on, as the Catechism says, a-walking in the same all the days of your life, and *you*'ll know what Durdles means.'

'It is a bitter cold place,' Mr. Jasper assents, with an antipathetic shiver.

'And if it's bitter cold for you, up in the chancel, with a lot of live breath smoking out about you, what the bitterness is to Durdles, down in the crypt among the earthy damps there, and the dead breath of the old 'uns,' returns that individual, 'Durdles leaves you to judge. — Is this to be put in hand at once, Mr. Sapsea?'

Mr. Sapsea, with an Author's anxiety to rush into publication, replies that it cannot be out of hand too soon.

'You had better let me have the key then,' says Durdles.

'Why, man, it is not to be put inside the monument!'

'Durdles knows where it's to be put, Mr. Sapsea; no man better. Ask 'ere a man in Cloisterham whether Durdles knows his work.'

Mr. Sapsea rises, takes a key from a drawer, unlocks an iron safe let into the wall, and takes from it another key.

'When Durdles puts a touch or a finish upon his work, no matter where, inside or outside, Durdles likes to look at his work all round, and see that his work is a-doing him credit,' Durdles explains, doggedly.

The key proffered him by the bereaved widower being a large one, he slips his two-foot rule into a side-pocket of his flannel trousers made for it, and deliberately opens his flannel coat, and opens the mouth of a large breast-pocket within it before taking the key to place it in that repository.

'Why, Durdles!' exclaims Jasper, looking on amused, 'you are undermined with pockets!'

'And I carries weight in 'em too, Mr. Jasper. Feel those!' producing two other large keys.

'Hand me Mr. Sapsea's likewise. Surely this is the heaviest of the three.'

'You'll find 'em much of a muchness, I expect,' says Durdles. 'They all belong to monuments. They all open Durdles's work. Durdles keeps the keys of his work mostly. Not that they're much used.'

'By the bye,' it comes into Jasper's mind to say, as he idly examines the keys, 'I have been going to ask you, many a day, and have always forgotten. You know they sometimes call you Stony Durdles, don't you?'

'Cloisterham knows me as Durdles, Mr. Jasper.'

'I am aware of that, of course. But the boys sometimes ——'

'O! if you mind them young imps of boys ——' Durdles gruffly interrupts.

'I don't mind them any more than you do. But there was a discussion the other day among the Choir, whether Stony stood for Tony;' clinking one key against another.

('Take care of the wards, Mr. Jasper.')

'Or whether Stony stood for Stephen;' clinking with a change of keys.

('You can't make a pitch pipe of 'em, Mr. Jasper.')

'Or whether the name comes from your trade. How stands the fact?'

Mr. Jasper weighs the three keys in his hand, lifts his head from his idly stooping attitude over the fire, and delivers the keys to Durdles with an ingenuous and friendly face.

But the stony one is a gruff one likewise, and that hazy state of his is always an uncertain state, highly conscious of its dignity, and prone to take offence. He drops his two keys back into his pocket one by one, and buttons them up; he takes his dinner-bundle from the chair-back on which he hung it when he came in; he distributes the weight he carries, by tying the third key up in it, as though he were an Ostrich, and liked to dine off cold iron; and he gets out of the room, deigning no word of answer.

Mr. Sapsea then proposes a hit at backgammon, which, seasoned with his own improving conversation, and terminating in a supper of cold roast beef and salad, beguiles the golden evening until pretty late. Mr. Sapsea's wisdom being, in its delivery to mortals, rather of the diffuse than the epigrammatic order, is by no means expended even then; but his visitor intimates that he will come back for more of the precious commodity on future occasions, and Mr. Sapsea lets him off for the present, to ponder on the instalment he carries away.

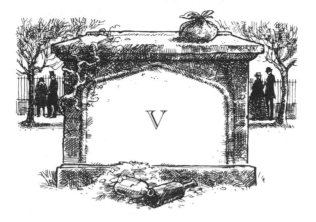

Mr. Durdles and Friend

JOHN JASPER, on his way home through the Close, is brought to a stand-still by the spectacle of Stony Durdles, dinner-bundle and all, leaning his back against the iron railing of the burial-ground enclosing it from the old cloister-arches; and a hideous small boy in rags flinging stones at him as a well-defined mark in the moonlight. Sometimes the stones hit him, and sometimes they miss him, but Durdles seems indifferent to either fortune. The hideous small boy, on the contrary, whenever he hits Durdles, blows a whistle of triumph through a jagged gap, convenient for the purpose, in the front of his mouth, where half his teeth are wanting; and whenever he misses him, yelps out 'Mulled agin!' and tries to atone for the failure by taking a more correct and vicious aim.

'What are you doing to the man?' demands Jasper, stepping out into the moonlight from the shade.

'Making a cock-shy of him,' replies the hideous small boy.

'Give me those stones in your hand.'

'Yes, I'll give 'em you down your throat, if you come a-ketching hold of me,' says the small boy, shaking himself loose, and backing. 'I'll smash your eye, if you don't look out!'

'Baby-Devil that you are, what has the man done to you?'

'He won't go home.'

'What is that to you?'

'He gives me a 'apenny to pelt him home if I ketches him out too late,' says the boy. And then chants, like a little savage, half stumbling and half dancing among the rags and laces of his dilapidated boots:—

> 'Widdy widdy wen!
> I—ket—ches—Im—out—ar—ter—ten,
> Widdy widdy wy!
> Then—E—don't—go—then—I—shy—
> Widdy Widdy Wake-cock warning!'

— with a comprehensive sweep on the last word, and one more delivery at Durdles.

This would seem to be a poetical note of preparation, agreed upon, as a caution to Durdles to stand clear if he can, or to betake himself homeward.

Widdy Warning

John Jasper invites the boy with a beck of his head to follow him (feeling it hopeless to drag him, or coax him), and crosses to the iron railing where the Stony (and stoned) One is profoundly meditating.

'Do you know this thing, this child?' asks Jasper, at a loss for a word that will define this thing.

'Deputy,' says Durdles, with a nod.

'Is that its — his — name?'

'Deputy,' assents Durdles.

'I'm man-servant up at the Travellers' Twopenny in Gas Works Garding,' this thing explains. 'All us man-servants at Travellers' Lodgings is named Deputy. When we're chock full and the Travellers is all a-bed I come out for my 'elth.' Then withdrawing into the road, and taking aim, he resumes:—

> 'Widdy widdy wen!
> I—ket—ches—Im—out—ar—ter—'

'Hold your hand,' cries Jasper, 'and don't throw while I stand so near him, or I'll kill you! Come, Durdles; let me walk home with you to-night. Shall I carry your bundle?'

'Not on any account,' replies Durdles, adjusting it. 'Durdles was making his reflections here when you come up, sir, surrounded by his works, like a popular Author.— Your own brother-in-law;' introducing a sarcophagus within the railing, white and cold in the moonlight. 'Mrs. Sapsea;' introducing the monument of that devoted wife. 'Late Incumbent;' introducing the Reverend Gentleman's broken column. 'Departed Assessed Taxes;' introducing a vase and towel, standing on what might represent the cake of soap. 'Former pastrycook and Muffin-maker, much respected;' introducing gravestone. 'All safe and sound here, sir, and all Durdles's work. Of the common folk, that is merely bundled up in turf and brambles, the less said the better. A poor lot, soon forgot.'

'This creature, Deputy, is behind us,' says Jasper, looking back. 'Is he to follow us?'

The relations between Durdles and Deputy are of a capricious kind; for, on Durdles's turning himself about with the slow gravity of beery soddenness, Deputy makes a pretty wide circuit into the road and stands on the defensive.

'You never cried Widdy Warning before you begun to-night,' says Durdles, unexpectedly reminded of, or imagining, an injury.

'Yer lie, I did,' says Deputy, in his only form of polite contradiction.

'Own brother, sir,' observes Durdles, turning himself about again, and as unexpectedly forgetting his offence as he had recalled or conceived it; 'own brother to Peter the Wild Boy! But I gave him an object in life.'

'At which he takes aim?' Mr. Jasper suggests.

'That's it, sir,' returns Durdles, quite satisfied; 'at which he takes aim. I took him in hand and gave him an object. What was he before? A destroyer. What work did he do? Nothing but destruction. What did he earn by it? Short terms in Cloisterham Jail. Not a person, not a piece of property, not a winder, not a horse, nor a dog, nor a cat, nor a bird, nor a fowl, nor a pig, but what he stoned, for want of an enlightened object. I put that enlightened object before him, and now he can turn his honest halfpenny by the three penn'orth a week.'

'I wonder he has no competitors.'

'He has plenty, Mr. Jasper, but he stones 'em all away. Now, I don't know what this scheme of mine comes to,' pursues Durdles, considering about it with the same sodden gravity; 'I don't know what you may precisely call it. It ain't a sort of a — scheme of a — National Education?'

'I should say not,' replies Jasper.

'*I* should say not,' assents Durdles; 'then we won't try to give it a name.'

'He still keeps behind us,' repeats Jasper, looking over his shoulder; 'is he to follow us?'

'We can't help going round by the Travellers' Twopenny, if we go the short way, which is the back way,' Durdles answers, 'and we'll drop him there.'

So they go on; Deputy, as a rear rank one, taking open order, and invading the silence of the hour and place by stoning every wall, post, pillar, and other inanimate object, by the deserted way.

'Is there anything new down in the crypt, Durdles?' asks John Jasper.

'Anything old, I think you mean,' growls Durdles. 'It ain't a spot for novelty.'

'Any new discovery on your part, I meant.'

'There's a old 'un under the seventh pillar on the left as you go down the broken steps of the little underground chapel as formerly was; I make him out (so fur as I've made him out yet) to be one of them old 'uns with a crook. To judge from the size of the passages in the walls, and of the steps and doors, by which they come and went, them crooks must have been a good deal in the way of the old 'uns! Two on 'em meeting promiscuous must have hitched one another by the mitre pretty often, I should say.'

Without any endeavour to correct the literality of this opinion, Jasper surveys his companion — covered from head to foot with old mortar, lime, and stone grit — as though he, Jasper, were getting imbued with a romantic interest in his weird life.

'Yours is a curious existence.'

Without furnishing the least clue to the question, whether he receives this as a compliment or as quite the reverse, Durdles gruffly answers: 'Yours is another.'

'Well! inasmuch as my lot is cast in the same old earthy, chilly, never-changing place, Yes. But there is much more mystery and interest in your connection with the Cathedral than in mine. Indeed, I am beginning to have some idea of asking you to take me on as a sort of student, or free 'prentice, under you, and to let me go about with you sometimes, and see some of these odd nooks in which you pass your days.'

The Stony One replies, in a general way, 'All right. Everybody knows where to find Durdles, when he's wanted.' Which, if not strictly true, is approximately so, if taken to express that Durdles may always be found in a state of vagabondage somewhere.

'What I dwell upon most,' says Jasper, pursuing his subject of romantic interest, 'is the remarkable accuracy with which you would seem to find out where people are buried. — What is the matter? That bundle is in your way; let me hold it.'

Durdles has stopped and backed a little (Deputy, attentive to all his movements, immediately skirmishing into the road), and was looking about for some ledge or corner to place his bundle on, when thus relieved of it.

'Just you give me my hammer out of that,' says Durdles, 'and I'll show you.'

Clink, clink. And his hammer is handed him.

'Now, lookee here. You pitch your note, don't you, Mr. Jasper?'

'Yes.'

'So I sound for mine. I take my hammer, and I tap.' (Here he strikes the pavement, and the attentive Deputy skirmishes at a rather wider range, as supposing that his head may be in requisition.) 'I tap, tap, tap. Solid! I go on tapping. Solid still! Tap again. Holloa! Hollow! Tap again, persevering. Solid in hollow! Tap, tap, tap, to try it better. Solid in hollow; and inside solid, hollow again! There you are! Old 'un crumbled away in stone coffin, in vault!'

'Astonishing!'

'I have even done this,' says Durdles, drawing out his two-foot rule (Deputy meanwhile skirmishing nearer, as suspecting that Treasure may be about to be discovered, which may somehow lead to his own enrichment, and the delicious treat of the discoverers being hanged by the neck, on his evidence, until they are dead). 'Say that hammer of mine's a wall — my work. Two; four; and two is six,' measuring on the pavement. 'Six foot inside that wall is Mrs. Sapsea.'

'Not really Mrs. Sapsea?'

'Say Mrs. Sapsea. Her wall's thicker, but say Mrs. Sapsea. Durdles taps that wall represented by that hammer, and says, after good sounding: "Something betwixt us!" Sure enough, some rubbish has been left in that same six-foot space by Durdles's men!'

Jasper opines that such accuracy 'is a gift.'

'I wouldn't have it as a gift,' returns Durdles, by no means receiving the observation in good part. 'I worked it out for myself. Durdles comes by *his* knowledge through grubbing deep for it, and having it up by the roots when it don't want to come. — Holloa you Deputy!'

'Widdy!' is Deputy's shrill response, standing off again.

'Catch that ha'penny. And don't let me see any more of you to-night, after we come to the Travellers' Twopenny.'

'Warning!' returns Deputy, having caught the halfpenny, and appearing by this mystic word to express his assent to the arrangement.

They have but to cross what was once the vineyard, belonging to what was once the Monastery, to come into the narrow back lane wherein stands the crazy wooden house of two low stories currently known as the Travellers' Twopenny:— a house all warped and distorted, like the morals of the travellers, with scant remains of a lattice-work porch over the door, and also of a rustic fence before its stamped-out garden; by reason of the travellers being so bound to the premises by a tender sentiment (or so fond of having a fire by the roadside in the course of the day), that they can never be persuaded or threatened into departure, without violently possessing themselves of some wooden forget-me-not, and bearing it off.

The semblance of an inn is attempted to be given to this wretched place by fragments of conventional red curtaining in the windows, which rags are made muddily transparent in the night-season by feeble lights of rush or cotton dip burning dully in the close air of the inside. As Durdles and Jasper come near, they are addressed by an inscribed paper lantern over the door, setting forth the purport of the house. They are also addressed by some half-dozen other hideous small boys — whether twopenny lodgers or followers or hangers-on of such, who knows! — who, as if attracted by some carrion-scent of Deputy in the air, start into the moonlight, as vultures might gather in the desert, and instantly fall to stoning him and one another.

'Stop, you young brutes,' cries Jasper angrily, 'and let us go by!'

This remonstrance being received with yells and flying stones, according to a custom of late years comfortably established among the police regulations of our English communities, where Christians are stoned on all sides, as if the days of Saint Stephen were revived, Durdles remarks of the young savages, with some point, that 'they haven't got an object,' and leads the way down the lane.

At the corner of the lane, Jasper, hotly enraged, checks his companion and looks back. All is silent. Next moment, a stone coming rattling at his hat, and a distant yell of 'Wake-Cock! Warning!' followed by a crow, as from some infernally-hatched Chanticleer, apprising him under whose victorious fire he stands, he turns the corner into safety, and takes Durdles home: Durdles stumbling among the litter of his stony yard as if he were going to turn head foremost into one of the unfinished tombs.

John Jasper returns by another way to his gatehouse, and entering softly with his key, finds his fire still burning. He takes from a locked press a peculiar-looking pipe, which he fills — but not with tobacco — and, having adjusted the contents of the bowl, very carefully, with a little instrument, ascends an inner staircase of only a few steps, leading to two rooms. One of these is his own sleeping chamber: the other is his nephew's. There is a light in each.

His nephew lies asleep, calm and untroubled. John Jasper stands looking down upon him, his unlighted pipe in his hand, for some time, with a fixed and deep attention. Then, hushing his footsteps, he passes to his own room, lights his pipe, and delivers himself to the Spectres it invokes at midnight.

Philanthropy in Minor Canon Corner

THE Reverend Septimus Crisparkle (Septimus, because six little brother Crisparkles before him went out, one by one, as they were born, like six weak little rushlights, as they were lighted), having broken the thin morning ice near Cloisterham Weir with his amiable head, much to the invigoration of his frame, was now assisting his circulation by boxing at a looking-glass with great science and prowess. A fresh and healthy portrait the looking-glass presented of the Reverend Septimus, feinting and dodging with the utmost artfulness, and hitting out from the shoulder with the utmost straightness, while his radiant features teemed with innocence, and soft-hearted benevolence beamed from his boxing-gloves.

It was scarcely breakfast-time yet, for Mrs. Crisparkle — mother, not wife of the Reverend Septimus — was only just down, and waiting for the urn. Indeed, the Reverend Septimus left off at this very moment to take the pretty old lady's entering face between his boxing-gloves and kiss it. Having done so with tenderness, the Reverend Septimus turned to again, countering with his left, and putting in his right, in a tremendous manner.

'I say, every morning of my life, that you'll do it at last, Sept,' remarked the old lady, looking on; 'and so you will.'

'Do what, Ma dear?'

'Break the pier-glass, or burst a blood-vessel.'

'Neither, please God, Ma dear. Here's wind, Ma. Look at this!'

In a concluding round of great severity, the Reverend Septimus administered and escaped all sorts of punishment, and wound up by getting the old lady's cap into Chancery — such is the technical term used in scientific circles by the learned in the Noble Art — with a lightness of touch that hardly stirred the lightest lavender or cherry riband on it. Magnanimously releasing the defeated, just in time to get his gloves into a drawer and feign to be looking out of window in a contemplative state of mind when a servant entered, the Reverend Septimus then gave place to the urn and other preparations for breakfast. These completed, and the two alone again, it was pleasant to see (or would have been, if there had been any one to see it, which there never was), the old lady standing to say the Lord's Prayer aloud, and her son, Minor Canon nevertheless, standing with bent head to hear it, he being within five years of forty: much as he had stood to hear the same words from the same lips when he was within five months of four.

What is prettier than an old lady — except a young lady — when her eyes are bright, when her figure is trim and compact, when her face is cheerful and calm, when her dress is as the dress of a china shepherdess: so dainty in its colours, so individually assorted to herself, so neatly moulded on her? Nothing is prettier, thought the good Minor Canon frequently, when taking his seat at table opposite his long-widowed mother. Her thought at such times may be condensed into the two words that oftenest did duty together in all her conversations: 'My Sept!'

They were a good pair to sit breakfasting together in Minor Canon Corner, Cloisterham. For Minor Canon Corner was a quiet place in the shadow of the Cathedral, which the cawing of the rooks, the echoing footsteps of rare passers, the sound of the Cathedral bell, or the roll of the Cathedral organ, seemed to render more quiet than absolute silence. Swaggering fighting men had had their centuries of ramping and raving about Minor Canon Corner, and beaten serfs had had their centuries of drudging and dying there, and powerful monks had had their centuries of being sometimes useful and sometimes harmful there, and behold they were all gone out of Minor Canon Corner, and so much the better. Perhaps one of the highest uses of their ever having been there, was, that there might be left behind, that blessed air of tranquillity which pervaded Minor Canon Corner, and that serenely romantic state of the mind — productive for the most part of pity and forbearance — which is engendered by a sorrowful story that is all told, or a pathetic play that is played out.

Red-brick walls harmoniously toned down in colour by time, strong-rooted ivy, latticed windows, panelled rooms, big oaken beams in little places, and stone-walled gardens where annual fruit yet ripened upon monkish trees, were the principal surroundings of pretty old Mrs. Crisparkle and the Reverend Septimus as they sat at breakfast.

'And what, Ma dear,' inquired the Minor Canon, giving proof of a wholesome and vigorous appetite, 'does the letter say?'

The pretty old lady, after reading it, had just laid it down upon the breakfast-cloth. She handed it over to her son.

Now, the old lady was exceedingly proud of her bright eyes being so clear that she could read writing without spectacles. Her son was also so proud of the circumstance, and so dutifully bent on her deriving the utmost possible gratification from it, that he had invented the pretence that he himself could *not* read writing without spectacles. Therefore he now assumed a pair, of grave and prodigious proportions, which not only seriously inconvenienced his nose and his breakfast, but seriously impeded his perusal of the letter. For, he had the eyes of a microscope and a telescope combined, when they were unassisted.

'It's from Mr. Honeythunder, of course,' said the old lady, folding her arms.

'Of course,' assented her son. He then lamely read on:

> '"Haven of Philanthropy,
> '"Chief Offices, London, Wednesday.

'"DEAR MADAM,

'"I write in the —;" In the what's this? What does he write in?'

'In the chair,' said the old lady.

The Reverend Septimus took off his spectacles, that he might see her face, as he exclaimed:

'Why, what should he write in?'

'Bless me, bless me, Sept,' returned the old lady, 'you don't see the context! Give it back to me, my dear.'

Glad to get his spectacles off (for they always made his eyes water), her son obeyed: murmuring that his sight for reading manuscript got worse and worse daily.

'"I write,"' his mother went on, reading very perspicuously and precisely, '"from the chair, to which I shall probably be confined for some hours."'

Septimus looked at the row of chairs against the wall, with a half-protesting and half-appealing countenance.

'"We have,"' the old lady read on with a little extra emphasis, '"a meeting of our Convened Chief Composite Committee of Central and District Philanthropists, at our Head Haven as above; and it is their unanimous pleasure that I take the chair."'

Septimus breathed more freely, and muttered: 'O! if he comes to *that*, let him.'

'"Not to lose a day's post, I take the opportunity of a long report being read, denouncing a public miscreant ——"'

'It is a most extraordinary thing,' interposed the gentle Minor Canon, laying down his knife and fork to rub his ear in a vexed manner, 'that these Philanthropists are always denouncing somebody. And it is another most extraordinary thing that they are always so violently flush of miscreants!'

'"Denouncing a public miscreant——"' — the old lady resumed, '"to get our little affair of business off my mind. I have spoken with my two wards, Neville and Helena Landless, on the subject of their defective education, and they give in to the plan proposed; as I should have taken good care they did, whether they liked it or not."'

'And it is another most extraordinary thing,' remarked the Minor Canon in the same tone as before, 'that these philanthropists are so given to seizing their fellow-creatures by the scruff of the neck, and (as one may say) bumping them into the paths of peace. — I beg your pardon, Ma dear, for interrupting.'

'"Therefore, dear Madam, you will please prepare your son, the Rev. Mr. Septimus, to expect Neville as an inmate to be read with, on Monday next. On the same day Helena will accompany him to Cloisterham, to take up her quarters at the Nuns' House, the establishment recommended by yourself and son jointly. Please likewise to prepare for her reception and tuition there. The terms in both cases are understood to be exactly as stated to me in writing by yourself, when I opened a correspondence with you on this subject, after the honour of being introduced to you at your sister's house in town here. With compliments to the Rev. Mr. Septimus, I am, Dear Madam, Your affectionate brother (In Philanthropy), LUKE HONEYTHUNDER."'

'Well, Ma,' said Septimus, after a little more rubbing of his ear, 'we must try it. There can be no doubt that we have room for an inmate, and that I have time to bestow upon him, and inclination too. I must confess to feeling rather glad that he is not Mr. Honeythunder himself. Though that seems wretchedly prejudiced — does it not? — for I never saw him. Is he a large man, Ma?'

'I should call him a large man, my dear,' the old lady replied after some hesitation, 'but that his voice is so much larger.'

'Than himself?'

'Than anybody.'

'Hah!' said Septimus. And finished his breakfast as if the flavour of the Superior Family Souchong, and also of the ham and toast and eggs, were a little on the wane.

Mrs. Crisparkle's sister, another piece of Dresden china, and matching her so neatly that they would have made a delightful pair of ornaments for the two ends of any capacious old-fashioned chimneypiece, and by right should never have been seen apart, was the childless wife of a clergyman holding Corporation preferment in London City. Mr. Honeythunder in his public character of Professor of Philanthropy had come to know Mrs. Crisparkle during the last re-matching of the china ornaments (in other words during her last annual visit to her sister), after a public occasion of a philanthropic nature, when certain devoted orphans of tender years had been glutted with plum buns, and plump bumptiousness. These were all the antecedents known in Minor Canon Corner of the coming pupils.

'I am sure you will agree with me, Ma,' said Mr. Crisparkle, after thinking the matter over, 'that the first thing to be done, is, to put these young people as much at their ease as possible. There is nothing disinterested in the notion, because we cannot be at our ease with them unless they are at their ease with us. Now, Jasper's nephew is down here at present; and like takes to like, and youth takes to youth. He is a cordial young fellow, and we will have him to meet the brother and sister at dinner. That's three. We can't think of asking him, without asking Jasper. That's four. Add Miss Twinkleton and the fairy bride that is to be, and that's six. Add our two selves, and that's eight. Would eight at a friendly dinner at all put you out, Ma?'

'Nine would, Sept,' returned the old lady, visibly nervous.

'My dear Ma, I particularise eight.'

'The exact size of the table and the room, my dear.'

So it was settled that way: and when Mr. Crisparkle called with his mother upon Miss Twinkleton, to arrange for the reception of Miss Helena Landless at the Nuns' House, the two other invitations having reference to that establishment were proffered and accepted. Miss Twinkleton did, indeed, glance at the globes, as regretting that they were not formed to be taken out into society; but became reconciled to leaving them behind. Instructions were then despatched to the Philanthropist for the departure and arrival, in good time for dinner, of Mr. Neville and Miss Helena; and stock for soup became fragrant in the air of Minor Canon Corner.

In those days there was no railway to Cloisterham, and Mr. Sapsea said there never would be. Mr. Sapsea said more; he said there never should be. And yet, marvellous to consider, it has come to pass, in these days, that Express Trains don't think Cloisterham worth stopping at, but yell and whirl through it on their larger errands, casting the dust off their wheels as a testimony against its insignificance. Some remote fragment of Main Line to somewhere else, there was, which was going to ruin the Money Market if it failed, and Church and State if it succeeded, and (of course), the Constitution, whether or no; but even that had already so unsettled Cloisterham traffic, that the traffic, deserting the high road, came sneaking in from an unprecedented part of the country by a back stable-way, for many years labelled at the corner: 'Beware of the Dog.'

To this ignominious avenue of approach, Mr. Crisparkle repaired, awaiting the arrival of a short, squat omnibus, with a disproportionate heap of luggage on the roof — like a little Elephant with infinitely too much Castle — which was then the daily service between Cloisterham and external mankind. As this vehicle lumbered up, Mr. Crisparkle could hardly see anything else of it for a large outside passenger seated on the box, with his elbows squared, and his hands on his knees, compressing the driver into a most uncomfortably small compass, and glowering about him with a strongly-marked face.

'Is this Cloisterham?' demanded the passenger, in a tremendous voice.

'It is,' replied the driver, rubbing himself as if he ached, after throwing the reins to the ostler. 'And I never was so glad to see it.'

'Tell your master to make his box-seat wider, then,' returned the passenger. 'Your master is morally bound — and ought to be legally, under ruinous penalties — to provide for the comfort of his fellow-man.'

The driver instituted, with the palms of his hands, a superficial perquisition into the state of his skeleton; which seemed to make him anxious.

'Have I sat upon you?' asked the passenger.

'You have,' said the driver, as if he didn't like it at all.

'Take that card, my friend.'

'I think I won't deprive you on it,' returned the driver, casting his eyes over it with no great favour, without taking it. 'What's the good of it to me?'

'Be a Member of that Society,' said the passenger.

'What shall I get by it?' asked the driver.

'Brotherhood,' returned the passenger, in a ferocious voice.

'Thankee,' said the driver, very deliberately, as he got down; 'my mother was contented with myself, and so am I. I don't want no brothers.'

'But you must have them,' replied the passenger, also descending, 'whether you like it or not. I am your brother.'

'I say!' expostulated the driver, becoming more chafed in temper, 'not too fur! The worm *will*, when——'

But here Mr. Crisparkle interposed, remonstrating aside, in a friendly voice: 'Joe, Joe, Joe! don't forget yourself, Joe, my good fellow!' and then, when Joe peaceably touched his hat, accosting the passenger with: 'Mr. Honeythunder?'

'That is my name, sir.'

'My name is Crisparkle.'

'Reverend Mr. Septimus? Glad to see you, sir. Neville and Helena are inside. Having a little succumbed of late, under the pressure of my public labours, I thought I would take a mouthful of fresh air, and come down with them, and return at night. So you are the Reverend Mr. Septimus, are you?' surveying him on the whole with disappointment, and twisting a double eyeglass by its ribbon, as if he were roasting it, but not otherwise using it. 'Hah! I expected to see you older, sir.'

'I hope you will,' was the good-humoured reply.

'Eh?' demanded Mr. Honeythunder.

'Only a poor little joke. Not worth repeating.'

'Joke? Ay; I never see a joke,' Mr. Honeythunder frowningly retorted. 'A joke is wasted upon me, sir. Where are they? Helena and Neville, come here! Mr. Crisparkle has come down to meet you.'

An unusually handsome lithe young fellow, and an unusually handsome lithe girl; much alike; both very dark, and very rich in colour; she of almost the gipsy type; something untamed about them both; a certain air upon them of hunter and huntress; yet withal a certain air of being the objects of the chase, rather than the followers. Slender, supple, quick of eye and limb; half shy, half defiant; fierce of look; an indefinable kind of pause coming and going on their whole expression, both of face and form, which might be equally likened to the pause before a crouch or a bound. The rough mental notes made in the first five minutes by Mr. Crisparkle would have read thus, *verbatim*.

He invited Mr. Honeythunder to dinner, with a troubled mind (for the discomfiture of the dear old china shepherdess lay heavy on it), and gave his arm to Helena Landless. Both she and her brother, as they walked all together through the ancient streets, took great delight in what he pointed out of the Cathedral and the Monastery ruin, and wondered — so his notes ran on — much as if they were beautiful barbaric captives brought from some wild tropical dominion. Mr. Honeythunder walked in the middle of the road, shouldering the natives out of his way, and loudly developing a scheme he had, for making a raid on all the unemployed persons in the United Kingdom, laying them every one by the heels in jail, and forcing them, on pain of prompt extermination, to become philanthropists.

Mrs. Crisparkle had need of her own share of philanthropy when she beheld this very large and very good excrescence on the little party. Always something in the nature of a Boil upon the face of society, Mr. Honeythunder expanded into an inflammatory Wen in Minor Canon Corner. Though it was not literally true, as was facetiously charged against him by public unbelievers, that he called aloud to his fellow-creatures: 'Curse your souls and bodies, come here and be blessed!' still his philanthropy was of that gunpowderous sort that the difference between it and animosity was hard to determine. You were to abolish military force, but you were first to bring all commanding officers who had done their duty, to trial by court-martial for that offence, and shoot them. You were to abolish war, but were to make converts by making war upon them, and charging them with loving war as the apple of their eye. You were to have no capital punishment, but were first to sweep off the face of the earth all legislators, jurists, and judges, who were of the contrary opinion. You were to have universal concord, and were to get it by eliminating all the people who wouldn't, or conscientiously couldn't, be concordant. You were to love your brother as yourself, but after an indefinite interval of maligning him (very much as if you hated him), and calling him all manner of names. Above all things, you were to do nothing in private, or on your own account. You were to go to the offices of the Haven of Philanthropy, and put your name down as a Member and a Professing Philanthropist. Then, you were to pay up your subscription, get your card of membership and your riband and medal, and were evermore to live upon a platform, and evermore to say what Mr. Honeythunder said, and what the Treasurer said, and what the sub-Treasurer said, and what the Committee said, and what the sub-Committee said, and what the Secretary said, and what the Vice-Secretary said. And this was usually said in the unanimously-carried resolution under hand and seal, to the effect: 'That this assembled Body of Professing Philanthropists views, with indignant scorn and contempt, not unmixed with utter detestation and loathing abhorrence' — in short, the baseness of all those who do not belong to it, and pledges itself to make as many obnoxious statements as possible about them, without being at all particular as to facts.

The dinner was a most doleful breakdown. The philanthropist deranged the symmetry of the table, sat himself in the way of the waiting, blocked up the thoroughfare, and drove Mr. Tope (who assisted the parlour-maid) to the verge of distraction by passing plates and dishes on, over his own head. Nobody could talk to anybody, because he held forth to everybody at once, as if the company had no individual existence, but were a Meeting. He impounded the Reverend Mr. Septimus, as an official personage to be addressed, or kind of human peg to hang his oratorical hat on, and fell into the exasperating habit, common among such orators, of impersonating him as a wicked and weak opponent. Thus, he would ask: 'And will you, sir, now stultify yourself by telling me' — and so forth, when the innocent man had not opened his lips, nor meant to open them. Or he would say: 'Now see, sir, to what a position you are reduced. I will leave you no escape. After exhausting all the resources of fraud and falsehood, during years upon years; after exhibiting a combination of dastardly meanness with ensanguined daring, such as the world has not often witnessed; you have now the hypocrisy to bend the knee before the most degraded of mankind, and to sue and whine and howl for mercy!' Whereat the unfortunate Minor Canon would look, in part indignant and in part perplexed; while his worthy mother sat bridling, with tears in her eyes, and the remainder of the party lapsed into a sort of gelatinous state, in which there was no flavour or solidity, and very little resistance.

But the gush of philanthropy that burst forth when the departure of Mr. Honeythunder began to impend, must have been highly gratifying to the feelings of that distinguished man. His coffee was produced, by the special activity of Mr. Tope, a full hour before he wanted it. Mr. Crisparkle sat with his watch in his hand for about the same period, lest he should overstay his time. The four young people were unanimous in believing that the Cathedral clock struck three-quarters, when it actually struck but one. Miss Twinkleton estimated the distance to the omnibus at five-and-twenty minutes' walk, when it was really five. The affectionate kindness of the whole circle hustled him into his greatcoat, and shoved him out into the moonlight, as if he were a fugitive traitor with whom they sympathised, and a troop of horses were at the back door. Mr. Crisparkle and his new charge, who took him to the omnibus, were so fervent in their apprehensions of his catching cold, that they shut him up in it instantly and left him, with still half-an-hour to spare.

More Confidences than One

'I KNOW very little of that gentleman, sir,' said Neville to the Minor Canon as they turned back.

'You know very little of your guardian?' the Minor Canon repeated.

'Almost nothing!'

'How came he——'

'To *be* my guardian? I'll tell you, sir. I suppose you know that we come (my sister and I) from Ceylon?'

'Indeed, no.'

'I wonder at that. We lived with a stepfather there. Our mother died there, when we were little children. We have had a wretched existence. She made him our guardian, and he was a miserly wretch who grudged us food to eat, and clothes to wear. At his death, he passed us over to this man; for no better reason that I know of, than his being a friend or connexion of his, whose name was always in print and catching his attention.'

'That was lately, I suppose?'

'Quite lately, sir. This stepfather of ours was a cruel brute as well as a grinding one. It is well he died when he did, or I might have killed him.'

Mr. Crisparkle stopped short in the moonlight and looked at his hopeful pupil in consternation.

'I surprise you, sir?' he said, with a quick change to a submissive manner.

'You shock me; unspeakably shock me.'

The pupil hung his head for a little while, as they walked on, and then said: 'You never saw him beat your sister. I have seen him beat mine, more than once or twice, and I never forgot it.'

'Nothing,' said Mr. Crisparkle, 'not even a beloved and beautiful sister's tears under dastardly ill-usage;' he became less severe, in spite of himself, as his indignation rose; 'could justify those horrible expressions that you used.'

'I am sorry I used them, and especially to you, sir. I beg to recall them.

But permit me to set you right on one point. You spoke of my sister's tears. My sister would have let him tear her to pieces, before she would have let him believe that he could make her shed a tear.'

Mr. Crisparkle reviewed those mental notes of his, and was neither at all surprised to hear it, nor at all disposed to question it.

'Perhaps you will think it strange, sir,' — this was said in a hesitating voice — 'that I should so soon ask you to allow me to confide in you, and to have the kindness to hear a word or two from me in my defence?'

'Defence?' Mr. Crisparkle repeated. 'You are not on your defence, Mr. Neville.'

'I think I am, sir. At least I know I should be, if you were better acquainted with my character.'

'Well, Mr. Neville,' was the rejoinder. 'What if you leave me to find it out?'

'Since it is your pleasure, sir,' answered the young man, with a quick change in his manner to sullen disappointment: 'since it is your pleasure to check me in my impulse, I must submit.'

There was that in the tone of this short speech which made the conscientious man to whom it was addressed uneasy. It hinted to him that he might, without meaning it, turn aside a trustfulness beneficial to a mis-shapen young mind and perhaps to his own power of directing and improving it. They were within sight of the lights in his windows, and he stopped.

'Let us turn back and take a turn or two up and down, Mr. Neville, or you may not have time to finish what you wish to say to me. You are hasty in thinking that I mean to check you. Quite the contrary. I invite your confidence.'

'You have invited it, sir, without knowing it, ever since I came here. I say "ever since," as if I had been here a week. The truth is, we came here (my sister and I) to quarrel with you, and affront you, and break away again.'

'Really?' said Mr. Crisparkle, at a dead loss for anything else to say.

'You see, we could not know what you were beforehand, sir; could we?'

'Clearly not,' said Mr. Crisparkle.

'And having liked no one else with whom we have ever been brought into contact, we had made up our minds not to like you.'

'Really?' said Mr. Crisparkle again.

'But we do like you, sir, and we see an unmistakable difference between your house and your reception of us, and anything else we have ever known. This — and my happening to be alone with you — and everything around us seeming so quiet and peaceful after Mr. Honeythunder's departure — and Cloisterham being so old and grave and beautiful, with the moon shining on it — these things inclined me to open my heart.'

'I quite understand, Mr. Neville. And it is salutary to listen to such influences.'

'In describing my own imperfections, sir, I must ask you not to suppose that I am describing my sister's. She has come out of the disadvantages of our miserable life, as much better than I am, as that Cathedral tower is higher than those chimneys.'

Mr. Crisparkle in his own breast was not so sure of this.

'I have had, sir, from my earliest remembrance, to suppress a deadly and bitter hatred. This has made me secret and revengeful. I have been always tyrannically held down by the strong hand. This has driven me, in my weakness, to the resource of being false and mean. I have been stinted of education, liberty, money, dress, the very necessaries of life, the commonest pleasures of childhood, the commonest possessions of youth. This has caused me to be utterly wanting in I don't know what emotions, or remembrances, or good instincts — I have not even a name for the thing, you see! — that you have had to work upon in other young men to whom you have been accustomed.'

'This is evidently true. But this is not encouraging,' thought Mr. Crisparkle as they turned again.

'And to finish with, sir: I have been brought up among abject and servile dependents, of an inferior race, and I may easily have contracted some affinity with them. Sometimes, I don't know but that it may be a drop of what is tigerish in their blood.'

'As in the case of that remark just now,' thought Mr. Crisparkle.

'In a last word of reference to my sister, sir (we are twin children), you ought to know, to her honour, that nothing in our misery ever subdued her, though it often cowed me. When we ran away from it (we ran away four times in six years, to be soon brought back and cruelly punished), the flight was always of her planning and leading. Each time she dressed as a boy, and showed the daring of a man. I take it we were seven years old when we first decamped; but I remember, when I lost the pocket-knife with which she was to have cut her hair short, how desperately she tried to tear it out, or bite it off. I have nothing further to say, sir, except that I hope you will bear with me and make allowance for me.'

'Of that, Mr. Neville, you may be sure,' returned the Minor Canon, 'I don't preach more than I can help, and I will not repay your confidence with a sermon. But I entreat you to bear in mind, very seriously and steadily, that if I am to do you any good, it can only be with your own assistance; and that you can only render that, efficiently, by seeking aid from Heaven.'

'I will try to do my part, sir.'

'And, Mr. Neville, I will try to do mine. Here is my hand on it. May God bless our endeavours!'

They were now standing at his house-door, and a cheerful sound of voices and laughter was heard within.

'We will take one more turn before going in,' said Mr. Crisparkle, 'for I want to ask you a question. When you said you were in a changed mind concerning me, you spoke, not only for yourself, but for your sister too?'

'Undoubtedly I did, sir.'

'Excuse me, Mr. Neville, but I think you have had no opportunity of communicating with your sister, since I met you. Mr. Honeythunder was very eloquent; but perhaps I may venture to say, without ill-nature, that he rather monopolised the occasion. May you not have answered for your sister without sufficient warrant?'

Neville shook his head with a proud smile.

'You don't know, sir, yet, what a complete understanding can exist between my sister and me, though no spoken word — perhaps hardly as much as a look — may have passed between us. She not only feels as I have described, but she very well knows that I am taking this opportunity of speaking to you, both for her and for myself.'

Mr. Crisparkle looked in his face, with some incredulity; but his face expressed such absolute and firm conviction of the truth of what he said, that Mr. Crisparkle looked at the pavement, and mused until they came to his door again.

'I will ask for one more turn, sir, this time,' said the young man, with a rather heightened colour rising in his face. 'But for Mr. Honeythunder's — I think you called it eloquence, sir?' (somewhat slyly.)

'I — yes, I called it eloquence,' said Mr. Crisparkle.

'But for Mr. Honeythunder's eloquence, I might have had no need to ask you what I am going to ask you. This Mr. Edwin Drood, sir: I think that's the name?'

'Quite correct,' said Mr. Crisparkle. 'D-r-double o-d.'

'Does he — or did he — read with you, sir?'

'Never, Mr. Neville. He comes here visiting his relation, Mr Jasper.'

'Is Miss Bud his relation too, sir?'

('Now, why should he ask that, with sudden superciliousness?' thought Mr. Crisparkle.) Then he explained, aloud, what he knew of the little story of their betrothal.

'O! *that's* it, is it?' said the young man. 'I understand his air of proprietorship now!'

This was said so evidently to himself, or to anybody rather than Mr. Crisparkle, that the latter instinctively felt as if to notice it would be almost tantamount to noticing a passage in a letter which he had read by chance over the writer's shoulder. A moment afterwards they re-entered the house.

Mr. Jasper was seated at the piano as they came into his drawing-room, and was accompanying Miss Rosebud while she sang. It was a consequence of his playing the accompaniment without notes, and of her being a heedless little creature, very apt to go wrong, that he followed her lips most attentively, with his eyes as well as hands; carefully and softly hinting the key-note from time to time. Standing with an arm drawn round her, but with a face far more intent on Mr. Jasper than on her singing, stood Helena, between whom and her brother an instantaneous recognition passed, in which Mr. Crisparkle saw, or thought he saw, the understanding that had been spoken of, flash out. Mr. Neville then took his admiring station, leaning against the piano, opposite the singer; Mr. Crisparkle sat down by the china shepherdess; Edwin Drood gallantly furled and unfurled Miss Twinkleton's fan; and that lady passively claimed that sort of exhibitor's proprietorship in the accomplishment on view, which Mr. Tope, the Verger, daily claimed in the Cathedral service.

The song went on. It was a sorrowful strain of parting, and the fresh young voice was very plaintive and tender. As Jasper watched the pretty lips, and ever and again hinted the one note, as though it were a low whisper from himself, the voice became less steady, until all at once the singer broke into a burst of tears, and shrieked out, with her hands over her eyes: 'I can't bear this! I am frightened! Take me away!'

With one swift turn of her lithe figure, Helena laid the little beauty on a

In the Drawing Room

sofa, as if she had never caught her up. Then, on one knee beside her, and with one hand upon her rosy mouth, while with the other she appealed to all the rest, Helena said to them: 'It's nothing; it's all over; don't speak to her for one minute, and she is well!'

Jasper's hands had, in the same instant, lifted themselves from the keys, and were now poised above them, as though he waited to resume. In that attitude he yet sat quiet: not even looking round, when all the rest had changed their places and were reassuring one another.

'Pussy's not used to an audience; that's the fact,' said Edwin Drood. 'She got nervous, and couldn't hold out. Besides, Jack, you are such a conscientious master, and require so much, that I believe you make her afraid of you. No wonder.'

'No wonder,' repeated Helena.

'There, Jack, you hear! You would be afraid of him, under similar circumstances, wouldn't you, Miss Landless?'

'Not under any circumstances,' returned Helena.

Jasper brought down his hands, looked over his shoulder, and begged to thank Miss Landless for her vindication of his character. Then he fell to dumbly playing, without striking the notes, while his little pupil was taken to an open window for air, and was otherwise petted and restored. When she was brought back, his place was empty. 'Jack's gone, Pussy,' Edwin told her. 'I am more than half afraid he didn't like to be charged with being the Monster who had frightened you.' But she answered never a word, and shivered, as if they had made her a little too cold.

Miss Twinkleton now opining that indeed these were late hours, Mrs. Crisparkle, for finding ourselves outside the walls of the Nuns' House, and that we who undertook the formation of the future wives and mothers of England (the last words in a lower voice, as requiring to be communicated in confidence) were really bound (voice coming up again) to set a better example than one of rakish habits, wrappers were put in requisition, and the two young cavaliers volunteered to see the ladies home. It was soon done, and the gate of the Nuns' House closed upon them.

The boarders had retired, and only Mrs. Tisher in solitary vigil awaited the new pupil. Her bedroom being within Rosa's, very little introduction or explanation was necessary, before she was placed in charge of her new friend, and left for the night.

'This is a blessed relief, my dear,' said Helena. 'I have been dreading all day, that I should be brought to bay at this time.'

'There are not many of us,' returned Rosa, and we are good-natured girls; at least the others are; I can answer for them.'

'I can answer for you,' laughed Helena, searching the lovely little face with her dark, fiery eyes, and tenderly caressing the small figure. 'You will be a friend to me, won't you?'

'I hope so. But the idea of my being a friend to you seems too absurd, though.'

'Why?'

'O, I am such a mite of a thing, and you are so womanly and handsome. You seem to have resolution and power enough to crush me. I shrink into nothing by the side of your presence even.'

'I am a neglected creature, my dear, unacquainted with all accomplishments, sensitively conscious that I have everything to learn, and deeply ashamed to own my ignorance.'

'And yet you acknowledge everything to me!' said Rosa.

'My pretty one, can I help it? There is a fascination in you.'

'O! is there though?' pouted Rosa, half in jest and half in earnest. 'What a pity Master Eddy doesn't feel it more!'

Of course her relations towards that young gentleman had been already imparted in Minor Canon Corner.

'Why, surely he must love you with all his heart!' cried Helena, with an earnestness that threatened to blaze into ferocity if he didn't.

'Eh? O, well, I suppose he does,' said Rosa, pouting again; 'I am sure I have no right to say he doesn't. Perhaps it's my fault. Perhaps I am not as nice to him as I ought to be. I don't think I am. But it *is* so ridiculous!'

Helena's eyes demanded what was.

'*We* are,' said Rosa, answering as if she had spoken. 'We are such a ridiculous couple. And we are always quarrelling.'

'Why?'

'Because we both know we are ridiculous, my dear!' Rosa gave that answer as if it were the most conclusive answer in the world.

Helena's masterful look was intent upon her face for a few moments, and then she impulsively put out both her hands and said:

'You will be my friend and help me?'

'Indeed, my dear, I will,' replied Rosa, in a tone of affectionate childishness that went straight and true to her heart; 'I will be as good a friend as such a mite of a thing can be to such a noble creature as you. And be a friend to me, please; I don't understand myself: and I want a friend who can understand me, very much indeed.'

Helena Landless kissed her, and retaining both her hands said:

'Who is Mr. Jasper?'

Rosa turned aside her head in answering: 'Eddy's uncle, and my music-master.'

'You do not love him?'

'Ugh!' She put her hands up to her face, and shook with fear or horror.

'You know that he loves you?'

'O, don't, don't, don't!' cried Rosa, dropping on her knees, and clinging to her new resource. 'Don't tell me of it! He terrifies me. He haunts my thoughts, like a dreadful ghost. I feel that I am never safe from him. I feel as if he could pass in through the wall when he is spoken of.' She actually did look round, as if she dreaded to see him standing in the shadow behind her.

'Try to tell me about it, darling.'

'Yes, I will, I will. Because you are so strong. But hold me the while, and stay with me afterwards.'

'My child! You speak as if he had threatened you in some dark way.'

'He has never spoken to me about — that. Never.'

'What has he done?'

'He has made a slave of me with his looks. He has forced me to understand him, without his saying a word; and he has forced me to keep silence, without his uttering a threat. When I play, he never moves his eyes from my hands. When I sing, he never moves his eyes from my lips. When he corrects me, and strikes a note, or a chord, or plays a passage, he himself is in the sounds, whispering that he pursues me as a lover, and commanding me to keep his secret. I avoid his eyes, but he forces me to see them without looking at them. Even when a glaze comes over them (which is sometimes the case), and he seems to wander away into a frightful sort of dream in which he threatens most, he obliges me to know it, and to know that he is sitting close at my side, more terrible to me than ever.'

'What is this imagined threatening, pretty one? What is threatened?'

'I don't know. I have never even dared to think or wonder what it is.'

'And was this all, to-night?'

'This was all; except that to-night when he watched my lips so closely as I was singing, besides feeling terrified I felt ashamed and passionately hurt. It was as if he kissed me, and I couldn't bear it, but cried out. You must never breathe this to any one. Eddy is devoted to him. But you said to-night that you would not be afraid of him, under any circumstances, and that gives me — who am so much afraid of him — courage to tell only you. Hold me! Stay with me! I am too frightened to be left by myself.'

The lustrous gipsy-face drooped over the clinging arms and bosom, and the wild black hair fell down protectingly over the childish form. There was a slumbering gleam of fire in the intense dark eyes, though they were then softened with compassion and admiration. Let whomsoever it most concerned look well to it!

Daggers Drawn

THE two young men, having seen the damsels, their charges, enter the courtyard of the Nuns' House, and finding themselves coldly stared at by the brazen door-plate, as if the battered old beau with the glass in his eye were insolent, look at one another, look along the perspective of the moonlit street, and slowly walk away together.

'Do you stay here long, Mr. Drood?' says Neville.

'Not this time,' is the careless answer. 'I leave for London again, to-morrow. But I shall be here, off and on, until next Midsummer; then I shall take my leave of Cloisterham, and England too; for many a long day, I expect.'

'Are you going abroad?'

'Going to wake up Egypt a little,' is the condescending answer.

'Are you reading?'

'Reading?' repeats Edwin Drood, with a touch of contempt. 'No. Doing, working, engineering. My small patrimony was left a part of the capital of the Firm I am with, by my father, a former partner; and I am a charge upon the Firm until I come of age; and then I step into my modest share in the concern. Jack — you met him at dinner — is, until then, my guardian and trustee.'

'I heard from Mr. Crisparkle of your other good fortune.'

'What do you mean by my other good fortune?'

Neville has made his remark in a watchfully advancing, and yet furtive and shy manner, very expressive of that peculiar air already noticed, of being at once hunter and hunted. Edwin has made his retort with an abruptness not at all polite. They stop and interchange a rather heated look.

'I hope,' says Neville, 'there is no offence, Mr. Drood, in my innocently referring to your betrothal?'

'By George!' cries Edwin, leading on again at a somewhat quicker pace;

'everybody in this chattering old Cloisterham refers to it. I wonder no public-house has been set up, with my portrait for the sign of The Betrothed's Head. Or Pussy's portrait. One or the other.'

'I am not accountable for Mr. Crisparkle's mentioning the matter to me, quite openly,' Neville begins.

'No; that's true; you are not,' Edwin Drood assents.

'But,' resumes Neville, 'I am accountable for mentioning it to you. And I did so, on the supposition that you could not fail to be highly proud of it.'

Now, there are these two curious touches of human nature working the secret springs of this dialogue. Neville Landless is already enough impressed by Little Rosebud, to feel indignant that Edwin Drood (far below her) should hold his prize so lightly. Edwin Drood is already enough impressed by Helena, to feel indignant that Helena's brother (far below her) should dispose of him so coolly, and put him out of the way so entirely.

However, the last remark had better be answered. So, says Edwin:

'I don't know, Mr. Neville' (adopting that mode of address from Mr. Crisparkle), 'that what people are proudest of, they usually talk most about; I don't know either, that what they are proudest of, they most like other people to talk about. But I live a busy life, and I speak under correction by you readers, who ought to know everything, and I daresay do.'

By this time they had both become savage; Mr. Neville out in the open; Edwin Drood under the transparent cover of a popular tune, and a stop now and then to pretend to admire picturesque effects in the moonlight before him.

'It does not seem to me very civil in you,' remarks Neville, at length, 'to reflect upon a stranger who comes here, not having had your advantages, to try to make up for lost time. But, to be sure, *I* was not brought up in "busy life," and my ideas of civility were formed among Heathens.'

'Perhaps, the best civility, whatever kind of people we are brought up among,' retorts Edwin Drood, 'is to mind our own business. If you will set me that example, I promise to follow it.'

'Do you know that you take a great deal too much upon yourself?' is the angry rejoinder, 'and that in the part of the world I come from, you would be called to account for it?'

'By whom, for instance?' asks Edwin Drood, coming to a halt, and surveying the other with a look of disdain.

But, here a startling right hand is laid on Edwin's shoulder, and Jasper stands between them. For, it would seem that he, too, has strolled round by the Nuns' House, and has come up behind them on the shadowy side of the road.

'Ned, Ned, Ned!' he says; 'we must have no more of this. I don't like this. I have overheard high words between you two. Remember, my dear boy, you are almost in the position of host to-night. You belong, as it were, to the place, and in a manner represent it towards a stranger. Mr. Neville is a stranger, and you should respect the obligations of hospitality. And, Mr. Neville,' laying his left hand on the inner shoulder of that young gentleman, and thus walking on between them, hand to shoulder on either side; 'you will pardon me; but I appeal to you to govern your temper too. Now, what is amiss? But why ask! Let there be nothing amiss, and the question is superfluous. We are all three on a good understanding, are we not?'

After a silent struggle between the two young men who shall speak last, Edwin Drood strikes in with: 'So far as I am concerned, Jack, there is no anger in me.'

'Nor in me,' says Neville Landless, though not so freely; or perhaps so carelessly. 'But if Mr. Drood knew all that lies behind me, far away from here, he might know better how it is that sharp-edged words have sharp edges to wound me.'

'Perhaps,' says Jasper, in a soothing manner, 'we had better not qualify our good understanding. We had better not say anything having the appearance of a remonstrance or condition; it might not seem generous. Frankly and freely, you see there is no anger in Ned. Frankly and freely, there is no anger in you, Mr. Neville?'

'None at all, Mr. Jasper.' Still, not quite so frankly or so freely; or, be it said once again, not quite so carelessly perhaps.

'All over, then! Now, my bachelor gatehouse is a few yards from here, and the heater is on the fire, and the wine and glasses are on the table, and it is not a stone's throw from Minor Canon Corner. Ned, you are up and away to-morrow. We will carry Mr. Neville in with us, to take a stirrup-cup.'

'With all my heart, Jack.'

'And with all mine, Mr. Jasper.' Neville feels it impossible to say less, but would rather not go. He has an impression upon him that he has lost hold of his temper; feels that Edwin Drood's coolness, so far from being infectious, makes him red-hot.

Mr. Jasper, still walking in the centre, hand to shoulder on either side, beautifully turns the Refrain of a drinking song, and they all go up to his rooms. There, the first object visible, when he adds the light of a lamp to that of the fire, is the portrait over the chimneypiece. It is not an object calculated to improve the understanding between the two young men, as rather awkwardly reviving the subject of their difference. Accordingly, they both glance at it consciously, but say nothing. Jasper, however (who would appear from his conduct to have gained but an imperfect clue to the cause of their late high words), directly calls attention to it.

'You recognise that picture, Mr. Neville?' shading the lamp to throw the light upon it.

'I recognise it, but it is far from flattering the original.'

'O, you are hard upon it! it was done by Ned, who made me a present of it.'

'I am sorry for that, Mr. Drood.' Neville apologises, with a real intention to apologise; 'if I had known I was in the artist's presence——'

'O, a joke, sir, a mere joke,' Edwin cuts in, with a provoking yawn. 'A little humouring of Pussy's points! I'm going to paint her gravely, one of these days, if she's good.'

The air of leisurely patronage and indifference with which this is said, as the speaker throws himself back in a chair and clasps his hands at the back of his head, as a rest for it, is very exasperating to the excitable and excited Neville. Jasper looks observantly from the one to the other, slightly smiles, and turns his back to mix a jug of mulled wine at the fire. It seems to require much mixing and compounding.

'I suppose, Mr. Neville,' says Edwin, quick to resent the indignant protest against himself in the face of young Landless, which is fully as visible as the portrait, or the fire, or the lamp: 'I suppose that if you painted the picture of your lady love——'

'I can't paint,' is the hasty interruption.

'That's your misfortune, and not your fault. You would if you could. But if you could, I suppose you would make her (no matter what she was in reality), Juno, Minerva, Diana, and Venus, all in one. Eh?'

'I have no lady love, and I can't say.'

'If I were to try my hand,' says Edwin, with a boyish boastfulness getting up in him, 'on a portrait of Miss Landless — in earnest, mind you; in earnest — you should see what I could do!'

'My sister's consent to sit for it being first got, I suppose? As it never will be got, I am afraid I shall never see what you can do. I must bear the loss.'

Jasper turns round from the fire, fills a large goblet glass for Neville, fills a large goblet glass for Edwin, and hands each his own; then fills for himself, saying:

'Come, Mr. Neville, we are to drink to my nephew, Ned. As it is his foot that is in the stirrup — metaphorically — our stirrup-cup is to be devoted to him. Ned, my dearest fellow, my love!'

Jasper sets the example of nearly emptying his glass, and Neville follows it. Edwin Drood says, 'Thank you both very much,' and follows the double example.

'Look at him,' cries Jasper, stretching out his hand admiringly and tenderly, though rallyingly too. 'See where he lounges so easily, Mr. Neville! The world is all before him where to choose. A life of stirring work and interest, a life of change and excitement, a life of domestic ease and love! Look at him!'

Edwin Drood's face has become quickly and remarkably flushed with the wine; so has the face of Neville Landless. Edwin still sits thrown back in his chair, making that rest of clasped hands for his head.

'See how little he heeds it all!' Jasper proceeds in a bantering vein. 'It is hardly worth his while to pluck the golden fruit that hangs ripe on the tree for him. And yet consider the contrast, Mr. Neville. You and I have no prospect of stirring work and interest, or of change and excitement, or of domestic ease and love. You and I have no prospect (unless you are more fortunate than I am, which may easily be), but the tedious unchanging round of this dull place.'

'Upon my soul, Jack,' says Edwin, complacently, 'I feel quite apologetic for having my way smoothed as you describe. But you know what I know Jack, and it may not be so very easy as it seems, after all. May it, Pussy?' To the portrait, with a snap of his thumb and finger. 'We have got to hit it off yet; haven't we Pussy? You know what I mean, Jack.'

His speech has become thick and indistinct. Jasper, quiet and self-possessed, looks to Neville, as expecting his answer or comment. When Neville speaks, *his* speech is also thick and indistinct.

'It might have been better for Mr. Drood to have known some hardships,' he says, defiantly.

'Pray,' retorts Edwin, turning merely his eyes in that direction, 'pray why might it have been better for Mr. Drood to have known some hardships?'

'Ay,' Jasper assents, with an air of interest; 'let us know why?'

'Because they might have made him more sensible,' says Neville, 'of good fortune that is not by any means necessarily the result of his own merits.'

Mr. Jasper quickly looks to his nephew for his rejoinder.

'Have *you* known hardships, may I ask?' says Edwin Drood, sitting upright.

Mr. Jasper quickly looks to the other for his retort.

'I have.'

'And what have they made *you* sensible of?'

Mr. Jasper's play of eyes between the two holds good throughout the dialogue, to the end.

'I have told you once before to-night.'

'You have done nothing of the sort.'

'I tell you I have. That you take a great deal too much upon yourself.'

'You added something else to that, if I remember?'

'Yes, I did say something else.'

'Say it again.'

'I said that in the part of the world I come from, you would be called to account for it.'

'Only there?' cries Edwin Drood, with a contemptuous laugh. 'A long way off, I believe? Yes; I see! That part of the world is at a safe distance.'

'Say here, then,' rejoins the other, rising in a fury. 'Say anywhere! Your vanity is intolerable, your conceit is beyond endurance; you talk as if you were some rare and precious prize, instead of a common boaster. You are a common fellow, and a common boaster.'

'Pooh, pooh,' says Edwin Drood, equally furious, but more collected; 'how should you know? You may know a black common fellow, or a black common boaster, when you see him (and no doubt you have a large acquaintance that way); but you are no judge of white men.'

This insulting allusion to his dark skin infuriates Neville to that violent degree, that he flings the dregs of his wine at Edwin Drood, and is in the act of flinging the goblet after it, when his arm is caught in the nick of time by Jasper.

'Ned, my dear fellow!' he cries in a loud voice; 'I entreat you, I command you, to be still!' There has been a rush of all the three, and a clattering of glasses and overturning of chairs. 'Mr. Neville, for shame! Give this glass to me. Open your hand, sir. I WILL have it!'

But Neville throws him off, and pauses for an instant, in a raging passion, with the goblet yet in his uplifted hand. Then, he dashes it down under the grate, with such force that the broken splinters fly out again in a shower; and he leaves the house.

When he first emerges into the night air, nothing around him is still or steady; nothing around him shows like what it is; he only knows that he stands with a bare head in the midst of a blood-red whirl, waiting to be struggled with, and to struggle to the death.

But, nothing happening, and the moon looking down upon him as if he were dead after a fit of wrath, he holds his steam-hammer beating head and heart, and staggers away. Then, he becomes half-conscious of having heard himself bolted and barred out, like a dangerous animal; and thinks what shall he do?

Some wildly passionate ideas of the river dissolve under the spell of the moonlight on the Cathedral and the graves, and the remembrance of his sister, and the thought of what he owes to the good man who has but that very day won his confidence and given him his pledge. He repairs to Minor Canon Corner, and knocks softly at the door.

It is Mr. Crisparkle's custom to sit up last of the early household, very softly touching his piano and practising his favourite parts in concerted vocal music. The south wind that goes where it lists, by way of Minor Canon Corner on a still night, is not more subdued than Mr. Crisparkle at such times, regardful of the slumbers of the china shepherdess.

His knock is immediately answered by Mr. Crisparkle himself. When he opens the door, candle in hand, his cheerful face falls, and disappointed amazement is in it.

'Mr. Neville! In this disorder! Where have you been?'

'I have been to Mr. Jasper's, sir. With his nephew.'

'Come in.'

The Minor Canon props him by the elbow with a strong hand (in a strictly scientific manner, worthy of his morning trainings), and turns him into his own little book-room, and shuts the door.

'I have begun ill, sir. I have begun dreadfully ill.'

'Too true. You are not sober, Mr. Neville.'

'I am afraid I am not, sir, though I can satisfy you at another time that I have had a very little indeed to drink, and that it overcame me in the strangest and most sudden manner.'

'Mr. Neville, Mr. Neville,' says the Minor Canon, shaking his head with a sorrowful smile; 'I have heard that said before.'

'I think — my mind is much confused, but I think — it is equally true of Mr. Jasper's nephew, sir.'

'Very likely,' is the dry rejoinder.

'We quarrelled, sir. He insulted me most grossly. He had heated that tigerish blood I told you of to-day, before then.'

'Mr. Neville,' rejoins the Minor Canon, mildly, but firmly: 'I request you not to speak to me with that clenched right hand. Unclench it, if you please.'

'He goaded me, sir,' pursues the young man, instantly obeying, 'beyond my power of endurance. I cannot say whether or no he meant it at first, but he did it. He certainly meant it at last. In short, sir,' with an irrepressible outburst, 'in the passion into which he lashed me, I would have cut him down if I could, and I tried to do it.'

'You have clenched that hand again,' is Mr. Crisparkle's quiet commentary.

'I beg your pardon, sir.'

'You know your room, for I showed it you before dinner; but I will accompany you to it once more. Your arm, if you please. Softly, for the house is all a-bed.'

Scooping his hand into the same scientific elbow-rest as before, and backing it up with the inert strength of his arm, as skilfully as a Police Expert, and with an apparent repose quite unattainable by novices, Mr. Crisparkle conducts his pupil to the pleasant and orderly old room prepared for him. Arrived there, the young man throws himself into a chair, and, flinging his arms upon his reading-table, rests his head upon them with an air of wretched self-reproach.

The gentle Minor Canon has had it in his thoughts to leave the room, without a word. But looking round at the door, and seeing this dejected figure, he turns back to it, touches it with a mild hand, says 'Good night!' A sob is his only acknowledgment. He might have had many a worse; perhaps, could have had few better.

Another soft knock at the outer door attracts his attention as he goes down-stairs. He opens it to Mr. Jasper, holding in his hand the pupil's hat.

'We have had an awful scene with him,' says Jasper, in a low voice.

'Has it been so bad as that?'

'Murderous!'

Mr. Crisparkle remonstrates: 'No, no, no. Do not use such strong words.'

'He might have laid my dear boy dead at my feet. It is no fault of his, that he did not. But that I was, through the mercy of God, swift and strong with him, he would have cut him down on my hearth.'

The phrase smites home. 'Ah!' thinks Mr. Crisparkle, 'his own words!'

'Seeing what I have seen to-night, and hearing what I have heard,' adds Jasper, with great earnestness, 'I shall never know peace of mind when there is danger of those two coming together, with no one else to interfere. It was horrible. There is something of the tiger in his dark blood.'

'Ah!' thinks Mr. Crisparkle, 'so he said!'

'You, my dear sir,' pursues Jasper, taking his hand, 'even you, have accepted a dangerous charge.'

'You need have no fear for me, Jasper,' returns Mr. Crisparkle, with a quiet smile. 'I have none for myself.'

'I have none for myself,' returns Jasper, with an emphasis on the last pronoun, 'because I am not, nor am I in the way of being, the object of his hostility. But you may be, and my dear boy has been. Good night!'

Mr. Crisparkle goes in, with the hat that has so easily, so almost imperceptibly, acquired the right to be hung up in his hall; hangs it up; and goes thoughtfully to bed.

Birds in the Bush

Rosa, having no relation that she knew of in the world, had, from the seventh year of her age, known no home but the Nuns' House, and no mother but Miss Twinkleton. Her remembrance of her own mother was of a pretty little creature like herself (not much older than herself it seemed to her), who had been brought home in her father's arms, drowned. The fatal accident had happened at a party of pleasure. Every fold and colour in the pretty summer dress, and even the long wet hair, with scattered petals of ruined flowers still clinging to it, as the dead young figure, in its sad, sad beauty lay upon the bed, were fixed indelibly in Rosa's recollection. So were the wild despair and the subsequent bowed-down grief of her poor young father, who died broken-hearted on the first anniversary of that hard day.

The betrothal of Rosa grew out of the soothing of his year of mental distress by his fast friend and old college companion, Drood: who likewise had been left a widower in his youth. But he, too, went the silent road into which all earthly pilgrimages merge, some sooner, and some later; and thus the young couple had come to be as they were.

The atmosphere of pity surrounding the little orphan girl when she first came to Cloisterham, had never cleared away. It had taken brighter hues as she grew older, happier, prettier; now it had been golden, now roseate, and now azure; but it had always adorned her with some soft light of its own. The general desire to console and caress her, had caused her to be treated in the beginning as a child much younger than her years; the same desire had caused her to be still petted when she was a child no longer. Who should be her favourite, who should anticipate this or that small present, or do her this or that small service; who should take her home for the holidays; who should write to her the oftenest when they were separated, and whom she would most rejoice to see again when they were reunited; even these gentle rivalries were not without their slight dashes of bitterness in the Nuns' House. Well for the poor Nuns in their day, if they hid no harder strife under their veils and rosaries!

Thus Rosa had grown to be an amiable, giddy, wilful, winning little creature; spoilt, in the sense of counting upon kindness from all around her; but not in the sense of repaying it with indifference. Possessing an exhaustless well of affection in her nature, its sparkling waters had freshened and brightened the Nuns' House for years, and yet its depths had never yet been moved: what might betide when that came to pass; what developing changes might fall upon the heedless head, and light heart, then; remained to be seen.

By what means the news that there had been a quarrel between the two young men overnight, involving even some kind of onslaught by Mr. Neville upon Edwin Drood, got into Miss Twinkleton's establishment before breakfast, it is impossible to say. Whether it was brought in by the birds of the air, or came blowing in with the very air itself, when the casement windows were set open; whether the baker brought it kneaded into the bread, or the milkman delivered it as part of the adulteration of his milk; or the housemaids, beating the dust out of their mats against the gateposts, received it in exchange deposited on the mats by the town atmosphere; certain it is that the news permeated every gable of the old building before Miss Twinkleton was down, and that Miss Twinkleton herself received it through Mrs. Tisher, while yet in the act of dressing; or (as she might have expressed the phrase to a parent or guardian of a mythological turn) of sacrificing to the Graces.

Miss Landless's brother had thrown a bottle at Mr. Edwin Drood.

Miss Landless's brother had thrown a knife at Mr. Edwin Drood.

A knife became suggestive of a fork; and Miss Landless's brother had thrown a fork at Mr. Edwin Drood.

As in the governing precedence of Peter Piper, alleged to have picked the peck of pickled pepper, it was held physically desirable to have evidence of the existence of the peck of pickled pepper which Peter Piper was alleged to have picked; so, in this case, it was held psychologically important to know why Miss Landless's brother threw a bottle, knife, or fork — or bottle, Knife, *and* fork — for the cook had been given to understand it was all three — at Mr. Edwin Drood?

Well, then. Miss Landless's brother had said he admired Miss Bud. Mr. Edwin Drood had said to Miss Landless's brother that he had no business to admire Miss Bud. Miss Landless's brother had then 'up'd' (this was the cook's exact information) with the bottle, knife, fork, and decanter (the decanter now coolly flying at everybody's head, without the least introduction), and thrown them all at Mr. Edwin Drood.

Poor little Rosa put a forefinger into each of her ears when these rumours began to circulate, and retired into a corner, beseeching not to be told any more; but Miss Landless, begging permission of Miss Twinkleton to go and speak with her brother, and pretty plainly showing that she would take it if it were not given, struck out the more definite course of going to Mr. Crisparkle's for accurate intelligence.

When she came back (being first closeted with Miss Twinkleton, in order that anything objectionable in her tidings might be retained by that discreet filter), she imparted to Rosa only, what had taken place; dwelling with a flushed cheek cn the provocation her brother had received, but almost limiting it to that last gross affront as crowning 'some other words between them,' and, out of consideration for her new friend, passing lightly over the fact that the other words had originated in her lover's taking things in general so very easily. To Rosa direct, she brought a petition from her brother that she would forgive him; and, having delivered it with sisterly earnestness, made an end of the subject.

It was reserved for Miss Twinkleton to tone down the public mind of the Nuns' House. That lady, therefore, entering in a stately manner what plebeians might have called the school-room, but what, in the patrician language of the head of the Nuns' House, was euphuistically, not to say round-aboutedly, denominated 'the apartment allotted to study,' and saying with a forensic air, 'Ladies!' all rose. Mrs. Tisher at the same time grouped herself behind her chief, as representing Queen Elizabeth's first historical female friend at Tilbury fort. Miss Twinkleton then proceeded to remark that Rumour, Ladies, had been represented by the bard of Avon — needless were it to mention the immortal SHAKESPEARE, also called the Swan of his native river, not improbably with some reference to the ancient superstition that that bird of graceful plumage (Miss Jennings will please stand upright) sang sweetly on the approach of death, for which we have no ornithological authority, — Rumour, Ladies, had been represented by that bard — hem! —

'who drew
The celebrated Jew,'

as painted full of tongues. Rumour in Cloisterham (Miss Ferdinand will honour me with her attention) was no exception to the great limner's portrait of Rumour elsewhere. A slight *fracas* between two young gentlemen occurring last night within a hundred miles of these peaceful walls (Miss Ferdinand, being apparently incorrigible, will have the kindness to write out this evening, in the original language, the first four fables of our vivacious neighbour, Monsieur La Fontaine) had been very grossly exaggerated by Rumour's voice. In the first alarm and anxiety arising from our sympathy with a sweet young friend, not wholly to be dissociated from one of the gladiators in the bloodless arena in question (the impropriety of Miss Reynolds's appearing to stab herself in the hand with a pin, is far too obvious, and too glaringly unlady-like, to be pointed out), we descended from our maiden elevation to discuss this uncongenial and this unfit theme. Responsible inquiries having assured us that it was but one of those 'airy nothings' pointed at by the Poet (whose name and date of birth Miss Giggles will supply within half an hour), we would now discard the subject, and concentrate our minds upon the grateful labours of the day.

But the subject so survived all day, nevertheless, that Miss Ferdinand got into new trouble by surreptitiously clapping on a paper moustache at dinner-time, and going through the motions of aiming a water-bottle at Miss Giggles, who drew a table-spoon in defence.

Now, Rosa thought of this unlucky quarrel a great deal, and thought of it with an uncomfortable feeling that she was involved in it, as cause, or consequence, or what not, through being in a false position altogether as to her marriage engagement. Never free from such uneasiness when she was with her affianced husband, it was not likely that she would be free from it when they were apart. To-day, too, she was cast in upon herself, and deprived of the relief of talking freely with her new friend, because the quarrel had been with Helena's brother, and Helena undisguisedly avoided the subject as a delicate and difficult one to herself. At this critical time, of all times, Rosa's guardian was announced as having come to see her.

Mr. Grewgious had been well selected for his trust, as a man of incorruptible integrity, but certainly for no other appropriate quality discernible on the surface. He was an arid, sandy man, who, if he had been put into a grinding-mill, looked as if he would have ground immediately into high-dried snuff. He had a scanty flat crop of hair, in colour and consistency like some very mangy yellow fur tippet; it was so unlike hair, that it must have been a wig, but for the stupendous improbability of anybody's voluntarily sporting such a head. The little play of feature that his face presented, was cut deep into it, in a few hard curves that made it more like work; and he had certain notches in his forehead, which looked as though Nature had been about to touch them into sensibility or refinement, when she had impatiently thrown away the chisel, and said: 'I really cannot be worried to finish off this man; let him go as he is.'

With too great length of throat at his upper end, and too much ankle-bone and heel at his lower; with an awkward and hesitating manner; with a shambling walk; and with what is called a near sight — which perhaps prevented his observing how much white cotton stocking he displayed to the public eye, in contrast with his black suit — Mr. Grewgious still had some strange capacity in him of making on the whole an agreeable impression.

Mr. Grewgious was discovered by his ward, much discomfited by being in Miss Twinkleton's company in Miss Twinkleton's own sacred room. Dim forebodings of being examined in something, and not coming well out of it, seemed to oppress the poor gentleman when found in these circumstances.

'My dear, how do you do? I am glad to see you. My dear, how much improved you are. Permit me to hand you a chair, my dear.'

Miss Twinkleton rose at her little writing-table, saying, with general sweetness, as to the polite Universe: 'Will you permit me to retire?'

'By no means, madam, on my account. I beg that you will not move.'

'I must entreat permission to *move,*' returned Miss Twinkleton, repeating the word with a charming grace; 'but I will not withdraw, since you are so obliging. If I wheel my desk to this corner window, shall I be in the way?'

'Madam! In the way!'

'You are very kind. — Rosa, my dear, you will be under no restraint, I am sure.'

Here Mr. Grewgious, left by the fire with Rosa, said again: 'My dear, how do you do? I am glad to see you, my dear.' And having waited for her to sit down, sat down himself.

'My visits,' said Mr. Grewgious, 'are, like those of the angels — not that I compare myself to an angel.'

'No sir,' said Rosa.

'Not by any means,' assented Mr. Grewgious. 'I merely refer to my visits, which are few and far between. The angels are, we know very well, up-stairs.'

Miss Twinkleton looked round with a kind of stiff stare.

'I refer, my dear,' said Mr. Grewgious, laying his hand on Rosa's, as the possibility thrilled through his frame of his otherwise seeming to take the awful liberty of calling Miss Twinkleton my dear; 'I refer to the other young ladies.'

Miss Twinkleton resumed her writing.

Mr. Grewgious, with a sense of not having managed his opening point quite as neatly as he might have desired, smoothed his head from back to front as if he had just dived, and were pressing the water out — this smoothing action, however superfluous, was habitual with him — and took a pocket-book from his coat-pocket, and a stump of black-lead pencil from his waistcoat-pocket.

'I made,' he said, turning the leaves: 'I made a guiding memorandum or so — as I usually do, for I have no conversational powers whatever — to which I will, with your permission, my dear, refer. "Well and happy." Truly. You are well and happy, my dear? You look so.'

'Yes, indeed, sir,' answered Rosa.

'For which,' said Mr. Grewgious, with a bend of his head towards the corner window, 'our warmest acknowledgements are due, and I am sure are rendered, to the maternal kindness and the constant care and consideration of the lady whom I have now the honour to see before me.'

This point, again, made but a lame departure from Mr. Grewgious, and never got to its destination; for, Miss Twinkleton, feeling that the courtesies required her to be by this time quite outside the conversation, was biting the end of her pen, and looking upward, as waiting for the descent of an idea from any member of the Celestial Nine who might have one to spare.

Mr. Grewgious smoothed his smooth head again, and then made another reference to his pocket-book; lining out 'well and happy,' as disposed of.

'"Pounds, shillings, and pence," is my next note. A dry subject for a young lady, but an important subject too. Life is pounds, shillings, and pence. Death is —' A sudden recollection of the death of her two parents seemed to stop him, and he said in a softer tone, and evidently inserting the negative as an after-thought: 'Death is *not* pounds, shillings, and pence.'

His voice was as hard and dry as himself, and Fancy might have ground it straight, like himself, into high-dried snuff. And yet, through the very limited means of expression that he possessed, he seemed to express kindness. If Nature had but finished him off, kindness might have been recognisable in his face at this moment. But if the notches in his forehead wouldn't fuse together, and if his face would work and couldn't play, what could he do, poor man!

'"Pounds, shillings, and pence." You find your allowance always sufficient for your wants, my dear?'

Rosa wanted for nothing, and therefore it was ample.

'And you are not in debt?'

Rosa laughed at the idea of being in debt. It seemed, to her inexperience, a comical vagary of the imagination. Mr. Grewgious stretched his near sight to be sure that this was her view of the case. 'Ah!' he said, as comment, with a furtive glance towards Miss Twinkleton, and lining out pounds, shillings, and pence: 'I spoke of having got among the angels! So I did!'

Rosa felt what his next memorandum would prove to be, and was blushing and folding a crease in her dress with one embarrassed hand, long before he found it.

'"Marriage." Hem!' Mr. Grewgious carried his smoothing hand down over his eyes and nose, and even chin, before drawing his chair a little nearer, and speaking a little more confidentially: 'I now touch, my dear, upon the point that is the direct cause of my troubling you with the present visit. Otherwise, being a particularly Angular man, I should not have intruded here. I am the last man to intrude into a sphere for which I am so entirely unfitted. I feel, on these premises, as if I was a bear — with the cramp — in a youthful Cotillion.'

His ungainliness gave him enough of the air of his simile to set Rosa off laughing heartily.

'It strikes you in the same light,' said Mr. Grewgious, with perfect calmness. 'Just so. To return to my memorandum. Mr. Edwin has been to and fro here, as was arranged. You have mentioned that, in your quarterly letters to me. And you like him, and he likes you.'

'I *like* him very much, sir,' rejoined Rosa.

'So I said, my dear,' returned her guardian, for whose ear the timid emphasis was much too fine. 'Good. And you correspond.'

'We write to one another,' said Rosa, pouting, as she recalled their epistolary differences.

'Such is the meaning that I attach to the word "correspond" in this application, my dear,' said Mr. Grewgious. 'Good. All goes well, time works on, and at this next Christmas-time it will become necessary, as a matter of form, to give the exemplary lady in the corner window, to whom we are so much indebted, business notice of your departure in the ensuing half-year. Your relations with her are far more than business relations, no doubt; but a residue of business remains in them, and business is business ever. I am a particularly Angular man,' proceeded Mr. Grewgious, as if it suddenly occurred to him to mention it, 'and I am not used to give anything away. If, for these two reasons, some competent Proxy would give *you* away, I should take it very kindly.'

Rosa intimated, with her eyes on the ground, that she thought a substitute might be found, if required.

'Surely, surely,' said Mr. Grewgious. 'For instance, the gentleman who teaches Dancing here — he would know how to do it with graceful propriety. He would advance and retire in a manner satisfactory to the feelings of the officiating clergyman, and of yourself, and the bridegroom, and all parties concerned. I am — I am a particularly Angular man,' said Mr. Grewgious, as if he had made up his mind to screw it out at last: 'and should only blunder.'

Rosa sat still and silent. Perhaps her mind had not got quite so far as the ceremony yet, but was lagging on the way there.

'Memorandum, "Will." Now, my dear,' said Mr. Grewgious, referring to his notes, disposing of 'Marriage' with his pencil, and taking a paper from his pocket; 'although I have before possessed you with the contents of your father's will, I think it right at this time to leave a certified copy of it in your hands. And although Mr. Edwin is also aware of its contents, I think it right at this time likewise to place a certified copy of it in Mr. Jasper's hand ——'

'Not in his own!' asked Rosa, looking up quickly. 'Cannot the copy go to Eddy himself?'

'Why, yes, my dear, if you particularly wish it; but I spoke of Mr. Jasper as being his trustee.'

'I do particularly wish it, if you please,' said Rosa, hurriedly and earnestly; 'I don't like Mr. Jasper to come between us, in any way.'

'It is natural, I suppose,' said Mr. Grewgious, 'that your young husband should be all in all. Yes. You observe that I say, I suppose. The fact is, I am a particularly Unnatural man, and I don't know from my own knowledge.'

Rosa looked at him with some wonder.

'I mean,' he explained, 'that young ways were never my ways. I was the only offspring of parents far advanced in life, and I half believe I was born advanced in life myself. No personality is intended towards the name you will so soon change, when I remark that while the general growth of people seem to have come into existence, buds, I seem to have come into existence a chip. I was a chip — and a very dry one — when I first became aware of myself. Respecting the other certified copy, your wish shall be complied with. Respecting your inheritance, I think you know all. It is an annuity of two hundred and fifty pounds. The savings upon that annuity, and some other items to your credit, all duly carried to account, with vouchers, will place you in possession of a lump-sum of money, rather exceeding Seventeen Hundred Pounds. I am empowered to advance the cost of your preparations for your marriage out of that fund. All is told.'

'Will you please tell me,' said Rosa, taking the paper with a prettily knitted brow, but not opening it: 'whether I am right in what I am going to say? I can understand what you tell me, so very much better than what I read in law-writings. My poor papa and Eddy's father made their agreement together, as very dear and firm and fast friends, in order that we, too, might be very dear and firm and fast friends after them?'

'Just so.'

'For the lasting good of both of us, and the lasting happiness of both of us?'

'Just so.'

'That we might be to one another even much more than they had been to one another?'

'Just so.'

'It was not bound upon Eddy, and it was not bound upon me, by any forfeit, in case ——'

'Don't be agitated, my dear. In the case that it brings tears into your affectionate eyes even to picture to yourself — in the case of your not marrying one another — no, no forfeiture on either side. You would then have been my ward until you were of age. No worse would have befallen you. Bad enough perhaps!'

'And Eddy?'

'He would have come into his partnership derived from his father, and into its arrears to his credit (if any), on attaining his majority, just as now.'

Rosa, with her perplexed face and knitted brow, bit the corner of her attested copy, as she sat with her head on one side, looking abstractedly on the floor, and smoothing it with her foot.

'In short,' said Mr. Grewgious, 'this betrothal is a wish, a sentiment, a friendly project, tenderly expressed on both sides. That it was strongly felt, and that there was a lively hope that it would prosper, there can be no doubt. When you were both children, you began to be accustomed to it, and it *has* prospered. But circumstances alter cases; and I made this visit to-day, partly, indeed principally, to discharge myself of the duty of telling you, my dear, that two young people can only be betrothed in marriage (except as a matter of convenience, and therefore mockery and misery) of their own free will, their own attachment, and their own assurance (it may or it may not prove a mistaken one, but we must take our chance of that), that they are suited to each other, and will make each other happy. Is it to be supposed, for example, that if either of your fathers were living now, and had any mistrust on that subject, his mind would not be changed by the change of circumstances involved in the change of your years? Untenable, unreasonable, inconclusive, and preposterous!'

Mr. Grewgious said all this, as if he were reading it aloud; or, still more, as if he were repeating a lesson. So expressionless of any approach to spontaneity were his face and manner.

'I have now, my dear,' he added, blurring out 'Will' with his pencil, 'discharged myself of what is doubtless a formal duty in this case, but still a duty in such a case. Memorandum, "Wishes." My dear, is there any wish of yours that I can further?'

Rosa shook her head, with an almost plaintive air of hesitation in want of help.

'Is there any instruction that I can take from you with reference to your affairs?'

'I — I should like to settle them with Eddy first, if you please,' said Rosa, plaiting the crease in her dress.

'Surely, surely,' returned Mr. Grewgious. 'You two should be of one mind in all things. Is the young gentleman expected shortly?'

'He has gone away only this morning. He will be back at Christmas.'

'Nothing could happen better. You will, on his return at Christmas, arrange all matters of detail with him; you will then communicate with me; and I will discharge myself (as a mere business acquaintance) of my business responsibilities towards the accomplished lady in the corner window. They will accrue at that season.' Blurring pencil once again. 'Memorandum, "Leave." Yes. I will now, my dear, take my leave.'

'Could I,' said Rosa, rising, as he jerked out of his chair in his ungainly way: 'could I ask you, most kindly to come to me at Christmas, if I had anything particular to say to you?'

'Why, certainly, certainly,' he rejoined; apparently — if such a word can be used of one who had no apparent lights or shadows about him — complimented by the question. 'As a particularly Angular man, I do not fit smoothly into the social circle, and consequently I have no other engagement at Christmas-time than to partake, on the twenty-fifth, of a boiled turkey and celery sauce with a — with a particularly Angular clerk I have the good fortune to possess, whose father, being a Norfolk farmer, sends him up (the turkey up), as a present to me, from the neighbourhood of Norwich. I should be quite proud of your wishing to see me, my dear. As a professional Receiver of rents, so very few people *do* wish to see me, that the novelty would be bracing.'

For his ready acquiescence, the grateful Rosa put her hands upon his shoulders, stood on tiptoe, and instantly kissed him.

'Lord bless me!' cried Mr. Grewgious. 'Thank you, my dear! The honour is almost equal to the pleasure. Miss Twinkleton, madam, I have had a most satisfactory conversation with my ward, and I will now release you from the incumbrance of my presence.'

'Nay, sir,' rejoined Miss Twinkleton, rising with a gracious condescension: 'say not incumbrance. Not so, by any means. I cannot permit you to say so.'

'Thank you, madam. I have read in the newspapers,' said Mr. Grewgious, stammering a little, 'that when a distinguished visitor (not that I am one: far from it) goes to a school (not that this is one: far from it), he asks for a holiday, or some sort of grace. It being now the afternoon in the — College — of which you are the eminent head, the young ladies might gain nothing, except in name, by having the rest of the day allowed them. But if there is any young lady at all under a cloud, might I solicit ——'

'Ah, Mr. Grewgious, Mr. Grewgious!' cried Miss Twinkleton, with a chastely-rallying forefinger. 'O you gentlemen, you gentlemen! Fie for shame, that you are so hard upon us poor maligned disciplinarians of our sex, for your sakes! But as Miss Ferdinand is at present weighed down by an incubus' — Miss Twinkleton might have said a pen-and-ink-ubus of writing out Monsieur La Fontaine — 'go to her, Rosa my dear, and tell her the penalty is remitted, in deference to the intercession of your guardian, Mr. Grewgious.'

Miss Twinkleton here achieved a curtsey, suggestive of marvels happening to her respected legs, and which she came out of nobly, three yards behind her starting-point.

As he held it incumbent upon him to call on Mr. Jasper before leaving Cloisterham, Mr. Grewgious went to the gatehouse, and climbed its postern stair. But Mr. Jasper's door being closed, and presenting on a slip of paper the word 'Cathedral,' the fact of its being service-time was borne into the mind of Mr. Grewgious. So he descended the stair again, and crossing the Close, paused at the great western folding-door of the Cathedral, which stood open on the fine and bright, though short-lived, afternoon, for the airing of the place.

'Dear me,' said Mr. Grewgious, peeping in, 'it's like looking down the throat of Old Time.'

Old Time heaved a mouldy sigh from tomb and arch and vault; and gloomy shadows began to deepen in corners; and damps began to rise from green patches of stone; and jewels, cast upon the pavement of the nave from stained glass by the declining sun, began to perish. Within the grill-gate of the chancel, up the steps surmounted loomingly by the fast-darkening organ, white robes could be dimly seen, and one feeble voice, rising and falling in a cracked, monotonous mutter, could at intervals be faintly heard. In the free outer air, the river, the green pastures, and the brown arable lands, the teeming hills and dales, were reddened by the sunset: while the distant little windows in windmills and farm homesteads, shone, patches of bright beaten gold. In the Cathedral, all became gray, murky, and sepulchral, and the cracked monotonous mutter went on like a dying voice, until the organ and the choir burst forth, and drowned it in a sea of music. Then, the sea fell, and the dying voice made another feeble effort, and then the sea rose high, and beat its life out, and lashed the roof, and surged among the arches, and pierced the heights of the great tower; and then the sea was dry, and all was still.

Mr. Grewgious had by that time walked to the chancel-steps, where he met the living waters coming out.

'Nothing is the matter?' Thus Jasper accosted him, rather quickly. 'You have not been sent for?'

'Not at all, not at all. I came down of my own accord. I have been to my pretty ward's, and am now homeward bound again.'

'You found her thriving?'

'Blooming indeed. Most blooming. I merely came to tell her, seriously, what a betrothal by deceased parents is.'

'And what is it — according to your judgment?'

Mr. Grewgious noticed the whiteness of the lips that asked the question, and put it down to the chilling account of the Cathedral.

'I merely came to tell her that it could not be considered binding, against any such reason for its dissolution as a want of affection, or want of disposition to carry it into effect, on the side of either party.'

'May I ask, had you any especial reason for telling her that?'

Mr. Grewgious answered somewhat sharply: 'The especial reason of doing my duty, sir. Simply that.' Then he added: 'Come, Mr. Jasper; I know your affection for your nephew, and that you are quick to feel on his behalf. I assure you that this implies not the least doubt of, or disrespect to, your nephew.'

'You could not,' returned Jasper, with a friendly pressure of his arm, as they walked on side by side, 'speak more handsomely.'

Mr. Grewgious pulled off his hat to smooth his head, and, having smoothed it, nodded it contentedly, and put his hat on again.

'I will wager,' said Jasper, smiling — his lips were still so white that he was conscious of it, and bit and moistened them while speaking: 'I will wager that she hinted no wish to be released from Ned.'

'And you will win your wager, if you do,' retorted Mr. Grewgious. 'We should allow some margin for little maidenly delicacies in a young motherless creature, under such circumstances, I suppose; it is not in my line; what do you think?'

'There can be no doubt of it.'

'I am glad you say so. Because,' proceeded Mr. Grewgious, who had all this time very knowingly felt his way round to action on his remembrance of what she had said of Jasper himself: 'because she seems to have some little delicate instinct that all preliminary arrangements had best be made between Mr. Edwin Drood and herself, don't you see? She don't want us, don't you know?'

Jasper touched himself on the breast, and said, somewhat indistinctly: 'You mean me.'

Mr. Grewgious touched himself on the breast, and said: 'I mean us. Therefore, let them have their little discussions and councils together, when Mr. Edwin Drood comes back here at Christmas; and then you and I will step in, and put the final touches to the business.'

'So, you settled with her that you would come back at Christmas?' observed Jasper. 'I see! Mr. Grewgious, as you quite fairly said just now, there is such an exceptional attachment between my nephew and me, that I am more sensitive for the dear, fortunate, happy, happy fellow than for myself. But it is only right that the young lady should be considered, as you have pointed out, and that I should accept my cue from you. I accept it. I understand that at Christmas they will complete their preparations for May, and that their marriage will be put in final train by themselves, and that nothing will remain for us but to put ourselves in train also, and have everything ready for our formal release from our trusts, on Edwin's birthday.'

'That is my understanding,' assented Mr. Grewgious, as they shook hands to part. 'God bless them both!'

'God save them both!' cried Jasper.

'I said, bless them,' remarked the former, looking back over his shoulder.

'I said, save them,' returned the latter. 'Is there any difference?'

Smoothing the Way

IT has been often enough remarked that women have a curious power of divining the characters of men, which would seem to be innate and instinctive; seeing that it is arrived at through no patient process of reasoning, that it can give no satisfactory or sufficient account of itself, and that it pronounces in the most confident manner even against accumulated observation on the part of the other sex. But it has not been quite so often remarked that this power (fallible, like every other human attribute) is for the most part absolutely incapable of self-revision; and that when it has delivered an adverse opinion which by all human lights is subsequently proved to have failed, it is undistinguishable from prejudice, in respect of its determination not to be corrected. Nay, the very possibility of contradiction or disproof, however remote, communicates to this feminine judgment from the first, in nine cases out of ten, the weakness attendant on the testimony of an interested witness; so personally and strongly does the fair diviner connect herself with her divination.

'Now, don't you think, Ma dear,' said the Minor Canon to his mother one day as she sat at her knitting in his little book-room, 'that you are rather hard on Mr. Neville?'

'No, I do *not*, Sept,' returned the old lady.

'Let us discuss it, Ma.'

'I have no objection to discuss it, Sept. I trust, my dear, I am always open to discussion.' There was a vibration in the old lady's cap, as though she internally added: 'and I should like to see the discussion that would change *my* mind!'

'Very good, Ma,' said her conciliatory son. 'There is nothing like being open to discussion.'

'I hope not, my dear,' returned the old lady, evidently shut to it.

'Well! Mr. Neville, on that unfortunate occasion, commits himself under provocation.'

'And under mulled wine,' added the old lady.

'I must admit the wine. Though I believe the two young men were much alike in that regard.'

'I don't,' said the old lady.

'Why not, Ma?'

'Because I *don't*,' said the old lady. 'Still, I am quite open to discussion.'

'But, my dear Ma, I cannot see how we are to discuss, if you take that line.'

'Blame Mr. Neville for it, Sept, and not me,' said the old lady, with stately severity.

'My dear Ma! Why Mr. Neville?'

'Because,' said Mrs. Crisparkle, retiring on first principles, 'he came home intoxicated, and did great discredit to this house, and showed great disrespect to this family.'

'That is not to be denied, Ma. He was then, and he is now, very sorry for it.'

'But for Mr. Jasper's well-bred consideration in coming up to me, next day, after service, in the Nave itself, with his gown still on, and expressing his hope that I had not been greatly alarmed or had my rest violently broken, I believe I might never have heard of that disgraceful transaction,' said the old lady.

'To be candid, Ma, I think I should have kept if from you if I could: though I had not decidedly made up my mind. I was following Jasper out, to confer with him on the subject, and to consider the expediency of his and my jointly hushing the thing up on all accounts, when I found him speaking to you. Then it was too late.'

'Too late, indeed, Sept. He was still as pale as gentlemanly ashes at what had taken place in his rooms overnight.'

'If I *had* kept it from you, Ma, you may be sure it would have been for your peace and quiet, and for the good of the young men, and in my best discharge of my duty according to my lights.'

The old lady immediately walked across the room and kissed him: saying, 'Of course, my dear Sept, I am sure of that.'

'However, it became the town-talk,' said Mr. Crisparkle, rubbing his ear, as his mother resumed her seat, and her knitting, 'and passed out of my power.'

'And I said then, Sept,' returned the old lady, 'that I thought ill of Mr. Neville. And I say now, that I think ill of Mr. Neville. And I said then, and I say now, that I hope Mr. Neville may come to good, but I don't believe he will.' Here the cap vibrated again considerably.

'I am sorry to hear you say so, Ma ——'

'I am sorry to say so, my dear,' interposed the old lady, knitting on firmly, 'but I can't help it.'

'—— For,' pursued the Minor Canon, 'it is undeniable that Mr. Neville is exceedingly industrious and attentive, and that he improves apace, and that he has — I hope I may say — an attachment to me.'

'There is no merit in the last article, my dear,' said the old lady, quickly; 'and if he says there is, I think the worse of him for the boast.'

'But, my dear Ma, he never said there was.'

'Perhaps not,' returned the old lady; 'still, I don't see that it greatly signifies.'

There was no impatience in the pleasant look with which Mr. Crisparkle contemplated the pretty old piece of china as it knitted; but there was, certainly, a humorous sense of its not being a piece of china to argue with very closely.

'Besides, Sept, ask yourself what he would be without his sister. You know what an influence she has over him; you know what a capacity she has; you know that whatever he reads with you, he reads with her. Give her her fair share of your praise, and how much do you leave for him?'

At these words Mr. Crisparkle fell into a little reverie, in which he thought of several things. He thought of the times he had seen the brother and sister together in deep converse over one of his own old college books; now, in the rimy mornings, when he made those sharpening pilgrimages to Cloisterham Weir; now, in the sombre evenings, when he faced the wind at sunset, having climbed his favourite outlook, a beetling fragment of monastery ruin; and the two studious figures passed below him along the margin of the river, in which the town fires and lights already shone, making the landscape bleaker. He thought how the consciousness had stolen upon him that in teaching one, he was teaching two; and how he had almost insensibly adapted his explanations to both minds — that with which his own was daily in contact, and that which he only approached through it. He thought of the gossip that had reached him from the Nuns' House, to the effect that Helena, whom he had mistrusted as so proud and fierce, submitted herself to the fairy-bride (as he called her), and learnt from her what she knew. He thought of the picturesque alliance between these two, externally so very different. He thought — perhaps most of all — could it be that these things were yet but so many weeks old, and had become an integral part of his life?

As, whenever the Reverend Septimus fell a-musing, his good mother took it to be an infallible sign that he 'wanted support,' the blooming old lady made all haste to the dining-room closet, to produce from it the support embodied in a glass of Constantia and a home-made biscuit. It was a most wonderful closet, worthy of Cloisterham and of Minor Canon Corner. Above it, a portrait of Handel in a flowing wig beamed down at the spectator, with a knowing air of being up to the contents of the closet, and a musical air of intending to combine all its harmonies in one delicious fugue. No common closet with a vulgar door on hinges, openable all at once, and leaving nothing to be disclosed by degrees, this rare closet had a lock in mid-air, where two perpendicular slides met; the one falling down, and the other pushing up. The upper slide, on being pulled down (leaving the lower a double mystery), revealed deep shelves of pickle-jars, jam-pots, tin canisters, spice-boxes, and agreeably outlandish vessels of blue and white, the luscious lodgings of preserved tamarinds and ginger. Every benevolent inhabitant of this retreat had his name inscribed upon his stomach. The pickles, in a uniform of rich brown double-breasted buttoned coat, and yellow or sombre drab continuations, announced their portly forms, in printed capitals, as Walnut, Gherkin, Onion, Cabbage, Cauliflower, Mixed, and other members of that noble family. The jams, as being of a less masculine temperament, and as wearing curlpapers, announced themselves in feminine caligraphy, like a soft whisper, to be Raspberry, Gooseberry, Apricot, Plum, Damson, Apple, and Peach. The scene closing on these charmers, and the lower slide ascending, oranges were revealed, attended by a mighty japanned sugar-box, to temper their acerbity if unripe. Home-made biscuits waited at the Court of these Powers, accompanied by a goodly fragment of plum-cake, and various slender ladies' fingers, to be dipped into sweet wine and kissed. Lowest of all, a compact leaden vault enshrined the sweet wine and a stock of cordials: whence issued whispers of Seville Orange, Lemon, Almond, and Caraway-seed. There was a crowning air upon this closet of closets, of having been for ages hummed through by the Cathedral bell and organ, until those venerable bees had made sublimated honey of everything in store; and it was always observed that every dipper among the shelves (deep, as has been noticed, and swallowing up head, shoulders, and elbows) came forth again mellow-faced, and seeming to have undergone a saccharine transfiguration.

The Reverend Septimus yielded himself up quite as willing a victim to a nauseous medicinal herb-closet, also presided over by the china shepherdess, as to this glorious cupboard. To what amazing infusions of gentian, peppermint, gilliflower, sage, parsley, thyme, rue, rosemary, and dandelion, did his courageous stomach submit itself! In what wonderful wrappers, enclosing layers of dried leaves, would he swathe his rosy and contented face, if his mother suspected him of a toothache! What botanical blotches would he cheerfully stick upon his cheek, or forehead, if the dear old lady convicted him of an imperceptible pimple there! Into this herbaceous penitentiary, situated on an upper staircase-landing: a low and narrow whitewashed cell, where bunches of dried leaves hung from rusty hooks in the ceiling, and were spread out upon shelves, in company with portentous bottles: would the Reverend Septimus submissively be led, like the highly popular lamb who has so long and unresistingly been led to the slaughter, and there would he, unlike that lamb, bore nobody but himself. Not even doing that much, so that the old lady were busy and pleased, he would quietly swallow what was given him, merely taking a corrective dip of hands and face into the great bowl of dried rose-leaves, and into the other great bowl of dried lavender, and then would go out, as confident in the sweetening powers of Cloisterham Weir and a wholesome mind, as Lady Macbeth was hopeless of those of all the seas that roll.

In the present instance the good Minor Canon took his glass of Constantia with an excellent grace, and, so supported to his mother's satisfaction, applied himself to the remaining duties of the day. In their orderly and punctual progress they brought round Vesper Service and twilight. The Cathedral being very cold, he set off for a brisk trot after service; the trot to end in a charge at his favourite fragment of ruin, which was to be carried by storm, without a pause for breath.

He carried it in a masterly manner, and, not breathed even then, stood looking down upon the river. The river at Cloisterham is sufficiently near the sea to throw up oftentimes a quantity of seaweed. An unusual quantity had come in with the last tide, and this, and the confusion of the water, and the restless dipping and flapping of the noisy gulls, and an angry light out seaward beyond the brown-sailed barges that were turning black, foreshadowed a stormy night. In his mind he was contrasting the wild and noisy sea with the quiet harbour of Minor Canon Corner, when Helena and Neville Landless passed below him. He had had the two together in his thoughts all day, and at once climbed down to speak to them together. The footing was rough in an uncertain light for any tread save that of a good

Mr. Crisparkle interrupts a favourite walk

climber; but the Minor Canon was as good a climber as most men, and stood beside them before many good climbers would have been half-way down.

'A wild evening, Miss Landless! Do you not find your usual walk with your brother too exposed and cold for the time of year? Or at all events, when the sun is down, and the weather is driving in from the sea?'

Helena thought not. It was their favourite walk. It was very retired.

'It is very retired,' assented Mr. Crisparkle, laying hold of his opportunity straightway, and walking on with them. 'It is a place of all others where one can speak without interruption, as I wish to do. Mr. Neville, I believe you tell your sister everything that passes between us?'

'Everything, sir'

'Consequently,' said Mr. Crisparkle, 'your sister is aware that I have repeatedly urged you to make some kind of apology for that unfortunate occurrence which befell on the night of your arrival here.'

In saying it he looked to her, and not to him; therefore it was she, and not he, who replied:

'Yes.'

'I call it unfortunate, Miss Helena,' resumed Mr. Crisparkle, 'forasmuch as it certainly has engendered a prejudice against Neville. There is a notion about, that he is a dangerously passionate fellow, of an uncontrollable and furious temper: he is really avoided as such.'

'I have no doubt he is, poor fellow,' said Helena, with a look of proud compassion at her brother, expressing a deep sense of his being ungenerously treated. 'I should be quite sure of it, from your saying so; but what you tell me is confirmed by suppressed hints and references that I meet with every day.'

'Now,' Mr. Crisparkle again resumed, in a tone of mild though firm persuasion, 'is not this to be regretted, and ought it not to be amended? These are early days of Neville's in Cloisterham, and I have no fear of his outliving such a prejudice, and proving himself to have been misunderstood. But how much wiser to take action at once, than to trust to uncertain time! Besides, apart from its being politic, it is right. For there can be no question that Neville was wrong.'

'He was provoked,' Helena submitted.

'He was the assailant,' Mr. Crisparkle submitted.

They walked on in silence, until Helena raised her eyes to the Minor Canon's face, and said, almost reproachfully: 'O Mr. Crisparkle, would you have Neville throw himself at young Drood's feet, or at Mr. Jasper's, who maligns him every day? In your heart you cannot mean it. From your heart you could not do it, if his case were yours.'

'I have represented to Mr. Crisparkle, Helena,' said Neville, with a glance of deference towards his tutor, 'that if I could do it from my heart, I would. But I cannot, and I revolt from the pretence. You forget, however, that to put the case to Mr. Crisparkle as his own, is to suppose Mr. Crisparkle to have done what I did.'

'I ask his pardon,' said Helena.

'You see,' remarked Mr. Crisparkle, again laying hold of his opportunity, though with a moderate and delicate touch, 'you both instinctively acknowledge that Neville did wrong. Then why stop short, and not otherwise acknowledge it?'

'Is there no difference,' asked Helena, with a little faltering in her manner, 'between submission to a generous spirit, and submission to a base or trivial one?'

Before the worthy Minor Canon was quite ready with his argument in reference to this nice distinction, Neville struck in:

'Help me to clear myself with Mr. Crisparkle, Helena. Help me to convince him that I cannot be the first to make concessions without mockery and falsehood. My nature must be changed before I can do so, and it is not changed. I am sensible of inexpressible affront, and deliberate aggravation of inexpressible affront, and I am angry. The plain truth is, I am still as angry when I recall that night as I was that night.'

'Neville,' hinted the Minor Canon, with a steady countenance, 'you have repeated that former action of your hands, which I so much dislike.'

'I am sorry for it, sir, but it was involuntary. I confessed that I was still as angry.'

'And I confess,' said Mr. Crisparkle, 'that I hoped for better things.'

'I am sorry to disappoint you sir, but it would be far worse to deceive you, and I should deceive you grossly if I pretended that you had softened me in this respect. The time may come when your powerful influence will do even that with the difficult pupil whose antecedents you know; but it has not come yet. Is this so, and in spite of my struggles against myself, Helena?'

She, whose dark eyes were watching the effect of what he said on Mr. Crisparkle's face, replied — to Mr. Crisparkle, not to him: 'It is so.' After a short pause, she answered the slightest look of inquiry conceivable, in her brother's eyes, with as slight an affirmative bend of her own head; and he went on:

'I have never yet had the courage to say to you, sir, what in full openness I ought to have said when you first talked with me on this subject. It is not easy to say, and I have been withheld by a fear of its seeming ridiculous, which is very strong upon me down to this last moment, and might, but for my sister, prevent my being quite open with you even now. — I admire Miss Bud, sir, so very much, that I cannot bear her being treated with conceit or indifference; and even if I did not feel that I had an injury against young Drood on my own account, I should feel that I had an injury against him on hers.'

Mr. Crisparkle, in utter amazement, looked at Helena for corroboration, and met in her expressive face full corroboration, and a plea for advice.

'The young lady of whom you speak is, as you know, Mr. Neville, shortly to be married,' said Mr. Crisparkle, gravely; 'therefore your admiration, if it be of that special nature which you seem to indicate, is outrageously misplaced. Moreover, it is monstrous that you should take upon yourself to be the young lady's champion against her chosen husband.

Besides, you have seen them only once. The young lady has become your sister's friend; and I wonder that your sister, even on her behalf, has not checked you in this irrational and culpable fancy.'

'She has tried, sir, but uselessly. Husband or no husband, that fellow is incapable of the feeling with which I am inspired towards the beautiful young creature whom he treats like a doll. I say he is as incapable of it, as he is unworthy of her. I say she is sacrificed in being bestowed upon him. I say that I love her, and despise and hate him!' This with a face so flushed, and a gesture so violent, that his sister crossed to his side, and caught his arm, remonstrating, 'Neville, Neville!'

Thus recalled to himself, he quickly became sensible of having lost the guard he had set upon his passionate tendency, and covered his face with his hand, as one repentant and wretched.

Mr. Crisparkle, watching him attentively, and at the same time meditating how to proceed, walked on for some paces in silence. Then he spoke:

'Mr. Neville, Mr. Neville, I am sorely grieved to see in you more traces of a character as sullen, angry, and wild, as the night now closing in. They are of too serious an aspect to leave me the resource of treating the infatuation you have disclosed, as undeserving serious consideration. I give it very serious consideration, and I speak to you accordingly. This feud between you and young Drood must not go on. I cannot permit it to go on any longer, knowing what I now know from you, and you living under my roof. Whatever prejudiced and unauthorised constructions your blind and envious wrath may put upon his character, it is a frank, good-natured character. I know I can trust to it for that. Now, pray observe what I am about to say. On reflection, and on your sister's representation, I am willing to admit that, in making peace with young Drood, you have a right to be met half-way. I will engage that you shall be, and even that young Drood shall make the first advance. This condition fulfilled, you will pledge me the honour of a Christian gentleman that the quarrel is for ever at an end on your side. What may be in your heart when you give him your hand, can only be known to the Searcher of all hearts; but it will never go well with you, if there be any treachery there. So far, as to that; next as to what I must again speak of as your infatuation. I understand it to have been confided to me, and to be known to no other person save your sister and yourself. Do I understand aright?'

Helena answered in a low voice: 'It is only known to us three who are here together.'

'It is not at all known to the young lady, your friend?'

'On my soul, no!'

'I require you, then, to give me your similar and solemn pledge, Mr. Neville, that it shall remain the secret it is, and that you will take no other action whatsoever upon it than endeavouring (and that most earnestly) to erase it from your mind. I will not tell you that it will soon pass; I will not tell you that it is the fancy of the moment; I will not tell you that such caprices have their rise and fall among the young and ardent every hour; I will leave you undisturbed in the belief that it has few parallels or none, that it will abide with you a long time, and that it will be very difficult to conquer. So much the more weight shall I attach to the pledge I require from you, when it is unreservedly given.'

The young man twice or thrice essayed to speak, but failed.

'Let me leave you with your sister, whom it is time you took home,' said Mr. Crisparkle. 'You will find me alone in my room by-and-by.'

'Pray do not leave us yet,' Helena implored him. 'Another minute.'

'I should not,' said Neville, pressing his hand upon his face, 'have needed so much as another minute, if you had been less patient with me, Mr. Crisparkle, less considerate of me, and less unpretendingly good and true. O, if in my childhood I had known such a guide!'

'Follow your guide now, Neville,' murmured Helena, 'and follow him to Heaven!'

There was that in her tone which broke the good Minor Canon's voice, or it would have repudiated her exaltation of him. As it was, he laid a finger on his lips, and looked towards her brother.

'To say that I give both pledges, Mr. Crisparkle, out of my innermost heart, and to say that there is no treachery in it, is to say nothing!' Thus Neville, greatly moved. 'I beg your forgiveness for my miserable lapse into a burst of passion.'

'Not mine, Neville, not mine. You know with whom forgiveness lies, as the highest attribute conceivable. Miss Helena, you and your brother are twin children. You came into this world with the same dispositions, and you passed your younger days together surrounded by the same adverse circumstances. What you have overcome in yourself, can you not overcome in him? You see the rock that lies in his course. Who but you can keep him clear of it?'

'Who but you, sir?' replied Helena. 'What is my influence, or my weak wisdom, compared with yours!'

'You have the wisdom of Love,' returned the Minor Canon, 'and it was the highest wisdom ever known upon this earth, remember. As to mine — but the less said of that commonplace commodity the better. Good night!'

She took the hand he offered her, and gratefully and almost reverently raised it to her lips.

'Tut!' said the Minor Canon softly, 'I am much overpaid!' and turned away.

Retracing his steps towards the Cathedral Close, he tried, as he went along in the dark, to think out the best means of bringing to pass what he had promised to effect, and what must somehow be done. 'I shall probably be asked to marry them,' he reflected, 'and I would they were married and gone! But this presses first.' He debated principally whether he should write to young Drood, or whether he should speak to Jasper. The consciousness of being popular with the whole Cathedral establishment inclined him to the latter course, and the well-timed sight of the lighted gatehouse decided him to take it. 'I will strike while the iron is hot,' he said, 'and see him now.'

Jasper was lying asleep on a couch before the fire, when, having ascended the postern-stair, and received no answer to his knock at the door, Mr. Crisparkle gently turned the handle and looked in. Long afterwards he had cause to remember how Jasper sprang from the couch in a delirious state between sleeping and waking, and crying out: 'What is the matter? Who did it?'

'It is only I, Jasper. I am sorry to have disturbed you.'

The glare of his eyes settled down into a look of recognition, and he moved a chair or two, to make a way to the fireside.

'I was dreaming at a great rate, and am glad to be disturbed from an indigestive after-dinner sleep. Not to mention that you are always welcome.'

'Thank you. I am not confident,' returned Mr. Crisparkle, as he sat himself down in the easy-chair placed for him, 'that my subject will at first sight be quite as welcome as myself; but I am a minister of peace, and I pursue my subject in the interests of peace. In a word, Jasper, I want to establish peace between these two young fellows.'

A very perplexed expression took hold of Mr. Jasper's face; a very perplexing expression too, for Mr. Crisparkle could make nothing of it.

'How?' was Jasper's inquiry, in a low and slow voice, after a silence.

'For the "How" I come to you. I want to ask you to do me the great favour and service of interposing with your nephew (I have already interposed with Mr. Neville), and getting him to write you a short note, in his lively way, saying that he is willing to shake hands. I know what a good-natured fellow he is, and what influence you have with him. And without in the least defending Mr. Neville, we must all admit that he was bitterly stung.'

Jasper turned that perplexed face towards the fire. Mr. Crisparkle continuing to observe it, found it even more perplexing than before, inasmuch as it seemed to denote (which could hardly be) some close internal calculation.

'I know that you are not prepossessed in Mr. Neville's favour,' the Minor Canon was going on, when Jasper stopped him:

'You have cause to say so. I am not, indeed.'

'Undoubtedly; and I admit his lamentable violence of temper, though I hope he and I will get the better of it between us. But I have exacted a very solemn promise from him as to his future demeanour towards your nephew, if you do kindly interpose; and I am sure he will keep it.'

'You are always responsible and trustworthy, Mr. Crisparkle. Do you really feel sure that you can answer for him so confidently?'

'I do.'

The perplexed and perplexing look vanished.

'Then you relieve my mind of a great dread, and a heavy weight,' said Jasper; 'I will do it.'

Mr. Crisparkle, delighted by the swiftness and completeness of his success, acknowledged it in the handsomest terms.

'I will do it,' repeated Jasper, 'for the comfort of having your guarantee against my vague and unfounded fears. You will laugh — but do you keep a Diary?'

'A line for a day; not more.'

'A line for a day would be quite as much as my uneventful life would need, Heaven knows,' said Jasper, taking a book from a desk, 'but that my

Diary is, in fact, a Diary of Ned's life too. You will laugh at this entry; you will guess when it was made:

'"Past midnight. — After what I have just now seen, I have a morbid dread upon me of some horrible consequences resulting to my dear boy, that I cannot reason with or in any way contend against. All my efforts are vain. The demoniacal passion of this Neville Landless, his strength in his fury, and his savage rage for the destruction of its object, appal me. So profound is the impression, that twice since I have gone into my dear boy's room, to assure myself of his sleeping safely, and not lying dead in his blood."

'Here is another entry next morning:

'"Ned up and away. Light-hearted and unsuspicious as ever. He laughed when I cautioned him, and said he was as good a man as Neville Landless any day. I told him that might be, but he was not as bad a man. He continued to make light of it, but I travelled with him as far as I could, and left him most unwillingly. I am unable to shake off these dark intangible presentiments of evil — if feelings founded upon staring facts are to be so called."

'Again and again,' said Jasper, in conclusion, twirling the leaves of the book before putting it by, 'I have relapsed into these moods, as other entries show. But I have now your assurance at my back, and shall put it in my book, and make it an antidote to my black humours.'

'Such an antidote, I hope,' returned Mr. Crisparkle, 'as will induce you before long to consign the black humours to the flames. I ought to be the last to find any fault with you this evening, when you have met my wishes so freely; but I must say, Jasper, that your devotion to your nephew has made you exaggerative here.'

'You are my witness,' said Jasper, shrugging his shoulders, 'what my state of mind honestly was, that night, before I sat down to write, and in what words I expressed it. You remember objecting to a word I used, as being too strong? It was a stronger word than any in my Diary.'

'Well, well. Try the antidote,' rejoined Mr. Crisparkle; 'and may it give you a brighter and better view of the case! We will discuss it no more now. I have to thank you for myself, and I thank you sincerely.'

'You shall find,' said Jasper, as they shook hands, 'that I will not do the thing you wish me to do, by halves. I will take care that Ned, giving way at all, shall give way thoroughly.'

On the third day after this conversation, he called on Mr. Crisparkle with the following letter:

'MY DEAR JACK,

'I am touched by your account of your interview with Mr. Crisparkle, whom I much respect and esteem. At once I openly say that I forgot myself on that occasion quite as much as Mr. Landless did, and that I wish that bygone to be a bygone, and all to be right again.

'Look here, dear old boy. Ask Mr. Landless to dinner on Christmas Eve (the better the day the better the deed), and let there be only we three, and let us shake hands all round there and then, and say no more about it.

'My dear Jack,
'Ever your most affectionate,
'EDWIN DROOD.

'P.S. Love to Miss Pussy at the next music-lesson.'

'You expect Mr. Neville, then?' said Mr. Crisparkle.
'I count upon his coming,' said Mr. Jasper.

A Picture and a Ring

BEHIND the most ancient part of Holborn, London, where certain gabled houses some centuries of age still stand looking on the public way, as if disconsolately looking for the Old Bourne that has long run dry, is a little nook composed of two irregular quadrangles, called Staple Inn. It is one of those nooks, the turning into which out of the clashing street, imparts to the relieved pedestrian the sensation of having put cotton in his ears, and velvet soles on his boots. It is one of those nooks where a few smoky sparrows twitter in smoky trees, as though they called to one another, 'Let us play at country,' and where a few feet of garden-mould and a few yards of gravel enable them to do that refreshing violence to their tiny understandings. Moreover, it is one of those nooks which are legal nooks; and it contains a little Hall, with a little lantern in its roof: to what obstructive purposes devoted, and at whose expense, this history knoweth not.

In the days when Cloisterham took offence at the existence of a railroad afar off, as menacing that sensitive constitution, the property of us Britons: the odd fortune of which sacred institution it is to be in exactly equal degrees croaked about, trembled for, and boasted of, whatever happens to anything, anywhere in the world: in those days no neighbouring architecture of lofty proportions had arisen to overshadow Staple Inn. The westering sun bestowed bright glances on it, and the south-west wind blew into it unimpeded.

Neither wind nor sun, however, favoured Staple Inn one December afternoon towards six o'clock, when it was filled with fog, and candles shed murky and blurred rays through the windows of all its then-occupied sets of chambers; notably from a set of chambers in a corner house in the little inner quadrangle, presenting in black and white over its ugly portal the mysterious inscription:

P

J   T

1747

In which set of chambers, never having troubled his head about the inscription, unless to bethink himself at odd times on glancing up at it, that haply it might mean Perhaps John Thomas, or Perhaps Joe Tyler, sat Mr. Grewgious writing by his fire.

Who could have told, by looking at Mr. Grewgious, whether he had ever known ambition or disappointment? He had been bred to the Bar, and had laid himself out for chamber practice; to draw deeds; 'convey the wise it call,' as Pistol says. But Conveyancing and he had made such a very indifferent marriage of it that they had separated by consent — if there can be said to be separation where there has never been coming together.

No. Coy Conveyancing would not come to Mr. Grewgious. She was wooed, not won, and they went their several ways. But an Arbitration being blown towards him by some unaccountable wind, and he gaining great credit in it as one indefatigable in seeking out right and doing right, a pretty fat Receivership was next blown into his pocket by a wind more traceable to its source. So, by chance, he had found his niche. Receiver and Agent now, to two rich estates, and deputing their legal business, in an amount worth having, to a firm of solicitors on the floor below, he had snuffed out his ambition (supposing him to have ever lighted it), and had settled down with his snuffers for the rest of his life under the dry vine and fig-tree of P. J. T., who planted in seventeen-forty-seven.

Many accounts and account-books, many files of correspondence, and several strong boxes, garnished Mr. Grewgious's room. They can scarcely be represented as having lumbered it, so conscientious and precise was their orderly arrangement. The apprehension of dying suddenly, and leaving one fact or one figure with any incompleteness or obscurity attaching to it, would have stretched Mr. Grewgious stone-dead any day. The largest fidelity to a trust was the life-blood of the man. There are sorts of life-blood that course more quickly, more gaily, more attractively; but there is no better sort in circulation.

There was no luxury in his room. Even its comforts were limited to its being dry and warm, and having a snug though faded fireside. What may be called its private life was confined to the hearth, and an easy-chair, and an old-fashioned occasional round table that was brought out upon the rug after business hours, from a corner where it elsewise remained turned up like a shining mahogany shield. Behind it, when standing thus on the defensive, was a closet, usually containing something good to drink. An outer room was the clerk's room; Mr. Grewgious's sleeping-room was across the common stair; and he held some not empty cellarage at the bottom of the common stair. Three hundred days in the year, at least, he crossed over to the hotel in Furnival's Inn for his dinner, and after dinner crossed back again, to make the most of these simplicities until it should become broad business day once more, with P. J. T., date seventeen-forty-seven.

As Mr. Grewgious sat and wrote by his fire that afternoon, so did the clerk of Mr. Grewgious sit and write by *his* fire. A pale, puffy-faced, dark-haired person of thirty, with big dark eyes that wholly wanted lustre, and a dissatisfied doughy complexion, that seemed to ask to be sent to the baker's, this attendant was a mysterious being, possessed of some strange power over Mr. Grewgious. As though he had been called into existence, like a fabulous Familiar, by a magic spell which had failed when required to dismiss him, he stuck tight to Mr. Grewgious's stool, although Mr. Grewgious's comfort and convenience would manifestly have been advanced by dispossessing him. A gloomy person with tangled locks, and a general air of having been reared under the shadow of that baleful tree of Java which has given shelter to more lies than the whole botanical kingdom, Mr. Grewgious, nevertheless, treated him with unaccountable consideration.

'Now, Bazzard,' said Mr. Grewgious, on the entrance of his clerk: looking up from his papers as he arranged them for the night: 'what is in the wind besides fog?'

'Mr. Drood,' said Bazzard.

'What of him?'

'Has called,' said Bazzard.

'You might have shown him in.'

'I am doing it,' said Bazzard.

The visitor came in accordingly.

'Dear me!' said Mr. Grewgious, looking round his pair of office candles. 'I thought you had called and merely left your name and gone. How do you do, Mr. Edwin? Dear me, you're choking!'

'It's this fog,' returned Edwin; 'and it makes my eyes smart, like Cayenne pepper.'

'Is it really so bad as that? Pray undo your wrappers. It's fortunate I have so good a fire; but Mr. Bazzard has taken care of me.'

'No I haven't,' said Mr. Bazzard at the door.

'Ah! then it follows that I must have taken care of myself without observing it,' said Mr. Grewgious. 'Pray be seated in my chair. No. I beg! Coming out of such an atmosphere, in *my* chair.'

Edwin took the easy-chair in the corner; and the fog he had brought in with him, and the fog he took off with his greatcoat and neck-shawl, was speedily licked up by the eager fire.

'I look,' said Edwin, smiling, 'as if I had come to stop.'

'— By the by,' cried Mr. Grewgious; 'excuse my interrupting you; do stop. The fog may clear in an hour or two. We can have dinner in from just across Holborn. You had better take your Cayenne pepper here than outside; pray stop and dine.'

'You are very kind,' said Edwin, glancing about him as though attracted by the notion of a new and relishing sort of gipsy-party.

'Not at all,' said Mr Grewgious; '*you* are very kind to join issue with a bachelor in chambers, and take pot-luck. And I'll ask,' said Mr. Grewgious, dropping his voice, and speaking with a twinkling eye, as if inspired with a bright thought: 'I'll ask Bazzard. He mightn't like it else. — Bazzard!'

Bazzard reappeared.

'Dine presently with Mr. Drood and me.'

'If I am ordered to dine, of course I will, sir,' was the gloomy answer.

'Save the man!' cried Mr. Grewgious. 'You're not ordered; you're invited.'

'Thank you, sir,' said Bazzard; 'in that case I don't care if I do.'

'That's arranged. And perhaps you wouldn't mind,' said Mr. Grewgious, 'stepping over to the hotel in Furnival's, and asking them to send in materials for laying the cloth. For dinner we'll have a tureen of the hottest and strongest soup available, and we'll have the best made-dish that can be recommended, and we'll have a joint (such as a haunch of mutton), and we'll have a goose, or a turkey, or any little stuffed thing of that sort that may happen to be in the bill of fare — in short, we'll have whatever there is on hand.'

These liberal directions Mr. Grewgious issued with his usual air of reading an inventory, or repeating a lesson, or doing anything else by rote. Bazzard, after drawing out the round table, withdrew to execute them.

'I was a little delicate, you see,' said Mr. Grewgious, in a lower tone, after his clerk's departure, 'about employing him in the foraging or commissariat department. Because he mightn't like it.'

'He seems to have his own way, sir,' remarked Edwin.

'His own way?' returned Mr. Grewgious. 'O dear no! Poor fellow, you quite mistake him. If he had his own way, he wouldn't be here.'

'I wonder where he would be!' Edwin thought. But he only thought it, because Mr. Grewgious came and stood himself with his back to the other corner of the fire, and his shoulder-blades against the chimneypiece, and collected his skirts for easy conversation.

'I take it, without having the gift of prophecy, that you have done me the favour of looking in to mention that you are going down yonder — where I can tell you, you are expected — and to offer to execute any little commission from me to my charming ward, and perhaps to sharpen me up a bit in any proceedings? Eh, Mr. Edwin?'

'I called, sir, before going down, as an act of attention.'

'Of attention!' said Mr. Grewgious. 'Ah! of course, not of impatience?'

'Impatience, sir?'

Mr. Grewgious had meant to be arch — not that he in the remotest degree expressed that meaning — and had brought himself into scarcely supportable proximity with the fire, as if to burn the fullest effect of his archness into himself, as other subtle impressions are burnt into hard metals. But his archness suddenly flying before the composed face and manner of his visitor, and only the fire remaining, he started and rubbed himself.

'I have lately been down yonder,' said Mr. Grewgious, rearranging his skirts; 'and that was what I referred to, when I said I could tell you you are expected.'

'Indeed, sir! Yes; I knew that Pussy was looking out for me.'

'Do you keep a cat down there?' asked Mr. Grewgious.

Edwin coloured a little as he explained: 'I call Rosa Pussy.'

'O, really,' said Mr. Grewgious, smoothing down his head; 'that's very affable.'

Edwin glanced at his face, uncertain whether or no he seriously objected to the appellation. But Edwin might as well have glanced at the face of a clock.

'A pet name, sir,' he explained again.

'Umps,' said Mr. Grewgious, with a nod. But with such an

extraordinary compromise between an unqualified assent and a qualified dissent, that his visitor was much disconcerted.

'Did PRosa —' Edwin began by way of recovering himself.

'PRosa?' repeated Mr. Grewgious.

'I was going to say Pussy, and changed my mind; — did she tell you anything about the Landlesses?'

'No,' said Mr. Grewgious. 'What is the Landlesses? An estate? A villa? A farm?'

'A brother and sister. The sister is at the Nuns' House, and has become a great friend of P——'

'PRosa's,' Mr. Grewgious struck in, with a fixed face.

'She is a strikingly handsome girl, sir, and I thought she might have been described to you, or presented to you perhaps?'

'Neither,' said Mr. Grewgious. 'But here is Bazzard.'

Bazzard returned, accompanied by two waiters — an immovable waiter, and a flying waiter; and the three brought in with them as much fog as gave a new roar to the fire. The flying waiter, who had brought everything on his shoulders, laid the cloth with amazing rapidity and dexterity; while the immovable waiter, who had brought nothing, found fault with him. The flying waiter then highly polished all the glasses he had brought, and the immovable waiter looked through them. The flying waiter then flew across Holborn for the soup, and flew back again, and then took another flight for the made-dish, and flew back again, and then took another flight for the joint and poultry, and flew back again, and between whiles took supplementary flights for a great variety of articles, as it was discovered from time to time that the immovable waiter had forgotten them all. But let the flying waiter cleave the air as he might, he was always reproached on his return by the immovable waiter for bringing fog with him, and being out of breath. At the conclusion of the repast, by which time the flying waiter was severely blown, the immovable waiter gathered up the tablecloth under his arm with a grand air, and having sternly (not to say with indignation) looked on at the flying waiter while he set the clean glasses round, directed a valedictory glance towards Mr. Grewgious, conveying: 'Let it be clearly understood between us that the reward is mine, and that Nil is the claim of this slave,' and pushed the flying waiter before him out of the room.

It was like a highly-finished miniature painting representing My Lords of the Circumlocution Department, Commandership-in-Chief of any sort, Government. It was quite an edifying little picture to be hung on the line in the National Gallery.

As the fog had been the proximate cause of this sumptuous repast, so the fog served for its general sauce. To hear the out-door clerks sneezing, wheezing, and beating their feet on the gravel was a zest far surpassing Doctor Kitchener's. To bid, with a shiver, the unfortunate flying waiter shut the door before he had opened it, was a condiment of a profounder flavour than Harvey. And here let it be noticed, parenthetically, that the leg of this young man, in its application to the door, evinced the finest sense of touch: always preceding himself and tray (with something of an angling air about it), by some seconds: and always lingering after he and the tray had disappeared, like Macbeth's leg when accompanying him off the stage with reluctance to the assassination of Duncan.

The host had gone below to the cellar, and had brought up bottles of ruby, straw-coloured, and golden drinks, which had ripened long ago in lands where no fogs are, and had since lain slumbering in the shade. Sparkling and tingling after so long a nap, they pushed at their corks to help the corkscrew (like prisoners helping rioters to force their gates), and danced out gaily. If P. J. T. in seventeen-forty-seven, or in any other year of his period, drank such wines — then, for a certainty, P. J. T. was Pretty Jolly Too.

Externally, Mr. Grewgious showed no signs of being mellowed by these glowing vintages. Instead of his drinking them, they might have been poured over him in his high-dried snuff form, and run to waste, for any lights and shades they caused to flicker over his face. Neither was his manner influenced. But, in his wooden way, he had observant eyes for Edwin; and when at the end of dinner, he motioned Edwin back to his own easy-chair in the fireside corner, and Edwin sank luxuriously into it after very brief remonstrance, Mr. Grewgious, as he turned his seat round towards the fire too, and smoothed his head and face, might have been seen looking at his visitor between his smoothing fingers.

'Bazzard!' said Mr. Grewgious, suddenly turning to him.

'I follow you, sir,' returned Bazzard; who had done his work of consuming meat and drink in a workmanlike manner, though mostly in speechlessness.

'I drink to you, Bazzard; Mr. Edwin, success to Mr. Bazzard!'

'Success to Mr. Bazzard!' echoed Edwin, with a totally unfounded appearance of enthusiasm, and with the unspoken addition: 'What in, I wonder!'

'And May!' pursued Mr. Grewgious — 'I am not at liberty to be definite — May! — my conversational powers are so very limited that I know I shall not come well out of this — May! — it ought to be put imaginatively, but I have no imagination — May! — the thorn of anxiety is as nearly the mark as I am likely to get — May it come out at last!'

Mr. Bazzard, with a frowning smile at the fire, put a hand into his tangled locks, as if the thorn of anxiety were there; then into his waistcoat, as if it were there; then into his pockets, as if it were there. In all these movements he was closely followed by the eyes of Edwin, as if that young gentleman expected to see the thorn in action. It was not produced, however, and Mr. Bazzard merely said: 'I follow you, sir, and I thank you.'

'I am going,' said Mr. Grewgious, jingling his glass on the table with one hand, and bending aside under cover of the other, to whisper to Edwin, 'to drink to my ward. But I put Bazzard first. He mightn't like it else.'

This was said with a mysterious wink; or what would have been a wink, if, in Mr. Grewgious's hands, it could have been quick enough. So Edwin winked responsively, without the least idea what he meant by doing so.

'And now,' said Mr. Grewgious, 'I devote a bumper to the fair and fascinating Miss Rosa. Bazzard, the fair and fascinating Miss Rosa!'

'I follow you, sir,' said Bazzard, 'and I pledge you!'

'And so do I!' said Edwin.

'Lord bless me,' cried Mr. Grewgious, breaking the blank silence which of course ensued: though why these pauses *should* come upon us when we have performed any small social rite, not directly inducive of self-examination or mental despondency, who can tell? 'I am a particularly Angular man, and yet I fancy (if I may use the word, not having a morsel of fancy), that I could draw a picture of a true lover's state of mind, to-night.'

'Let us follow you, sir,' said Bazzard, 'and have the picture.'

'Mr. Edwin will correct it where it's wrong,' resumed Mr. Grewgious, 'and will throw in a few touches from the life. I dare say it is wrong in many particulars, and wants many touches from the life, for I was born a Chip, and have neither soft sympathies nor soft experiences. Well! I hazard the guess that the true lover's mind is completely permeated by the beloved object of his affections. I hazard the guess that her dear name is precious to him, cannot be heard or repeated without emotion, and is preserved sacred. If he has any distinguishing appellation of fondness for her, it is reserved for her, and is not for common ears. A name that it would be a privilege to call her by, being alone with her own bright self, it would be a liberty, a coldness, an insensibility, almost a breach of good faith, to flaunt elsewhere.'

It was wonderful to see Mr. Grewgious sitting bolt upright, with his hands on his knees, continuously chopping this discourse out of himself: much as a charity boy with a very good memory might get his catechism said: and evincing no correspondent emotion whatever, unless in a certain occasional little tingling perceptible at the end of his nose.

'My picture,' Mr. Grewgious proceeded, 'goes on to represent (under correction from you, Mr. Edwin), the true lover as ever impatient to be in the presence or vicinity of the beloved object of his affections; as caring very little for his ease in any other society; and as constantly seeking that. If I was to say seeking that, as a bird seeks its nest, I should make an ass of myself, because that would trench upon what I understand to be poetry; and I am so far from trenching upon poetry at any time, that I never, to my knowledge, got within ten thousand miles of it. And I am besides totally unacquainted with the habits of birds, except the birds of Staple Inn, who seek their nests on ledges, and in gutter-pipes and chimneypots, not constructed for them by the beneficent hand of Nature. I beg, therefore, to be understood as foregoing the bird's-nest. But my picture does represent the true lover as having no existence separable from that of the beloved object of his affections, and as living at once a doubled life and a halved life. And if I do not clearly express what I mean by that, it is either for the reason that having no conversational powers, I cannot express what I mean, or that having no meaning, I do not mean what I fail to express. Which, to the best of my belief, is not the case.'

Edwin had turned red and turned white, as certain points of this picture came into the light. He now sat looking at the fire, and bit his lip.

'The speculations of an Angular man,' resumed Mr. Grewgious, still sitting and speaking exactly as before, 'are probably erroneous on so globular a topic. But I figure to myself (subject, as before, to Mr. Edwin's correction), that there can be no coolness, no lassitude, no doubt, no indifference, no half fire and half smoke state of mind, in a real lover. Pray am I at all near the mark in my picture?'

As abrupt in his conclusion as in his commencement and progress, he jerked this inquiry at Edwin, and stopped when one might have supposed him in the middle of his oration.

'I should say, sir,' stammered Edwin, 'as you refer the question to me——'

'Yes,' said Mr. Grewgious, 'I refer it to you, as an authority.'

'I should say, then, sir,' Edwin went on, embarrassed, 'that the picture you have drawn is generally correct; but I submit that perhaps you may be rather hard upon the unlucky lover.'

'Likely so,' assented Mr. Grewgious, 'likely so. I am a hard man in the grain.'

'He may not show,' said Edwin, 'all he feels; or he may not——'

There he stopped so long, to find the rest of his sentence, that Mr. Grewgious rendered his difficulty a thousand times the greater by unexpectedly striking in with:

'No to be sure; he *may* not!'

After that, they all sat silent; the silence of Mr. Bazzard being occasioned by slumber.

'His responsibility is very great, though,' said Mr. Grewgious at length, with his eyes on the fire.

Edwin nodded assent, with *his* eyes on the fire.

'And let him be sure that he trifles with no one,' said Mr. Grewgious; 'neither with himself, nor with any other.'

Edwin bit his lip again, and still sat looking at the fire.

'He must not make a plaything of a treasure. Woe betide him if he does! Let him take that well to heart,' said Mr. Grewgious.

Though he said these things in short sentences, much as the supposititious charity boy just now referred to might have repeated a verse or two from the Book of Proverbs, there was something dreamy (for so literal a man) in the way in which he now shook his right forefinger at the live coals in the grate, and again fell silent.

But not for long. As he sat upright and stiff in his chair, he suddenly rapped his knees, like the carved image of some queer Joss or other coming out of its reverie, and said: 'We must finish this bottle, Mr. Edwin. Let me help you. I'll help Bazzard too, though he *is* asleep. He mightn't like it else.'

He helped them both, and helped himself, and drained his glass, and stood it bottom upward on the table, as though he had just caught a bluebottle in it.

'And now, Mr. Edwin,' he proceeded, wiping his mouth and hands upon his handkerchief: 'to a little piece of business. You received from me, the other day, a certified copy of Miss Rosa's father's will. You knew its contents before, but you received it from me as a matter of business. I should have sent it to Mr. Jasper, but for Miss Rosa's wishing it to come straight to you, in preference. You received it?'

'Quite safely, sir.'

'You should have acknowledged its receipt,' said Mr. Grewgious; 'business being business all the world over. However, you did not.'

'I meant to have acknowledged it when I first came in this evening, sir.'

'Not a business-like acknowledgement,' returned Mr. Grewgious; 'however, let that pass. Now, in that document you have observed a few words of kindly allusion to its being left to me to discharge a little trust, confided to me in conversation, at such time as I in my discretion may think best.'

'Yes, sir.'

'Mr. Edwin, it came into my mind just now, when I was looking at the fire, that I could, in my discretion, acquit myself of that trust at no better time than the present. Favour me with your attention, half a minute.'

He took a bunch of keys from his pocket, singled out by the candle-light the key he wanted, and then, with a candle in his hand, went to a bureau or escritoire, unlocked it, touched the spring of a little secret drawer, and took from it an ordinary ring-case made for a single ring. With this in his hand, he returned to his chair. As he held it up for the young man to see, his hand trembled.

'Mr. Edwin, this rose of diamonds and rubies delicately set in gold, was a ring belonging to Miss Rosa's mother. It was removed from her dead hand, in my presence, with such distracted grief as I hope it may never be my lot to contemplate again. Hard man as I am, I am not hard enough for that. See how bright these stones shine!' opening the case. 'And yet the eyes that were so much brighter, and that so often looked upon them with a light and a proud heart, have been ashes among ashes, and dust among dust, some years! If I had any imagination (which it is needless to say I have not), I might imagine that the lasting beauty of these stones was almost cruel.'

He closed the case again as he spoke.

'This ring was given to the young lady who was drowned so early in her beautiful and happy career, by her husband, when they first plighted their faith to one another. It was he who removed it from her unconscious hand, and it was he who, when his death drew very near, placed it in mine. The trust in which I received it, was, that, you and Miss Rosa growing to manhood and womanhood, and your betrothal prospering and coming to maturity, I should give it to you to place upon her finger. Failing those desired results, it was to remain in my possession.'

Some trouble was in the young man's face, and some indecision was in the action of his hand, as Mr. Grewgious, looking steadfastly at him, gave him the ring.

'Your placing it on her finger,' said Mr. Grewgious, 'will be the solemn seal upon your strict fidelity to the living and the dead. You are going to her, to make the last irrevocable preparations for your marriage. Take it with you.'

The young man took the little case, and placed it in his breast.

'If anything should be amiss, if anything should be even slightly wrong, between you; if you should have any secret consciousness that you are committing yourself to this step for no higher reason than because you have long been accustomed to look forward to it; then,' said Mr. Grewgious, 'I charge you once more, by the living and by the dead, to bring that ring back to me!'

Here Bazzard awoke himself by his own snoring; and, as is usual in such cases, sat apoplectically staring at vacancy, as defying vacancy to accuse him of having been asleep.

'Bazzard!' said Mr. Grewgious, harder than ever.

'I follow you, sir,' said Bazzard, 'and I have been following you.'

'In discharge of a trust, I have handed Mr. Edwin Drood a ring of diamonds and rubies. You see?'

Edwin reproduced the little case, and opened it; and Bazzard looked into it.

'I follow you both, sir,' returned Bazzard, 'and I witness the transaction.'

Evidently anxious to get away and be alone, Edwin Drood now resumed his outer clothing, muttering something about time and appointments. The fog was reported no clearer (by the flying waiter, who alighted from a speculative flight in the coffee interest), but he went out into it; and Bazzard, after his manner, 'followed' him.

Mr. Grewgious, left alone, walked softly and slowly to and fro, for an hour and more. He was restless to-night, and seemed dispirited.

'I hope I have done right,' he said. 'The appeal to him seemed necessary. It was hard to lose the ring, and yet it must have gone from me very soon.'

He closed the empty little drawer with a sigh, and shut and locked the escritoire, and came back to the solitary fireside.

'Her ring,' he went on. 'Will it come back to me? My mind hangs about her ring very uneasily to-night. But that is explainable. I have had it so long, and I have prized it so much! I wonder——'

He was in a wondering mood as well as a restless; for, though he checked himself at that point, and took another walk, he resumed his wondering when he sat down again.

'I wonder (for the ten-thousandth time, and what a weak fool I, for what can it signify now!) whether he confided the charge of their orphan child to me, because he knew — Good God, how like her mother she has become!

'I wonder whether he ever so much as suspected that someone doted on her, at a hopeless, speechless distance, when he struck in and won her. I wonder whether it ever crept into his mind who that unfortunate someone was!

'I wonder whether I shall sleep to-night! At all events, I will shut out the world with the bedclothes, and try.'

Mr. Grewgious crossed the staircase to his raw and foggy bedroom, and was soon ready for bed. Dimly catching sight of his face in the misty looking-glass, he held his candle to it for a moment.

'A likely some one, *you,* to come into anybody's thoughts in such an aspect!' he exclaimed. 'There! there! there! Get to bed, poor man, and cease to jabber!'

With that, he extinguished his light, pulled up the bedclothes around him, and with another sigh shut out the world. And yet there are such unexplored romantic nooks in the unlikeliest men, that even old tinderous and touchwoody P. J. T. Possibly Jabbered Thus, at some odd times, in or about seventeen-forty-seven.

A Night with Durdles

WHEN Mr. Sapsea has nothing better to do, towards evening, and finds the contemplation of his own profundity becoming a little monotonous in spite of the vastness of the subject, he often takes an airing in the Cathedral Close and thereabout. He likes to pass the churchyard with a swelling air of proprietorship, and to encourage in his breast a sort of benignant-landlord feeling, in that he has been bountiful towards that meritorious tenant, Mrs. Sapsea, and has publicly given her a prize. He likes to see a stray face or two looking in through the railings, and perhaps reading his inscription. Should he meet a stranger coming from the churchyard with a quick step, he is morally convinced that the stranger is 'with a blush retiring,' as monumentally directed.

Mr. Sapsea's importance has received enhancement, for he has become Mayor of Cloisterham. Without mayors, and many of them, it cannot be disputed that the whole framework of society — Mr. Sapsea is confident that he invented that forcible figure — would fall to pieces. Mayors have been knighted for 'going up' with addresses: explosive machines intrepidly discharging shot and shell into the English Grammar. Mr. Sapsea may 'go up' with an address. Rise, Sir Thomas Sapsea! Of such is the salt of the earth.

Mr. Sapsea has improved the acquaintance of Mr. Jasper, since their first meeting to partake of port, epitaph, backgammon, beef, and salad. Mr. Sapsea has been received at the gatehouse with kindred hospitality; and on that occasion Mr. Jasper seated himself at the piano, and sang to him, tickling his ears — figuratively — long enough to present a considerable area for tickling. What Mr. Sapsea likes in that young man is, that he is always ready to profit by the wisdom of his elders, and that he is sound, sir, at the core. In proof of which, he sang to Mr. Sapsea that evening, no kickshaw ditties, favourites with national enemies, but gave him the genuine George the Third home-brewed; exhorting him (as 'my brave boys') to reduce to a smashed condition all other islands but this island, and all continents, peninsulas, isthmuses, promontories, and other geographical forms of land soever, besides sweeping the seas in all directions. In short, he rendered it pretty clear that Providence made a distinct mistake in originating so small a nation of hearts of oak, and so many other verminous peoples.

Mr. Sapsea, walking slowly this moist evening near the churchyard with his hands behind him, on the look-out for a blushing and retiring stranger, turns a corner, and comes instead into the goodly presence of the Dean, conversing with the Verger and Mr. Jasper. Mr. Sapsea makes his obeisance, and is instantly stricken far more ecclesiastical than any Archbishop of York or Canterbury.

'You are evidently going to write a book about us, Mr. Jasper,' quoth the Dean; 'to write a book about us. Well! We are very ancient, and we ought to make a good book. We are not so richly endowed in possessions as in age; but perhaps you will put *that* in your book, among other things, and call attention to our wrongs.'

Mr. Tope, as in duty bound, is greatly entertained by this.

'I really have no intention at all, sir,' replies Jasper, 'of turning author or archæologist. It is but a whim of mine. And even for my whim, Mr. Sapsea here is more accountable than I am.'

'How so, Mr. Mayor?' says the Dean, with a nod of good-natured recognition of his Fetch. 'How is that, Mr. Mayor?'

'I am not aware,' Mr. Sapsea remarks, looking about him for information, 'to what the Very Reverend the Dean does me the honour of referring.' And then falls to studying his original in minute points of detail.

'Durdles,' Mr. Tope hints.

'Ay!' the Dean echoes; 'Durdles, Durdles!'

'The truth is, sir,' explains Jasper, 'that my curiosity in the man was first really stimulated by Mr. Sapsea. Mr. Sapsea's knowledge of mankind and power of drawing out whatever is recluse or odd around him, first led to my bestowing a second thought upon the man: though of course I had met him constantly about. You would not be surprised by this, Mr. Dean, if you had seen Mr. Sapsea deal with him in his own parlour, as I did.'

'O!' cries Sapsea, picking up the ball thrown to him with ineffable complacency and pomposity; 'yes, yes. The Very Reverend the Dean refers to that? Yes. I happened to bring Durdles and Mr. Jasper together. I regard Durdles as a Character.'

'A character, Mr. Sapsea, that with a few skilled touches you turn inside out,' says Jasper.

'Nay, not quite that,' returns the lumbering auctioneer. 'I may have a little influence over him, perhaps; and a little insight into his character, perhaps. The Very Reverend the Dean will please to bear in mind that I have seen the world.' Here Mr. Sapsea gets a little behind the Dean, to inspect his coat-buttons.

'Well!' says the Dean, looking about him to see what has become of his copyist: 'I hope, Mr. Mayor, you will use your study and knowledge of

Durdles to the good purpose of exhorting him not to break our worthy and respected Choir-Master's neck; we cannot afford it; his head and voice are much too valuable to us.'

Mr. Tope is again highly entertained, and, having fallen into respectful convulsions of laughter, subsides into a deferential murmur, importing that surely any gentleman would deem it a pleasure and an honour to have his neck broken, in return for such a compliment from such a source.

'I will take it upon myself, sir,' observes Sapsea loftily, 'to answer for Mr. Jasper's neck. I will tell Durdles to be careful of it. He will mind what *I* say. How is it at present endangered?' he inquires, looking about him with magnificent patronage.

'Only by my making a moonlight expedition with Durdles among the tombs, vaults, towers, and ruins,' returns Jasper. 'You remember suggesting, when you brought us together, that, as a lover of the picturesque, it might be worth my while?'

'*I* remember!' replies the auctioneer. And the solemn idiot really believes that he does remember.

'Profiting by your hint,' pursues Jasper, 'I have had some day-rambles with the extraordinary old fellow, and we are to make a moonlight hole-and-corner exploration to-night.'

'And here he is,' says the Dean.

Durdles, with his dinner-bundle in his hand, is indeed beheld slouching towards them. Slouching nearer, and perceiving the Dean, he pulls off his hat, and is slouching away with it under his arm, when Mr. Sapsea stops him.

'Mind you take care of my friend,' is the injunction Mr. Sapsea lays upon him. 'What friend o' yourn is dead?' asks Durdles. 'No orders has come in for any friend o' yourn.'

'I mean my live friend there.'

'O! him?' says Durdles. 'He can take care of himself, can Mister Jarsper.'

'But do you take care of him too,' says Sapsea.

Whom Durdles (there being command in his tone) surlily surveys from head to foot.

'With submission to his Reverence the Dean, if you'll mind what concerns you, Mr. Sapsea, Durdles he'll mind what concerns him.'

'You're out of temper,' says Mr. Sapsea, winking to the company to observe how smoothly he will manage him. 'My friend concerns me, and Mr. Jasper is my friend. And you are my friend.'

'Don't you get into a bad habit of boasting,' retorts Durdles, with a grave cautionary nod. 'It'll grow upon you.'

'You are out of temper,' says Sapsea again; reddening, but again winking to the company.

'I own to it,' returns Durdles; 'I don't like liberties.'

Mr. Sapsea winks a third wink to the company, as who should say: 'I think you will agree with me that I have settled *his* business;' and stalks out of the controversy.

Durdles then gives the Dean a good evening, and adding, as he puts his hat on, 'You'll find me at home, Mister Jarsper, as agreed, when you want me; I'm a-going home to clean myself,' soon slouches out of sight. This going home to clean himself is one of the man's incomprehensible compromises with inexorable facts; he, and his hat, and his boots, and his clothes, never showing any trace of cleaning, but being uniformly in one condition of dust and grit.

The lamplighter now dotting the quiet Close with specks of light, and running at a great rate up and down his little ladder with that object — his little ladder under the sacred shadow of whose inconvenience generations had grown up, and which all Cloisterham would have stood aghast at the idea of abolishing — the Dean withdraws to his dinner, Mr. Tope to his tea, and Mr. Jasper to his piano. There, with no light but that of the fire, he sits chanting choir-music in a low and beautiful voice, for two or three hours; in short, until it has been for some time dark, and the moon is about to rise.

Then he closes his piano softly, softly changes his coat for a pea-jacket, with a goodly wicker-cased bottle in its largest pocket, and putting on a low-crowned, flap-brimmed hat, goes softly out. Why does he move so softly to-night? No outward reason is apparent for it. Can there be any sympathetic reason crouching darkly within him?

Repairing to Durdles's unfinished house, or hole in the city wall, and seeing a light within it, he softly picks his course among the gravestones, monuments, and stony lumber of the yard, already touched here and there, sidewise, by the rising moon. The two journeymen have left their two great saws sticking in their blocks of stone; and two skeleton journeymen out of the Dance of Death might be grinning in the shadow of their sheltering sentry-boxes, about to slash away at cutting out the gravestones of the next two people destined to die in Cloisterham. Likely enough, the two think little of that now, being alive, and perhaps merry. Curious, to make a guess at the two; — or say one of the two!

'Ho! Durdles!'

The light moves, and he appears with it at the door. He would seem to have been 'cleaning himself' with the aid of a bottle, jug, and tumbler; for no other cleansing instruments are visible in the bare brick room with rafters overhead and no plastered ceiling, into which he shows his visitor.

'Are you ready?'

'I am ready, Mister Jarsper. Let the old uns come out if they dare, when we go among their tombs. My spirit is ready for 'em.'

'Do you mean animal spirits, or ardent?'

'The one's the t'other,' answers Durdles, 'and I mean 'em both.'

He takes a lantern from a hook, puts a match or two in his pocket wherewith to light it, should there be need; and they go out together, dinner-bundle and all.

Surely an unaccountable sort of expedition! That Durdles himself, who is always prowling among old graves, and ruins, like a Ghoul — that he should be stealing forth to climb, and dive, and wander without an object, is nothing extraordinary; but that the Choir-Master or any one else should hold it worth his while to be with him, and to study moonlight effects in such company is another affair. Surely an unaccountable sort of expedition, therefore!

''Ware that there mound by the yard-gate, Mister Jarsper.'

'I see it. What is it?'

'Lime.'

Mr. Jasper stops, and waits for him to come up, for he lags behind. 'What you call quick-lime?'

'Ay!' says Durdles; 'quick enough to eat your boots. With a little handy stirring, quick enough to eat your bones.'

They go on, presently passing the red windows of the Travellers' Twopenny, and emerging into the clear moonlight of the Monks' Vineyard. This crossed, they come to Minor Canon Corner: of which the greater part lies in shadow until the moon shall rise higher in the sky.

The sound of a closing house-door strikes their ears, and two men come out. These are Mr. Crisparkle and Neville. Jasper, with a strange and sudden smile upon his face, lays the palm of his hand upon the breast of Durdles, stopping him where he stands.

At that end of Minor Canon Corner the shadow is profound in the existing state of the light: at that end, too, there is a piece of old dwarf wall, breast high, the only remaining boundary of what was once a garden, but is now the thoroughfare. Jasper and Durdles would have turned this wall in another instant; but, stopping so short, stand behind it.

'Those two are only sauntering,' Jasper whispers; 'they will go out into the moonlight soon. Let us keep quiet here, or they will detain us, or want to join us, or what not.'

Durdles nods assent, and falls to munching some fragments from his bundle. Jasper folds his arms upon the top of the wall, and, with his chin resting on them, watches. He takes no note whatever of the Minor Canon, but watches Neville, as though his eye were at the trigger of a loaded rifle, and he had covered him, and were going to fire. A sense of destructive power is so expressed in his face, that even Durdles pauses in his munching, and looks at him, with an unmunched something in his cheek.

Meanwhile Mr. Crisparkle and Neville walk to and fro, quietly talking together. What they say, cannot be heard consecutively; but Mr. Jasper has already distinguished his own name more than once.

'This is the first day of the week,' Mr. Crisparkle can be distinctly heard to observe, as they turn back; 'and the last day of the week is Christmas Eve.'

'You may be certain of me, sir.'

The echoes were favourable at those points, but as the two approach, the sound of their talking becomes confused again. The word 'confidence,' shattered by the echoes, but still capable of being pieced together, is uttered by Mr. Crisparkle. As they draw still nearer, this fragment of a reply is heard: 'Not deserved yet, but shall be, sir.' As they turn away again, Jasper again hears his own name, in connection with the words from Mr. Crisparkle: 'Remember that I said I answered for you confidently.' Then the sound of their talk becomes confused again; they halting for a little while, and some earnest action on the part of Neville succeeding. When they move once more, Mr. Crisparkle is seen to look up at the sky, and to point before him. They then slowly disappear; passing out into the moonlight at the opposite end of the Corner.

It is not until they are gone, that Mr. Jasper moves. But then he turns to

Durdles, and bursts into a fit of laughter. Durdles, who still has that suspended something in his cheek, and who sees nothing to laugh at, stares at him until Mr. Jasper lays his face down on his arms to have his laugh out. Then Durdles bolts the something, as if desperately resigning himself to indigestion.

Among those secluded nooks there is very little stir or movement after dark. There is little enough in the high tide of the day, but there is next to none at night. Besides that the cheerfully frequented High Street lies nearly parallel to the spot (the old Cathedral rising between the two), and is the natural channel in which the Cloisterham traffic flows, a certain awful hush pervades the ancient pile, the cloisters, and the churchyard, after dark, which not many people care to encounter. Ask the first hundred citizens of Cloisterham, met at random in the streets at noon, if they believed in Ghosts, they would tell you no; but put them to choose at night between these eerie Precincts and the thoroughfare of shops, and you would find that ninety-nine declared for the longer round and the more frequented way. The cause of this is not to be found in any local superstition that attaches to the Precincts — albeit a mysterious lady, with a child in her arms and a rope dangling from her neck, has been seen flitting about there by sundry witnesses as intangible as herself — but it is to be sought in the innate shrinking of dust with the breath of life in it from dust out of which the breath of life has passed; also, in the widely diffused, and almost as widely unacknowledged, reflection: 'If the dead do, under any circumstances, become visible to the living, these are such likely surroundings for the purpose that I, the living, will get out of them as soon as I can.'

Hence, when Mr. Jasper and Durdles pause to glance around them, before descending into the crypt by a small side door, of which the latter has a key, the whole expanse of moonlight in their view is utterly deserted. One might fancy that the tide of life was stemmed by Mr. Jasper's own gatehouse. The murmur of the tide is heard beyond; but no wave passes the archway, over which his lamp burns red behind his curtain, as if the building were a Lighthouse.

They enter, locking themselves in, descend the rugged steps, and are down in the Crypt. The lantern is not wanted, for the moonlight strikes in at the groined windows, bare of glass, the broken frames for which cast patterns on the ground. The heavy pillars which support the roof engender masses of black shade, but between them there are lanes of light. Up and down these lanes they walk, Durdles discoursing of the 'old uns' he yet counts on disinterring, and slapping a wall, in which he considers 'a whole family on 'em' to be stoned and earthed up, just as if he were a familiar friend of the family. The taciturnity of Durdles is for the time overcome by Mr. Jasper's wicker bottle, which circulates freely; — in the sense, that is to say, that its contents enter freely into Mr. Durdles's circulation, while Mr. Jasper only rinses his mouth once, and casts forth the rinsing.

They are to ascend the great Tower. On the steps by which they rise to the Cathedral, Durdles pauses for new store of breath. The steps are very dark, but out of the darkness they can see the lanes of light they have traversed. Durdles seats himself upon a step. Mr. Jasper seats himself upon another. The odour from the wicker bottle (which has somehow passed into Durdles's keeping) soon intimates that the cork has been taken out; but this is not ascertainable through the sense of sight, since neither can descry the other. And yet, in talking, they turn to one another, as though their faces could commune together.

'This is good stuff, Mister Jarsper!'

'It is very good stuff, I hope. I bought it on purpose.'

'They don't show, you see, the old uns don't, Mister Jarsper!'

'It would be a more confused world than it is, if they could.'

'Well, it *would* lead towards a mixing of things,' Durdles acquiesces: pausing on the remark, as if the idea of ghosts had not previously presented itself to him in a merely inconvenient light, domestically or chronologically. 'But do you think there may be Ghosts of other things, though not of men and women?'

'What things? Flower-beds and watering-pots? horses and harness?'

'No. Sounds.'

'What sounds?'

'Cries.'

'What cries do you mean? Chairs to mend?'

'No. I mean screeches. Now I'll tell you, Mr. Jarsper. Wait a bit till I put the bottle right.' Here the cork is evidently taken out again, and replaced again. 'There! *Now* it's right! This time last year, only a few days later, I happened to have been doing what was correct by the season, in the way of giving it the welcome it had a right to expect, when them town-boys set on me at their worst. At length I gave 'em the slip, and turned in here. And here I fell asleep. And what woke me? The ghost of a cry. The ghost of one terrific shriek, which shriek was followed by the ghost of the howl of a dog: a long, dismal, woeful howl, such as a dog gives when a person's dead. That was *my* last Christmas Eve.'

'What do you mean?' is the very abrupt, and, one might say, fierce retort.

'I mean that I made inquiries everywhere about, and, that no living ears but mine heard either that cry or that howl. So I say they was both ghosts; though why they came to me, I've never made out.'

'I thought you were another kind of man,' says Jasper, scornfully.

'So I thought myself,' answers Durdles with his usual composure; 'and yet I was picked out for it.'

Jasper had risen suddenly, when he asked him what he meant, and he now says, 'Come; we shall freeze here; lead the way.'

Durdles complies, not over-steadily; opens the door at the top of the steps with the key he has already used; and so emerges on the Cathedral level, in a passage at the side of the chancel. Here, the moonlight is so very bright again that the colours of the nearest stained-glass window are thrown upon their faces. The appearance of the unconscious Durdles, holding the door open for his companion to follow, as if from the grave, is ghastly enough, with a purple band across his face, and a yellow splash upon his brow; but he bears the close scrutiny of his companion in an insensible way, although it is prolonged while the latter fumbles among his pockets for a key confided to him that will open an iron gate, so to enable them to pass to the staircase of the great tower.

'That and the bottle are enough for you to carry,' he says, giving it to Durdles; 'hand your bundle to me; I am younger and longer-winded than you.' Durdles hesitates for a moment between bundle and bottle; but gives the preference to the bottle as being by far the better company, and consigns the dry weight to his fellow-explorer.

Then they go up the winding staircase of the great tower, toilsomely, turning and turning, and lowering their heads to avoid the stairs above, or the rough stone pivot around which they twist. Durdles has lighted his lantern, by drawing from the cold, hard wall a spark of that mysterious fire which lurks in everything, and, guided by this speck, they clamber up among the cobwebs and the dust. Their way lies through strange places. Twice or thrice they emerge into level, low-arched galleries, whence they can look down into the moon-lit nave; and where Durdles, waving his lantern, waves the dim angels' heads upon the corbels of the roof, seeming to watch their progress. Anon they turn into narrower and steeper staircases, and the night-air begins to blow upon them, and the chirp of some startled jackdaw or frightened rook precedes the heavy beating of wings in a confined space, and the beating down of dust and straws upon their heads. At last, leaving their light behind a stair — for it blows fresh up here — they look down on Cloisterham, fair to see in the moonlight: its ruined habitations and sanctuaries of the dead, at the tower's base: its moss-softened red-tiled roofs and red-brick houses of the living, clustered beyond: its river winding down from the mist on the horizon, as though that were its source, and already heaving with a restless knowledge of its approach towards the sea.

Once again, an unaccountable expedition this! Jasper (always moving softly with no visible reason) contemplates the scene, and especially that stillest part of it which the Cathedral overshadows. But he contemplates Durdles quite as curiously, and Durdles is by times conscious of his watchful eyes.

Only by times, because Durdles is growing drowsy. As aëronauts lighten the load they carry, when they wish to rise, similarly Durdles has lightened the wicker bottle in coming up. Snatches of sleep surprise him on his legs, and stop him in his talk. A mild fit of calenture seizes him, in which he deems that the ground so far below, is on a level with the tower, and would as lief walk off the tower into the air as not. Such is his state when they begin to come down. And as aëronauts make themselves heavier when they wish to descend, similarly Durdles charges himself with more liquid from the wicker bottle, that he may come down the better.

The iron gate attained and locked — but not before Durdles has tumbled twice, and cut an eyebrow open once — they descend into the crypt again, with the intent of issuing forth as they entered. But, while returning among those lanes of light, Durdles becomes so very uncertain, both of foot and speech, that he half drops, half throws himself down, by one of the heavy pillars, scarcely less heavy than itself, and indistinctly appeals to his companion for forty winks of a second each.

'If you will have it so, or must have it so,' replies Jasper, 'I'll not leave you here. Take them, while I walk to and fro.'

Durdles is asleep at once; and in his sleep he dreams a dream.

In the Crypt

It is not much of a dream, considering the vast extent of the domains of dreamland, and their wonderful productions; it is only remarkable for being unusually restless and unusually real. He dreams of lying there, asleep, and yet counting his companion's footsteps as he walks to and fro. He dreams that the footsteps die away into distance of time and of space, and that something touches him, and that something falls from his hand. Then something clinks and gropes about, and he dreams that he is alone for so long a time, that the lanes of light take new directions as the moon advances in her course. From succeeding unconsciousness he passes into a dream of slow uneasiness from cold; and painfully awakes to a perception of the lanes of light — really changed, much as he had dreamed — and Jasper walking among them, beating his hands and feet.

'Holloa!' Durdles cries out, unmeaningly alarmed.

'Awake at last?' says Jasper, coming up to him. 'Do you know that your forties have stretched into thousands?'

'No.'

'They have though.'

'What's the time?'

'Hark! The bells are going in the Tower!'

They strike four quarters, and then the great bell strikes.

'Two!' cries Durdles, scrambling up; 'why didn't you try to wake me, Mister Jarsper?'

'I did. I might as well have tried to wake the dead — your own family of dead, up in the corner there.'

'Did you touch me?'

'Touch you! Yes. Shook you.'

As Durdles recalls that touching something in his dream, he looks down on the pavement, and sees the key of the crypt door lying close to where he himself lay.

'I dropped you, did I?' he says, picking it up, and recalling that part of his dream. As he gathers himself up again into an upright position, or into a position as nearly upright as he ever maintains, he is again conscious of being watched by his companion.

'Well?' says Jasper, smiling, 'are you quite ready? Pray don't hurry.'

'Let me get my bundle right, Mister Jarsper, and I'm with you.'

As he ties it afresh, he is once more conscious that he is very narrowly observed.

'What do you suspect me of, Mister Jarsper?' he asks, with drunken displeasure. 'Let them as has any suspicions of Durdles name 'em.'

'I've no suspicions of you, my good Mr. Durdles; but I have suspicions that my bottle was filled with something stiffer than either of us supposed. And I also have suspicions,' Jasper adds, taking it from the pavement and turning it bottom upwards, 'that it's empty.'

Durdles condescends to laugh at this. Continuing to chuckle when his laugh is over, as though remonstrant with himself on his drinking powers, he rolls to the door and unlocks it. They both pass out, and Durdles relocks it, and pockets his key.

'A thousand thanks for a curious and interesting night,' says Jasper, giving him his hand; 'you can make your own way home?'

'I should think so!' answers Durdles. 'If you was to offer Durdles the affront to show him his way home, he wouldn't go home.

> Durdles wouldn't go home till morning;
> And *then* Durdles wouldn't go home,

Durdles wouldn't.' This with the utmost defiance.

'Good-night, then.'

'Good-night, Mister Jarsper.'

Each is turning his own way, when a sharp whistle rends the silence, and the jargon is yelped out;

> 'Widdy widdy wen!
> I—ket—ches—Im—out—ar—ter—ten.
> Widdy widdy wy!
> Then—E—don't—go—then—I—shy—
> Widdy Widdy Wake-cock warning!'

Instantly afterwards, a rapid fire of stones rattles at the Cathedral wall, and the hideous small boy is beheld opposite, dancing in the moonlight.

'What! Is that baby-devil on the watch there!' cries Jasper in a fury: so quickly roused, and so violent, that he seems an older devil himself. 'I shall shed the blood of that impish wretch! I know I shall do it!' Regardless of the fire, though it hits him more than once, he rushes at Deputy, collars him, and tries to bring him across. But Deputy is not to be so easily brought across. With a diabolical insight into the strongest part of his position, he is no sooner taken by the throat than he curls up his legs, forces his assailant to hang him, as it were, and gurgles in his throat, and screws his body, and twists, as already undergoing the first agonies of strangulation. There is nothing for it but to drop him. He instantly gets himself together, backs over to Durdles, and cries to his assailant, gnashing the great gap in front of his mouth with rage and malice:

'I'll blind yer, s'elp me! I'll stone yer eyes out, s'elp me! If I don't have yer eyesight, bellows me!' At the same time dodging behind Durdles, and snarling at Jasper, now from this side of him, and now from that: prepared, if pounced upon, to dart away in all manner of curvilinear directions, and, if run down after all, to grovel in the dust, and cry: 'Now, hit me when I'm down! Do it!'

'Don't hurt the boy, Mister Jarsper,' urges Durdles, shielding him. 'Recollect yourself.'

'He followed us to-night, when we first came here!'

'Yer lie, I didn't!' replies Deputy, in his one form of polite contradiction.

'He has been prowling near us ever since!'

'Yer lie, I haven't,' returns Deputy. 'I'd only jist come out for my 'elth when I see you two a-coming out of the Kinfreederel. If

> I—ket—ches—Im—out—ar—ter—ten!'

(with the usual rhythm and dance, though dodging behind Durdles), 'it ain't *my* fault, is it?'

'Take him home, then,' retorts Jasper, ferociously, though with a strong check upon himself, 'and let my eyes be rid of the sight of you!'

Deputy, with another sharp whistle, at once expressing his relief, and his commencement of a milder stoning of Mr. Durdles, begins stoning that respectable gentleman home, as if he were a reluctant ox. Mr. Jasper goes to his gatehouse, brooding. And thus, as everything comes to an end, the unaccountable expedition comes to an end — for the time.

Both at their Best

MISS TWINKLETON'S establishment was about to undergo a serene hush. The Christmas recess was at hand. What had once, and at no remote period, been called, even by the erudite Miss Twinkleton herself, 'the half;' but what was now called, as being more elegant, and more strictly collegiate, 'the term,' would expire to-morrow. A noticeable relaxation of discipline had for some few days pervaded the Nuns' House. Club suppers had occurred in the bedrooms, and a dressed tongue had been carved with a pair of scissors, and handed round with the curling tongs. Portions of marmalade had likewise been distributed on a service of plates constructed of curlpaper; and cowslip wine had been quaffed from the small squat measuring glass in which little Rickitts (a junior of weakly constitution) took her steel drops daily. The housemaids had been bribed with various fragments of riband, and sundry pairs of shoes more or less down at heel, to make no mention of crumbs in the beds; the airiest costumes had been worn on these festive occasions; and the daring Miss Ferdinand had even surprised the company with a sprightly solo on the comb-and-curlpaper, until suffocated in her own pillow by two flowing-haired executioners.

Nor were these the only tokens of dispersal. Boxes appeared in the bedrooms (where they were capital at other times), and a surprising amount of packing took place, out of all proportion to the amount packed. Largess, in the form of odds and ends of cold cream and pomatum, and also of hairpins, was freely distributed among the attendants. On charges of inviolable secrecy, confidences were interchanged respecting golden youth of England expected to call, 'at home,' on the first opportunity. Miss Giggles (deficient in sentiment) did indeed profess that she, for her part, acknowledged such homage by making faces at the golden youth; but this young lady was outvoted by an immense majority.

On the last night before a recess, it was always expressly made a point of honour that nobody should go to sleep, and that Ghosts should be encouraged by all possible means. This compact invariably broke down, and all the young ladies went to sleep very soon, and got up very early.

The concluding ceremony came off at twelve o'clock on the day of departure; when Miss Twinkleton, supported by Mrs. Tisher, held a drawing-room in her own apartment (the globes already covered with brown Holland), where glasses of white wine and plates of cut pound-cake were discovered on the table. Miss Twinkleton then said: Ladies, another revolving year had brought us round to that festive period at which the first feelings of our nature bounded in our — Miss Twinkleton was annually going to add 'bosoms,' but annually stopped on the brink of that expression, and substituted 'hearts.' Hearts; our hearts. Hem! Again a revolving year, ladies, had brought us to a pause in our studies — let us hope our greatly advanced studies — and, like the mariner in his bark, the warrior in his tent, the captive in his dungeon, and the traveller in his various conveyances, we yearned for home. Did we say, on such an occasion, in the opening words of Mr. Addison's impressive tragedy:

> 'The dawn is overcast, the morning lowers,
> And heavily in clouds brings on the day,
> The great, th' important day——?'

Not so. From horizon to zenith all was *couleur de rose*, for all was redolent of our relations and friends. Might *we* find *them* prospering as *we* expected; might *they* find *us* prospering as *they* expected! Ladies, we would now, with our love to one another, wish one another good-bye, and happiness, until we met again. And when the time should come for our resumption of those pursuits which (here a general depression set in all round), pursuits which, pursuits which; — then let us ever remember what was said by the Spartan General, in words too trite for repetition, at the battle it were superfluous to specify.

The handmaidens of the establishment, in their best caps, then handed the trays, and the young ladies sipped and crumbled, and the bespoken coaches began to choke the street. Then leave-taking was not long about; and Miss Twinkleton, in saluting each young lady's cheek, confided to her an exceedingly neat letter, addressed to her next friend at law, 'with Miss Twinkleton's best compliments' in the corner. This missive she handed with an air as if it had not the least connexion with the bill, but were something in the nature of a delicate and joyful surprise.

So many times had Rosa seen such dispersals, and so very little did she know of any other Home, that she was contented to remain where she was, and was even better contented than ever before, having her latest friend with her. And yet her latest friendship had a blank place in it of which she could not fail to be sensible. Helena Landless, having been a party to her brother's revelation about Rosa, and having entered into that compact of silence with Mr. Crisparkle, shrank from any allusion to Edwin Drood's name. Why she so avoided it, was mysterious to Rosa, but she perfectly perceived the fact. But for the fact, she might have relieved her own little perplexed heart of some of its doubts and hesitations, by taking Helena into her confidence. As it was, she had no such vent: she could only ponder on her own difficulties, and wonder more and more why this avoidance of

Edwin's name should last, now that she knew — for so much Helena had told her — that a good understanding was to be reestablished between the two young men, when Edwin came down.

It would have made a pretty picture, so many pretty girls kissing Rosa in the cold porch of the Nuns' House, and that sunny little creature peeping out of it (unconscious of sly faces carved on spout and gable peeping at her), and waving farewells to the departing coaches, as if she represented the spirit of rosy youth abiding in the place to keep it bright and warm in its desertion. The hoarse High Street became musical with the cry, in various silvery voices, 'Good-bye, Rosebud darling!' and the effigy of Mr. Sapsea's father over the opposite doorway seemed to say to mankind: 'Gentlemen, favour me with your attention to this charming little last lot left behind, and bid with a spirit worthy of the occasion!' Then the staid street, so unwontedly sparkling, youthful, and fresh for a few rippling moments, ran dry, and Cloisterham was itself again.

If Rosebud in her bower now waited Edwin Drood's coming with an uneasy heart, Edwin for his part was uneasy too. With far less force of purpose in his composition than the childish beauty, crowned by acclamation fairy queen of Miss Twinkleton's establishment, he had a conscience, and Mr. Grewgious had pricked it. That gentleman's steady convictions of what was right and what was wrong in such a case as his, were neither to be frowned aside nor laughed aside. They would not be moved. But for the dinner in Staple Inn, and but for the ring he carried in the breast pocket of his coat, he would have drifted into their wedding-day without another pause for real thought, loosely trusting that all would go well, left alone. But that serious putting him on his truth to the living and the dead had brought him to a check. He must either give the ring to Rosa, or he must take it back. Once put into this narrowed way of action, it was curious that he began to consider Rosa's claims upon him more unselfishly than he had ever considered them before, and began to be less sure of himself than he had ever been in all his easy-going days.

'I will be guided by what she says, and by how we get on,' was his decision, walking from the gatehouse to the Nuns' House. 'Whatever comes of it, I will bear his words in mind, and try to be true to the living and the dead.'

Rosa was dressed for walking. She expected him. It was a bright, frosty day, and Miss Twinkleton had already graciously sanctioned fresh air. Thus they got out together before it became necessary for either Miss Twinkleton, or the deputy high-priest Mrs. Tisher, to lay even so much as one of those usual offerings on the shrine of Propriety.

'My dear Eddy,' said Rosa, when they had turned out of the High Street, and had got among the quiet walks in the neighbourhood of the Cathedral and the river: 'I want to say something very serious to you. I have been thinking about it for a long, long time.'

'I want to be serious with you too, Rosa dear. I mean to be serious and earnest.'

'Thank you, Eddy. And you will not think me unkind because I begin, will you? You will not think I speak for myself only, because I speak first? That would not be generous, would it? And I know you are generous!'

He said, 'I hope I am not ungenerous to you, Rosa.' He called her Pussy no more. Never again.

'And there is no fear,' pursued Rosa, 'of our quarrelling, is there? Because, Eddy,' clasping her hand on his arm, 'we have so much reason to be very lenient to each other!'

'We will be, Rosa.'

'That's a dear good boy! Eddy, let us be courageous. Let us change to brother and sister from this day forth.'

'Never be husband and wife?'

'Never!'

Neither spoke again for a little while. But after that pause he said, with some effort:

'Of course I know that this has been in both our minds, Rosa, and of course I am in honour bound to confess freely that it does not originate with you.'

'No, nor with you, dear,' she returned, with pathetic earnestness. 'That sprung up between us. You are not truly happy in our engagement; I am not truly happy in it. O, I am so sorry, so sorry!' And there she broke into tears.

'I am deeply sorry too, Rosa. Deeply sorry for you.'

'And I for you, poor boy! And I for you!'

This pure young feeling, this gentle and forbearing feeling of each towards the other, brought with it its reward in a softening light that seemed to shine on their position. The relations between them did not look wilful, or capricious, or a failure, in such a light; they became elevated into something more self-denying, honourable, affectionate, and true.

'If we knew yesterday,' said Rosa, as she dried her eyes, 'and we did know yesterday, and on many, many yesterdays, that we were far from right together in those relations which were not of our own choosing, what better could we do to-day than change them? It is natural that we should be sorry, and you see how sorry we both are; but how much better to be sorry now than then!'

'When, Rosa?'

'When it would be too late. And then we should be angry, besides.'

Another silence fell upon them.

'And you know,' said Rosa innocently, 'you couldn't like me then; and you can always like me now, for I shall not be a drag upon you, or a worry to you. And I can always like you now, and your sister will not tease or trifle with you. I often did when I was not your sister, and I beg your pardon for it.'

'Don't let us come to that, Rosa; or I shall want more pardoning than I like to think of.'

'No, indeed, Eddy; you are too hard, my generous boy, upon yourself. Let us sit down, brother, on these ruins, and let me tell you how it was with us. I think I know, for I have considered about it very much since you were here last time. You liked me, didn't you? You thought I was a nice little thing?'

'Everybody thinks that, Rosa.'

'Do they?' She knitted her brow musingly for a moment, and then flashed out with the bright little induction: 'Well, but say they do. Surely it was not enough that you should think of me only as other people did; now, was it?'

The point was not to be got over. It was not enough.

'And that is just what I mean; that is just how it was with us,' said Rosa. 'You liked me very well, and you had grown used to me, and had grown used to the idea of our being married. You accepted the situation as an inevitable kind of thing, didn't you? It was to be, you thought, and why discuss or dispute it?'

It was new and strange to him to have himself presented to himself so clearly, in a glass of her holding up. He had always patronised her, in his superiority to her share of woman's wit. Was that but another instance of something radically amiss in the terms on which they had been gliding towards a life-long bondage?

'All this that I say of you is true of me as well, Eddy. Unless it was, I might not be bold enough to say it. Only, the difference between us was, that by little and little there crept into my mind a habit of thinking about it, instead of dismissing it. My life is not so busy as yours, you see, and I have not so many things to think of. So I thought about it very much, and I cried about it very much too (though that was not your fault, poor boy); when all at once my guardian came down, to prepare for my leaving the Nuns' House. I tried to hint to him that I was not quite settled in my mind, but I hesitated and failed, and he didn't understand me. But he is a good, good man. And he put before me so kindly, and yet so strongly, how seriously we ought to consider, in our circumstances, that I resolved to speak to you the next moment we were alone and grave. And if I seemed to come to it easily just now, because I came to it all at once, don't think it was so really, Eddy, for O, it was very, very hard, and O, I am very, very sorry!'

Her full heart broke into tears again. He put his arm about her waist, and they walked by the river-side together.

'Your guardian has spoken to me too, Rosa dear. I saw him before I left London.' His right hand was in his breast, seeking the ring; but he checked it, as he thought: 'If I am to take it back, why should I tell her of it?'

'And that made you more serious about it, didn't it, Eddy? And if I had not spoken to you, as I have, you would have spoken to me? I hope you can tell me so? I don't like it to be *all* my doing, though it *is* so much better for us.'

'Yes, I should have spoken; I should have put everything before you; I came intending to do it. But I never could have spoken to you as you have spoken to me, Rosa.'

'Don't say you mean so coldly or unkindly, Eddy, please, if you can help it.'

'I mean so sensibly and delicately, so wisely and affectionately.'

'That's my dear brother!' She kissed his hand in a little rapture. 'The dear girls will be dreadfully disappointed,' added Rosa, laughing, with the dewdrops glistening in her bright eyes. 'They have looked forward to it so, poor pets!'

'Ah! but I fear it will be a worse disappointment to Jack,' said Edwin Drood, with a start. 'I never thought of Jack!'

Her swift and intent look at him as he said the words could no more be recalled than a flash of lightning can. But it appeared as though she would have instantly recalled it, if she could; for she looked down, confused, and breathed quickly.

'You don't doubt its being a blow to Jack, Rosa?'

She merely replied, and that evasively and hurriedly: Why should she? She had not thought about it. He seemed, to her, to have so little to do with it.

'My dear child! can you suppose that any one so wrapped up in another — Mrs. Tope's expression: not mine — as Jack is in me, could fail to be struck all of a heap by such a sudden and complete change in my life? I say sudden, because it will be sudden to *him*, you know.'

She nodded twice or thrice, and her lips parted as if she would have assented. But she uttered no sound, and her breathing was no slower.

'How shall I tell Jack?' said Edwin, ruminating. If he had been less occupied with the thought, he must have seen her singular emotion. 'I never thought of Jack. It must be broken to him, before the town-crier knows it. I dine with the dear fellow tomorrow and next day — Christmas Eve and Christmas Day — but it would never do to spoil his feast-days. He always worries about me, and moddley-coddleys in the merest trifles. The news is sure to overset him. How on earth shall this be broken to Jack?'

'He must be told, I suppose?' said Rosa.

'My dear Rosa! who ought to be in our confidence, if not Jack?'

'My guardian promised to come down, if I should write and ask him. I am going to do so. Would you like to leave it to him?'

'A bright idea!' cried Edwin. 'The other trustee. Nothing more natural. He comes down, he goes to Jack, he relates what we have agreed upon, and he states our case better than we could. He has already spoken feelingly to you, he has already spoken feelingly to me, and he'll put the whole thing feelingly to Jack. That's it! I am not a coward, Rosa, but to tell you a secret, I am a little afraid of Jack.'

'No, no! you are not afraid of him!' cried Rosa, turning white, and clasping her hands.

'Why, sister Rosa, sister Rosa, what do you see from the turret?' said Edwin, rallying her. 'My dear girl!'

'You frightened me.'

'Most unintentionally, but I am as sorry as if I had meant to do it. Could you possibly suppose for a moment, from any loose way of speaking of mine, that I was literally afraid of the dear fond fellow? What I mean is, that he is subject to a kind of paroxysm, or fit — I saw him in it once — and I don't know but that so great a surprise, coming upon him direct from me whom he is so wrapped up in, might bring it on perhaps. Which — and this is the secret I was going to tell you — is another reason for your guardian's making the communication. He is so steady, precise, and exact, that he will talk Jack's thoughts into shape, in no time: whereas with me Jack is always impulsive and hurried, and, I may say, almost womanish.'

Rosa seemed convinced. Perhaps from her own very different point of view of 'Jack,' she felt comforted and protected by the interposition of Mr. Grewgious between herself and him.

And now, Edwin Drood's right hand closed again upon the ring in its little case, and again was checked by the consideration: 'It is certain, now, that I am to give it back to him; then why should I tell her of it?' That pretty sympathetic nature which could be so sorry for him in the blight of their childish hopes of happiness together, and could so quietly find itself alone in a new world to weave fresh wreaths of such flowers as it might prove to bear, the old world's flowers being withered, would be grieved by those sorrowful jewels; and to what purpose? Why should it be? They were but a sign of broken joys and baseless projects; in their very beauty they were (as the unlikeliest of men had said) almost a cruel satire on the loves, hopes, plans, of humanity, which are able to forecast nothing, and are so much brittle dust. Let them be. He would restore them to her guardian when he came down; he in his turn would restore them to the cabinet from which he had unwillingly taken them; and there, like old letters or old vows, or other records of old aspirations come to nothing, they would be disregarded, until, being valuable, they were sold into circulation again, to repeat their former round.

Let them be. Let them lie unspoken of, in his breast. However distinctly or indistinctly he entertained these thoughts, he arrived at the conclusion, Let them be. Among the mighty store of wonderful chains that are for ever forging, day and night, in the vast iron-works of time and circumstance, there was one chain forged in the moment of that small conclusion, riveted to the foundations of heaven and earth, and gifted with invincible force to hold and drag.

They walked on by the river. They began to speak of their separate plans. He would quicken his departure from England, and she would remain where she was, at least as long as Helena remained. The poor dear girls should have their disappointment broken to them gently, and, as the first preliminary, Miss Twinkleton should be confided in by Rosa, even in advance of the reappearance of Mr. Grewgious. It should be made clear in all quarters that she and Edwin were the best of friends. There had never been so serene an understanding between them since they were first affianced. And yet there was one reservation on each side; on hers, that she intended through her guardian to withdraw herself immediately from the tuition of her music-master; on his, that he did already entertain some wandering speculations whether it might ever come to pass that he would know more of Miss Landless.

The bright, frosty day declined as they walked and spoke together. The sun dipped in the river far behind them, and the old city lay red before them, as their walk drew to a close. The moaning water cast its seaweed duskily at their feet, when they turned to leave its margin; and the rooks hovered above them with hoarse cries, darker splashes in the darkening air.

'I will prepare Jack for my flitting soon,' said Edwin, in a low voice, 'and I will but see your guardian when he comes, and then go before they speak together. It will be better done without my being by. Don't you think so?'

'Yes.'

'We know we have done right, Rosa?'

'Yes.'

'We know we are better so, even now?'

'And shall be far, far better so by-and-by.'

Still there was that lingering tenderness in their hearts towards the old positions they were relinquishing, that they prolonged their parting. When they came among the elm-trees by the Cathedral, where they had last sat together, they stopped as by consent, and Rosa raised her face to his, as she had never raised it in the old days; — for they were old already.

'God bless you, dear! Good-bye!'

'God bless you, dear! Good-bye!'

They kissed each other fervently.

'Now, please take me home, Eddy, and let me be by myself.'

'Don't look round, Rosa,' he cautioned her, as he drew her arm through his, and led her away. 'Didn't you see Jack?'

'No! Where?'

'Under the trees. He saw us, as we took leave of each other. Poor fellow! he little thinks we have parted. This will be a blow to him, I am much afraid!'

She hurried on, without resting, and hurried on until they had passed under the gatehouse into the street; once there, she asked:

'Has he followed us? You can look without seeming to. Is he behind?'

'No. Yes, he is! He has just passed out under the gateway. The dear, sympathetic old fellow likes to keep us in sight. I am afraid he will be bitterly disappointed!'

She pulled hurriedly at the handle of the hoarse old bell, and the gate soon opened. Before going in, she gave him one last, wide, wondering look, as if she would have asked him with imploring emphasis: 'O! don't you understand?' And out of that look he vanished from her view.

When Shall These Three Meet Again?

CHRISTMAS EVE in Cloisterham. A few strange faces in the streets; a few other faces, half strange and half familiar, once the faces of Cloisterham children, now the faces of men and women who come back from the outer world at long intervals to find the city wonderfully shrunken in size, as if it had not washed by any means well in the meanwhile. To these, the striking of the Cathedral clock, and the cawing of the rooks from the Cathedral tower, are like voices of their nursery time. To such as these, it has happened in their dying hours afar off, that they have imagined their chamber-floor to be strewn with the autumnal leaves fallen from the elm-trees in the Close: so have the rustling sounds and fresh scents of their earliest impressions revived when the circle of their lives was very nearly traced, and the beginning and the end were drawing close together.

Seasonable tokens are about. Red berries shine here and there in the lattices of Minor Canon Corner; Mr. and Mrs. Tope are daintily sticking sprigs of holly into the carvings and sconces of the Cathedral stalls, as if they were sticking them into the coat-buttonholes of the Dean and Chapter. Lavish profusion is in the shops: particularly in the articles of currants, raisins, spices, candied peel, and moist sugar. An unusual air of gallantry and dissipation is abroad; evinced in an immense bunch of mistletoe hanging in the greengrocer's shop doorway, and a poor little Twelfth Cake, culminating in the figure of a Harlequin — such a very poor little Twelfth Cake, that one would rather called it a Twenty-fourth Cake or a Forty-eighth Cake — to be raffled for at the pastrycook's, terms one shilling per member. Public amusements are not wanting. The Wax-Work which made so deep an impression on the reflective mind of the Emperor of China is to be seen by particular desire during Christmas Week only, on the premises of the bankrupt livery-stable-keeper up the lane; and a new grand comic Christmas pantomime is to be produced at the Theatre: the latter heralded by the portrait of Signor Jacksonini the clown, saying 'How do you do to-morrow?' quite as large as life, and almost as miserably. In short, Cloisterham is up and doing: though from this description the High School and Miss Twinkleton's are to be excluded. From the former establishment the scholars have gone home, every one of them in love with one of Miss Twinkleton's young ladies (who knows nothing about it); and only the handmaidens flutter occasionally in the windows of the latter. It is noticed, by the bye, that these damsels become, within the limits of decorum, more skittish when thus intrusted with the concrete representations of their sex, than when dividing the representation with Miss Twinkleton's young ladies.

Three are to meet at the gatehouse to-night. How does each one of the three get through the day?

Neville Landless, though absolved from his books for the time by Mr. Crisparkle — whose fresh nature is by no means insensible to the charms of a holiday — reads and writes in his quiet room, with a concentrated air, until it is two hours past noon. He then sets himself to clearing his table, to arranging his books, and to tearing up and burning his stray papers. He makes a clean sweep of all untidy accumulations, puts all his drawers in order, and leaves no note or scrap of paper undestroyed, save such memoranda as bear directly on his studies. This done, he turns to his wardrobe, selects a few articles of ordinary wear — among them, change of stout shoes and socks for walking — and packs these in a knapsack. This knapsack is new, and he bought it in the High Street yesterday. He also purchased, at the same time and at the same place, a heavy walking-stick; strong in the handle for the grip of the hand, and iron-shod. He tries this, swings it, poises it, and lays it by, with the knapsack, on a window-seat. By this time his arrangements are complete.

He dresses for going out, and is in the act of going — indeed has left his room, and has met the Minor Canon on the staircase, coming out of his bedroom upon the same story — when he turns back again for his walking-stick, thinking he will carry it now. Mr. Crisparkle, who has paused on the staircase, sees it in his hand on his immediately reappearing, takes it from him, and asks him with a smile how he chooses a stick?

'Really I don't know that I understand the subject,' he answers. 'I chose it for its weight.'

'Much too heavy, Neville; *much* too heavy.'

'To rest upon in a long walk, sir?'

'Rest upon?' repeats Mr. Crisparkle, throwing himself into pedestrian form. 'You don't rest upon it; you merely balance with it.'

'I shall know better, with practice, sir. I have not lived in a walking country, you know.'

'True,' says Mr. Crisparkle. 'Get into a little training, and we will have a few score miles together. I should leave you nowhere now. Do you come back before dinner?'

'I think not, as we dine early.'

Mr. Crisparkle gives him a bright nod and a cheerful goodbye; expressing (not without intention) absolute confidence and ease.

Neville repairs to the Nuns' House, and requests that Miss Landless may be informed that her brother is there, by appointment. He waits at the gate, not even crossing the threshold; for he is on his parole not to put himself in Rosa's way.

His sister is at least as mindful of the obligation they have taken on themselves as he can be, and loses not a moment in joining him. They meet affectionately, avoid lingering there, and walk towards the upper inland country.

'I am not going to tread upon forbidden ground, Helena,' says Neville, when they have walked some distance and are turning; 'you will understand in another moment that I cannot help referring to — what shall I say? — my infatuation.'

'Had you not better avoid it, Neville? You know that I can hear nothing.'

'You can hear, my dear, what Mr. Crisparkle has heard, and heard with approval.'

'Yes; I can hear so much.'

'Well, it is this. I am not only unsettled and unhappy myself, but I am conscious of unsettling and interfering with other people. How do I know that, but for my unfortunate presence, you, and — and — the rest of that former party, our engaging guardian excepted, might be dining cheerfully in Minor Canon Corner to-morrow? Indeed it probably would be so. I can see too well that I am not high in the old lady's opinion, and it is easy to understand what an irksome clog I must be upon the hospitalities of her orderly house — especially at this time of year — when I must be kept asunder from this person, and there is such a reason for my not being brought into contact with that person, and an unfavourable reputation has preceded me with such another person; and so on. I have put this very gently to Mr. Crisparkle, for you know his self-denying ways; but still I have put it. What I have laid much greater stress upon at the same time is, that I am engaged in a miserable struggle with myself, and that a little change and absence may enable me to come through it the better. So, the weather being bright and hard, I am going on a walking expedition, and intend taking myself out of everybody's way (my own included, I hope) to-morrow morning.'

'When to come back?'

'In a fortnight.'

'And going quite alone?'

'I am much better without company, even if there were any one but you to bear me company, my dear Helena.'

'Mr. Crisparkle entirely agrees, you say?'

'Entirely. I am not sure but that at first he was inclined to think it rather a moody scheme, and one that might do a brooding mind harm. But we took a moonlight walk last Monday night, to talk it over at leisure, and I represented the case to him as it really is. I showed him that I do want to conquer myself, and that, this evening well got over, it is surely better that I should be away from here just now, than here. I could hardly help meeting certain people walking together here, and that could do no good, and is certainly not the way to forget. A fortnight hence, that chance will probably be over, for the time; and when it again arises for the last time, why, I can again go away. Farther, I really do feel hopeful of bracing exercise and wholesome fatigue. You know that Mr. Crisparkle allows such things their full weight in the preservation of his own sound mind in his own sound body, and that his just spirit is not likely to maintain one set of natural laws for himself and another for me. He yielded to my view of the matter, when convinced that I was honestly in earnest; and so, with his full consent, I start to-morrow morning. Early enough to be not only out of the streets, but out of hearing of the bells, when the good people go to church.'

Helena thinks it over, and thinks well of it. Mr. Crisparkle doing so, she would do so; but she does originally, out of her own mind, think well of it, as a healthy project, denoting a sincere endeavour and an active attempt at self-correction. She is inclined to pity him, poor fellow, for going away solitary on the great Christmas festival; but she feels it much more to the purpose to encourage him. And she does encourage him.

He will write to her?

He will write to her every alternate day, and tell her all his adventures.

Does he send clothes on in advance of him?

'My dear Helena, no. Travel like a pilgrim, with wallet and staff. My wallet — or my knapsack — is packed, and ready for strapping on; and here is my staff!'

He hands it to her; she makes the same remark as Mr. Crisparkle, that it is very heavy; and gives it back to him, asking what wood it is? Iron-wood.

Up to this point he has been extremely cheerful. Perhaps, the having to carry his case with her, and therefore to present it in its brightest aspect, has roused his spirits. Perhaps, the having done so with success, is followed by a revulsion. As the day closes in, and the city-lights begin to spring up before them, he grows depressed.

'I wish I were not going to this dinner, Helena.'

'Dear Neville, is it worth while to care much about it? Think how soon it will be over.'

'How soon it will be over!' he repeats gloomily. 'Yes. But I don't like it.'

There may be a moment's awkwardness, she cheeringly represents to him, but it can only last a moment. He is quite sure of himself.

'I wish I felt as sure of everything else, as I feel of myself,' he answers her.

'How strangely you speak, dear! What do you mean?'

'Helena, I don't know. I only know that I don't like it. What a strange dead weight there is in the air!'

She calls his attention to those copperous clouds beyond the river, and says that the wind is rising. He scarcely speaks again, until he takes leave of her, at the gate of the Nuns' House. She does not immediately enter, when they have parted, but remains looking after him along the street. Twice he passes the gatehouse, reluctant to enter. At length, the Cathedral clock chiming one quarter, with a rapid turn he hurries in.

And so *he* goes up the postern stair.

Edwin Drood passes a solitary day. Something of deeper moment than he had thought, has gone out of his life; and in the silence of his own chamber he wept for it last night. Though the image of Miss Landless still hovers in the background of his mind, the pretty little affectionate creature, so much firmer and wiser than he had supposed, occupies its stronghold. It is with some misgiving of his own unworthiness that he thinks of her, and of what they might have been to one another, if he had been more in earnest some time ago; if he had set a higher value on her; if, instead of accepting his lot in life as an inheritance of course, he had studied the right way to its appreciation and enhancement. And still, for all this, and though there is a sharp heartache in all this, the vanity and caprice of youth sustain that handsome figure of Miss Landless in the background of his mind.

That was a curious look of Rosa's when they parted at the gate. Did it mean that she saw below the surface of his thoughts, and down into their twilight depths? Scarcely that, for it was a look of astonished and keen inquiry. He decides that he cannot understand it, though it was remarkably expressive.

As he only waits for Mr. Grewgious now, and will depart immediately after having seen him, he takes a sauntering leave of the ancient city and its neighbourhood. He recalls the time when Rosa and he walked here or there, mere children, full of the dignity of being engaged. Poor children! he thinks, with a pitying sadness.

Finding that his watch has stopped, he turns into the jeweller's shop, to have it wound and set. The jeweller is knowing on the subject of a bracelet, which he begs leave to submit, in a general and quite aimless way. It would suit (he considers) a young bride, to perfection; especially if of a rather diminutive style of beauty. Finding the bracelet but coldly looked at, the jeweller invites attention to a tray of rings for gentlemen; here is a style of ring, now, he remarks — a very chaste signet — which gentlemen are much given to purchasing, when changing their condition. A ring of a very responsible appearance. With the date of their wedding-day engraved inside, several gentlemen have preferred it to any other kind of memento.

The rings are as coldly viewed as the bracelet. Edwin tells the tempter that he wears no jewellery but his watch and chain, which were his father's; and his shirt-pin.

'That I was aware of,' is the jeweller's reply, 'for Mr. Jasper dropped in for a watch-glass the other day, and, in fact, I showed these articles to him, remarking that if he *should* wish to make a present to a gentleman relative, on any particular occasion — But he said with a smile that he had an inventory in his mind of all the jewellery his gentleman relative ever wore; namely, his watch and chain, and his shirt-pin.' Still (the jeweller considers) that might not apply to all times, though applying to the present time. 'Twenty minutes past two, Mr. Drood, I set your watch at. Let me recommend you not to let it run down, sir.'

Edwin takes his watch, puts it on, and goes out, thinking: 'Dear old Jack! If I were to make an extra crease in my neckcloth, he would think it worth noticing!'

He strolls about and about, to pass the time until the dinner-hour. It somehow happens that Cloisterham seems reproachful to him to-day; has fault to find with him, as if he had not used it well; but is far more pensive with him than angry. His wonted carelessness is replaced by a wistful looking at, and dwelling upon, all the old landmarks. He will soon be far away, and may never see them again, he thinks. Poor youth! Poor youth!

As dusk draws on, he paces the Monks' Vineyard. He has walked to and fro, full half an hour by the Cathedral chimes, and it has closed in dark, before he becomes quite aware of a woman crouching on the ground near a wicket gate in a corner. The gate commands a cross bye-path, little used in the gloaming; and the figure must have been there all the time, though he has but gradually and lately made it out.

He strikes into that path, and walks up to the wicket. By the light of a lamp near it, he sees that the woman is of a haggard appearance, and that her weazen chin is resting on her hands, and that her eyes are staring — with an unwinking, blind sort of steadfastness — before her.

"I'll tell you something."

Always kindly, but moved to be unusually kind this evening, and having bestowed kind words on most of the children and aged people he has met, he at once bends down, and speaks to this woman.

'Are you ill?'

'No, deary,' she answers, without looking at him, and with no departure from her strange blind stare.

'Are you blind?'

'No, deary.'

'Are you lost, homeless, faint? What is the matter, that you stay here in the cold so long, without moving?'

By slow and stiff efforts, she appears to contract her vision until it can rest upon him; and then a curious film passes over her, and she begins to shake.

He straightens himself, recoils a step, and looks down at her in a dread amazement; for he seems to know her.

'Good Heaven!' he thinks, next moment. 'Like Jack that night!'

As he looks down at her, she looks up at him, and whimpers: 'My lungs is weakly; my lungs is dreffle bad. Poor me, poor me, my cough is rattling dry!' and coughs in confirmation horribly.

'Where do you come from?'

'Come from London, deary.' (Her cough still rending her.)

'Where are you going to?'

'Back to London, deary. I came here, looking for a needle in a haystack, and I ain't found it. Look'ee, deary; give me three-and-sixpence, and don't you be afeard for me. I'll get back to London then, and trouble no one. I'm in a business. — Ah, me! It's slack, it's slack, and times is very bad! — but I can make a shift to live by it.'

'Do you eat opium?'

'Smokes it,' she replies with difficulty, still racked by her cough. 'Give me three-and-sixpence, and I'll lay it out well, and get back. If you don't give me three-and-sixpence, don't give me a brass farden. And if you do give me three-and-sixpence, deary, I'll tell you something.'

He counts the money from his pocket, and puts it in her hand. She instantly clutches it tight, and rises to her feet with a croaking laugh of satisfaction.

'Bless ye! Hark'ee, dear genl'mn. What's your Chris'en name?'

'Edwin.'

'Edwin, Edwin, Edwin,' she repeats, trailing off into a drowsy repetition of the word; and then asks suddenly: 'Is the short of that name Eddy?'

'It is sometimes called so,' he replies, with the colour starting to his face.

'Don't sweethearts call it so?' she asks, pondering.

'How should I know?'

'Haven't you a sweetheart, upon your soul?'

'None.'

She is moving away, with another 'Bless ye, and thank'ee, deary!' when he adds: 'You were to tell me something; you may as well do so.'

'So I was, so I was. Well, then. Whisper. You be thankful that your name ain't Ned.'

He looks at her quite steadily, as he asks: 'Why?'

'Because it's a bad name to have just now.'

'How a bad name?'

'A threatened name. A dangerous name.'

'The proverb says that threatened men live long,' he tells her, lightly.

'Then Ned — so threatened is he, wherever he may be while I am a-talking to you, deary — should live to all eternity!' replies the woman.

She has leaned forward to say it in his ear, with her forefinger shaking before his eyes, and now huddles herself together, and with another 'Bless ye, and thank'ee!' goes away in the direction of the Travellers' Lodging House.

This is not an inspiriting close to a dull day. Alone, in a sequestered place, surrounded by vestiges of old time and decay, it rather has a tendency to call a shudder into being. He makes for the better-lighted streets, and resolves as he walks on to say nothing of this to-night, but to mention it to Jack (who alone calls him Ned), as an odd coincidence, to-morrow; of course only as a coincidence, and not as anything better worth remembering.

Still, it holds to him, as many things much better worth remembering never did. He has another mile or so, to linger out before the dinner-hour; and, when he walks over the bridge and by the river, the woman's words are in the rising wind, in the angry sky, in the troubled water, in the flickering lights. There is some solemn echo of them even in the Cathedral chime, which strikes a sudden surprise to his heart as he turns in under the archway of the gatehouse.

And so *he* goes up the postern stair.

John Jasper passes a more agreeable and cheerful day than either of his guests. Having no music-lessons to give in the holiday season, his time is his own, but for the Cathedral services. He is early among the shopkeepers, ordering little table luxuries that his nephew likes. His nephew will not be with him long, he tells his provision-dealers, and so must be petted and made much of. While out on his hospitable preparations, he looks in on Mr. Sapsea; and mentions that dear Ned, and that inflammable young spark of Mr. Crisparkle's, are to dine at the gatehouse to-day, and make up their difference. Mr. Sapsea is by no means friendly towards the inflammable young spark. He says that his complexion is 'Un-English.' And when Mr. Sapsea has once declared anything to be Un-English, he considers that thing everlastingly sunk in the bottomless pit.

John Jasper is truly sorry to hear Mr. Sapsea speak thus, for he knows right well that Mr. Sapsea never speaks without a meaning, and that he has a subtle trick of being right. Mr. Sapsea (by a very remarkable coincidence) is of exactly that opinion.

Mr. Jasper is in beautiful voice this day. In the pathetic supplication to have his heart inclined to keep this law, he quite astonishes his fellows by his melodious power. He has never sung difficult music with such skill and harmony, as in this day's Anthem. His nervous temperament is occasionally prone to take difficult music a little too quickly; to-day his time is perfect.

These results are probably attained through a grand composure of the spirits. The mere mechanism of his throat is a little tender, for he wears, both with his singing-robe and with his ordinary dress, a large black scarf of strong close-woven silk, slung loosely round his neck. But his composure is so noticeable, that Mr. Crisparkle speaks of it as they come out from Vespers.

'I must thank you, Jasper, for the pleasure with which I have heard you to-day. Beautiful! Delightful! You could not have so outdone yourself, I hope, without being wonderfully well.'

'I *am* wonderfully well.'

'Nothing unequal,' says the Minor Canon, with a smooth motion of his hand: 'nothing unsteady, nothing forced, nothing avoided; all thoroughly done in a masterly manner, with perfect self-command.'

'Thank you. I hope so, if it is not too much to say.'

'One would think, Jasper, you had been trying a new medicine for that occasional indisposition of yours.'

'No, really? That's well observed; for I have.'

'Then stick to it, my good fellow,' says Mr. Crisparkle, clapping him on the shoulder with friendly encouragement, 'stick to it.'

'I will.'

'I congratulate you,' Mr. Crisparkle pursues, as they come out of the Cathedral, 'on all accounts.'

'Thank you again. I will walk round to the Corner with you, if you don't object; I have plenty of time before my company come; and I want to say a word to you, which I think you will not be displeased to hear.'

'What is it?'

'Well. We were speaking, the other evening, of my black humours.'

Mr. Crisparkle's face falls, and he shakes his head deploringly.

'I said, you know, that I should make you an antidote to those black humours; and you said you hoped I would consign them to the flames.'

'And I still hope so, Jasper.'

'With the best reason in the world! I mean to burn this year's Diary at the year's end.'

'Because you ——?' Mr. Crisparkle brightens greatly as he thus begins.

'You anticipate me. Because I feel that I have been out of sorts, gloomy, bilious, brain-oppressed, whatever it may be. You said I had been exaggerative. So I have.'

Mr. Crisparkle's brightened face brightens still more.

'I couldn't see it then, because I *was* out of sorts; but I am in a healthier state now, and I acknowledge it with genuine pleasure. I made a great deal of a very little; that's the fact.'

'It does me good,' cries Mr. Crisparkle, 'to hear you say it!'

'A man leading a monotonous life,' Jasper proceeds, 'and getting his nerves, or his stomach, out of order, dwells upon an idea until it loses its proportions. That was my case with the idea in question. So I shall burn the evidence of my case, when the book is full, and begin the next volume with a clearer vision.'

'This is better,' says Mr. Crisparkle, stopping at the steps of his own door to shake hands, 'than I could have hoped.'

'Why, naturally,' returns Jasper. 'You had but little reason to hope that I should become more like yourself. You are always training yourself to be, mind and body, as clear as crystal, and you always are, and never change; whereas I am a muddy, solitary, moping weed. However, I have got over that mope. Shall I wait, while you ask if Mr. Neville has left for my place? If not, he and I may walk round together.'

'I think,' says Mr. Crisparkle, opening the entrance-door with his key, 'that he left some time ago; at least I know he left, and I think he has not come back. But I'll inquire. You won't come in?'

'My company wait,' said Jasper, with a smile.

The Minor Canon disappears, and in a few moments returns. As he thought, Mr. Neville has not come back; indeed, as he remembers now, Mr. Neville said he would probably go straight to the gatehouse.

'Bad manners in a host!' says Jasper. 'My company will be there before me! What will you bet that I don't find my company embracing?'

'I will bet — or I would, if ever I did bet,' returns Mr. Crisparkle, 'that your company will have a gay entertainer this evening.'

Jasper nods, and laughs good-night!

He retraces his steps to the Cathedral door, and turns down past it to the gatehouse. He sings, in a low voice and with delicate expression, as he walks along. It still seems as if a false note were not within his power to-night, and as if nothing could hurry or retard him. Arriving thus under the arched entrance of his dwelling, he pauses for an instant in the shelter to pull off that great black scarf, and hang it in a loop upon his arm. For that brief time, his face is knitted and stern. But it immediately clears, as he resumes his singing, and his way.

And so *he* goes up the postern stair.

The red light burns steadily all the evening in the lighthouse on the margin of the tide of busy life. Softened sounds and hum of traffic pass it and flow on irregularly into the lonely Precincts; but very little else goes by, save violent rushes of wind. It comes on to blow a boisterous gale.

The Precincts are never particularly well lighted; but the strong blasts of wind blowing out many of the lamps (in some instances shattering the frames too, and bringing the glass rattling to the ground), they are unusually dark to-night. The darkness is augmented and confused, by flying dust from the earth, dry twigs from the trees, and great ragged fragments from the rooks' nests up in the tower. The trees themselves so toss and creak, as this tangible part of the darkness madly whirls about, that they seem in peril of being torn out of the earth: while ever and again a crack, and a rushing fall, denote that some large branch has yielded to the storm.

Not such power of wind has blown for many a winter night. Chimneys topple in the streets, and people hold to posts and corners, and to one another, to keep themselves upon their feet. The violent rushes abate not, but increase in frequency and fury until at midnight, when the streets are empty, the storm goes thundering along them, rattling at all the latches, and tearing at all the shutters, as if warning the people to get up and fly with it, rather than have the roofs brought down upon their brains.

Still, the red light burns steadily. Nothing is steady but the red light.

All through the night the wind blows, and abates not. But early in the morning, when there is barely enough light in the east to dim the stars, it begins to lull. From that time, with occasional wild charges, like a wounded monster dying, it drops and sinks; and at full daylight it is dead.

It is then seen that the hands of the Cathedral clock are torn off; that lead from the roof has been stripped away, rolled up, and blown into the Close;

and that some stones have been displaced upon the summit of the great tower. Christmas morning though it be, it is necessary to send up workmen, to ascertain the extent of the damage done. These, led by Durdles, go aloft; while Mr. Tope and a crowd of early idlers gather down in Minor Canon Corner, shading their eyes and watching for their appearance up there.

This cluster is suddenly broken and put aside by the hands of Mr. Jasper; all the gazing eyes are brought down to the earth by his loudly inquiring of Mr. Crisparkle, at an open window:

'Where is my nephew?'

'He has not been here. Is he not with you?'

'No. He went down to the river last night, with Mr. Neville, to look at the storm, and has not been back. Call Mr. Neville!'

'He left this morning, early.'

'Left this morning early? Let me in! let me in!'

There is no more looking up at the tower, now. All the assembled eyes are turned on Mr. Jasper, white, half-dressed, panting, and clinging to the rail before the Minor Canon's house.

Impeached

NEVILLE LANDLESS had started so early and walked at so good a pace, that when the church-bells began to ring in Cloisterham for morning service, he was eight miles away. As he wanted his breakfast by that time, having set forth on a crust of bread, he stopped at the next roadside tavern to refresh.

Visitors in want of breakfast — unless they were horses or cattle, for which class of guests there was preparation enough in the way of water-trough and hay — were so unusual at the sign of The Tilted Wagon, that it took a long time to get the wagon into the track of tea and toast and bacon. Neville in the interval, sitting in a sanded parlour, wondering in how long a time after he had gone, the sneezy fire of damp fagots would begin to make somebody else warm.

Indeed, The Tilted Wagon, as a cool establishment on the top of a hill, where the ground before the door was puddled with damp hoofs and trodden straw; where a scolding landlady slapped a moist baby (with one red sock on and one wanting), in the bar; where the cheese was cast aground upon a shelf, in company with a mouldy tablecloth and a green-handled knife, in a sort of cast-iron canoe; where the pale-faced bread shed tears of crumb over its shipwreck in another canoe; where the family linen, half washed and half dried, led a public life of lying about; where everything to drink was drunk out of mugs, and everything else was suggestive of a rhyme to mugs; The Tilted Wagon, all these things considered, hardly kept its painted promise of providing good entertainment for Man and Beast. However, Man, in the present case, was not critical, but took what entertainment he could get, and went on again after a longer rest than he needed.

He stopped at some quarter of a mile from the house, hesitating whether to pursue the road, or to follow a cart track between two high hedgerows, which led across the slope of a breezy heath, and evidently struck into the road again by-and-by. He decided in favour of this latter track, and pursued it with some toil; the rise being steep, and the way worn into deep ruts.

He was labouring along, when he became aware of some other pedestrians behind him. As they were coming up at a faster pace than his, he stood aside, against one of the high banks, to let them pass. But their manner was very curious. Only four of them passed. Other four slackened speed, and loitered as intending to follow him when he should go on. The remainder of the party (half-a-dozen perhaps) turned, and went back at a great rate.

He looked at the four behind him, and he looked at the four before him. They all returned his look. He resumed his way. The four in advance went on, constantly looking back; the four in the rear came closing up.

When they all ranged out from the narrow track upon the open slope of the heath, and this order was maintained, let him diverge as he would to either side, there was no longer room to doubt that he was beset by these fellows. He stopped, as a last test; and they all stopped.

'Why do you attend upon me in this way?' he asked the whole body. 'Are you a pack of thieves?'

'Don't answer him,' said one of the number; he did not see which. 'Better be quiet.'

'Better be quiet?' repeated Neville. 'Who said so?' Nobody replied.

'It's good advice, whichever of you skulkers gave it,' he went on angrily. 'I will not submit to be penned in between four men there, and four men there. I wish to pass, and I mean to pass, those four in front.'

They were all standing still; himself included.

'If eight men, or four men, or two men, set upon one,' he proceeded, growing more enraged, 'the one has no chance but to set his mark upon some of them. And, by the Lord, I'll do it, if I am interrupted any farther!'

Shouldering his heavy stick, and quickening his pace, he shot on to pass the four ahead. The largest and strongest man of the number changed swiftly to the side on which he came up, and dexterously closed with him and went down with him; but not before the heavy stick had descended smartly.

'Let him be!' said this man in a suppressed voice, as they struggled together on the grass. 'Fair play! His is the build of a girl to mine, and he's got a weight strapped to his back besides. Let him alone. I'll manage him.'

After a little rolling about, in a close scuffle which caused the faces of both to be besmeared with blood, the man took his knee from Neville's chest, and rose, saying: 'There! Now take him arm-in-arm, any two of you!'

It was immediately done.

'As to our being a pack of thieves, Mr. Landless,' said the man, as he spat out some blood, and wiped more from his face; 'you know better than that at midday. We wouldn't have touched you if you hadn't forced us. We're going to take you round to the high road, anyhow, and you'll find help enough against thieves there, if you want it. — Wipe his face, somebody; see how it's a-trickling down him!'

When his face was cleansed, Neville recognised in the speaker, Joe, driver of the Cloisterham omnibus, whom he had seen but once, and that on the day of his arrival.

'And what I recommend you for the present, is, don't talk, Mr. Landless. You'll find a friend waiting for you, at the high road — gone ahead by the other way when we split into two parties — and you had much better say nothing till you come up with him. Bring that stick along, somebody else, and let's be moving!'

Utterly bewildered, Neville stared around him and said not a word. Walking between his two conductors, who held his arms in theirs, he went on, as in a dream, until they came again into the high road, and into the midst of a little group of people. The men who had turned back were among the group; and its central figures were Mr. Jasper and Mr. Crisparkle. Neville's conductors took him up to the Minor Canon, and there released him, as an act of deference to that gentleman.

'What is all this, sir? What is the matter? I feel as if I had lost my senses!' cried Neville, the group closing in around him.

'Where is my nephew?' asked Mr. Jasper, wildly.

'Where is your nephew?' repeated Neville. 'Why do you ask me?'

'I ask you,' retorted Jasper, 'because you were the last person in his company, and he is not to be found.'

'Not to be found!' cried Neville, aghast.

'Stay, stay,' said Mr. Crisparkle. 'Permit me, Jasper. Mr. Neville, you are confounded; collect your thoughts; it is of great importance that you should collect your thoughts; attend to me.'

'I will try, sir, but I seem mad.'

'You left Mr. Jasper last night with Edwin Drood?'

'Yes.'

'At what hour?'

'Was it at twelve o'clock?' asked Neville, with his hand to his confused head, and appealing to Jasper.

'Quite right,' said Mr. Crisparkle; 'the hour Mr. Jasper has already named to me. You went down to the river together?'

'Undoubtedly. To see the action of the wind there.'

'What followed? How long did you stay there?'

'About ten minutes; I should say not more. We then walked together to your house, and he took leave of me at the door.'

'Did he say that he was going down to the river again?'

'No. He said that he was going straight back.'

The bystanders looked at one another, and at Mr. Crisparkle. To whom Mr. Jasper, who had been intensely watching Neville, said, in a low, distinct, suspicious voice: 'What are those stains upon his dress?'

All eyes were turned towards the blood upon his clothes.

'And here are the same stains upon this stick!' said Jasper, taking it from the hand of the man who held it. 'I know the stick to be his, and he carried it last night. What does this mean?'

'In the name of God, say what it means, Neville!' urged Mr. Crisparkle.

'That man and I,' said Neville, pointing out his late adversary, 'had a struggle for the stick just now, and you may see the same marks on him, sir. What was I to suppose, when I found myself molested by eight people? Could I dream of the true reason when they would give me none at all?'

They admitted that they had thought it discreet to be silent, and that the struggle had taken place. And yet the very men who had seen it looked darkly at the smears which the bright cold air had already dried.

'We must return, Neville,' said Mr. Crisparkle; 'of course you will be glad to come back to clear yourself?'

'Of course, sir.'

'Mr. Landless will walk at my side,' the Minor Canon continued, looking around him. 'Come, Neville!'

They set forth on the walk back; and the others, with one exception, straggled after them at various distances. Jasper walked on the other side of Neville, and never quitted that position. He was silent, while Mr. Crisparkle more than once repeated his former questions, and while Neville repeated his former answers; also, while they both hazarded some explanatory conjectures. He was obstinately silent, because Mr. Crisparkle's manner directly appealed to him to take some part in the discussion, and no appeal would move his fixed face. When they drew near to the city, and it was suggested by the Minor Canon that they might do well in calling on the Mayor at once, he assented with a stern nod; but he spake no word until they stood in Mr. Sapsea's parlour.

Mr. Sapsea being informed by Mr. Crisparkle of the circumstances under which they desired to make a voluntary statement before him, Mr. Jasper broke silence by declaring that he placed his whole reliance, humanly speaking, on Mr. Sapsea's penetration. There was no conceivable reason why his nephew should have suddenly absconded, unless Mr. Sapsea could suggest one, and then he would defer. There was no intelligible likelihood of his having returned to the river, and been accidentally drowned in the dark, unless it should appear likely to Mr. Sapsea, and then again he would defer. He washed his hands as clean as he could of all horrible suspicions, unless it should appear to Mr. Sapsea that some such were inseparable from his last companion before his disappearance (not on good terms with previously), and then, once more, he would defer. His own state of mind, he being distracted with doubts, and labouring under dismal apprehensions, was not to be safely trusted; but Mr. Sapsea's was.

Mr. Sapsea expressed his opinion that the case had a dark look; in short (and here his eyes rested full on Neville's countenance), an Un-English complexion. Having made this grand point, he wandered into a denser haze and maze of nonsense than even a mayor might have been expected to disport himself in, and came out of it with the brilliant discovery that to take the life of a fellow-creature was to take something that didn't belong to you. He wavered whether or no he should at once issue his warrant for the committal of Neville Landless to jail, under circumstances of grave suspicion; and he might have gone so far as to do it but for the indignant protest of the Minor Canon: who undertook for the young man's remaining in his own house, and being produced by his own hands, whenever demanded. Mr. Jasper then understood Mr. Sapsea to suggest that the river should be dragged, that its banks should be rigidly examined, that particulars of the disappearance should be sent to all outlying places and to London, and that placards and advertisements should be widely circulated imploring Edwin Drood, if for any unknown reason he had withdrawn himself from his uncle's home and society, to take pity on that loving kinsman's sore bereavement and distress, and somehow inform him that he was yet alive. Mr. Sapsea was perfectly understood, for this was exactly his meaning (though he had said nothing about it); and measures were taken towards all these ends immediately.

It would be difficult to determine which was the more oppressed with horror and amazement: Neville Landless, or John Jasper. But that Jasper's position forced him to be active, while Neville's forced him to be passive, there would have been nothing to choose between them. Each was bowed down and broken.

Jasper searches the river

With the earliest light of the next morning, men were at work upon the river, and other men — most of whom volunteered for the service — were examining the banks. All the livelong day the search went on; upon the river, with barge and pole, and drag and net; upon the muddy and rushy shore, with jack-boots, hatchet, spade, rope, dogs, and all imaginable appliances. Even at night, the river was specked with lanterns, and lurid with fires; far-off creeks, into which the tide washed as it changed, had their knots of watchers, listening to the lapping of the stream, and looking out for any burden it might bear; remote shingly causeways near the sea, and lonely points off which there was a race of water, had their unwonted flaring cressets and rough-coated figures when the next day dawned; but no trace of Edwin Drood revisited the light of the sun.

All that day, again, the search went on. Now, in barge and boat; and now ashore among the osiers, or tramping amidst mud and stakes and jagged stones in low-lying places, where solitary watermarks and signals of strange shapes showed like spectres, John Jasper worked and toiled. But to no purpose; for still no trace of Edwin Drood revisited the light of the sun.

Setting his watches for that night again, so that vigilant eyes should be kept on every change of tide, he went home exhausted. Unkempt and disordered, bedaubed with mud that had dried upon him, and with much of his clothing torn to rags, he had but just dropped into his easy-chair, when Mr. Grewgious stood before him.

'This is strange news,' said Mr. Grewgious.

'Strange and fearful news.'

Jasper had merely lifted up his heavy eyes to say it, and now dropped them again as he drooped, worn out, over one side of his easy-chair.

Mr. Grewgious smoothed his head and face, and stood looking at the fire.

'How is your ward?' asked Jasper, after a time, in a faint, fatigued voice.

'Poor little thing! You may imagine her condition.'

'Have you seen his sister?' inquired Jasper, as before.

'Whose?'

The curtness of the counter-question, and the cool, slow manner in which, as he put it, Mr. Grewgious moved his eyes from the fire to his companion's face, might at any other time have been exasperating. In his depression and exhaustion, Jasper merely opened his eyes to say: 'The suspected young man's.'

'Do you suspect him?' asked Mr. Grewgious.

'I don't know what to think. I cannot make up my mind.'

'Nor I,' said Mr. Grewgious. 'But as you spoke of him as the suspected young man, I thought you *had* made up your mind. — I have just left Miss Landless.'

'What is her state?'

'Defiance of all suspicion, and unbounded faith in her brother.'

'Poor thing!'

'However,' pursued Mr. Grewgious, 'it is not of her that I came to speak. It is of my ward. I have a communication to make that will surprise you. At least, it has surprised me.'

Jasper, with a groaning sigh, turned wearily in his chair.

'Shall I put it off till to-morrow?' said Mr. Grewgious. 'Mind, I warn you, that I think it will surprise you!'

More attention and concentration came into John Jasper's eyes as they caught sight of Mr. Grewgious smoothing his head again, and again looking at the fire; but now, with a compressed and determined mouth.

'What is it?' demanded Jasper, becoming upright in his chair.

'To be sure,' said Mr. Grewgious, provokingly slowly and internally, as he kept his eyes on the fire: 'I might have known it sooner; she gave me the opening; but I am such an exceedingly Angular man, that it never occurred to me; I took all for granted.'

'What is it?' demanded Jasper once more.

Mr. Grewgious, alternately opening and shutting the palms of his hands as he warmed them at the fire, and looking fixedly at him sideways, and never changing either his action or his look in all that followed, went on to reply.

'This young couple, the lost youth and Miss Rosa, my ward, though so long betrothed, and so long recognising their betrothal, and so near being married ——'

Mr. Grewgious saw a staring white face, and two quivering white lips, in the easy-chair, and saw two muddy hands gripping its sides. But for the hands, he might have thought he had never seen the face.

'—— This young couple came gradually to the discovery (made on both sides pretty equally, I think), that they would be happier and better, both in their present and their future lives, as affectionate friends, or say rather as brother and sister, than as husband and wife.'

Mr. Grewgious saw a lead-coloured face in the easy-chair, and on its surface dreadful starting drops or bubbles, as if of steel.

'This young couple formed at length the healthy resolution of interchanging their discoveries, openly, sensibly, and tenderly. They met for that purpose. After some innocent and generous talk, they agreed to dissolve their existing, and their intended, relations, for ever and ever.'

Mr. Grewgious saw a ghastly figure rise, open-mouthed, from the easy-chair, and lift its outspread hands towards its head.

'One of this young couple, and that one your nephew, fearful, however, that in the tenderness of your affection for him you would be bitterly disappointed by so wide a departure from his projected life, forbore to tell you the secret, for a few days, and left it to be disclosed by me, when I should come down to speak to you, and he would be gone. I speak to you, and he is gone.'

Mr. Grewgious saw the ghastly figure throw back its head, clutch its hair with its hands, and turn with a writhing action from him.

'I have now said all I have to say: except that this young couple parted, firmly, though not without tears and sorrow, on the evening when you last saw them together.'

Mr. Grewgious heard a terrible shriek, and saw no ghastly figure, sitting or standing; saw nothing but a heap of torn and miry clothes upon the floor.

Not changing his action even then, he opened and shut the palms of his hands as he warmed them, and looked down at it.

Devoted

WHEN John Jasper recovered from his fit or swoon, he found himself being tended by Mr. and Mrs. Tope, whom his visitor had summoned for the purpose. His visitor, wooden of aspect, sat stiffly in a chair, with his hands upon his knees, watching his recovery.

'There! You've come to nicely now, sir,' said the tearful Mrs. Tope; 'you were thoroughly worn out, and no wonder!'

'A man,' said Mr. Grewgious, with his usual air of repeating a lesson, 'cannot have his rest broken, and his mind cruelly tormented, and his body overtaxed by fatigue, whithout being thoroughly worn out.'

'I fear I have alarmed you?' Jasper apologised faintly, when he was helped into his easy-chair.

'Not at all, I thank you,' answered Mr. Grewgious.

'You are too considerate.'

'Not at all, I thank you,' answered Mr. Grewgious again.

'You must take some wine, sir,' said Mrs. Tope, 'and the jelly that I had ready for you, and that you wouldn't put your lips to at noon, though I warned you what would come of it, you know, and you not breakfasted; and you must have a wing of the roast fowl that has been put back twenty times if it's been put back once. It shall all be on table in five minutes, and this good gentleman belike will stop and see you take it.'

This good gentleman replied with a snort, which might mean yes, or no, or anything or nothing, and which Mrs. Tope would have found highly mystifying, but that her attention was divided by the service of the table.

'You will take something with me?' said Jasper, as the cloth was laid.

'I couldn't get a morsel down my throat, I thank you,' answered Mr. Grewgious.

Jasper both ate and drank almost voraciously. Combined with the hurry in his mode of doing it, was an evident indifference to the taste of what he took, suggesting that he ate and drank to fortify himself against any other failure of the spirits, far more than to gratify his palate. Mr. Grewgious in the meantime sat upright, with no expression in his face, and a hard kind of imperturbably polite protest all over him: as though he would have said, in reply to some invitation to discourse; 'I couldn't originate the faintest approach to an observation on any subject whatever, I thank you.'

'Do you know,' said Jasper, when he had pushed away his plate and glass, and had sat meditating for a few minutes: 'do you know that I find some crumbs of comfort in the communication with which you have so much amazed me?'

'*Do* you?' returned Mr. Grewgious, pretty plainly adding the unspoken clause; 'I don't, I thank you!'

'After recovering from the shock of a piece of news of my dear boy, so entirely unexpected, and so destructive of all the castles I had built for him; and after having had time to think of it; yes.'

'I shall be glad to pick up your crumbs,' said Mr. Grewgious, dryly.

'Is there not, or is there — if I deceive myself, tell me so, and shorten my pain — is there not, or is there, hope that, finding himself in this new position, and becoming sensitively alive to the awkward burden of explanation, in this quarter, and that, and the other, with which it would load him, he avoided the awkwardness, and took to flight?'

'Such a thing might be,' said Mr. Grewgious, pondering.

'Such a thing has been. I have read of cases in which people, rather than face a seven days' wonder, and have to account for themselves to the idle and impertinent, have taken themselves away, and been long unheard of.'

'I believe such things have happened,' said Mr. Grewgious, pondering still.

'When I had, and could have, no suspicion,' pursued Jasper, eagerly following the new track, 'that the dear lost boy had withheld anything from me — most of all, such a leading matter as this — what gleam of light was there for me in the whole black sky? When I supposed that his intended wife was here, and his marriage close at hand, how could I entertain the possibility of his voluntarily leaving this place, in a manner that would be so unaccountable, capricious, and cruel? But now that I know what you have told me, is there no little chink through which day pierces? Supposing him to have disappeared of his own act, is not his disappearance more accountable and less cruel? The fact of his having just parted from your ward, is in itself a sort of reason for his going away. It does not make his mysterious departure the less cruel to me, it is true; but it relieves it of cruelty to her.'

Mr. Grewgious could not but assent to this.

'And even as to me,' continued Jasper, still pursuing the new track, with ardour, and, as he did so, brightening with hope: 'he knew that you were coming to me; he knew that you were intrusted to tell me what you have told me; if your doing so has awakened a new train of thought in my perplexed mind, it reasonably follows that, from the same premises, he might have foreseen the inferences that I should draw. Grant that he did foresee them; and even the cruelty to me — and who am I! — John Jasper, Music Master, vanishes!' —

Once more, Mr. Grewgious could not but assent to this.

'I have had my distrusts, and terrible distrusts they have been,' said Jasper; 'but your disclosure, overpowering as it was at first — showing me that my own dear boy had had a great disappointing reservation from me, who so fondly loved him, kindles hope within me. You do not extinguish it when I state it, but admit it to be a reasonable hope. I begin to believe it possible:' here he clasped his hands: 'that he may have disappeared from among us of his own accord, and that he may yet be alive and well.'

Mr. Crisparkle came in at the moment. To whom Mr. Jasper repeated:

'I begin to believe it possible that he may have disappeared of his own accord, and may yet be alive and well.'

Mr. Crisparkle taking a seat, and inquiring: 'Why so?' Mr. Jasper repeated the arguments he had just set forth. If they had been less plausible than they were, the good Minor Canon's mind would have been in a state of preparation to receive them, as exculpatory of his unfortunate pupil. But he, too, did really attach great importance to the lost young man's having been, so immediately before his disappearance, placed in a new and embarrassing relation towards every one acquainted with his projects and affairs; and the fact seemed to him to present the question in a new light.

'I stated to Mr. Sapsea, when we waited on him,' said Jasper: as he really had done: 'that there was no quarrel or difference between the two young men at their last meeting. We all know that their first meeting was unfortunately very far from amicable; but all went smoothly and quietly when they were last together at my house. My dear boy was not in his usual spirits; he was depressed — I noticed that — and I am bound henceforth to dwell upon the circumstance the more, now that I know there was a special reason for his being depressed: a reason, moreover, which may possibly have induced him to absent himself.'

'I pray to Heaven it may turn out so!' exclaimed Mr. Crisparkle.

'*I* pray to Heaven it may turn out so!' repeated Jasper. 'You know — and Mr. Grewgious should now know likewise — that I took a great prepossession against Mr. Neville Landless, arising out of his furious conduct on that first occasion. You know that I came to you, extremely apprehensive, on my dear boy's behalf, of his mad violence. You know that I even entered in my Diary, and showed the entry to you, that I had dark forebodings against him. Mr. Grewgious ought to be possessed of the whole case. He shall not, through any suppression of mine, be informed of a part of it, and kept in ignorance of another part of it. I wish him to be good enough to understand that the communication he has made to me has hopefully influenced my mind, in spite of its having been, before this mysterious occurrence took place, profoundly impressed against young Landless.'

This fairness troubled the Minor Canon much. He felt that he was not as open in his own dealing. He charged against himself reproachfully that he had suppressed, so far, the two points of a second strong outbreak of temper against Edwin Drood on the part of Neville, and of the passion of jealousy having, to his own certain knowledge, flamed up in Neville's breast against him. He was convinced of Neville's innocence of any part in the ugly disappearance; and yet so many little circumstances combined so wofully against him, that he dreaded to add two more to their cumulative weight. He was among the truest of men; but he had been balancing in his mind, much to its distress, whether his volunteering to tell these two fragments of truth, at this time, would not be tantamount to a piecing together of falsehood in the place of truth.

However, here was a model before him. He hesitated no longer. Addressing Mr. Grewgious, as one placed in authority by the revelation he had brought to bear on the mystery (and surpassingly Angular Mr. Grewgious became when he found himself in that unexpected position), Mr. Crisparkle bore his testimony to Mr. Jasper's strict sense of justice, and, expressing his absolute confidence in the complete clearance of his pupil from the least taint of suspicion, sooner or later, avowed that his confidence in that young gentleman had been formed, in spite of his confidential knowledge that his temper was of the hottest and fiercest, and that it was directly incensed against Mr. Jasper's nephew, by the circumstance of his romantically supposing himself to be enamoured of the same young lady. The sanguine reaction manifest in Mr. Jasper was proof even against this unlooked-for declaration. It turned him paler; but he repeated that he would cling to the hope he had derived from Mr. Grewgious; and that if no trace of his dear boy were found, leading to the dreadful inference that he had been made away with, he would cherish unto the last stretch of possibility the idea, that he might have absconded of his own wild will.

Now, it fell out that Mr. Crisparkle, going away from this conference still very uneasy in his mind, and very much troubled on behalf of the young man whom he held as a kind of prisoner in his own house, took a memorable night walk.

He walked to Cloisterham Weir.

He often did so, and consequently there was nothing remarkable in his footsteps tending that way. But the preoccupation of his mind so hindered him from planning any walk, or taking heed of the objects he passed, that his first consciousness of being near the Weir, was derived from the sound of the falling water close at hand.

'How did I come here!' was his first thought, as he stopped.

'Why did I come here!' was his second.

Then, he stood intently listening to the water. A familiar passage in his reading, about airy tongues that syllable men's names, rose so unbidden to his ear, that he put it from him with his hand, as if it were tangible.

It was starlight. The Weir was full two miles above the spot to which the young men had repaired to watch the storm. No search had been made up here, for the tide had been running strongly down, at that time of the night of Christmas Eve, and the likeliest places for the discovery of a body, if a fatal accident had happened under such circumstances, all lay — both when the tide ebbed, and when it flowed again — between that spot and the sea. The water came over the Weir, with its usual sound on a cold starlight night, and little could be seen of it; yet Mr. Crisparkle had a strange idea that something unusual hung about the place.

He reasoned with himself: What was it? Where was it? Put it to the proof. Which sense did it address?

No sense reported anything unusual there. He listened again, and his sense of hearing again checked the water coming over the Weir, with its usual sound on a cold starlight night.

Knowing very well that the mystery with which his mind was occupied, might of itself give the place this haunted air, he strained those hawk's eyes of his for the correction of his sight. He got closer to the Weir, and peered at its well-known posts and timbers. Nothing in the least unusual was remotely shadowed forth. But he resolved that he would come back early in the morning.

The Weir ran through his broken sleep, all night, and he was back again at sunrise. It was a bright frosty morning. The whole composition before him, when he stood where he had stood last night, was clearly discernible in its minutest details. He had surveyed it closely for some minutes, and was about to withdraw his eyes, when they were attracted keenly to one spot.

He turned his back upon the Weir, and looked far away at the sky, and at the earth, and then looked again at that one spot. It caught his sight again immediately, and he concentrated his vision upon it. He could not lose it now, though it was but such a speck in the landscape. It fascinated his sight. His hands began plucking off his coat. For it struck him that at that spot — a corner of the Weir — something glistened, which did not move and come over with the glistening water-drops, but remained stationary.

He assured himself of this, threw off his clothes, he plunged into the icy water, and swam for the spot. Climbing the timbers, he took from them, caught among their interstices by its chain, a gold watch, bearing engraved upon its back E. D.

He brought the watch to the bank, swam to the Weir again, climbed it, and dived off. He knew every hole and corner of all the depths, and dived and dived and dived, until he could bear the cold no more. His notion was, that he would find the body; he only found a shirt-pin sticking in some mud and ooze.

With these discoveries he returned to Cloisterham, and, taking Neville Landless with him, went straight to the Mayor. Mr. Jasper was sent for, the watch and shirt-pin were identified, Neville was detained, and the wildest frenzy and fatuity of evil report rose against him. He was of that vindictive and violent nature, that but for his poor sister, who alone had influence over him, and out of whose sight he was never to be trusted, he would be in the daily commission of murder. Before coming to England he had caused to be whipped to death sundry 'Natives' — nomadic persons, encamping now in Asia, now in Africa, now in the West Indies, and now at the North Pole — vaguely supposed in Cloisterham to be always black, always of great virtue, always calling themselves Me, and everybody else Massa or Missie (according to sex), and always reading tracts of the obscurest meaning, in broken English, but always accurately understanding them in the purest mother tongue. He had nearly brought Mrs. Crisparkle's grey hairs with sorrow to the grave. (Those original expressions were Mr. Sapsea's.) He had repeatedly said he would have Mr. Crisparkle's life. He had repeatedly said he would have everybody's life, and become in effect the last man. He had been brought down to Cloisterham, from London, by an eminent Philanthropist, and why? Because that Philanthropist had expressly declared: 'I owe it to my fellow-creatures that he should be, in the words of BENTHAM, where he is the cause of the greatest danger to the smallest number.'

These dropping shots from the blunderbusses of blunderheadedness might not have hit him in a vital place. But he had to stand against a trained and well-directed fire of arms of precision too. He had notoriously threatened the lost young man, and had, according to the showing of his own faithful friend and tutor who strove so hard for him, a cause of bitter animosity (created by himself, and stated by himself), against that ill-starred fellow. He had armed himself with an offensive weapon for the fatal night, and he had gone off early in the morning, after making preparations for departure. He had been found with traces of blood on him; truly, they might have been wholly caused as he represented, but they might not, also. On a search-warrant being issued for the examination of his room, clothes, and so forth, it was discovered that he had destroyed all his papers, and rearranged all his possessions, on the very afternoon of the disappearance. The watch found at the Weir was challenged by the jeweller as one he had wound and set for Edwin Drood, at twenty minutes past two on the same afternoon; and it had run down, before being cast into the water; and it was the jeweller's positive opinion that it had never been re-wound. This would justify the hypothesis that the watch was taken from him not long after he left Mr. Jasper's house at midnight, in company with the last person seen with him, and that it had been thrown away after being retained some hours. Why thrown away? If he had been murdered, and so artfully disfigured, or concealed, or both, as that the murderer hoped identification to be impossible, except from something that he wore, assuredly the murderer would seek to remove from the body the most lasting, the best known, and the most easily recognisable, things upon it. Those things would be the watch and shirt-pin. As to his opportunities of casting them into the river; if he were the object of these suspicions, they were easy. For, he had been seen by many persons, wandering about on that side of the city — indeed on all sides of it — in a miserable and seemingly half-distracted manner. As to the choice of the spot, obviously such criminating evidence had better take its chance of being found anywhere, rather than upon himself, or in his possession. Concerning the reconciliatory nature of the appointed meeting between the two young men, very little could be made of that in young Landless's favour; for it distinctly appeared that the meeting originated, not with him, but with Mr. Crisparkle, and that it had been urged on by Mr. Crisparkle; and who could say how unwillingly, or in what ill-conditioned mood, his enforced pupil had gone to it? The more his case was looked into, the weaker it became in every point. Even the broad suggestion that the lost young man had absconded, was rendered additionally improbable on the showing of the young lady from whom he had so lately parted; for, what did she say, with great earnestness and sorrow, when interrogated? That he had, expressly and enthusiastically, planned with her, that he would await the arrival of her guardian, Mr. Grewgious. And yet, be it observed, he disappeared before that gentleman appeared.

On the suspicions thus urged and supported, Neville was detained, and re-detained, and the search was pressed on every hand, and Jasper laboured night and day. But nothing more was found. No discovery being made, which proved the lost man to be dead, it at length became necessary to release the person suspected of having made away with him. Neville was set at large. Then, a consequence ensued which Mr. Crisparkle had too well foreseen. Neville must leave the place, for the place shunned him and cast him out. Even had it not been so, the dear old china shepherdess would have worried herself to death with fears for her son, and with general trepidation occasioned by their having such an inmate. Even had that not been so, the authority to which the Minor Canon deferred officially, would have settled the point.

'Mr. Crisparkle,' quoth the Dean, 'human justice may err, but it must act according to its lights. The days of taking sanctuary are past. This young man must not take sanctuary with us.'

'You mean that he must leave my house, sir?'

'Mr. Crisparkle,' returned the prudent Dean, 'I claim no authority in your house. I merely confer with you, on the painful necessity you find yourself under, of depriving this young man of the great advantages of your counsel and instruction.'

'It is very lamentable, sir,' Mr. Crisparkle represented.

'Very much so,' the Dean assented.

'And if it be a necessity ——' Mr. Crisparkle faltered.

'As you unfortunately find it to be,' returned the Dean.

Mr. Crisparkle bowed submissively: 'It is hard to prejudge his case, sir, but I am sensible that ——'

'Just so. Perfectly. As you say, Mr. Crisparkle,' interposed the Dean nodding his head smoothly, 'there is nothing else to be done. No doubt, no doubt. There is no alternative, as your good sense has discovered.'

'I am entirely satisfied of his perfect innocence, sir, nevertheless.'

'We-e-ell!' said the Dean, in a more confidential tone, and slightly glancing around him, 'I would not say so, generally. Not generally. Enough of suspicion attaches to him to — no, I think I would not say so, generally.'

Mr. Crisparkle bowed again.

'It does not become us, perhaps,' pursued the Dean, 'to be partisans. Not partisans. We clergy keep our hearts warm and our heads cool, and we hold a judicious middle course.'

'I hope you do not object, sir, to my having stated in public, emphatically, that he will reappear here, whenever any new suspicion may be awakened, or any new circumstance may come to light in this extraordinary matter?'

'Not at all,' returned the Dean. 'And yet, do you know, I don't think,' with a very nice and neat emphasis on those two words: 'I *don't think* I would state it emphatically. State it? Ye-e-es! But emphatically? No-o-o. I *think* not. In point of fact, Mr. Crisparkle, keeping our hearts warm and our heads cool, we clergy need do nothing emphatically.'

So Minor Canon Row knew Neville Landless no more; and he went whithersoever he would, or could, with a blight upon his name and fame.

It was not until then that John Jasper silently resumed his place in the choir. Haggard and red-eyed, his hopes plainly had deserted him, his sanguine mood was gone, and all his worst misgivings had come back. A day or two afterwards, while unrobing, he took his Diary from a pocket of his coat, turned the leaves, and with an impressive look, and without one spoken word, handed this entry to Mr. Crisparkle to read:

'My dear boy is murdered. The discovery of the watch and shirt-pin convinces me that he was murdered that night, and that his jewellery was taken from him to prevent identification by its means. All the delusive hopes I had founded on his separation from his betrothed wife, I give to the winds. They perish before this fatal discovery. I now swear, and record the oath on this page, That I nevermore will discuss this mystery with any human creature until I hold the clue to it in my hand. That I never will relax in my secrecy or in my search. That I will fasten the crime of the murder of my dear dead boy upon the murderer. And, That I devote myself to his destruction.'

Philanthropy, Professional
and Unprofessional

FULL half a year had come and gone, and Mr. Crisparkle sat in a waiting-room in the London chief offices of the Haven of Philanthropy, until he could have audience of Mr. Honeythunder.

In his college days of athletic exercises, Mr. Crisparkle had known professors of the Noble Art of fisticuffs, and had attended two or three of their gloved gatherings. He had now an opportunity of observing that as to the phrenological formation of the backs of their heads, the Professing Philanthropists were uncommonly like the Pugilists. In the development of all those organs which constitute, or attend, a propensity to 'pitch into' your fellow-creatures, the Philanthropists were remarkably favoured. There were several Professors passing in and out, with exactly the aggressive air upon them of being ready for a turn-up with any Novice who might happen to be on hand, that Mr. Crisparkle well remembered in the circles of the Fancy. Preparations were in progress for a moral little Mill somewhere on the rural circuit, and other Professors were backing this or that Heavy-Weight as good for such or such speech-making hits, so very much after the manner of the sporting publicans, that the intended Resolutions might have been Rounds. In an official manager of these displays much celebrated for his platform tactics, Mr. Crisparkle recognised (in a suit of black) the counterpart of a deceased benefactor of his species, an eminent public character, once known to fame as Frosty-faced Fogo, who in days of yore superintended the formation of the magic circle with the ropes and stakes. There were only three conditions of resemblance wanting between these Professors and those. Firstly, the Philanthropists were in very bad training: much too fleshy, and presenting, both in face and figure, a superabundance of what is known to Pugilistic Experts as Suet Pudding. Secondly, the Philanthropists had not the good temper of the Pugilists, and used worse language. Thirdly, their fighting code stood in great need of revision, as empowering them not only to bore their man to the ropes, but to bore him to the confines of distraction; also to hit him when he was down, hit him anywhere and anyhow, kick him, stamp upon him, gouge him, and maul him behind his back without mercy. In these last particulars the Professors of the Noble Art were much nobler than the Professors of Philanthropy.

Mr. Crisparkle was so completely lost in musing on these similarities and dissimilarities, at the same time watching the crowd which came and went by, always, as it seemed, on errands of antagonistically snatching something from somebody, and never giving anything to anybody, that his name was called before he heard it. On his at length responding, he was shown by a miserably shabby and underpaid stipendiary Philanthropist (who could hardly have done worse if he had taken service with a declared enemy of the human race) to Mr. Honeythunder's room.

'Sir,' said Mr. Honeythunder, in his tremendous voice, like a schoolmaster issuing orders to a boy of whom he had a bad opinion, 'sit down'.

Mr. Crisparkle seated himself.

Mr. Honeythunder having signed the remaining few score of a few thousand circulars, calling upon a corresponding number of families without means to come forward, stump up instantly, and be Philanthropists, or go to the Devil, another shabby stipendiary Philanthropist (highly disinterested, if in earnest) gathered these into a basket and walked off with them.

'Now, Mr. Crisparkle,' said Mr. Honeythunder, turning his chair half round towards him when they were alone, and squaring his arms with his hands on his knees, and his brows knitted, as if he added, I am going to make short work of *you:* 'Now, Mr. Crisparkle, we entertain different views, you and I, sir, of the sanctity of human life.'

'Do we?' returned the Minor Canon.

'We do, sir.'

'Might I ask you,' said the Minor Canon: 'what are your views on that subject?'

'That human life is a thing to be held sacred, sir.'

'Might I ask you,' pursued the Minor Canon as before: 'what you suppose to be my views on that subject?'

'By George, sir!' returned the Philanthropist, squaring his arms still more, as he frowned on Mr. Crisparkle: 'they are best known to yourself.'

'Readily admitted. But you began by saying that we took different views, you know. Therefore (or you could not say so) you must have set up some views as mine. Pray, what views *have* you set up as mine?'

'Here is a man — and a young man,' said Mr. Honeythunder, as if that made the matter infinitely worse, and he could have easily borne the loss of an old one, 'swept off the face of the earth by a deed of violence. What do you call that?'

'Murder,' said the Minor Canon.

'What do you call the doer of that deed, sir?'

'A murderer,' said the Minor Canon.

'I am glad to hear you admit so much, sir,' retorted Mr. Honeythunder, in his most offensive manner; 'and I candidly tell you that I didn't expect it.' Here he lowered heavily at Mr. Crisparkle again.

'Be so good as to explain what you mean by those very unjustifiable expressions.'

'I don't sit here, sir,' returned the Philanthropist, raising his voice to a roar, 'to be browbeaten.'

'As the only other person present, no one can possibly know that better than I do,' returned the Minor Canon very quietly. 'But I interrupt your explanation.'

'Murder!' proceeded Mr. Honeythunder, in a kind of boisterous reverie, with his platform folding of his arms, and his platform nod of abhorrent reflection after each short sentiment of a word. 'Bloodshed! Abel! Cain! I hold no terms with Cain. I repudiate with a shudder the red hand when it is offered me.'

Instead of instantly leaping into his chair and cheering himself hoarse, as the Brotherhood in public meeting assembled would infallibly have done on this cue, Mr. Crisparkle merely reversed the quiet crossing of his legs, and said mildly: 'Don't let me interrupt your explanation — when you begin it.'

'The Commandments say, no murder. NO murder, sir!' proceeded Mr. Honeythunder, platformally pausing as if he took Mr. Crisparkle to task for having distinctly asserted that they said: You may do a little murder, and then leave off.

'And they also say, you shall bear no false witness,' observed Mr. Crisparkle.

'Enough!' bellowed Mr. Honeythunder, with a solemnity and severity that would have brought the house down at a meeting, 'E — e — nough! My late wards being now of age, and I being released from a trust which I cannot contemplate without a thrill of horror, there are the accounts which you have undertaken to accept on their behalf, and there is a statement of the balance which you have undertaken to receive, and which you cannot receive too soon. And let me tell you, sir, I wish that, as a man and a Minor Canon, you were better employed,' with a nod. 'Better employed,' with another nod. 'Bet — ter em — ployed!' with another and the three nods added up.

Mr. Crisparkle rose; a little heated in the face, but with perfect command of himself.

'Mr. Honeythunder,' he said, taking up the papers referred to: 'my being better or worse employed than I am at present is a matter of taste and opinion. You might think me better employed in enrolling myself a member of your Society.'

'Ay, indeed, sir!' retorted Mr. Honeythunder, shaking his head in a threatening manner. 'It would have been better for you if you had done that long ago!'

'I think otherwise.'

'Or,' said Mr. Honeythunder, shaking his head again, 'I might think one of your profession better employed in devoting himself to the discovery and punishment of guilt than in leaving that duty to be undertaken by a layman.'

'I may regard my profession from a point of view which teaches me that its first duty is towards those who are in necessity and tribulation, who are desolate and oppressed,' said Mr. Crisparkle. 'However, as I have quite clearly satisfied myself that it is no part of my profession to make professions, I say no more of that. But I owe it to Mr. Neville, and to Mr. Neville's sister (and in a much lower degree to myself), to say to you that I *know* I was in the full possession and understanding of Mr. Neville's mind and heart at the time of this occurrence; and that, without in the least colouring or concealing what was to be deplored in him and required to be corrected, I feel certain that his tale is true. Feeling that certainty, I befriend him. As long as that certainty shall last, I will befriend him. And if any consideration could shake me in this resolve, I should be so ashamed of myself for my meanness, that no man's good opinion — no, nor no woman's — so gained, could compensate me for the loss of my own.'

Good fellow! manly fellow! And he was so modest, too. There was no more self-assertion in the Minor Canon than in the schoolboy who had stood in the breezy playing-fields keeping a wicket. He was simply and staunchly true to his duty alike in the large case and in the small. So all true souls ever are. So every true soul ever was, ever is, and ever will be. There is nothing little to the really great in spirit.

'Then who do you make out did the deed?' asked Mr. Honeythunder, turning on him abruptly.

'Heaven forbid,' said Mr. Crisparkle, 'that in my desire to clear one man I should lightly criminate another! I accuse no one.'

'Tcha!' ejaculated Mr. Honeythunder with great disgust; for this was by no means the principle on which the Philanthropic Brotherhood usually proceeded. 'And, sir, you are not a disinterested witness, we must bear in mind.'

'How am I an interested one?' inquired Mr. Crisparkle, smiling innocently, at a loss to imagine.

'There was a certain stipend, sir, paid to you for your pupil, which may have warped your judgment a bit,' said Mr. Honeythunder, coarsely.

'Perhaps I expect to retain it still?' Mr. Crisparkle returned, enlightened; 'do you mean that too?'

'Well, sir,' returned the professional Philanthropist, getting up and thrusting his hands down into his trousers-pockets, 'I don't go about measuring people for caps. If people find I have any about me that fit 'em, they can put 'em on and wear 'em, if they like. That's their look out: not mine.'

Mr. Crisparkle eyed him with a just indignation, and took him to task thus:

'Mr. Honeythunder, I hoped when I came in here that I might be under no necessity of commenting on the introduction of platform manners or platform manœuvres among the decent forbearances of private life. But you have given me such a specimen of both, that I should be a fit subject for both if I remained silent respecting them. They are detestable.'

'They don't suit *you*, I dare say, sir.'

'They are,' repeated Mr. Crisparkle, without noticing the interruption, 'detestable. They violate equally the justice that should belong to Christians, and the restraints that should belong to gentlemen. You assume a great crime to have been committed by one whom I, acquainted with the attendant circumstances, and having numerous reasons on my side, devoutly believe to be innocent of it. Because I differ from you on that vital point, what is your platform resource? Instantly to turn upon me, charging that I have no sense of the enormity of the crime itself, but am its aider and abettor! So, another time — taking me as representing your opponent in other cases — you set up a platform credulity; a moved and seconded and carried-unanimously profession of faith in some ridiculous delusion or mischievous imposition. I decline to believe it, and you fall back upon your platform resource of proclaiming that I believe nothing; that because I will not bow down to a false God of your making, I deny the true God! Another time you make the platform discovery that War is a calamity, and you propose to abolish it by a string of twisted resolutions tossed into the air like the tail of a kite. I do not admit the discovery to be yours in the least, and I have not a grain of faith in your remedy. Again, your platform resource of representing me as revelling in the horrors of a battle-field like a fiend incarnate! Another time, in another of your undiscriminating platform rushes, you would punish the sober for the drunken. I claim consideration for the comfort, convenience, and refreshment of the sober; and you presently make platform proclamation that I have a depraved desire to turn Heaven's creatures into swine and wild beasts! In all such cases your movers, and your seconders, and your supporters — your regular Professors of all degrees, run amuck like so many mad Malays; habitually attributing the lowest and basest motives with the utmost recklessness (let me call your attention to a recent instance in yourself for which you should blush), and quoting figures which you know to be as wilfully onesided as a statement of any complicated account that should be all Creditor side and no Debtor, or all Debtor side and no Creditor. Therefore it is, Mr. Honeythunder, that I consider the platform a sufficiently bad example and a sufficiently bad school, even in public life; but hold that, carried into private life, it becomes an unendurable nuisance.'

'These are strong words, sir!' exclaimed the Philanthropist.

'I hope so,' said Mr. Crisparkle. 'Good morning.'

He walked out of the Haven at a great rate, but soon fell into his regular brisk pace, and soon had a smile upon his face as he went along, wondering what the china shepherdess would have said if she had seen him pounding Mr. Honeythunder in the late little lively affair. For Mr. Crisparkle had just enough of harmless vanity to hope that he had hit hard, and to glow with the belief that he had trimmed the Philanthropic jacket pretty handsomely.

He took himself to Staple Inn, but not to P. J. T. and Mr. Grewgious. Full many a creaking stair he climbed before he reached some attic rooms in a corner, turned the latch of their unbolted door, and stood beside the table of Neville Landless.

An air of retreat and solitude hung about the rooms and about their inhabitant. He was much worn, and so were they. Their sloping ceilings, cumbrous rusty locks and grates, and heavy wooden bins and beams, slowly mouldering withal, had a prisonous look, and he had the haggard face of a prisoner. Yet the sunlight shone in at the ugly garret-window, which had a penthouse to itself thrust out among the tiles; and on the cracked and smoke-blackened parapet beyond, some of the deluded sparrows of the place rheumatically hopped, like little feathered cripples who had left their crutches in their nests; and there was a play of living leaves at hand that changed the air, and made an imperfect sort of music in it that would have been melody in the country.

The rooms were sparely furnished, but with good store of books. Everything expressed the abode of a poor student. That Mr. Crisparkle had been either chooser, lender, or donor of the books, or that he combined the three characters, might have been easily seen in the friendly beam of his eyes upon them as he entered.

'How goes it, Neville?'

'I am in good heart, Mr. Crisparkle, and working away.'

'I wish your eyes were not quite so large and not quite so bright,' said the Minor Canon, slowly releasing the hand he had taken in his.

'They brighten at the sight of you,' returned Neville. 'If you were to fall away from me, they would soon be dull enough.'

'Rally, rally!' urged the other, in a stimulating tone. 'Fight for it, Neville!'

'If I were dying, I feel as if a word from you would rally me; if my pulse had stopped, I feel as if your touch would make it beat again,' said Neville. 'But I *have* rallied, and am doing famously.'

Mr. Crisparkle turned him with his face a little more towards the light.

'I want to see a ruddier touch here, Neville,' he said, indicating his own healthy cheek by way of pattern. 'I want more sun to shine upon you.'

Neville drooped suddenly, as he replied in a lowered voice: 'I am not hardy enough for that, yet. I may become so, but I cannot bear it yet. If you had gone through those Cloisterham streets as I did; if you had seen, as I did, those averted eyes, and the better sort of people silently giving me too much room to pass, that I might not touch them or come near them, you wouldn't think it quite unreasonable that I cannot go about in the daylight.'

'My poor fellow!' said the Minor Canon, in a tone so purely sympathetic that the young man caught his hand, 'I never said it was unreasonable; never thought so. But I should like you to do it.'

'And that would give me the strongest motive to do it. But I cannot yet. I cannot persuade myself that the eyes of even the stream of strangers I pass in this vast city look at me without suspicion. I feel marked and tainted, even when I go out — as I do only — at night. But the darkness covers me then, and I take courage from it.'

Mr. Crisparkle laid a hand upon his shoulder, and stood looking down at him.

'If I could have changed my name,' said Neville, 'I would have done so. But as you wisely pointed out to me, I can't do that, for it would look like guilt. If I could have gone to some distant place, I might have found relief in that, but the thing is not to be thought of, for the same reason. Hiding and escaping would be the construction in either case. It seems a little hard to be so tied to a stake, and innocent; but I don't complain.'

'And you must expect no miracle to help you, Neville,' said Mr. Crisparkle, compassionately.

'No, sir, I know that. The ordinary fulness of time and circumstances is all I have to trust to.'

'It will right you at last, Neville.'

'So I believe, and I hope I may live to know it.'

But perceiving that the despondent mood into which he was falling cast a shadow on the Minor Canon, and (it may be) feeling that the broad hand upon his shoulder was not then quite as steady as its own natural strength had rendered it when it first touched him just now, he brightened and said:

'Excellent circumstances for study, anyhow! and you know, Mr. Crisparkle, what need I have of study in all ways. Not to mention that you have advised me to study for the difficult profession of the law, specially, and that of course I am guiding myself by the advice of such a friend and helper. Such a good friend and helper!'

He took the fortifying hand from his shoulder, and kissed it. Mr. Crisparkle beamed at the books, but not so brightly as when he had entered.

'I gather from your silence on the subject that my late guardian is adverse, Mr. Crisparkle?'

The Minor Canon answered: 'Your late guardian is a — a most unreasonable person, and it signifies nothing to any reasonable person whether he is *ad*verse, or *per*verse, or the *re*verse.'

'Well for me that I have enough with economy to live upon,' sighed Neville, half wearily and half cheerily, 'while I wait to be learned, and wait to be righted! Else I might have proved the proverb, that while the grass grows, the steed starves!'

He opened some books as he said it, and was soon immersed in their interleaved and annotated passages; while Mr. Crisparkle sat beside him, expounding, correcting, and advising. The Minor Canon's Cathedral duties made these visits of his difficult to accomplish, and only to be compassed at intervals of many weeks. But they were as serviceable as they were precious to Neville Landless.

When they had got through such studies as they had in hand, they stood leaning on the window-sill, and looking down upon the patch of garden. 'Next week,' said Mr. Crisparkle, 'you will cease to be alone, and will have a devoted companion.'

'And yet,' returned Neville, 'this seems an uncongenial place to bring my sister to.'

'I don't think so,' said the Minor Canon. 'There is duty to be done here; and there are womanly feeling, sense, and courage wanted here.'

'I meant,' explained Neville, 'that the surroundings are so dull and unwomanly, and that Helena can have no suitable friend or society here.'

'You have only to remember,' said Mr. Crisparkle, 'that you are here yourself, and that she has to draw you into the sunlight.'

They were silent for a little while, and then Mr. Crisparkle began anew.

'When we first spoke together, Neville, you told me that your sister had risen out of the disadvantages of your past lives as superior to you as the tower of Cloisterham Cathedral is higher than the chimneys of Minor Canon Corner. Do you remember that?'

'Right well!'

'I was inclined to think it at the time an enthusiastic flight. No matter what I think it now. What I would emphasise is, that under the head of Pride your sister is a great and opportune example to you.'

'Under *all* heads that are included in the composition of a fine character, she is.'

'Say so; but take this one. Your sister has learnt how to govern what is proud in her nature. She can dominate it even when it is wounded through her sympathy with you. No doubt she has suffered deeply in those same streets where you suffered deeply. No doubt her life is darkened by the cloud that darkens yours. But bending her pride into a grand composure that is not haughty or aggressive, but is a sustained confidence in you and in the truth, she has won her way through those streets until she passes along them as high in the general respect as any one who treads them. Every day and hour of her life since Edwin Drood's disappearance, she has faced malignity and folly — for you — as only a brave nature well directed can. So it will be with her to the end. Another and weaker kind of pride might sink broken-hearted, but never such a pride as hers: which knows no shrinking, and can get no mastery over her.'

The pale cheek beside him flushed under the comparison, and the hint implied in it.

'I will do all I can to imitate her,' said Neville.

'Do so, and be a truly brave man, as she is a truly brave woman,' answered Mr. Crisparkle stoutly. 'It is growing dark. Will you go my way with me, when it is quite dark? Mind! it is not I who wait for darkness.'

Neville replied, that he would accompany him directly. But Mr. Crisparkle said he had a moment's call to make on Mr. Grewgious as an act of courtesy, and would run across to that gentleman's chambers, and rejoin Neville on his own doorstep, if he would come down there to meet him.

Mr. Grewgious, bolt upright as usual, sat taking his wine in the dusk at his open window; his wineglass and decanter on the round table at his elbow; himself and his legs on the window-seat; only one hinge in his whole body, like a bootjack.

'How do you do, reverend sir?' said Mr. Grewgious, with abundant offers of hospitality, which were as cordially declined as made. 'And how is your charge getting on over the way in the set that I had the pleasure of recommending to you as vacant and eligible?'

Mr. Crisparkle replied suitably.

'I am glad you approve of them,' said Mr. Grewgious, 'because I entertain a sort of fancy for having him under my eye.'

As Mr. Grewgious had to turn his eye up considerably before he could see the chambers, the phrase was to be taken figuratively and not literally.

'And how did you leave Mr. Jasper, reverend sir?' said Mr. Grewgious.

Mr. Crisparkle had left him pretty well.

'And where did you leave Mr. Jasper, reverend sir?'

Mr. Crisparkle had left him at Cloisterham.

'And when did you leave Mr. Jasper, reverend sir?'

That morning.

'Umps!' said Mr. Grewgious. 'He didn't say he was coming, perhaps?'

'Coming where?'

'Anywhere, for instance?' said Mr. Grewgious.

'No.'

'Because here he is,' said Mr. Grewgious, who had asked all these questions, with his preoccupied glance directed out at window. 'And he don't look agreeable, does he?'

Mr. Crisparkle was craning towards the window, when Mr. Grewgious added:

'If you will kindly step round here behind me, in the gloom of the room, and will cast your eye at the second-floor landing window in yonder house, I think you will hardly fail to see a slinking individual in whom I recognise our local friend.'

'You are right!' cried Mr. Crisparkle.

'Umps!' said Mr. Grewgious. Then he added, turning his face so abruptly that his head nearly came into collision with Mr. Crisparkle's: 'what should you say that our local friend was up to?'

The last passage he had been shown in the Diary returned on Mr. Crisparkle's mind with the force of a strong recoil, and he asked Mr. Grewgious if he thought it possible that Neville was to be harassed by the keeping of a watch upon him?

'A watch?' repeated Mr. Grewgious musingly. 'Ay!'

'Which would not only of itself haunt and torture his life,' said Mr. Crisparkle warmly, 'but would expose him to the torment of a perpetually reviving suspicion, whatever he might do, or wherever he might go.'

'Ay!' said Mr. Grewgious, musingly still. 'Do I see him waiting for you?'

'No doubt you do.'

'Then *would* you have the goodness to excuse my getting up to see you out, and to go out to join him, and to go the way that you were going, and to take no notice of our local friend?' said Mr. Grewgious. 'I entertain a sort of fancy for having *him* under my eye to-night, do you know?'

Mr. Crisparkle, with a significant nod, complied; and rejoining Neville, went away with him. They dined together, and parted at the yet unfinished and undeveloped railway station: Mr. Crisparkle to get home; Neville to walk the streets, cross the bridges, make a wide round of the city in the friendly darkness, and tire himself out.

It was midnight when he returned from his solitary expedition and climbed his staircase. The night was hot, and the windows of the staircase were all wide open. Coming to the top, it gave him a passing chill of surprise (there being no rooms but his up there) to find a stranger sitting on the window-sill, more after the manner of a venturesome glazier than an amateur ordinarily careful of his neck; in fact, so much more outside the window than inside, as to suggest the thought that he must have come up by the water-spout instead of the stairs.

The stranger said nothing until Neville put his key in his door; then, seeming to make sure of his identity from the action, he spoke:

'I beg your pardon,' he said, coming from the window with a frank and smiling air, and a prepossessing address; 'the beans.'

Neville was quite at a loss.

'Runners,' said the visitor. 'Scarlet. Next door at the back.'

'O,' returned Neville. 'And the mignonette and wall-flower?'

'The same,' said the visitor.

'Pray walk in.'

'Thank you.'

Neville lighted his candles, and the visitor sat down. A handsome gentleman, with a young face, but with an older figure in its robustness and its breadth of shoulder; say a man of eight-and-twenty, or at the utmost thirty; so extremely sunburnt that the contrast between his brown visage and the white forehead shaded out of doors by his hat, and the glimpses of white throat below the neckerchief, would have been almost ludicrous but for his broad temples, bright blue eyes, clustering brown hair, and laughing teeth.

'I have noticed,' said he; '— my name is Tartar.'

Neville inclined his head.

'I have noticed (excuse me) that you shut yourself up a good deal, and that you seem to like my garden aloft here. If you would like a little more of it, I could throw out a few lines and stays between my windows and yours, which the runners would take to directly. And I have some boxes, both of mignonette and wall-flower, that I could shove on along the gutter (with a boathook I have by me) to your windows, and draw back again when they wanted watering or gardening, and shove on again when they were ship-shape; so that they would cause you no trouble. I couldn't take this liberty without asking your permission, so I venture to ask it. Tartar, corresponding set, next door.'

'You are very kind.'

'Not at all. I ought to apologise for looking in so late. But having noticed (excuse me) that you generally walk out at night, I thought I should inconvenience you least by awaiting your return. I am always afraid of inconveniencing busy men, being an idle man.'

'I should not have thought so, from your appearance.'

'No? I take it as a compliment. In fact, I was bred in the Royal Navy, and was First Lieutenant when I quitted it. But, an uncle disappointed in the service leaving me his property on condition that I left the Navy, I accepted the fortune, and resigned my commission.'

'Lately, I presume?'

'Well, I had had twelve or fifteen years of knocking about first. I came here some nine months before you; I had had one crop before you came. I chose this place, because, having served last in a little corvette, I knew I should feel more at home where I had a constant opportunity of knocking my head against the ceiling. Besides, it would never do for a man who had been aboard ship from his boyhood to turn luxurious all at once. Besides, again; having been accustomed to a very short allowance of land all my life, I thought I'd feel my way to the command of a landed estate, by beginning in boxes.'

Whimsically as this was said, there was a touch of merry earnestness in it that made it doubly whimsical.

'However,' said the Lieutenant, 'I have talked quite enough about myself. It is not my way, I hope; it has merely been to present myself to you naturally. If you will allow me to take the liberty I have described, it will be a charity, for it will give me something more to do. And you are not to suppose that it will entail any interruption or intrusion on you, for that is far from my intention.'

Neville replied that he was greatly obliged, and that he thankfully accepted the kind proposal.

'I am very glad to take your windows in tow,' said the Lieutenant. 'From what I have seen of you when I have been gardening at mine, and you have been looking on, I have thought you (excuse me) rather too studious and delicate. May I ask, is your health at all affected?'

'I have undergone some mental distress,' said Neville, confused, 'which has stood me in the stead of illness.'

'Pardon me,' said Mr. Tartar.

With the greatest delicacy he shifted his ground to the windows again, and asked if he could look at one of them. On Neville's opening it, he immediately sprang out, as if he were going aloft with a whole watch in an emergency, and were setting a bright example.

'For Heaven's sake,' cried Neville, 'don't do that! Where are you going, Mr. Tartar? You'll be dashed to pieces!'

'All well!' said the Lieutenant, coolly looking about him on the housetop. 'All taut and trim here. Those lines and stays shall be rigged before you turn out in the morning. May I take this short cut home, and say good-night?'

'Mr. Tartar!' urged Neville. 'Pray! It makes me giddy to see you!'

But Mr. Tartar, with a wave of his hand and the deftness of a cat, had already dipped through his scuttle of scarlet runners without breaking a leaf, and 'gone below.'

Beanstalk country

Mr. Grewgious, his bedroom window-blind held aside with his hand, happened at that moment to have Neville's chambers under his eye for the last time that night. Fortunately his eye was on the front of the house and not the back, or this remarkable appearance and disappearance might have broken his rest as a phenomenon. But Mr. Grewgious seeing nothing there, not even a light in the windows, his gaze wandered from the windows to the stars, as if he would have read in them something that was hidden from him. Many of us would, if we could; but none of us so much as know our letters in the stars yet — or seem likely to do it, in this state of existence — and few languages can be read until their alphabets are mastered.

A Settler in Cloisterham

AT about this time a stranger appeared in Cloisterham; a white-haired personage, with black eyebrows. Being buttoned up in a tightish blue surtout, with a buff waistcoat and gray trousers, he had something of a military air; but he announced himself at the Crozier (the orthodox hotel, where he put up with a portmanteau) as an idle dog who lived upon his means; and he farther announced that he had a mind to take a lodging in the picturesque old city for a month or two, with a view of settling down there altogether. Both announcements were made in the coffee-room of the Crozier, to all whom it might or might not concern, by the stranger as he stood with his back to the empty fireplace, waiting for his fried sole, veal cutlet, and pint of sherry. And the waiter (business being chronically slack at the Crozier) represented all whom it might or might not concern, and absorbed the whole of the information.

This gentleman's white head was unusually large, and his shock of white hair was unusually thick and ample. 'I suppose, waiter,' he said, shaking his shock of hair, as a Newfoundland dog might shake his before sitting down to dinner, 'that a fair lodging for a single buffer might be found in these parts, eh?'

The waiter had no doubt of it.

'Something old,' said the gentleman. 'Take my hat down for a moment from that peg, will you? No, I don't want it; look into it. What do you see written there?'

The waiter read: 'Datchery.'

'Now you know my name,' said the gentleman; 'Dick Datchery. Hang it up again. I was saying something old is what I should prefer, something odd and out of the way; something venerable, architectural, and inconvenient.'

'We have a good choice of inconvenient lodgings in the town, sir, I think,' replied the waiter, with modest confidence in its resources that way; 'indeed, I have no doubt that we could suit you that far, however particular you might be. But an architectural lodging!' That seemed to trouble the waiter's head, and he shook it.

'Anything Cathedraly, now,' Mr. Datchery suggested.

'Mr. Tope,' said the waiter, brightening, as he rubbed his chin with his hand, 'would be the likeliest party to inform in that line.'

'Who is Mr. Tope?' inquired Dick Datchery.

The waiter explained that he was the Verger, and that Mrs. Tope had indeed once upon a time let lodgings herself or offered to let them; but that as nobody had ever taken them, Mrs. Tope's window-bill, long a Cloisterham Institution, had disappeared; probably had tumbled down one day, and never been put up again.

'I'll call on Mrs. Tope,' said Mr. Datchery, 'after dinner.'

So when he had done his dinner, he was duly directed to the spot, and sallied out for it. But the Crozier being an hotel of a most retiring disposition, and the waiter's directions being fatally precise, he soon became bewildered, and went boggling about and about the Cathedral Tower, whenever he could catch a glimpse of it, with a general impression on his mind that Mrs. Tope's was somewhere very near it, and that, like the children in the game of hot boiled beans and very good butter, he was warm in his search when he saw the Tower, and cold when he didn't see it.

He was getting very cold indeed when he came upon a fragment of burial-ground in which an unhappy sheep was grazing. Unhappy, because a hideous small boy was stoning it through the railings, and had already lamed it in one leg, and was much excited by the benevolent sportsmanlike purpose of breaking its other three legs, and bringing it down.

'It 'im agin!' cried the boy, as the poor creature leaped; 'and made a dint in his wool.'

'Let him be!' said Mr. Datchery. 'Don't you see you have lamed him?'

'Yer lie,' returned the sportsman. ''E went and lamed isself. I see 'im do it, and I giv' 'im a shy as a Widdy-warning to 'im not to go a-bruisin' 'is master's mutton any more.'

'Come here.'

'I won't; I'll come when yer can ketch me.'

'Stay there then, and show me which is Mr. Tope's.'

'Ow can I stay here and show you which is Topeseses, when Topeseses is t'other side the Kinfreederal, and over the crossings, and round ever so many corners? Stoo-pid! Ya-a-ah!'

'Show me where it is, and I'll give you something.'

'Come on, then.'

This brisk dialogue concluded, the boy led the way, and by-and-by stopped at some distance from an arched passage, pointing.

'Lookie yonder. You see that there winder and door?'

'That's Tope's?'

'Yer lie; it ain't. That's Jarsper's.'

'Indeed?' said Mr. Datchery, with a second look of some interest.

'Yes, and I ain't a-goin' no nearer 'IM, I tell yer.'

'Why not?'

"'Cos I ain't a-goin' to be lifted off my legs and 'ave my braces bust and be choked; not if I knows it, and not by 'Im. Wait till I set a jolly good flint a-flyin' at the back o' is jolly old 'ed some day! Now look t'other side the harch; not the side where Jarsper's door is; t'other side.'

'I see.'

'A little way in, o' that side, there's a low door, down two steps. That's Topeseses with 'is name on a hoval plate.'

'Good. See here,' said Mr. Datchery, producing a shilling. 'You owe me half of this.'

'Yer lie; I don't owe yer nothing; I never seen yer.'

'I tell you you owe me half of this, because I have no sixpence in my pocket. So the next time you meet me you shall do something else for me, to pay me.'

'All right, give us 'old.'

'What is your name, and where do you live?'

'Deputy. Travellers' Twopenny, 'cross the green.'

The boy instantly darted off with the shilling, lest Mr. Datchery should repent, but stopped at a safe distance, on the happy chance of his being uneasy in his mind about it, to goad him with a demon dance expressive of its irrevocability.

Mr. Datchery, taking off his hat to give that shock of white hair of his another shake, seemed quite resigned, and betook himself whither he had been directed.

Mr. Tope's official dwelling, communicating by an upper stair with Mr. Jasper's (hence Mrs. Tope's attendance on that gentleman), was of very modest proportions, and partook of the character of a cool dungeon. Its ancient walls were massive, and its rooms rather seemed to have been dug out of them, than to have been designed beforehand with any reference to them. The main door opened at once on a chamber of no describable shape, with a groined roof, which in its turn opened on another chamber of no describable shape, with another groined roof: their windows small, and in the thickness of the walls. These two chambers, close as to their atmosphere, and swarthy as to their illumination by natural light, were the apartments which Mrs. Tope had so long offered to an unappreciative city. Mr. Datchery, however, was more appreciative. He found that if he sat with the main door open he would enjoy the passing society of all comers to and fro by the gateway, and would have light enough. He found that if Mr. and Mrs. Tope, living overhead, used for their own egress and ingress a little side stair that came plump into the Precincts by a door opening outward, to the surprise and inconvenience of a limited public of pedestrians in a narrow way, he would be alone, as in a separate residence. He found the rent moderate, and everything as quaintly inconvenient as he could desire. He agreed, therefore, to take the lodging then and there, and money down, possession to be had next evening, on condition that reference was permitted him to Mr. Jasper as occupying the gatehouse, of which on the other side of the gateway, the Verger's hole-in-the-wall was an appanage or subsidiary part.

The poor dear gentleman was very solitary and very sad, Mrs. Tope said, but she had no doubt he would 'speak for her.' Perhaps Mr. Datchery had heard something of what had occurred there last winter?

Mr. Datchery had as confused a knowledge of the event in question, on trying to recall it, as he well could have. He begged Mrs. Tope's pardon when she found it incumbent on her to correct him in every detail of his summary of the facts, but pleaded that he was merely a single buffer getting through life upon his means as idly as he could, and that so many people were so constantly making away with so many other people, as to render it difficult for a buffer of an easy temper to preserve the circumstances of the several cases unmixed in his mind.

Mr. Jasper proving willing to speak for Mrs. Tope, Mr. Datchery, who had sent up his card, was invited to ascend the postern staircase. The Mayor was there, Mr. Tope said; but he was not to be regarded in the light of company, as he and Mr. Jasper were great friends.

'I beg pardon,' said Mr. Datchery, making a leg with his hat under his arm, as he addressed himself equally to both gentlemen; 'a selfish precaution on my part, and not personally interesting to anybody but myself. But as a buffer living on his means, and having an idea of doing it in this lovely place in peace and quiet, for remaining span of life, I beg to ask if the Tope family are quite respectable?'

Mr. Jasper could answer for that without the slightest hesitation.

'That is enough, sir,' said Mr. Datchery.

'My friend the Mayor,' added Mr. Jasper, presenting Mr. Datchery with a courtly motion of his hand towards that potentate; 'whose recommendation is actually much more important to a stranger than that of an obscure person like myself, will testify in their behalf, I am sure.'

'The Worshipful the Mayor,' said Mr. Datchery, with a low bow, 'places me under an infinite obligation.'

'Very good people, sir, Mr. and Mrs. Tope,' said Mr. Sapsea, with condescension. 'Very good opinions. Very well behaved. Very respectful. Much approved by the Dean and Chapter.'

'The Worshipful the Mayor gives them a character,' said Mr. Datchery, 'of which they may indeed be proud. I would ask His Honour (if I might be permitted) whether there are not many objects of great interest in the city which is under his beneficent sway?'

'We are, sir,' returned Mr. Sapsea, 'an ancient city, and an ecclesiastical city. We are a constitutional city, as it becomes such a city to be, and we uphold and maintain our glorious privileges.'

'His Honour,' said Mr. Datchery, bowing, 'inspires me with a desire to know more of the city, and confirms me in my inclination to end my days in the city.'

'Retired from the Army, sir?' suggested Mr. Sapsea.

'His Honour the Mayor does me too much credit,' returned Mr. Datchery.

'Navy, sir?' suggested Mr. Sapsea.

'Again,' repeated Mr. Datchery, 'His Honour the Mayor does me too much credit.'

'Diplomacy is a fine profession,' said Mr. Sapsea, as a general remark.

'There, I confess, His Honour the Mayor is too many for me,' said Mr.

Datchery, with an ingenious smile and bow; 'even a diplomatic bird must fall to such a gun.'

Now this was very soothing. Here was a gentleman of a great, not to say a grand, address, accustomed to rank and dignity, really setting a fine example how to behave to a Mayor. There was something in that third-person style of being spoken to, that Mr. Sapsea found particularly recognisant of his merits and position.

'But I crave pardon,' said Mr. Datchery. 'His Honour the Mayor will bear with me, if for a moment I have been deluded into occupying his time, and have forgotten the humble claims upon my own, of my hotel, the Crozier.'

'Not at all, sir,' said Mr. Sapsea. 'I am returning home, and if you would like to take the exterior of our Cathedral in your way, I shall be glad to point it out.'

'His Honour the Mayor,' said Mr. Datchery, 'is more than kind and gracious.'

As Mr. Datchery, when he had made his acknowledgments to Mr. Jasper, could not be induced to go out of the room before the Worshipful, the Worshipful led the way down-stairs; Mr. Datchery following with his hat under his arm, and his shock of white hair streaming in the evening breeze.

'Might I ask His Honour,' said Mr. Datchery, 'whether that gentleman we have just left is the gentleman of whom I have heard in the neighbourhood as being much afflicted by the loss of a nephew, and concentrating his life on avenging the loss?'

'That is the gentleman. John Jasper, sir.'

'Would His Honour allow me to inquire whether there are strong suspicions of any one?'

'More than suspicions, sir,' returned Mr. Sapsea; 'all but certainties.'

'Only think now!' cried Mr. Datchery.

'But proof, sir, proof must be built up stone by stone,' said the Mayor. 'As I say, the end crowns the work. It is not enough that Justice should be morally certain; she must be immorally certain — legally, that is.'

'His Honour,' said Mr. Datchery, 'reminds me of the nature of the law. Immoral. How true!'

'As I say, sir,' pompously went on the Mayor, 'the arm of the law is a strong arm, and a long arm. That is the way I put it. A strong arm and a long arm.'

'How forcible! — And yet, again, how true!' murmured Mr. Datchery.

'And without betraying what I call the secrets of the prison-house,' said Mr. Sapsea; 'the secrets of the prison-house is the term I used on the bench.'

'And what other term than His Honour's would express it?' said Mr. Datchery.

'Without, I say, betraying them, I predict to you, knowing the iron will of the gentleman we have just left (I take the bold step of calling it iron, on account of its strength), that in this case the long arm will reach, and the strong arm will strike. — This is our Cathedral, sir. The best judges are pleased to admire it, and the best among our townsmen own to being a little vain of it.'

All this time Mr. Datchery had walked with his hat under his arm, and his white hair streaming. He had an odd momentary appearance upon him of having forgotten his hat, when Mr. Sapsea now touched it; and he clapped his hand up to his head as if with some vague expectation of finding another hat upon it.

'Pray be covered, sir,' entreated Mr. Sapsea; magnificently implying: 'I shall not mind it, I assure you.'

'His Honour is very good, but I do it for coolness,' said Mr. Datchery.

Then Mr. Datchery admired the Cathedral, and Mr. Sapsea pointed it out as if he himself had invented and built it: there were a few details indeed of which he did not approve, but those he glossed over, as if the workmen had made mistakes in his absence. The Cathedral disposed of, he led the way by the churchyard, and stopped to extol the beauty of the evening — by chance — in the immediate vicinity of Mrs. Sapsea's epitaph.

'And by the by,' said Mr. Sapsea, appearing to descend from an elevation to remember it all of a sudden; like Apollo shooting down from Olympus to pick up his forgotten lyre; '*that* is one of our small lions. The partiality of our people has made it so, and strangers have been seen taking a copy of it now and then. I am not a judge of it myself, for it is a little work of my own. But it was troublesome to turn, sir; I may say, difficult to turn with elegance.'

Mr. Datchery became so ecstatic over Mr. Sapsea's composition, that, in spite of his intention to end his days in Cloisterham, and therefore his probably having in reserve many opportunities of copying it, he would have transcribed it into his pocket-book on the spot, but for the slouching towards them of its material producer and perpetuator, Durdles, whom Mr. Sapsea hailed, not sorry to show him a bright example of behaviour to superiors.

'Ah, Durdles! This is the mason, sir; one of our Cloisterham worthies; everybody here knows Durdles. Mr. Datchery, Durdles; a gentleman who is going to settle here.'

'I wouldn't do it if I was him,' growled Durdles. 'We're a heavy lot.'

'You surely don't speak for yourself, Mr. Durdles,' returned Mr. Datchery, 'any more than for His Honour.'

'Who's His Honour?' demanded Durdles.

'His Honour the Mayor.'

'I never was brought afore him,' said Durdles, with anything but the look of a loyal subject of the mayoralty, 'and it'll be time enough for me to Honour him when I am. Until which, and when, and where,

> "Mister Sapsea is his name,
> England is his nation,
> Cloisterham's his dwelling-place,
> Aukshneer's his occupation."'

Here, Deputy (preceded by a flying oyster-shell) appeared upon the scene, and requested to have the sum of threepence instantly 'chucked' to him by Mr. Durdles, whom he had been vainly seeking up and down, as lawful wages overdue. While that gentleman, with his bundle under his arm, slowly found and counted out the money, Mr. Sapsea informed the new settler of Durdles's habits, pursuits, abode, and reputation. 'I suppose a curious stranger might come to see you, and your works, Mr. Durdles, at any odd time?' said Mr. Datchery upon that.

'Any gentleman is welcome to come and see me any evening if he brings liquor for two with him,' returned Durdles, with a penny between his teeth and certain halfpence in his hands; 'or if he likes to make it twice two, he'll be doubly welcome.'

'I shall come. Master Deputy, what do you owe me?'

'A job.'

'Mind you pay me honestly with the job of showing me Mr. Durdles's house when I want to go there.'

Deputy, with a piercing broadside of whistle through the whole gap in his mouth, as a receipt in full for all arrears, vanished.

The Worshipful and the Worshipper then passed on together until they parted, with many ceremonies, at the Worshipful's door; even then the Worshipper carried his hat under his arm, and gave his streaming white hair to the breeze.

Said Mr. Datchery to himself that night, as he looked at his white hair in the gas-lighted looking-glass over the coffee-room chimneypiece at the Crozier, and shook it out: 'For a single buffer, of an easy temper, living idly on his means, I have had a rather busy afternoon!'

Shadow on the Sun-Dial

AGAIN Miss Twinkleton has delivered her valedictory address, with the accompaniments of white-wine and pound-cake, and again the young ladies have departed to their several homes. Helena Landless has left the Nuns' House to attend her brother's fortunes, and pretty Rosa is alone.

Cloisterham is so bright and sunny in these summer days, that the Cathedral and the monastery-ruin show as if their strong walls were transparent. A soft glow seems to shine from within them, rather than upon them from without, such is their mellowness as they look forth on the hot corn-fields and the smoking roads that distantly wind among them. The Cloisterham gardens blush with ripening fruit. Time was when travel-stained pilgrims rode in clattering parties through the city's welcome shades; time is when wayfarers, leading a gipsy life between haymaking time and harvest, and looking as if they were just made of the dust of the earth, so very dusty are they, lounge about on cool door-steps, trying to mend their unmendable shoes, or giving them to the city kennels as a hopeless job, and seeking others in the bundles that they carry, along with their yet unused sickles swathed in bands of straw. At all the more public pumps there is much cooling of bare feet, together with much bubbling and gurgling of drinking with hand to spout on the part of these Bedouins; the Cloisterham police meanwhile looking askant from their beats with suspicion, and manifest impatience that the intruders should depart from within the civic bounds, and once more fry themselves on the simmering high-roads.

On the afternoon of such a day, when the last Cathedral service is done, and when that side of the High Street on which the Nuns' House stands is in grateful shade, save where its quaint old garden opens to the west between the boughs of trees, a servant informs Rosa, to her terror, that Mr. Jasper desires to see her.

If he had chosen his time for finding her at a disadvantage, he could have done no better. Perhaps he has chosen it. Helena Landless is gone, Mrs. Tisher is absent on leave, Miss Twinkleton (in her amateur state of existence) has contributed herself and a veal pie to a picnic.

'O why, why, why, did you say I was at home!' cried Rosa, helplessly.

The maid replies, that Mr. Jasper never asked the question. That he said he knew she was at home, and begged she might be told that he asked to see her.

'What shall I do! what shall I do!' thinks Rosa, clasping her hands.

Possessed by a kind of desperation, she adds in the next breath, that she will come to Mr. Jasper in the garden. She shudders at the thought of being shut up with him in the house; but many of its windows command the garden, and she can be seen as well as heard there, and can shriek in the free air and run away. Such is the wild idea that flutters through her mind.

She has never seen him since the fatal night, except when she was questioned before the Mayor, and then he was present in gloomy watchfulness, as representing his lost nephew and burning to avenge him. She hangs her garden-hat on her arm, and goes out. The moment she sees him from the porch, leaning on the sun-dial, the old horrible feeling of being compelled by him, asserts its hold upon her. She feels that she would even then go back, but that he draws her feet towards him. She cannot resist, and sits down, with her head bent, on the garden-seat beside the sun-dial. She cannot look up at him for abhorrence, but she has perceived that he is dressed in deep mourning. So is she. It was not so at first; but the lost has long been given up, and mourned for, as dead.

He would begin by touching her hand. She feels the intention, and draws her hand back. His eyes are then fixed upon her, she knows, though her own see nothing but the grass.

'I have been waiting,' he begins, 'for some time, to be summoned back to my duty near you.'

After several times forming her lips, which she knows he is closely watching, into the shape of some other hesitating reply, and then into none, she answers: 'Duty, sir?'

'The duty of teaching you, serving you as your faithful music-master.'

'I have left off that study.'

'Not left off, I think. Discontinued. I was told by your guardian that you discontinued it under the shock that we have all felt so acutely. When will you resume?'

'Never, sir.'

'Never? You could have done no more if you had loved my dear boy.'

'I did love him!' cried Rosa, with a flash of anger.

'Yes; but not quite — not quite in the right way, shall I say? Not in the intended and expected way. Much as my dear boy was, unhappily, too self-conscious and self-satisfied (I'll draw no parallel between him and you in that respect) to love as he should have loved, or as any one in his place would have loved — must have loved!'

She sits in the same still attitude, but shrinking a little more.

'Then, to be told that you discontinued your study with me, was to be politely told that you abandoned it altogether?' he suggested.

'Yes,' says Rosa, with sudden spirit. 'The politeness was my guardian's, not mine. I told him that I was resolved to leave off, and that I was determined to stand by my resolution.'

'And you still are?'

'I still am, sir. And I beg not to be questioned any more about it. At all events, I will not answer any more; I have that in my power.'

She is so conscious of his looking at her with a gloating admiration of the touch of anger on her, and the fire and animation it brings with it, that even as her spirit rises, it falls again, and she struggles with a sense of shame, affront, and fear, much as she did that night at the piano.

'I will not question you any more, since you object to it so much; I will confess ——'

'I do not wish to hear you, sir,' cries Rosa, rising.

This time he does touch her with his outstretched hand. In shrinking from it, she shrinks into her seat again.

'We must sometimes act in opposition to our wishes,' he tells her in a low voice. 'You must do so now, or do more harm to others than you can ever set right.'

'What harm?'

'Presently, presently. You question *me*, you see, and surely that's not fair when you forbid me to question you. Nevertheless, I will answer the question presently. Dearest Rosa! Charming Rosa!'

She starts up again.

This time he does not touch her. But his face looks so wicked and menacing, as he stands leaning against the sun-dial — setting, as it were, his black mark upon the very face of day — that her flight is arrested by horror as she looks at him.

'I do not forget how many windows command a view of us,' he says, glancing towards them. 'I will not touch you again; I will come no nearer to you than I am. Sit down, and there will be no mighty wonder in your music-master's leaning idly against a pedestal and speaking with you, remembering all that has happened, and our shares in it. Sit down, my beloved.'

She would have gone once more — was all but gone — and once more his face, darkly threatening what would follow if she went, has stopped her. Looking at him with the expression of the instant frozen on her face, she sits down on the seat again.

'Rosa, even when my dear boy was affianced to you, I loved you madly; even when I thought his happiness in having you for his wife was certain, I loved you madly; even when I strove to make him more ardently devoted to you, I loved you madly; even when he gave me the picture of your lovely face so carelessly traduced by him, which I feigned to hang always in my sight for his sake, but worshipped in torment for years, I loved you madly; in the distasteful work of the day, in the wakeful misery of the night, girded by sordid realities, or wandering through Paradises and Hells of visions into which I rushed, carrying your image in my arms, I loved you madly.'

If anything could make his words more hideous to her than they are in themselves, it would be the contrast between the violence of his look and delivery, and the composure of his assumed attitude.

'I endured it all in silence. So long as you were his, or so long as I supposed you to be his, I hid my secret loyally. Did I not?'

This lie, so gross, while the mere words in which it is told are so true, is more than Rosa can endure. She answers with kindling indignation: 'You were as false throughout, sir, as you are now. You were false to him, daily and hourly. You know that you made my life unhappy by your pursuit of me. You know that you made me afraid to open his generous eyes, and that you forced me, for his own trusting, good, good sake, to keep the truth from him, that you were a bad, bad man!'

His preservation of his easy attitude rendering his working features and his convulsive hands absolutely diabolical, he returns, with a fierce extreme of admiration:

'How beautiful you are! You are more beautiful in anger than in repose. I don't ask you for your love; give me yourself and your hatred; give me yourself and that pretty rage; give me yourself and that enchanting scorn; it will be enough for me.'

Impatient tears rise to the eyes of the trembling little beauty, and her face flames; but as she again rises to leave him in indignation, and seek protection within the house, he stretched out his hand towards the porch, as though he invited her to enter it.

'I told you, you rare charmer, you sweet witch, that you must stay and hear me, or do more harm than can ever be undone. You asked me what harm. Stay, and I will tell you. Go, and I will do it!'

Again Rosa quails before his threatening face, though innocent of its meaning, and she remains. Her panting breathing comes and goes as if it would choke her; but with a repressive hand upon her bosom, she remains.

'I have made my confession that my love is mad. It is so mad, that had the ties between me and my dear lost boy been one silken thread less strong, I might have swept even him from your side when you favoured him.'

A film comes over the eyes she raises for an instant, as though he had turned her faint.

'Even him,' he repeats. 'Yes, even him! Rosa, you see me and you hear me. Judge for yourself whether any other admirer shall love you and live, whose life is in my hand.'

'What do you mean, sir?'

'I mean to show you how mad my love is. It was hawked through the late inquiries by Mr. Crisparkle, that young Landless had confessed to him that he was a rival of my lost boy. That is an inexpiable offence in my eyes. The same Mr. Crisparkle knows under my hand that I have devoted myself to the murderer's discovery and destruction, be he whom he might, and that I determined to discuss the mystery with no one until I should hold the clue in which to entangle the murderer as in a net. I have since worked patiently to wind and wind it round him; and it is slowly winding as I speak.'

'Your belief, if you believe in the criminality of Mr. Landless, is not Mr. Crisparkle's belief, and he is a good man,' Rosa retorts.

'My belief is my own; and I reserve it, worshipped of my soul! Circumstances may accumulate so strongly *even against an innocent man*, that directed, sharpened, and pointed, they may slay him. One wanting link discovered by perseverance against a guilty man, proves his guilt, however slight its evidence before, and he dies. Young Landless stands in deadly peril either way.'

'If you really suppose,' Rosa pleads with him, turning paler, 'that I favour Mr. Landless, or that Mr. Landless has ever in any way addressed himself to me, you are wrong.'

He puts that from him with a slighting action of his hand and a curled lip.

'I was going to show you how madly I love you. More madly now than ever, for I am willing to renounce the second object that has arisen in my life to divide it with you; and henceforth to have no object in existence but you only. Miss Landless has become your bosom friend. You care for her peace of mind?'

'I love her dearly.'

'You care for her good name?'

'I have said, sir, I love her dearly.'

'I am unconsciously,' he observes with a smile, as he folds his hands upon the sun-dial and leans his chin upon them, so that his talk would seem from the windows (faces occasionally come and go there) to be of the airiest and playfullest — 'I am unconsciously giving offence by questioning again. I will simply make statements, therefore, and not put questions. You do care for your bosom friend's good name, and you do care for her peace of mind. Then remove the shadow of the gallows from her, dear one!'

'You dare propose to me to ——'

'Darling, I dare propose to you. Stop there. If it be bad to idolise you, I am the worst of men; if it be good, I am the best. My love for you is above all other love, and my truth to you is above all other truth. Let me have hope and favour, and I am a forsworn man for your sake.'

Rosa puts her hands to her temples, and, pushing back her hair, looks wildly and abhorrently at him, as though she were trying to piece together what it is his deep purpose to present to her only in fragments.

'Reckon up nothing at this moment, angel, but the sacrifices that I lay at those dear feet, which I could fall down among the vilest ashes and kiss, and put upon my head as a poor savage might. There is my fidelity to my dear boy after death. Tread upon it!'

With an action of his hands, as though he cast down something precious.

'There is the inexpiable offence against my adoration of you. Spurn it!'

With a similar action.

'There are my labours in the cause of a just vengeance for six toiling months. Crush them!'

With another repetition of the action.

'There is my past and my present wasted life. There is the desolation of my heart and my soul. There is my peace; there is my despair. Stamp them into the dust; so that you take me, were it even mortally hating me!'

The frightful vehemence of the man, now reaching its full height, so additionally terrifies her as to break the spell that has held her to the spot. She swiftly moves towards the porch; but in an instant he is at her side, and speaking in her ear.

'Rosa, I am self-repressed again. I am walking calmly beside you to the house. I shall wait for some encouragement and hope. I shall not strike too soon. Give me a sign that you attend to me.'

She slightly and constrainedly moves her hand.

'Not a word of this to any one, or it will bring down the blow, as certainly as night follows day. Another sign that you attend to me.'

She moves her hand once more.

'I love you, love you, love you! If you were to cast me off now — but you will not — you would never be rid of me. No one should come between us. I would pursue you to the death.'

The handmaid coming out to open the gate for him, he quietly pulls off his hat as a parting salute, and goes away with no greater show of agitation than is visible in the effigy of Mr. Sapsea's father opposite. Rosa faints in going up-stairs, and is carefully carried to her room and laid down on her bed. A thunderstorm is coming on, the maids say, and the hot and stifling air has overset the pretty dear: no wonder; they have felt their own knees all of a tremble all day long.

Divers Flights

ROSA no sooner came to herself than the whole of the late interview was before her. It even seemed as if it had pursued her into her insensibility, and she had not had a moment's unconsciousness of it. What to do, she was at a frightened loss to know: the only one clear thought in her mind was, that she must fly from this terrible man.

But where could she take refuge, and how could she go? She had never breathed her dread of him to any one but Helena. If she went to Helena, and told her what had passed, that very act might bring down the irreparable mischief that he threatened he had the power, and that she knew he had the will, to do. The more fearful he appeared to her excited memory and imagination, the more alarming her responsibility appeared; seeing that a slight mistake on her part, either in action or delay, might let his malevolence loose on Helena's brother.

Rosa's mind throughout the last six months had been stormily confused. A half-formed, wholly unexpressed suspicion tossed in it, now heaving itself up, and now sinking into the deep; now gaining palpability, and now losing it. Jasper's self-absorption in his nephew when he was alive, and his unceasing pursuit of the inquiry how he came by his death, if he were dead, were themes so rife in the place, that no one appeared able to suspect the possibility of foul play at his hands. She had asked herself the question, 'Am I so wicked in my thoughts as to conceive a wickedness that others cannot imagine?' Then she had considered, Did the suspicion come of her previous recoiling from him before the fact? And if so, was not that a proof of its baselessness? Then she had reflected, 'What motive could he have, according to my accusation?' She was ashamed to answer in her mind, 'The motive of gaining *me!*' And covered her face, as if the lightest shadow of the idea of founding murder on such an idle vanity were a crime almost as great.

She ran over in her mind again, all that he had said by the sundial in the garden. He had persisted in treating the disappearance as murder, consistently with his whole public course since the finding of the watch and shirt-pin. If he were afraid of the crime being traced out, would he not rather encourage the idea of a voluntary disappearance? He had even declared that if the ties between him and his nephew had been less strong, he might have swept 'even him' away from her side. Was that like his having really done so? He had spoken of laying his six months' labours in the cause of a just vengeance at her feet. Would he have done that, with that violence of passion, if they were a pretence? Would he have ranged them with his desolate heart and soul, his wasted life, his peace and his despair? The very first sacrifice that he represented himself as making for her, was his fidelity to his dear boy after death. Surely these facts were strong against a fancy that scarcely dared to hint itself. And yet he was so terrible a man! In short, the poor girl (for what could she know of the criminal intellect, which its own professed students perpetually misread, because they persist in trying to reconcile it with the average intellect of average men, instead of identifying it as a horrible wonder apart) could get by no road to any other conclusion than that he *was* a terrible man, and must be fled from.

She had been Helena's stay and comfort during the whole time. She had constantly assured her of her full belief in her brother's innocence, and of her sympathy with him in his misery. But she had never seen him since the disappearance, nor had Helena ever spoken one word of his avowal to Mr. Crisparkle in regard of Rosa, though as a part of the interest of the case it was well known far and wide. He was Helena's unfortunate brother, to her, and nothing more. The assurance she had given her odious suitor was strictly true, though it would have been better (she considered now) if she could have restrained herself from so giving it. Afraid of him as the bright and delicate little creature was, her spirit swelled at the thought of his knowing it from her own lips.

But where was she to go? Anywhere beyond his reach, was no reply to the question. Somewhere must be thought of. She determined to go to her guardian, and to go immediately. The feeling she had imparted to Helena on the night of their first confidence, was so strong upon her — the feeling of not being safe from him, and of the solid walls of the old convent being powerless to keep out his ghostly following of her — that no reasoning of her own could calm her terrors. The fascination of repulsion had been upon her so long, and now culminated so darkly, that she felt as if he had power to bind her by a spell. Glancing out at window, even now, as she rose to dress, the sight of the sun-dial on which he had leaned when he declared himself, turned her cold, and made her shrink from it, as though he had invested it with some awful quality from his own nature.

She wrote a hurried note to Miss Twinkleton, saying that she had sudden reason for wishing to see her guardian promptly, and had gone to him; also entreating the good lady not to be uneasy, for all was well with her. She hurried a few quite useless articles into a very little bag, left the note in a conspicuous place, and went out, softly closing the gate after her.

It was the first time she had ever been even in Cloisterham High Street alone. But knowing all its ways and windings very well, she hurried straight to the corner from which the omnibus departed. It was, at that very moment, going off.

'Stop and take me, if you please, Joe. I am obliged to go to London.'

In less than another minute she was on her road to the railway, under Joe's protection. Joe waited on her when she got there, put her safely into the railway carriage, and handed in the very little bag after her, as though it were some enormous trunk, hundredweights heavy, which she must on no account endeavour to lift.

'Can you go round when you get back, and tell Miss Twinkleton that you saw me safely off, Joe?'

'It shall be done, Miss.'

'With my love, please, Joe.'

'Yes, Miss — and I wouldn't mind having it myself!' But Joe did not articulate the last clause; only thought it.

Now that she was whirling away for London in real earnest, Rosa was at leisure to resume the thoughts which her personal hurry had checked. The indignant thought that his declaration of love soiled her; that she could only be cleansed from the stain of its impurity by appealing to the honest and true; supported her for a time against her fears, and confirmed her in her hasty resolution. But as the evening grew darker and darker, and the great city impended nearer and nearer, the doubts usual in such cases began to arise. Whether this was not a wild proceeding, after all; how Mr. Grewgious might regard it; whether she should find him at the journey's end; how she would act if he were absent; what might become of her, alone, in a place so strange and crowded; how if she had but waited and taken counsel first; whether, if she could now go back, she would not do it thankfully; a multitude of such uneasy speculations disturbed her, more and more as they accumulated. At length the train came into London over the housetops; and down below lay the gritty streets with their yet un-needed lamps a-glow, on a hot, light, summer night.

'Hiram Grewgious, Esquire, Staple Inn, London.' This was all Rosa knew of her destination; but it was enough to send her rattling away again in a cab, through deserts of gritty streets, where many people crowded at the corner of courts and byways to get some air, and where many other people walked with a miserably monotonous noise of shuffling of feet on hot paving-stones, and where all the people and all their surroundings were so gritty and so shabby!

There was music playing here and there, but it did not enliven the case. No barrel-organ mended the matter, and no big drum beat dull care away. Like the chapel bells that were also going here and there, they only seemed to evoke echoes from brick surfaces, and dust from everything. As to the flat wind-instruments, they seemed to have cracked their hearts and souls in pining for the country.

Her jingling conveyance stopped at last at a fast-closed gateway, which appeared to belong to somebody who had gone to bed very early, and was much afraid of housebreakers; Rosa, discharging her conveyance, timidly knocked at this gateway, and was let in, very little bag and all, by a watchman.

'Does Mr. Grewgious live here?'

'Mr. Grewgious lives there, Miss,' said the watchman, pointing further in.

So Rosa went further in, and, when the clocks were striking ten, stood on P.J.T.'s doorsteps, wondering what P.J.T. had done with his street-door.

Guided by the painted name of Mr. Grewgious, she went up-stairs and softly tapped and tapped several times. But no one answering, and Mr. Grewgious's door-handle yielding to her touch, she went in, and saw her guardian sitting on a window-seat at an open window, with a shaded lamp placed far from him on a table in a corner.

Rosa drew nearer to him in the twilight of the room. He saw her, and he said, in an undertone: 'Good Heaven!'

Rosa fell upon his neck, with tears, and then he said, returning her embrace:

'My child, my child! I thought you were your mother! — But what, what, what,' he added, soothingly, 'has happened? My dear, what has brought you here? Who has brought you here?'

'No one. I came alone.'

'Lord bless me!' ejaculated Mr. Grewgious. 'Came alone! Why didn't you write to me to come and fetch you?'

'I had no time. I took a sudden resolution. Poor, poor Eddy!'

'Ah, poor fellow, poor fellow!'

'His uncle has made love to me. I cannot bear it,' said Rosa, at once with a burst of tears, and a stamp of her little foot; 'I shudder with horror of him, and I have come to you to protect me and all of us from him, if you will?'

'I will,' cried Mr. Grewgious, with a sudden rush of amazing energy. 'Damn him!

> "Confound his politics!
> Frustrate his knavish tricks!
> On Thee his hopes to fix?
> Damn him again!"'

After this most extraordinary outburst, Mr. Grewgious, quite beside himself, plunged about the room, to all appearance undecided whether he was in a fit of loyal enthusiasm, or combative denunciation.

He stopped and said, wiping his face: 'I beg your pardon, my dear, but you will be glad to know I feel better. Tell me no more just now, or I might do it again. You must be refreshed and cheered. What did you take last? Was it breakfast, lunch, dinner, tea, or supper? And what will you take next? Shall it be breakfast, lunch, dinner, tea, or supper?'

The respectful tenderness with which, on one knee before her, he helped her to remove her hat, and disentangle her pretty hair from it, was quite a chivalrous sight. Yet who, knowing him only on the surface, would have expected chivalry — and of the true sort, too; not the spurious — from Mr. Grewgious?

'Your rest too must be provided for,' he went on; 'and you shall have the prettiest chamber in Furnival's. Your toilet must be provided for, and you shall have everything that an unlimited head chambermaid — by which expression I mean a head chambermaid not limited as to outlay — can procure. Is that a bag?' he looked hard at it; sooth to say, it required hard looking at to be seen at all in a dimly lighted room: 'and is it your property, my dear?'

'Yes, sir. I brought it with me.'

'It is not an extensive bag,' said Mr. Grewgious, candidly, 'though admirably calculated to contain a day's provision for a canary-bird. Perhaps you brought a canary-bird?'

Rosa smiled and shook her head.

'If you had, he should have been made welcome,' said Mr. Grewgious, 'and I think he would have been pleased to be hung upon a nail outside and pit himself against our Staple sparrows; whose execution must be admitted to be not quite equal to their intention. Which is the case with so many of us! You didn't say what meal, my dear. Have a nice jumble of all meals.'

Rosa thanked him, but said she could only take a cup of tea. Mr. Grewgious, after several times running out, and in again, to mention such supplementary items as marmalade, eggs, watercresses, salted fish, and frizzled ham, ran across to Furnival's without his hat, to give his various directions. And soon afterwards they were realised in practice, and the board was spread.

'Lord bless my soul,' cried Mr. Grewgious, putting the lamp upon it, and taking his seat opposite Rosa; 'what a new sensation for a poor old Angular bachelor, to be sure!'

Rosa's expressive little eyebrows asked him what he meant?

'The sensation of having a sweet young presence in the place, that whitewashes it, paints it, papers it, decorates it with gilding, and makes it Glorious!' said Mr. Grewgious. 'Ah me! Ah me!'

As there was something mournful in his sigh, Rosa, in touching him with her tea-cup, ventured to touch him with her small hand too.

'Thank you, my dear,' said Mr. Grewgious. 'Ahem! Let's talk!'

'Do you always live here, sir?' asked Rosa.

'Yes, my dear.'

'And always alone?'

'Always alone; except that I have daily company in a gentleman by the name of Bazzard, my clerk.'

'*He* doesn't live here?'

'No, he goes his way, after office hours. In fact, he is off duty here, altogether, just at present; and a firm down-stairs, with which I have business relations, lend me a substitute. But it would be extremely difficult to replace Mr. Bazzard.'

'He must be very fond of you,' said Rosa.

'He bears up against it with commendable fortitude if he is,' returned Mr. Grewgious, after considering the matter. 'But I doubt if he is. Not particularly so. You see, he is discontented, poor fellow.'

'Why isn't he contented?' was the natural inquiry.

'Misplaced,' said Mr. Grewgious, with great mystery.

Rosa's eyebrows resumed their inquisitive and perplexed expression.

'So misplaced,' Mr. Grewgious went on, 'that I feel constantly apologetic towards him. And he feels (though he doesn't mention it) that I have reason to be.'

Mr. Grewgious had by this time grown so very mysterious, that Rosa did not know how to go on. While she was thinking about it Mr. Grewgious suddenly jerked out of himself for the second time:

'Let's talk. We were speaking of Mr. Bazzard. It's a secret, and moreover it is Mr. Bazzard's secret; but the sweet presence at my table makes me so unusually expansive, that I feel I must impart it in inviolable confidence. What do you think Mr. Bazzard has done?'

'O dear!' cried Rosa, drawing her chair a little nearer, and her mind reverting to Jasper, 'nothing dreadful, I hope?'

'He has written a play,' said Mr. Grewgious, in a solemn whisper. 'A tragedy.'

Rosa seemed much relieved.

'And nobody,' pursued Mr. Grewgious in the same tone, 'will hear, on any account whatever, of bringing it out.'

Rosa looked reflective, and nodded her head slowly; as who should say, 'Such things are, and why are they!'

'Now, you know,' said Mr. Grewgious, '*I* couldn't write a play.'

'Not a bad one, sir?' said Rosa, innocently, with her eyebrows again in action.

'No. If I was under sentence of decapitation, and was about to be instantly decapitated, and an express arrived with a pardon for the condemned convict Grewgious if he wrote a play, I should be under the necessity of resuming the block, and begging the executioner to proceed to extremities, — meaning,' said Mr. Grewgious, passing his hand under his chin, 'the singular number, and this extremity.'

Rosa appeared to consider what she would do if the awkward supposititious case were hers.

'Consequently,' said Mr. Grewgious, 'Mr. Bazzard would have a sense of my inferiority to himself under any circumstances; but when I am his master, you know, the case is greatly aggravated.'

Mr. Grewgious shook his head seriously, as if he felt the offence to be a little too much, though of his own committing.

'How came you to be his master, sir?' asked Rosa.

'A question that naturally follows,' said Mr. Grewgious. 'Let's talk. Mr. Bazzard's father, being a Norfolk farmer, would have furiously laid about him with a flail, a pitch-fork, and every agricultural implement available for assaulting purposes, on the slightest hint of his son's having written a play. So the son, bringing to me the father's rent (which I receive), imparted his secret, and pointed out that he was determined to pursue his genius, and that it would put him in peril of starvation, and that he was not formed for it.'

'For pursuing his genius, sir?'

'No, my dear,' said Mr. Grewgious, 'for starvation. It was impossible to deny the position, that Mr. Bazzard was not formed to be starved, and Mr. Bazzard then pointed out that it was desirable that I should stand between him and a fate so perfectly unsuited to his formation. In that way Mr. Bazzard became my clerk, and he feels it very much.'

'I am glad he is grateful,' said Rosa.

'I didn't quite mean that, my dear. I mean, that he feels the degradation. There are some other geniuses that Mr. Bazzard has become acquainted with, who have also written tragedies, which likewise nobody will on any account whatever hear of bringing out, and these choice spirits dedicate their plays to one another in a highly panegyrical manner. Mr. Bazzard has been the subject of one of these dedications. Now, you know, *I* never had a play dedicated to *me!*'

Rosa looked at him as if she would have liked him to be the recipient of a thousand dedications.

'Which again, naturally, rubs against the grain of Mr. Bazzard,' said Mr. Grewgious. 'He is very short with me sometimes, and then I feel that he is meditating, "This blockhead is my master! A fellow who couldn't write a tragedy on pain of death, and who will never have one dedicated to him with the most complimentary congratulations on the high position he has taken in the eyes of posterity!" Very trying, very trying. However, in giving him directions, I reflect beforehand: "Perhaps he may not like this," or "He might take it ill if I asked that;" and so we get on very well. Indeed, better than I could have expected.'

'Is the tragedy named, sir?' asked Rosa.

'Strictly between ourselves,' answered Mr. Grewgious, 'it has a dreadfully appropriate name. It is called The Thorn of Anxiety. But Mr. Bazzard hopes — and I hope — that it will come out at last.'

It was not hard to divine that Mr. Grewgious had related the Bazzard history thus fully, at least quite as much for the recreation of his ward's mind from the subject that had driven her there, as for the gratification of his own tendency to be social and communicative.

'And now, my dear,' he said at this point, 'if you are not too tired to tell me more of what passed to-day — but only if you feel quite able — I should be glad to hear it. I may digest it the better, if I sleep on it to-night.'

Rosa, composed now, gave him a faithful account of the interview. Mr. Grewgious often smoothed his head while it was in progress, and begged to be told a second time those parts which bore on Helena and Neville. When Rosa had finished, he sat grave, silent, and meditative for a while.

'Clearly narrated,' was his only remark at last, 'and, I hope, clearly put away here,' smoothing his head again. 'See, my dear,' taking her to the open window, 'where they live! The dark windows over yonder.'

'I may go to Helena to-morrow?' asked Rosa.

'I should like to sleep on that question to-night,' he answered doubtfully. 'But let me take you to your own rest, for you must need it.'

With that Mr. Grewgious helped her to get her hat on again, and hung upon his arm the very little bag that was of no earthly use, and led her by the hand (with a certain stately awkwardness, as if he were going to walk a minuet) across Holborn, and into Furnival's Inn. At the hotel door, he confided her to the Unlimited head chambermaid, and said that while she went up to see her room, he would remain below, in case she should wish it exchanged for another, or should find that there was anything she wanted.

Rosa's room was airy, clean, comfortable, almost gay. The Unlimited had laid in everything omitted from the very little bag (that is to say, everything she could possibly need), and Rosa tripped down the great many stairs again, to thank her guardian for his thoughtful and affectionate care of her.

'Not at all, my dear,' said Mr. Grewgious, infinitely gratified; 'it is I who thank you for your charming confidence and for your charming company. Your breakfast will be provided for you in a neat, compact, and graceful little sitting-room (appropriate to your figure), and I will come to you at ten o'clock in the morning. I hope you don't feel very strange indeed, in this strange place.'

'O no, I feel so safe!'

'Yes, you may be sure that the stairs are fire-proof,' said Mr. Grewgious, 'and that any outbreak of the devouring element would be perceived and suppressed by the watchmen.'

'I did not mean that,' Rosa replied. 'I mean, I feel so safe from him.'

'There is a stout gate of iron bars to keep him out,' said Mr. Grewgious, smiling; 'and Furnival's is fire-proof, and specially watched and lighted, and *I* live over the way!' In the stoutness of his knight-errantry, he seemed to think the last-named protection all sufficient. In the same spirit he said to the gate-porter as he went out, 'If some one staying in the hotel should wish to send across the road to me in the night, a crown will be ready for the messenger.' In the same spirit, he walked up and down outside the iron gate for the best part of an hour, with some solicitude; occasionally looking in between the bars, as if he had laid a dove in a high roost in a cage of lions, and had it on his mind that she might tumble out.

Nothing occurred in the night to flutter the tired dove; and the dove arose refreshed. With Mr. Grewgious, when the clock struck ten in the morning, came Mr. Crisparkle, who had come at one plunge out of the river at Cloisterham.

'Miss Twinkleton was so uneasy, Miss Rosa,' he explained to her, 'and came round to Ma and me with your note, in such a state of wonder, that, to quiet her, I volunteered on this service by the very first train to be caught in the morning. I wished at the time that you had come to me; but now I think it best that you did *as* you did, and came to your guardian.'

'I did think of you,' Rosa told him; 'but Minor Canon Corner was so near him ——'

'I understand. It was quite natural.'

'I have told Mr. Crisparkle,' said Mr. Grewgious, 'all that you told me last night, my dear. Of course I should have written it to him immediately; but his coming was most opportune. And it was particularly kind of him to come, for he had but just gone.'

'Have you settled,' asked Rosa, appealing to them both, 'what is to be done for Helena and her brother?'

'Why really,' said Mr. Crisparkle, 'I am in great perplexity. If even Mr. Grewgious, whose head is much longer than mine, and who is a whole night's cogitation in advance of me, is undecided, what must I be!'

The Unlimited here put her head in at the door — after having rapped, and been authorised to present herself — announcing that a gentleman wished for a word with another gentleman named Crisparkle, if any such gentleman were there. If no such gentleman were there, he begged pardon for being mistaken.

'Such a gentleman is here,' said Mr. Crisparkle, 'but is engaged just now.'

'Is it a dark gentleman?' interposed Rosa, retreating on her guardian.

'No Miss, more of a brown gentleman.'

'You are sure not with black hair?' asked Rosa, taking courage.

'Quite sure of that, Miss. Brown hair and blue eyes.'

'Perhaps,' hinted Mr. Grewgious, with habitual caution, 'it might be well to see him, reverend sir, if you don't object. When one is in a difficulty or at a loss, one never knows in what direction a way out may chance to open. It is a business principle of mine, in such a case, not to close up any direction, but to keep an eye on every direction that may present itself. I could relate an anecdote in point, but that it would be premature.'

'If Miss Rosa will allow me, then? Let the gentleman come in,' said Mr. Crisparkle.

The gentleman came in; apologised, with a frank but modest grace, for not finding Mr. Crisparkle alone; turned to Mr. Crisparkle, and smilingly asked the unexpected question: 'Who am I?'

'You are the gentleman I saw smoking under the trees in Staple Inn, a few minutes ago.'

'True. There I saw you. Who else am I?'

Mr. Crisparkle concentrated his attention on a handsome face, much sunburnt; and the ghost of some departed boy seemed to rise, gradually and dimly, in the room.

The gentleman saw a struggling recollection lighten up the Minor Canon's features, and smiling again, said: 'What will you have for breakfast this morning? You are out of jam.'

'Wait a moment!' cried Mr. Crisparkle, raising his right hand. 'Give me another instant! Tartar!'

The two shook hands with the greatest heartiness, and then went the wonderful length — for Englishmen — of laying their hands each on the other's shoulders, and looking joyfully each into the other's face.

'My old fag!' said Mr. Crisparkle.

'My old master!' said Mr. Tartar.

'You saved me from drowning!' said Mr. Crisparkle.

'After which you took to swimming, you know!' said Mr. Tartar.

'God bless my soul!' said Mr. Crisparkle.

'Amen!' said Mr. Tartar.

And then they fell to shaking hands most heartily again.

'Imagine,' exclaimed Mr. Crisparkle, with glistening eyes: 'Miss Rosa Bud and Mr. Grewgious, imagine Mr. Tartar, when he was the smallest of juniors, diving for me, catching me, a big heavy senior, by the hair of the head, and striking out for the shore with me like a water-giant!'

'Imagine my not letting him sink, as I was his fag!' said Mr. Tartar. 'But the truth being that he was my best protector and friend, and did me more good than all the masters put together, an irrational impulse seized me to pick him up, or go down with him.'

'Hem! Permit me, sir, to have the honour,' said Mr. Grewgious, advancing with extended hand, 'for an honour I truly esteem it. I am proud to make your acquaintance. I hope you didn't take cold. I hope you were not inconvenienced by swallowing too much water. How have you been since?'

It was by no means apparent that Mr. Grewgious knew what he said, though it was very apparent that he meant to say something highly friendly and appreciative.

If Heaven, Rosa thought, had but sent such courage and skill to her poor mother's aid! And he to have been so slight and young then!

'I don't wish to be complimented upon it, I thank you; but I think I have an idea,' Mr. Grewgious announced, after taking a jog-trot or two across the room, so unexpected and unaccountable that they all stared at him, doubtful whether he was choking or had the cramp — 'I *think* I have an idea. I believe I have had the pleasure of seeing Mr. Tartar's name as tenant of the top set in the house next the top set in the corner?'

'Yes, sir,' returned Mr. Tartar. 'You are right so far.'

'I am right so far,' said Mr. Grewgious. 'Tick that off;' which he did, with his right thumb on his left. 'Might you happen to know the name of your neighbour in the top set on the other side of the party-wall?' coming very close to Mr. Tartar, to lose nothing of his face, in his shortness of sight.

'Landless.'

'Tick that off,' said Mr. Grewgious, taking another trot, and then coming back. 'No personal knowledge, I suppose, sir?'

'Slight, but some.'

'Tick that off,' said Mr. Grewgious, taking another trot, and again coming back. 'Nature of knowledge, Mr. Tartar?'

'I thought he seemed to be a young fellow in a poor way, and I asked his leave — only within a day or so — to share my flowers up there with him; that is to say, to extend my flower-garden to his windows.'

'Would you have the kindness to take seats?' said Mr. Grewgious. 'I *have* an idea!'

They complied; Mr. Tartar none the less readily, for being all abroad; and Mr. Grewgious, seated in the centre, with his hands upon his knees, thus stated his idea, with his usual manner of having got the statement by heart.

'I cannot as yet make up my mind whether it is prudent to hold open communication under present circumstances, and on the part of the fair member of the present company, with Mr. Neville or Miss Helena. I have reason to know that a local friend of ours (on whom I beg to bestow a passing but a hearty malediction, with the kind permission of my reverend friend) sneaks to and fro, and dodges up and down. When not doing so himself, he may have some informant skulking about, in the person of a watchman, porter, or such-like hanger-on of Staple. On the other hand, Miss Rosa very naturally wishes to see her friend Miss Helena, and it would seem important that at least Miss Helena (if not her brother too, through her) should privately know from Miss Rosa's lips what has occurred, and what has been threatened. Am I agreed with generally in the views I take?'

'I entirely coincide with them,' said Mr. Crisparkle, who had been very attentive.

'As I have no doubt I should,' added Mr. Tartar, smiling, 'if I understood them.'

'Fair and softly, sir,' said Mr. Grewgious; 'we shall fully confide in you directly, if you will favour us with your permission. Now, if our local friend should have any informant on the spot, it is tolerably clear that such informant can only be set to watch the chambers in the occupation of Mr. Neville. He reporting, to our local friend, who comes and goes there, our local friend would supply for himself, from his own previous knowledge, the identity of the parties. Nobody can be set to watch all Staple, or to concern himself with comers and goers to other sets of chambers: unless, indeed, mine.'

'I begin to understand to what you tend,' said Mr. Crisparkle, 'and highly approve of your caution.'

'I needn't repeat that I know nothing yet of the why and wherefore,' said Mr. Tartar; 'but I also understand to what you tend, so let me say at once that my chambers are freely at your disposal.'

'There!' cried Mr. Grewgious, smoothing his head triumphantly, 'now we have all got the idea. You have it, my dear?'

'I think I have,' said Rosa, blushing a little as Mr. Tartar looked quickly towards her.

'You see, you go over to Staple with Mr. Crisparkle and Mr. Tartar,' said Mr. Grewgious; 'I going in and out, and out and in alone, in my usual way; you go up with those gentlemen to Mr. Tartar's rooms; you look into Mr. Tartar's flower-garden; you wait for Miss Helena's appearance there, or you signify to Miss Helena that you are close by; and you communicate with her freely and no spy can be the wiser.'

'I am very much afraid I shall be —'

'Be what, my dear?' asked Mr. Grewgious, as she hesitated. 'Not frightened?'

'No, not that,' said Rosa, shyly; 'in Mr. Tartar's way. We seem to be appropriating Mr. Tartar's residence so very coolly.'

'I protest to you,' returned that gentleman, 'that I shall think the better of it for evermore, if your voice sounds in it only once.'

Rosa, not quite knowing what to say about that, cast down her eyes, and turning to Mr. Grewgious, dutifully asked if she should put her hat on? Mr. Grewgious being of opinion that she could not do better, she withdrew for the purpose. Mr. Crisparkle took the opportunity of giving Mr. Tartar a summary of the distresses of Neville and his sister; the opportunity was quite long enough, as the hat happened to require a little extra fitting on.

Mr. Tartar gave his arm to Rosa, and Mr. Crisparkle walked, detached, in front.

'Poor, poor Eddy!' thought Rosa, as they went along.

Mr. Tartar waved his right hand as he bent his head down over Rosa, talking in an animated way.

'It was not so powerful or so sun-browned when it saved Mr. Crisparkle,' thought Rosa, glancing at it; 'but it must have been very steady and determined even then.'

Mr. Tartar told her he had been a sailor, roving everywhere for years and years.

'When are you going to sea again?' asked Rosa.

'Never!'

Rosa wondered what the girls would say if they could see her crossing the wide street on the sailor's arm. And she fancied that the passers-by must think her very little and very helpless, contrasted with the strong figure that could have caught her up and carried her out of any danger, miles and miles without resting.

She was thinking further, that his far-seeing blue eyes looked as if they had been used to watch danger afar off, and to watch it without flinching, drawing nearer and nearer: when, happening to raise her own eyes, she found that he seemed to be thinking something about *them*.

This a little confused Rosebud, and may account for her never afterwards quite knowing how she ascended (with his help) to his garden in the air, and seemed to get into a marvellous country that came into sudden bloom like the country on the summit of the magic bean-stalk. May it flourish for ever!

XXI

A Gritty State of Things Comes On

MR. TARTAR'S chambers were the neatest, the cleanest, and the best-ordered chambers ever seen under the sun, moon, and stars. The floors were scrubbed to that extent, that you might have supposed the London blacks emancipated for ever, and gone out of the land for good. Every inch of brass-work in Mr. Tartar's possession was polished and burnished, till it shone like a brazen mirror. No speck, nor spot, nor spatter soiled the purity of any of Mr. Tartar's household gods, large, small, or middle-sized. His sitting-room was like the admiral's cabin, his bath-room was like a dairy, his sleeping-chamber, fitted all about with lockers and drawers, was like a seedsman's shop; and his nicely-balanced cot just stirred in the midst, as if it breathed. Everything belonging to Mr. Tartar had quarters of its own assigned to it: his maps and charts had their quarters; his books had theirs; his brushes had theirs; his boots had theirs; his clothes had theirs; his case-bottles had theirs; his telescopes and other instruments had theirs. Everything was readily accessible. Shelf, bracket, locker, hook, and drawer were equally within reach, and were equally contrived with a view to avoiding waste of room, and providing some snug inches or stowage for something that would have exactly fitted nowhere else. His gleaming little service of plate was so arranged upon his sideboard as that a slack salt-spoon would have instantly betrayed itself; his toilet implements were so arranged upon his dressing-table as that a toothpick of slovenly deportment could have been reported at a glance. So with the curiosities he had brought home from various voyages. Stuffed, dried, repolished, or otherwise preserved, according to their kind; birds, fishes, reptiles, arms, articles of dress, shells, seaweeds, grasses, or memorials of coral reef; each was displayed in its especial place, and each could have been displayed in no better place. Paint and varnish seemed to be kept somewhere out of sight, in constant readiness to obliterate stray finger-marks wherever any might become perceptible in

Mr. Tartar's chambers. No man-of-war was ever kept more spick and span from careless touch. On this bright summer day, a neat awning was rigged over Mr. Tartar's flower-garden as only a sailor can rig it; and there was a sea-going air upon the whole effect, so delightfully complete, that the flower-garden might have appertained to stern-windows afloat, and the whole concern might have bowled away gallantly with all on board, if Mr. Tartar had only clapped to his lips the speaking-trumpet that was slung in a corner, and given hoarse orders to heave the anchor up, look alive there, men, and get all sail upon her!

Mr. Tartar doing the honours of this gallant craft was of a piece with the rest. When a man rides an amiable hobby that shies at nothing and kicks nobody, it is only agreeable to find him riding it with a humorous sense of the droll side of the creature. When the man is a cordial and an earnest man by nature, and withal is perfectly fresh and genuine, it may be doubted whether he is ever seen to greater advantage than at such a time. So Rosa would have naturally thought (even if she hadn't been conducted over the ship with all the homage due to the First Lady of the Admiralty, or First Fairy of the Sea), that it was charming to see and hear Mr. Tartar half laughing at, and half rejoicing in, his various contrivances. So Rosa would have naturally thought, anyhow, that the sunburnt sailor showed to great advantage when, the inspection finished, he delicately withdrew out of his admiral's cabin, beseeching her to consider herself its Queen, and waving her free of his flower-garden with the hand that had had Mr. Crisparkle's life in it.

'Helena! Helena Landless! Are you there?'

'Who speaks to me? Not Rosa?' Then a second handsome face appearing.

'Yes, my darling!'

'Why, how did you come here, dearest?'

'I — I don't quite know,' said Rosa with a blush; 'unless I am dreaming!'

Why with a blush? For their two faces were alone with the other flowers. Are blushes among the fruits of the country of the magic bean-stalk?

'*I* am not dreaming,' said Helena, smiling. 'I should take more for granted if I were. How do we come together — or so near together — so very unexpectedly?'

Unexpectedly indeed, among the dingy gables and chimney-pots of P. J. T.'s connection, and the flowers that had sprung from the salt sea. But Rosa, waking, told in a hurry how they came to be together, and all the why and wherefore of that matter.

'And Mr. Crisparkle is here,' said Rosa, in rapid conclusion; 'and, could you believe it? long ago he saved his life!'

'I could believe any such thing of Mr. Crisparkle,' returned Helena, with a mantling face.

(More blushes in the bean-stalk country!)

'Yes, but it wasn't Mr. Crisparkle,' said Rosa, quickly putting in the correction.

'I don't understand, love.'

'It was very nice of Mr. Crisparkle to be saved,' said Rosa, 'and he couldn't have shown his high opinion of Mr. Tartar more expressively. But it was Mr. Tartar who saved him.'

A meeting in Beanstalk country

Helena's dark eyes looked very earnestly at the bright face among the leaves, and she asked, in a slower and more thoughtful tone:

'Is Mr. Tartar with you now, dear?'

'No; because he has given up his rooms to me — to us, I mean. It is such a beautiful place!'

'Is it?'

'It is like the inside of the most exquisite ship that ever sailed. It is like — it is like ——'

'Like a dream?' suggested Helena.

Rosa answered with a little nod, and smelled the flowers.

Helena resumed, after a short pause of silence, during which she seemed (or it was Rosa's fancy) to compassionate somebody: 'My poor Neville is reading in his own room, the sun being so very bright on this side just now. I think he had better not know that you are so near.'

'O, I think so too!' cried Rosa very readily.

'I suppose,' pursued Helena, doubtfully, 'that he must know by-and-by all you have told me; but I am not sure. Ask Mr. Crisparkle's advice, my darling. Ask him whether I may tell Neville as much or as little of what you have told me as I think best.'

Rosa subsided into her state-cabin, and propounded the question. The Minor Canon was for the free exercise of Helena's judgment.

'I thank him very much,' said Helena, when Rosa emerged again with her report. 'Ask him where it would be best to wait until any more maligning and pursuing of Neville on the part of this wretch shall disclose itself, or to try to anticipate it: I mean, so far as to find out whether any such goes on darkly about us?'

The Minor Canon found this point so difficult to give a confident opinion on, that, after two or three attempts and failures, he suggested a reference to Mr. Grewgious. Helena acquiescing, he betook himself (with a most unsuccessful assumption of lounging indifference) across the quadrangle to P. J. T.'s, and stated it. Mr. Grewgious held decidedly to the general principle, that if you could steal a march upon a brigand or a wild beast, you had better do it; and he also held decidedly to the special case, that John Jasper was a brigand and a wild beast in combination.

Thus advised, Mr. Crisparkle came back again and reported to Rosa, who in her turn reported to Helena. She now steadily pursuing her train of thought at her window, considered thereupon.

'We may count on Mr. Tartar's readiness to help us, Rosa?' she inquired.

O yes! Rosa shyly thought so. O yes, Rosa shyly believed she could almost answer for it. But should she ask Mr. Crisparkle? 'I think your authority on the point as good as his, my dear,' said Helena, sedately, 'and you needn't disappear again for that.' Odd of Helena!

'You see, Neville,' Helena pursued after more reflection, 'knows no one else here: he has not so much as exchanged a word with any one else here. If Mr. Tartar would call to see him openly and often; if he would spare a minute for the purpose, frequently; if he would even do so, almost daily; something might come of it.'

'Something might come of it, dear?' repeated Rosa, surveying her friend's beauty with a highly perplexed face. 'Something might?'

'If Neville's movements are really watched, and if the purpose really is to isolate him from all friends and acquaintance and wear his daily life out grain by grain (which would seem to be the threat to you), does it not appear likely,' said Helena, 'that his enemy would in some way communicate with Mr. Tartar to warn him off from Neville? In which case, we might not only know the fact, but might know from Mr. Tartar what the terms of the communication were.'

'I see!' cried Rosa. And immediately darted into her state-cabin again.

Presently her pretty face reappeared, with a greatly heightened colour, and she said that she had told Mr. Crisparkle, and that Mr. Crisparkle had fetched in Mr. Tartar, and that Mr. Tartar — 'who is waiting now, in case you want him,' added Rosa, with a half look back, and in not a little confusion between the inside of the state-cabin and out — had declared his readiness to act as she had suggested, and to enter on his task that very day.

'I thank him from my heart,' said Helena. 'Pray tell him so.'

Again not a little confused between the Flower-garden and the Cabin, Rosa dipped in with her message, and dipped out again with more assurances from Mr. Tartar, and stood wavering in a divided state between Helena and him, which proved that confusion is not always necessarily awkward, but may sometimes present a very pleasant appearance.

'And now, darling,' said Helena, 'we will be mindful of the caution that has restricted us to this interview for the present, and will part. I hear Neville moving too. Are you going back?'

'To Miss Twinkleton's?' asked Rosa.

'Yes.'

'O, I could never go there any more; I couldn't indeed, after that dreadful interview!' said Rosa.

'Then where *are* you going, pretty one?'

'Now I come to think of it, I don't know,' said Rosa. 'I have settled nothing at all yet, but my guardian will take care of me. Don't be uneasy, dear. I shall be sure to be somewhere.'

(It did seem likely.)

'And I shall hear of my Rosebud from Mr. Tartar?' inquired Helena.

'Yes, I suppose so; from ——' Rosa looked back again in a flutter, instead of supplying the name. 'But tell me one thing before we part, dearest Helena. Tell me that you are sure, sure, sure, I couldn't help it.'

'Help it, love?'

'Help making him malicious and revengeful. I couldn't hold any terms with him, could I?'

'You know how I love you, darling,' answered Helena, with indignation; 'but I would sooner see you dead at his wicked feet.'

'That's a great comfort to me! And you will tell your poor brother so, won't you? And you will give him my remembrance and my sympathy? And you will ask him not to hate me?'

With a mournful shake of the head, as if that would be quite a superfluous entreaty, Helena lovingly kissed her two hands to her friend, and her friend's two hands were kissed to her; and then she saw a third hand (a brown one) appear among the flowers and leaves, and help her friend out of sight.

The refection that Mr. Tartar produced in the Admiral's Cabin by merely touching the spring knob of a locker and the handle of a drawer, was a dazzling enchanted repast. Wonderful macaroons, glittering liqueurs, magically-preserved tropical spices, and jellies of celestial tropical fruits, displayed themselves profusely at an instant's notice. But Mr. Tartar could not make time stand still; and time, with his hard-hearted fleetness, strode on so fast, that Rosa was obliged to come down from the bean-stalk country to earth and her guardian's chambers.

'And now, my dear,' said Mr. Grewgious, 'what is to be done next? To put the same thought in another form; what is to be done with you?'

Rosa could only look apologetically sensible of being very much in her own way and in everybody else's. Some passing idea of living, fireproof, up a good many stairs in Furnival's Inn for the rest of her life, was the only thing in the nature of a plan that occurred to her.

'It has come into my thoughts,' said Mr. Grewgious, 'that as the respected lady, Miss Twinkleton, occasionally repairs to London in the recess, with the view of extending her connection, and being available for interviews with metropolitan parents, if any — whether, until we have time in which to turn ourselves round, we might invite Miss Twinkleton to come and stay with you for a month?'

'Stay where, sir?'

'Whether,' explained Mr. Grewgious, 'we might take a furnished lodging in town for a month, and invite Miss Twinkleton to assume the charge of you in it for that period?'

'And afterwards?' hinted Rosa.

'And afterwards,' said Mr. Grewgious, 'we should be no worse off than we are now.'

'I think that might smooth the way,' assented Rosa.

'Then let us,' said Mr. Grewgious, rising, 'go and look for a furnished lodging. Nothing could be more acceptable to me than the sweet presence of last evening, for all the remaining evenings of my existence; but these are not fit surroundings for a young lady. Let us set out in quest of adventures, and look for a furnished lodging. In the meantime, Mr. Crisparkle here, about to return home immediately, will no doubt kindly see Miss Twinkleton, and invite that lady to co-operate in our plan.'

Mr. Crisparkle, willingly accepting the commission, took his departure; Mr. Grewgious and his ward set forth on their expedition.

As Mr. Grewgious's idea of looking at a furnished lodging was to get on the opposite side of the street to a house with a suitable bill in the window, and stare at it; and then work his way tortuously to the back of the house, and stare at that; and then not go in, but make similar trials of another house, with the same result; their progress was but slow. At length he bethought himself of a widowed cousin, divers times removed, of Mr. Bazzard's, who had once solicited his influence in the lodger world, and who lived in Southampton Street, Bloomsbury Square. This lady's name, stated in uncompromising capitals of considerable size on a brass doorplate, and yet not lucidly as to sex or condition, was BILLICKIN.

Personal faintness, and an overpowering personal candour, were the distinguishing features of Mrs. Billickin's organisation. She came languishing out of her own exclusive back parlour, with the air of having been expressly brought-to for the purpose, from an accumulation of several swoons.

'I hope I see you well, sir,' said Mrs. Billickin, recognising her visitor with a bend.

'Thank you, quite well. And you, ma'am?' returned Mr. Grewgious.

'I am as well,' said Mrs. Billickin, becoming aspirational with excess of faintness, 'as I hever ham.'

'My ward and an elderly lady', said Mr. Grewgious, 'wish to find a genteel lodging for a month or so. Have you any apartments available, ma'am?'

'Mr. Grewgious,' returned Mrs. Billickin, 'I will not deceive you; far from it. I *have* apartments available.'

This with the air of adding: 'Convey me to the stake, if you will; but while I live, I will be candid.'

'And now, what apartments, ma'am?' asked Mr. Grewgious, cosily. To tame a certain severity apparent on the part of Mrs. Billickin.

'There is this sitting-room — which, call it what you will, it is the front parlour, Miss,' said Mrs. Billickin, impressing Rosa into the conversation: 'the back parlour being what I cling to and never part with; and there is two bedrooms at the top of the 'ouse with gas laid on. I do not tell you that your bedroom floors is firm, for firm they are not. The gas-fitter himself allowed, that to make a firm job, he must go right under your jistes, and it were not worth the outlay as a yearly tenant so to do. The piping is carried above your jistes, and it is best that it should be made known to you.'

Mr. Grewgious and Rosa exchanged looks of some dismay, though they had not the least idea what latent horrors this carriage of the piping might involve. Mrs. Billickin put her hand to her heart, as having eased it of a load.

'Well! The roof is all right, no doubt,' said Mr. Grewgious, plucking up a little.

'Mr. Grewgious,' returned Mrs. Billickin, 'if I was to tell you, sir, that to have nothink above you is to have a floor above you, I should put a deception upon you which I will not do. No, sir. Your slates WILL rattle loose at that elewation in windy weather, do your utmost, best or worst! I defy you, sir, be you what you may, to keep your slates tight, try how you can.' Here Mrs. Billickin, having been warm with Mr. Grewgious, cooled a little, not to abuse the moral power she held over him. 'Consequent,' proceeded Mrs. Billickin, more mildly, but still firmly in her incorruptible candour: 'consequent it would be worse than of no use for me to trapse and travel up to the top of the 'ouse with you, and for you to say, "Mrs. Billickin, what stain do I notice in the ceiling, for a stain I do consider it?" and for me to answer, "I do not understand you, sir." No, sir, I will not be so underhand. I *do* understand you before you pint it out. It is the wet, sir. It do come in, and it do not come in. You may lay dry there half your lifetime; but the time will come, and it is best that you should know it, when a dripping sop would be no name for you.'

Mr. Grewgious looked much disgraced by being prefigured in this pickle.

'Have you any other apartments, ma'am?' he asked.

'Mr. Grewgious,' returned Mrs. Billickin, with much solemnity, 'I have. You ask me have I, and my open and my honest answer sir, I have. The first and second floors is wacant, and sweet rooms.'

'Come, come! There's nothing against *them,*' said Mr. Grewgious, comforting himself.

'Mr. Grewgious,' replied Mrs. Billickin, 'pardon me, there is the stairs. Unless your mind is prepared for the stairs, it will lead to inevitable disappointment. You cannot, Miss,' said Mrs. Billickin, addressing Rosa reproachfully, 'place a first floor, and far less a second, on the level footing of a parlour. No, you cannot do it, Miss, it is beyond your power, and wherefore try?'

Mrs. Billickin put it very feelingly, as if Rosa had shown a headstrong determination to hold the untenable position.

'Can we see these rooms, ma'am?' inquired her guardian.

'Mr. Grewgious,' returned Mrs. Billickin, 'you can. I will not disguise it from you, sir; you can.'

Mrs. Billickin then sent into her back parlour for her shawl (it being a state fiction, dating from immemorial antiquity, that she could never go anywhere without being wrapped up), and having been enrolled by her attendant, led the way. She made various genteel pauses on the stairs for breath, and clutched at her heart in the drawing-room as if it had very nearly got loose, and she had caught it in the act of taking wing.

'And the second floor?' said Mr. Grewgious, on finding the first satisfactory.

'Mr. Grewgious,' replied Mrs. Billickin, turning upon him with ceremony, as if the time had now come when a distinct understanding on a difficult point must be arrived at, and a solemn confidence established, 'the second floor is over this.'

'Can we see that too, ma'am?'

'Yes, sir,' returned Mrs. Billickin, 'it is open as the day.'

That also proving satisfactory, Mr. Grewgious retired into a window with Rosa for a few words of consultation, and then asking for pen and ink, sketched out a line or two of agreement. In the meantime Mrs. Billickin took a seat, and delivered a kind of Index to, or Abstract of, the general question.

'Five-and-forty shillings per week by the month certain at the time of year,' said Mrs. Billickin, 'is only reasonable to both parties. It is not Bond Street nor yet St. James's Palace; but it is not pretended that it is. Neither is it attempted to be denied — for why should it? — that the Arching leads to a mews. Mewses must exist. Respecting attendance; two is kep', at liberal wages. Words *has* arisen as to tradesmen, but dirty shoes on fresh hearth-stoning was attributable, and no wish for a commission on your orders. Coals is either *by* the fire, or *per* the scuttle.' She emphasised the prepositions as marking a subtle but immense difference. 'Dogs is not viewed with faviour. Besides litter, they gets stole, and sharing suspicions is apt to creep in, and unpleasantness takes place.'

By this time Mr. Grewgious had his agreement-lines, and his earnest-money, ready. 'I have signed it for the ladies, ma'am,' he said, 'and you'll have the goodness to sign it for yourself, Christian and Surname, there, if you please.'

'Mr. Grewgious,' said Mrs. Billickin in a new burst of candour, 'no, sir! You must excuse the Christian name.'

Mr. Grewgious stared at her.

'The door-plate is used as a protection,' said Mrs. Billickin, 'and acts as such, and go from it I will not.'

Mr. Grewgious stared at Rosa.

'No, Mr. Grewgious, you must excuse me. So long as this 'ouse is known indefinite as Billickin's, and so long as it is a doubt with the riff-raff where Billickin may be hidin', near the street-door or down the airy, and what his weight and size, so long I feel safe. But commit myself to a solitary female statement, no, Miss! Nor would you for a moment wish,' said Mrs. Billickin, with a strong sense of injury, 'to take that advantage of your sex, if you were not brought to it by inconsiderable example.'

Rosa reddening as if she had made some most disgraceful attempt to overreach the good lady, besought Mr. Grewgious to rest content with any signature. And accordingly, in a baronial way, the sign-manual BILLICKIN got appended to the document.

Details were then settled for taking possession on the next day but one, when Miss Twinkleton might be reasonably expected; and Rosa went back to Furnival's Inn on her guardian's arm.

Behold Mr. Tartar walking up and down Furnival's Inn, checking himself when he saw them coming, and advancing towards them!

'It occurred to me,' hinted Mr. Tartar, 'that we might go up the river, the weather being so delicious and the tide serving. I have a boat of my own at the Temple Stairs.'

'I have not been up the river for this many a day,' said Mr. Grewgious, tempted.

'I was never up the river,' added Rosa.

Within half an hour they were setting this matter right by going up the river. The tide was running with them, the afternoon was charming. Mr. Tartar's boat was perfect. Mr. Tartar and Lobley (Mr. Tartar's man) pulled a pair of oars. Mr. Tartar had a yacht, it seemed, lying somewhere down by Greenhithe; and Mr. Tartar's man had charge of this yacht, and was detached upon his present service. He was a jolly-favoured man, with tawny hair and whiskers, and a big red face. He was the dead image of the sun in old woodcuts, his hair and whiskers answering for rays all around him. Resplendent in the bow of the boat, he was a shining sight, with a man-of-war's man's shirt on — or off, according to opinion — and his arms and breast tattooed all sorts of patterns. Lobley seemed to take it easily, and so did Mr. Tartar; yet their oars bent as they pulled, and the boat bounded under them. Mr. Tartar talked as if he were doing nothing, to Rosa who was really doing nothing, and to Mr. Grewgious who was doing this much that he steered all wrong; but what did that matter, when a turn of Mr. Tartar's skilful wrist, or a mere grin of Mr. Lobley's over the bow, put all to rights! The tide bore them on in the gayest and most sparkling manner, until they stopped to dine in some ever-lastingly-green garden, needing no matter-of-fact identification here; and then the tide obligingly turned — being devoted to that party alone for that day; and as they floated idly among some osier-beds, Rosa tried what she could do in the rowing way, and came off splendidly, being much assisted; and Mr. Grewgious tried what he could do, and came off on his back, doubled up with an oar under his chin, being not assisted at all. Then there was an interval of rest under boughs (such rest!) what time Mr. Lobley mopped, and, arranging cushions, stretchers, and the like, danced the tight-rope the whole length of the boat like a man to whom shoes were a superstition and stockings slavery; and then came the sweet return among delicious odours of limes in bloom, and musical ripplings; and, all too soon, the great black city cast its shadow on the waters, and its dark bridges spanned them as death spans life, and the everlastingly-green garden seemed to be left for everlasting, unregainable and far away.

'Cannot people get through life without gritty stages, I wonder?' Rosa thought next day, when the town was very gritty again, and everything had a strange and an uncomfortable appearance of seeming to wait for something that wouldn't come. No. She began to think, that, now the Cloisterham school-days had glided past and gone, the gritty stages would begin to set in at intervals and make themselves wearily known!

Yet what did Rosa expect? Did she expect Miss Twinkleton? Miss Twinkleton duly came. Forth from her back parlour issued the Billickin to receive Miss Twinkleton, and War was in the Billickin's eye from that fell moment.

Miss Twinkleton brought a quantity of luggage with her, having all Rosa's as well as her own. The Billickin took it ill that Miss Twinkleton's mind, being sorely disturbed by this luggage, failed to take in her personal identity with that clearness of perception which was due to its demands. Stateliness mounted her gloomy throne upon the Billickin's brow in consequence. And when Miss Twinkleton, in agitation taking stock of her trunks and packages, of which she had seventeen, particularly counted in the Billickin herself as number eleven, the B. found it necessary to repudiate.

'Things cannot too soon be put upon the footing,' said she, with a candour so demonstrative as to be almost obtrusive, 'that the person of the 'ouse is not a box nor yet a bundle, nor a carpetbag. No, I am 'ily obleeged to you, Miss Twinkleton, nor yet a beggar.'

This last disclaimer had reference to Miss Twinkleton's distractedly pressing two-and-sixpence on her, instead of the cabman.

Thus cast off, Miss Twinkleton wildly inquired, 'which gentleman' was to be paid? There being two gentlemen in that position (Miss Twinkleton having arrived with two cabs), each gentleman on being paid held forth his two-and-sixpence on the flat of his open hand, and, with a speechless stare and a dropped jaw, displayed his wrong to heaven and earth. Terrified by this alarming spectacle, Miss Twinkleton placed another shilling in each hand; at the same time appealing to the law in flurried accents, and recounting her luggage this time with the two gentlemen in, who caused the total to come out complicated. Meanwhile the two gentlemen, each looking very hard at the last shilling grumblingly, as if it might become eighteenpence if he kept his eyes on it, descended the doorsteps, ascended their carriages, and drove away, leaving Miss Twinkleton on a bonnet-box in tears.

The Billickin beheld this manifestation of weakness without sympathy, and gave directions for 'a young man to be got in' to wrestle with the luggage. When that gladiator had disappeared from the arena, peace ensued, and the new lodgers dined.

But the Billickin had somehow come to the knowledge that Miss Twinkleton kept a school. The leap from that knowledge to the inference that Miss Twinkleton set herself to teach *her* something, was easy. 'But you don't do it,' soliloquised the Billickin; '*I* am not your pupil, whatever she,' meaning Rosa, 'may be, poor thing!'

Miss Twinkleton, on the other hand, having changed her dress and recovered her spirits, was animated by a bland desire to improve the occasion in all ways, and to be as serene a model as possible. In a happy compromise between her two states of existence, she had already become, with her workbasket before her, the equably vivacious companion with a slight judicious flavouring of information, when the Billickin announced herself.

'I will not hide from you, ladies,' said the B., enveloped in the shawl of state, 'for it is not my character to hide neither my motives nor my actions, that I take the liberty to look in upon you to express a 'ope that your dinner was to your liking. Though not Professed but Plain, still her wages should be a sufficient object to her to stimilate to soar above mere roast and biled.'

'We dined very well indeed,' said Rosa, 'thank you.'

'Accustomed,' said Miss Twinkleton with a gracious air, which to the jealous ears of the Billickin seemed to add 'my good woman' — 'accustomed to a liberal and nutritious, yet plain and salutary diet, we have found no reason to bemoan our absence from the ancient city, and the methodical household, in which the quiet routine of our lot has been hitherto cast.'

'I did think it well to mention to my cook,' observed the Billickin with a gush of candour, 'which I 'ope you will agree with, Miss Twinkleton, was a right precaution, that the young lady being used to what we should consider here but poor diet, had better be brought forward by degrees. For, a rush from scanty feeding to generous feeding, and from what you may call messing to what you may call method, do require a power of constitution which is not often found in youth, particular when undermined by boarding-school!'

It will be seen that the Billickin now openly pitted herself against Miss Twinkleton, as one whom she had fully ascertained to be her natural enemy.

'Your remarks,' returned Miss Twinkleton, from a remote moral eminence, 'are well meant, I have no doubt; but you will permit me to observe that they develop a mistaken view of the subject, which can only be imputed to your extreme want of accurate information.'

'My informiation,' retorted the Billickin, throwing in an extra syllable for the sake of emphasis at once polite and powerful — 'my informiation, Miss Twinkleton, were my own experience, which I believe is usually considered to be good guidance. But whether so or not, I was put in youth to a very genteel boarding-school, the mistress being no less a lady than yourself, of about your own age or it may be some years younger, and a poorness of blood flowed from the table which has run through my life.'

'Very likely,' said Miss Twinkleton, still from her distant eminence; 'and very much to be deplored. — Rosa, my dear, how are you getting on with your work?'

'Miss Twinkleton,' resumed the Billickin, in a courtly manner, 'before retiring on the 'int, as a lady should, I wish to ask of yourself, as a lady, whether I am to consider that my words is doubted?'

'I am not aware on what ground you cherish such a supposition,' began Miss Twinkleton, when the Billickin neatly stopped her.

'Do not, if you please, put suppositions betwixt my lips where none such have been imparted by myself. Your flow of words is great, Miss Twinkleton, and no doubt is expected from you by your pupils, and no doubt is considered worth the money. *No* doubt, I am sure. But not paying for flows of words, and not asking to be favoured with them here, I wish to repeat my question.'

'If you refer to the poverty of your circulation,' began Miss Twinkleton, when again the Billickin neatly stopped her.

'I have used no such expressions.'

'If you refer, then, to the poorness of your blood ——'

'Brought upon me,' stipulated the Billickin, expressly, 'at a boarding-school ——'

'Then,' resumed Miss Twinkleton, 'all I can say is, that I am bound to believe, on your asseveration, that it is very poor indeed. I cannot forebear adding, that if that unfortunate circumstance influences your conversation, it is much to be lamented, and it is eminently desirable that your blood were richer. — Rosa, my dear, how are you getting on with your work?'

'Hem! Before retiring, Miss,' proclaimed the Billickin to Rosa, loftily cancelling Miss Twinkleton, 'I should wish it to be understood between yourself and me that my transactions in future is with you alone. I know no elderly lady here, Miss, none older than yourself.'

'A highly desirable arrangement, Rosa my dear,' observed Miss Twinkleton.

'It is not, Miss,' said the Billickin, with a sarcastic smile, 'that I possess the Mill I have heard of, in which old single ladies could be ground up young (what a gift it would be to some of us), but that I limit myself to you totally.'

'When I have any desire to communicate a request to the person of the house, Rosa my dear,' observed Miss Twinkleton with majestic cheerfulness, 'I will make it known to you, and you will kindly undertake, I am sure, that it is conveyed to the proper quarter.'

'Good-evening, Miss,' said the Billickin, at once affectionately and distantly. 'Being alone in my eyes, I wish you good-evening with best wishes, and do not find myself drove, I am truly 'appy to say, into expressing my contempt for an indiwidual, unfortunately for yourself, belonging to you.'

The Billickin gracefully withdrew with this parting speech, and from that time Rosa occupied the restless position of shuttlecock between these two battledores. Nothing could be done without a smart match being played out. Thus, on the daily-arising question of dinner, Miss Twinkleton would say, the three being present together:

'Perhaps, my love, you will consult with the person of the house, whether she can procure us a lamb's fry; or, failing that, a roast fowl.'

On which the Billickin would retort (Rosa not having spoken a word), 'If you was better accustomed to butcher's meat, Miss, you would not entertain the idea of a lamb's fry. Firstly, because lambs has long been sheep, and secondly, because there is such things as killing-days, and there is not. As to roast fowls, Miss, why you must be quite surfeited with roast fowls, letting alone your buying, when you market for yourself the agedest of poultry with the scaliest of legs, quite as if you was accustomed to picking 'em out for cheapness. Try a little inwention, Miss. Use yourself to 'ousekeeping a bit. Come now, think of somethink else.'

To this encouragement, offered with the indulgent toleration of a wise and liberal expert, Miss Twinkleton would rejoin, reddening:

'Or, my dear, you might propose to the person of the house a duck.'

'Well, Miss!' the Billickin would exclaim (still no word being spoken by Rosa), 'you do surprise me when you speak of ducks! Not to mention that they're getting out of season and very dear, it really strikes to my heart to see you have a duck; for the breast, which is the only delicate cuts in a duck, always goes in a direction which I cannot imagine where, and your own plate comes down so miserably skin-and-bony! Try again, Miss. Think more of yourself, and less of others. A dish of sweetbreads now, or a bit of mutton. Something at which you can get your equal chance.'

Occasionally the game would wax very brisk indeed, and would be kept up with a smartness rendering such an encounter as this quite tame. But the Billickin almost invariably made by far the higher score; and would come in with side hits of the most unexpected and extraordinary description, when she seemed without a chance.

All this did not improve the gritty state of things in London, or the air that London had acquired in Rosa's eyes of waiting for something that never came. Tired of working, and conversing with Miss Twinkleton, she suggested working and reading: to which Miss Twinkleton readily assented, as an admirable reader, of tried powers. But Rosa soon made the discovery that Miss Twinkleton didn't read fairly. She cut the love-scenes, interpolated passages in praise of female celibacy, and was guilty of other glaring pious frauds. As an instance in point, take the glowing passage: 'Ever dearest and best adored, — said Edward, clasping the dear head to his breast, and drawing the silken hair through his caressing fingers, from which he suffered it to fall like golden rain, — ever dearest and best adored, let us fly from the unsympathetic world and the sterile coldness of the stony-hearted, to the rich warm Paradise of Trust and Love.' Miss Twinkleton's fraudulent version tamely ran thus: 'Ever engaged to me with the consent of our parents on both sides, and the approbation of the silver-haired rector of the district, — said Edward, respectfully raising to his lips the taper fingers so skilful in embroidery, tambour, crochet, and other truly feminine arts, — let me call on thy papa ere to-morrow's dawn has sunk into the west, and propose a suburban establishment, lowly it may be, but within our means, where he will be always welcome as an evening guest, and where every arrangement shall invest economy, and constant interchange of scholastic acquirements with the attributes of the ministering angel to domestic bliss.'

As the days crept on and nothing happened, the neighbours began to say that the pretty girl at Billickin's, who looked so wistfully and so much out of the gritty windows of the drawing-room, seemed to be losing her spirits. The pretty girl might have lost them but for the accident of lighting on some books of voyages and sea-adventure. As a compensation against their romance, Miss Twinkleton, reading aloud, made the most of all the latitudes and longitudes, bearings, winds, currents, offsets, and other statistics (which she felt to be none the less improving because they expressed nothing whatever to her); while Rosa, listening intently, made the most of what was nearest to her heart. So they both did better than before.

The Dawn Again

ALTHOUGH Mr. Crisparkle and John Jasper met daily under the Cathedral roof, nothing at any time passed between them having reference to Edwin Drood, after the time, more than half a year gone by, when Jasper mutely showed the Minor Canon the conclusion and the resolution entered in his Diary. It is not likely that they ever met, though so often, without the thoughts of each reverting to the subject. It is not likely that they ever met, though so often, without a sensation on the part of each that the other was a perplexing secret to him. Jasper as the denouncer and pursuer of Neville Landless, and Mr. Crisparkle as his consistent advocate and protector, must at least have stood sufficiently in opposition to have speculated with keen interest on the steadiness and next direction of the other's designs. But neither ever broached the theme.

False pretence not being in the Minor Canon's nature, he doubtless displayed openly that he would at any time have revived the subject, and even desired to discuss it. The determined reticence of Jasper, however, was not to be so approached. Impassive, moody, solitary, resolute, so concentrated on one idea, and on its attendant fixed purpose, that he would share it with no fellow-creature, he lived apart from human life. Constantly exercising an Art which brought him into mechanical harmony with others, and which could not have been pursued unless he and they had been in the nicest mechanical relations and unison, it is curious to consider that the spirit of the man was in moral accordance or interchange with nothing around him. This indeed he had confided to his lost nephew, before the occasion for his present inflexibility arose.

That he must know of Rosa's abrupt departure, and that he must divine its cause, was not to be doubted. Did he suppose that he had terrified her into silence? or did he suppose that she had imparted to any one — to Mr. Crisparkle himself, for instance — the particulars of his last interview with her? Mr. Crisparkle could not determine this in his mind. He could not but admit, however, as a just man, that it was not, of itself, a crime to fall in love with Rosa, any more than it was a crime to offer to set love above revenge.

The dreadful suspicion of Jasper, which Rosa was so shocked to have received into her imagination, appeared to have no harbour in Mr. Crisparkle's. If it ever haunted Helena's thoughts or Neville's, neither gave it one spoken word of utterance. Mr. Grewgious took no pains to conceal his implacable dislike of Jasper, yet he never referred it, however distantly, to such a source. But he was a reticent as well as an eccentric man; and he made no mention of a certain evening when he warmed his hands at the gatehouse fire, and looked steadily down upon a certain heap of torn and miry clothes upon the floor.

Drowsy Cloisterham, whenever it awoke to a passing reconsideration of a story above six months old and dismissed by the bench of magistrates, was pretty equally divided in opinion whether John Jasper's beloved nephew had been killed by his treacherously passionate rival, or in an open struggle; or had, for his own purposes, spirited himself away. It then lifted up its head, to notice that the bereaved Jasper was still ever devoted to discovery and revenge; and then dozed off again. This was the condition of matters, all round, at the period to which the present history has now attained.

The Cathedral doors have closed for the night; and the Choir Master, on a short leave of absence for two or three services, sets his face towards London. He travels thither by the means by which Rosa travelled, and arrives, as Rosa arrived, on a hot, dusty evening.

His travelling baggage is easily carried in his hand, and he repairs with it on foot, to a hybrid hotel in a little square behind Aldersgate Street, near the General Post Office. It is hotel, boarding-house, or lodging-house, at its visitor's option. It announced itself, in the new Railway Advertisers, as a novel enterprise, timidly beginning to spring up. It bashfully, almost apologetically, gives the traveller to understand that it does not expect him, on the good old constitutional hotel plan, to order a pint of sweet blacking for his drinking, and throw it away; but insinuates that he may have his boots blacked instead of his stomach, and maybe also have bed, breakfast, attendance, and a porter up all night, for a certain fixed charge. From these and similar premises, many true Britons in the lowest spirits deduce that the times are levelling times, except in the article of high roads, of which there will shortly be not one in England.

He eats without appetite, and soon goes forth again. Eastward and still eastward through the stale streets he takes his way, until he reaches his destination: a miserable court, specially miserable among many such.

He ascends a broken staircase, opens a door, looks into a dark stifling room, and says: 'Are you alone here?'

'Alone, deary; worse luck for me, and better for you,' replies a croaking voice. 'Come in, come in, whoever you be: I can't see you till I light a match, yet I seem to know the sound of your speaking. I'm acquainted with you, ain't I?'

'Light your match, and try.'

'So I will, deary, so I will; but my hand that shakes, as I can't lay it on a match all in a moment. And I cough so, that, put my matches where I may, I never find 'em there. They jump and start, as I cough and cough, like live things. Are you off a voyage, deary?'

'No.'

'Not seafaring?'

'No.'

'Well, there's land customers, and there's water customers. I'm a mother to both. Different from Jack Chinaman t'other side the court. He ain't a father to neither. It ain't in him. And he ain't got the true secret of mixing, though he charges as much as me that has, and more if he can get it. Here's a match, and now where's the candle? If my cough takes me, I shall cough out twenty matches afore I gets a light.'

But she finds the candle, and lights it, before the cough comes on. It seizes her in the moment of success, and she sits down rocking herself to and fro, and gasping at intervals: 'O, my lungs is awful bad! my lungs is wore away to cabbage-nets!' until the fit is over. During its continuance she has had no power of sight, or any other power not absorbed in the struggle; but as it leaves her, she begins to strain her eyes, and as soon as she is able to articulate, she cries, staring:

'Why, it's you!'

'Are you so surprised to see me?'

'I thought I never should have seen you again, deary. I thought you was dead, and gone to Heaven.'

'Why?'

'I didn't suppose you could have kept away, alive, so long, from the poor old soul with the real receipt for mixing it. And you are in mourning too! Why didn't you come and have a pipe or two of comfort? Did they leave you money, perhaps, and so you didn't want comfort?'

'No.'

'Who was they as died, deary?'

'A relative.'

'Died of what, lovey?'

'Probably, Death.'

'We are short to-night!' cries the woman, with a propitiatory laugh. 'Short and snappish we are! But we're out of sorts for want of a smoke. We've got the all-overs, haven't us, deary? But this is the place to cure 'em in; this is the place where the all-overs is smoked off.'

'You may make ready, then,' replies the visitor, 'as soon as you like.'

He divests himself of his shoes, loosens his cravat, and lies across the foot of the squalid bed, with his head resting on his left hand.

'Now you begin to look like yourself,' says the woman approvingly. 'Now I begin to know my old customer indeed! Been trying to mix for yourself this long time, poppet?'

'I have been taking it now and then in my own way.'

'Never take it your own way. It ain't good for trade, and it ain't good for you. Where's my ink-bottle, and where's my thimble, and where's my little spoon? He's going to take it in a artful form now, my deary dear!'

Entering on her process, and beginning to bubble and blow at the faint spark enclosed in the hollow of her hands, she speaks from time to time, in a tone of snuffling satisfaction, without leaving off. When he speaks, he does so without looking at her, and as if his thoughts were already roaming away by anticipation.

'I've got a pretty many smokes ready for you, first and last, haven't I, chuckey?'

'A good many.'

'When you first come, you was quite new to it; warn't ye?'

'Yes, I was easily disposed of, then.'

'But you got on in the world, and was able by-and-by to take your pipe with the best of 'em, warn't ye?'

'Ah; and the worst.'

'It's just ready for you. What a sweet singer you was when you first come! Used to drop your head, and sing yourself off like a bird! It's ready for you now, deary.'

He takes it from her with great care, and puts the mouthpiece to his lips. She seats herself beside him, ready to refill the pipe. After inhaling a few whiffs in silence, he doubtingly accosts her with:

'Is it as potent as it used to be?'

'What do you speak of, deary?'

'What should I speak of, but what I have in my mouth?'

'It's just the same. Always the identical same.'

'It doesn't taste so. And it's slower.'

'You've got more used to it, you see.'

'That may be the cause, certainly. Look here.' He stops, becomes dreamy, and seems to forget that he has invited her attention. She bends over him, and speaks in his ear.

'I'm attending to you. Says you just now, Look here. Says I now, I'm attending to ye. We was talking just before of your being used to it.'

'I know all that. I was only thinking. Look here. Suppose you had something in your mind; something you were going to do.'

'Yes, deary; something I was going to do?'

'But had not quite determined to do.'

'Yes, deary.'

'Might or might not do, you understand.'

'Yes.' With the point of a needle she stirs the contents of the bowl.

'Should you do it in your fancy, when you were lying here doing this?'

She nods her head. 'Over and over again.'

'Just like me! I did it over and over again. I have done it hundreds of thousands of times in this room.'

'It's to be hoped it was pleasant to do, deary.'

'It *was* pleasant to do!'

He says this with a savage air, and a spring or start at her. Quite unmoved she retouches and replenishes the contents of the bowl with her little spatula. Seeing her intent upon the occupation, he sinks into his former attitude.

'It was a journey, a difficult and dangerous journey. That was the subject in my mind. A hazardous and perilous journey, over abysses where a slip would be destruction. Look down, look down! You see what lies at the bottom there?'

He has darted forward to say it, and to point at the ground, as though at some imaginary object far beneath. The woman looks at him, as his spasmodic face approaches close to hers, and not at his pointing. She seems to know what the influence of her perfect quietude would be; if so, she has not miscalculated it, for he subsides again.

'Well; I have told you I did it here hundreds of thousands of times. What do I say? I did it millions and billions of times. I did it so often, and through such vast expanses of time, that when it was really done, it seemed not worth the doing, it was done so soon.'

'That's the journey you have been away upon,' she quietly remarks.

He glares at her as he smokes; and then, his eyes becoming filmy, answers: 'That's the journey.'

Silence ensues. His eyes are sometimes closed and sometimes open. The woman sits beside him, very attentive to the pipe which is all the while at his lips.

'I'll warrant,' she observes, when he has been looking fixedly at her for some consecutive moments, with a singular appearance in his eyes of seeming to see her a long way off, instead of so near him: 'I'll warrant you made the journey in a many ways, when you made it so often?'

'No, always in one way.'

'Always in the same way?'

'Ay.'

'In the way in which it was really made at last?'

'Ay.'

'And always took the same pleasure in harping on it?'

'Ay.'

For the time he appears unequal to any other reply than this lazy monosyllabic assent. Probably to assure herself that it is not the assent of a mere automaton, she reverses the form of her next sentence.

'Did you never get tired of it, deary, and try to call up something else for a change?'

He struggles into a sitting posture, and retorts upon her: 'What do you mean? What did I want? What did I come for?'

She gently lays him back again, and before returning him the instrument he has dropped, revives the fire in it with her own breath; then says to him, coaxingly:

'Sure, sure, sure! Yes, yes, yes! Now I go along with you. You was too quick for me. I see now. You come o' purpose to take the journey. Why, I might have known it, through its standing by you so.'

He answers first with a laugh, and then with a passionate setting of his teeth: 'Yes, I came on purpose. When I could not bear my life, I came to get the relief, and I got it. It was one! It was one!' This repetition with extraordinary vehemence, and the snarl of a wolf.

She observes him very cautiously, as though mentally feeling her way to her next remark. It is: 'There was a fellow-traveller, deary.'

'Ha, ha, ha!' He breaks into a ringing laugh, or rather yell.

'To think,' he cries, 'how often fellow-traveller, and yet not know it!

To think how many times he went the journey, and never saw the road!'

The woman kneels upon the floor, with her arms crossed on the coverlet of the bed, close by him, and her chin upon them. In this crouching attitude she watches him. The pipe is falling from his mouth. She puts it back, and laying her hand upon his chest, moves him slightly from side to side. Upon that he speaks, as if she had spoken.

'Yes! I always made the journey first, before the changes of colours and the great landscapes and glittering processions began. They couldn't begin till it was off my mind. I had no room till then for anything else.'

Once more he lapses into silence. Once more she lays her hand upon his chest, and moves him slightly to and fro, as a cat might stimulate a half-slain mouse. Once more he speaks, as if she had spoken.

'What? I told you so. When it comes to be real at last, it is so short that it seems unreal for the first time. Hark!'

'Yes, deary. I'm listening.'

'Time and place are both at hand.'

He is on his feet, speaking in a whisper, and as if in the dark.

'Time, place, and fellow-traveller,' she suggests, adopting his tone, and holding him softly by the arm.

'How could the time be at hand unless the fellow-traveller was? Hush! The journey's made. It's over.'

'So soon?'

'That's what I said to you. So soon. Wait a little. This is a vision. I shall sleep it off. It has been too short and easy. I must have a better vision than this; this is the poorest of all. No struggle, no consciousness of peril, no entreaty — and yet I never saw *that* before.' With a start.

'Saw what, deary?'

'Look at it! Look what a poor, mean, miserable thing it is! *That* must be real. It's over.'

He has accompanied this incoherence with some wild unmeaning gestures; but they trail off into the progressive inaction of stupor, and he lies a log upon the bed.

The woman, however, is still inquisitive. With a repetition of her cat-like action she slightly stirs his body again, and listens; stirs again, and listens; whispers to it, and listens. Finding it past all rousing for the time, she slowly gets upon her feet, with an air of disappointment, and flicks the face with the back of her hand in turning from it.

But she goes no further away from it than the chair upon the hearth. She sits in it, with an elbow on one of its arms, and her chin upon her hand, intent upon him. 'I heard ye say once,' she croaks under her breath, 'I heard ye say once, when I was lying where you're lying, and you were making your speculations upon me, "Unintelligible!" I heard you say so, of two more than me. But don't ye be too sure always; don't be ye too sure, beauty!'

Unwinking, cat-like, and intent, she presently adds: 'Not so potent as it once was? Ah! Perhaps not at first. You may be more right there. Practice makes perfect. I may have learned the secret how to make ye talk, deary.'

He talks no more, whether or no. Twitching in an ugly way from time to time, both as to his face and limbs, he lies heavy and silent. The wretched

Jasper looks like himself again

candle burns down; the woman takes its expiring end between her fingers, lights another at it, crams the guttering frying morsel deep into the candlestick, and rams it home with the new candle, as if she were loading some ill-savoured and unseemly weapon of witchcraft; the new candle in its turn burns down; and still he lies insensible. At length what remains of the last candle is blown out, and daylight looks into the room.

It has not looked very long, when he sits up, chilled and shaking, slowly recovers consciousness of where he is, and makes himself ready to depart. The woman receives what he pays her with a grateful, 'Bless ye, bless ye, deary!' and seems, tired out, to begin making herself ready for sleep as he leaves the room.

But seeming may be false or true. It is false in this case; for the moment the stairs have ceased to creak under his tread, she glides after him, muttering emphatically: 'I'll not miss ye twice!'

There is no egress from the court but by its entrance. With a weird peep from the doorway, she watches for his looking back. He does not look back before disappearing, with a wavering step. She follows him, peeps from the court, sees him still faltering on without looking back, and holds him in view.

He repairs to the back of Aldersgate Street, where a door immediately opens to his knocking. She crouches in another doorway, watching that one, and easily comprehending that he puts up temporarily at that house. Her patience is unexhausted by hours. For sustenance she can, and does, buy bread within a hundred yards, and milk as it is carried past her.

He comes forth again at noon, having changed his dress, but carrying nothing in his hand, and having nothing carried for him. He is not going back into the country, therefore, just yet. She follows him a little way, hesitates, instantaneously turns confidently, and goes straight into the house he has quitted.

'Is the gentleman from Cloisterham indoors?'

'Just gone out.'

'Unlucky. When does the gentleman return to Cloisterham?'

'At six this evening.'

'Bless ye and thank ye. May the Lord prosper a business where a civil question, even from a poor soul, is so civilly answered!'

'I'll not miss ye twice!' repeats the poor soul in the street, and not so civilly. 'I lost ye last, where that omnibus you got into nigh your journey's end plied betwixt the station and the place. I wasn't so much as certain that you even went right on to the place. Now I know ye did. My gentleman from Cloisterham, I'll be there before ye, and bide your coming. I've swore my oath that I'll not miss ye twice!'

Accordingly, that same evening the poor soul stands in Cloisterham High Street, looking at the many quaint gables of the Nuns' House, and getting through the time as she best can until nine o'clock; at which hour she has reason to suppose that the arriving omnibus passengers may have some interest for her. The friendly darkness, at that hour, renders it easy for her to ascertain whether this be so or not; and it is so, for the passenger not to be missed twice arrives among the rest.

'Now let me see what becomes of you. Go on!'

An observation addressed to the air, and yet it might be addressed to the passenger, so compliantly does he go on along the High Street until he comes to an arched gateway, at which he unexpectedly vanishes. The poor soul quickens her pace; is swift, and close upon him entering under the gateway; but only sees a postern staircase on one side of it, and on the other side an ancient vaulted room, in which a large-headed, gray-haired gentleman is writing, under the odd circumstances of sitting open to the thoroughfare and eyeing all who pass, as if he were toll-taker of the gateway: though the way is free.

'Halloa!' he cries in a low voice, seeing her brought to a standstill: 'who are you looking for?'

'There was a gentleman passed in here this minute, sir.'

'Of course there was. What do you want with him?'

'Where do he live, deary?'

'Live? Up that staircase.'

'Bless ye! Whisper. What's his name, deary?'

'Surname Jasper, Christian name John. Mr. John Jasper.'

'Has he a calling, good gentleman?'

'Calling? Yes. Sings in the choir.'

'In the spire?'

'Choir.'

'What's that?'

Mr. Datchery rises from his papers, and comes to his doorstep. 'Do you know what a cathedral is?' he asks, jocosely.

The woman nods.

'What is it?'

She looks puzzled, casting about in her mind to find a definition, when it occurs to her that it is easier to point out the substantial object itself, massive against the dark-blue sky and the early stars.

'That's the answer. Go in there at seven to-morrow morning, and you may see Mr. John Jasper, and hear him too.'

'Thank ye! Thank ye!'

The burst of triumph in which she thanks him does not escape the notice of the single buffer of an easy temper living idly on his means. He glances at her; clasps his hands behind him, as the wont of such buffers is; and lounges along the echoing Precincts at her side.

'Or,' he suggests, with a backward hitch of his head, 'you can go up at once to Mr. Jasper's rooms there.'

The woman eyes him with a cunning smile, and shakes her head.

'O! you don't want to speak to him?'

She repeats her dumb reply, and forms with her lips a soundless 'No.'

'You can admire him at a distance three times a day, whenever you like. It's a long way to come for that, though.'

The woman looks up quickly. If Mr. Datchery thinks she is to be so induced to declare where she comes from, he is of a much easier temper than she is. But she acquits him of such an artful thought, as he lounges along, like the chartered bore of the city, with his uncovered gray hair blowing about, and his purposeless hands rattling the loose money in the pockets of his trousers.

The chink of the money has an attraction for her greedy ears. 'Wouldn't you help me to pay for my traveller's lodging, dear gentleman, and to pay my way along? I am a poor soul, I am indeed, and troubled with a grievous cough.'

'You know the travellers' lodging, I perceive, and are making directly for it,' is Mr. Datchery's bland comment, still rattling his loose money. 'Been here often, my good woman?'

'Once in all my life.'

'Ay, ay?'

They have arrived at the entrance to the Monks' Vineyard. An appropriate remembrance, presenting an exemplary model for imitation, is revived in the woman's mind by the sight of the place. She stops at the gate, and says energetically:

'By this token, though you mayn't believe it, That a young gentleman gave me three-and-sixpence as I was coughing my breath away on this very grass. I asked him for three-and-sixpence, and he gave it me.'

'Wasn't it a little cool to name your sum?' hints Mr. Datchery, still rattling. 'Isn't it customary to leave the amount open? Mightn't it have had the appearance, to the young gentleman — only the appearance — that he was rather dictated to?'

'Look'ee here, deary,' she replies, in a confidential and persuasive tone, 'I wanted the money to lay it out on a medicine as does me good, and as I deal in. I told the young gentleman so, and he gave it me, and I laid it out honest to the last brass farden. I want to lay out the same sum in the same way now; and if you'll give it me, I'll lay it out honest to the last brass farden again, upon my soul!'

'What's the medicine?'

'I'll be honest with you beforehand, as well as after. It's opium.'

Mr. Datchery, with a sudden change of countenance, gives her a sudden look.

'It's opium, deary. Neither more nor less. And it's like a human creetur so far, that you always hear what can be said against it, but seldom what can be said in its praise.'

Mr. Datchery begins very slowly to count out the sum demanded of him. Greedily watching his hands, she continues to hold forth on the great example set him.

'It was last Christmas Eve, just arter dark, the once that I was here afore, when the young gentleman gave me the three-and-six.'

Mr. Datchery stops in his counting, finds he has counted wrong, shakes his money together, and begins again.

'And the young gentleman's name,' she adds, 'was Edwin.'

Mr. Datchery drops some money, stoops to pick it up, and reddens with the exertion as he asks:

'How do you know the young gentleman's name?'

'I asked him for it, and he told it me. I only asked him the two questions, what was the Chris'en name, and whether he'd a sweetheart? And he answered, Edwin, and he hadn't.'

Mr. Datchery pauses with the selected coins in his hand, rather as if he were falling into a brown study of their value, and couldn't bear to part with them. The woman looks at him distrustfully, and with her anger brewing for the event of his thinking better of the gift; but he bestows it on her as if he were abstracting his mind from the sacrifice, and with many servile thanks she goes her way.

John Jasper's lamp is kindled, and his lighthouse is shining when Mr. Datchery returns alone towards it. As mariners on a dangerous voyage, approaching an iron-bound coast, may look along the beams of the warning light to the haven lying beyond it that may never be reached, so Mr. Datchery's wistful gaze is directed to this beacon, and beyond.

His object in now revisiting his lodging is merely to put on the hat which seems so superfluous an article in his wardrobe. It is half-past ten by the Cathedral clock when he walks out into the Precincts again; he lingers and looks about him, as though, the enchanted hour when Mr. Durdles may be stoned home having struck, he had some expectation of seeing the Imp who is appointed to the mission of stoning him.

In effect, that Power of Evil is abroad. Having nothing living to stone at the moment, he is discovered by Mr. Datchery in the unholy office of stoning the dead, through the railings of the churchyard. The Imp finds this a relishing and piquing pursuit; firstly, because their resting-place is announced to be sacred; and secondly, because the tall headstones are sufficiently like themselves, on their beat in the dark, to justify the delicious fancy that they are hurt when hit.

Mr. Datchery hails with him: 'Helloa, Winks!'

He acknowledges the hail with: 'Halloa, Dick!' Their acquaintance seemingly having been established on a familiar footing.

'But, I say,' he remonstrates, 'don't yer go a-making my name public. I never means to plead to no name, mind yer. When they says to me in the Lock-up, a-going to put me down in the book, "What's your name?" I says to them, "Find out." Likewise when they says, "What's your religion?" I says, "Find out."'

Which, it may be observed in passing, it would be immensely difficult for the State, however statistical, to do.

'Asides which,' adds the boy, 'there ain't no family of Winkses.'

'I think there must be.'

'Yer lie, there ain't. The travellers give me the name on account of my getting no settled sleep and being knocked up all night; whereby I gets one eye roused open afore I've shut the other. That's what Winks means. Deputy's the nighest name to indict me by: but yer wouldn't catch me pleading to that, neither.'

'Deputy be it always, then. We two are good friends; eh, Deputy?'

'Jolly good.'

'I forgave you the debt you owed me when we first became acquainted, and many of my sixpences have come your way since; eh, Deputy?'

'Ah! And what's more, yer ain't no friend o' Jarsper's. What did he go a-histing me off my legs for?'

'What indeed! But never mind him now. A shilling of mine is going your way to-night, Deputy. You have just taken in a lodger I have been speaking to; an infirm woman with a cough.'

'Puffer,' assents Deputy, with a shrewd leer of recognition, and smoking an imaginary pipe, with his head very much on one side and his eyes very much out of their places: 'Hopeum Puffer.'

'What is her name?'

''Er Royal Highness the Princess Puffer.'

'She has some other name than that; where does she live?'

'Up in London. Among the Jacks.'

'The sailors?'

'I said so; Jacks; and Chayner men: and hother Knifers.'

'I should like to know, through you, exactly where she lives.'

'All right. Give us 'old.'

A shilling passes; and, in that spirit of confidence which should pervade all business transactions between principals of honour, this piece of business is considered done.

'But here's a lark!' cries Deputy. 'Where did yer think 'Er Royal Highness is a-goin' to to-morrow morning? Blest if she ain't a-goin' to the KIN-FREE-DER-EL!' He greatly prolongs the word in his ecstasy, and smites his leg, and doubles himself up in a fit of shrill laughter.

'How do you know that, Deputy?'

'Cos she told me so just now. She said she must be hup and hout o' purpose. She ses, "Deputy, I must 'ave a early wash, and make myself as swell as I can, for I'm a-goin' to take a turn at the KIN-FREE-DER-EL!"' He separates the syllables with his former zest, and, not finding his sense of the ludicrous sufficiently relieved by stamping about on the pavement, breaks into a slow and stately dance, perhaps supposed to be performed by the Dean.

Mr. Datchery receives the communication with a well-satisfied though pondering face, and breaks up the conference. Returning to his quaint lodging, and sitting long over the supper of bread-and-cheese and salad and ale which Mrs. Tope has left prepared for him, he still sits when his supper is finished. At length he rises, throws open the door of a corner cupboard, and refers to a few uncouth chalked strokes on its inner side.

'I like,' says Mr. Datchery, 'the old tavern way of keeping scores. Illegible except to the scorer. The scorer not committed, the scored debited with what is against him. Hum; ha! A very small score this; a very poor score!'

He sighs over the contemplation of its poverty, takes a bit of chalk from one of the cupboard shelves, and pauses with it in his hand, uncertain what addition to make to the account.

'I think a moderate stroke,' he concludes, 'is all I am justified is scoring up;' so, suits the action to the word, closes the cupboard; and goes to bed.

A brilliant morning shines on the old city. Its antiquities and ruins are surpassingly beautiful, with a lusty ivy gleaming in the sun, and the rich trees waving in the balmy air. Changes of glorious light from moving boughs, songs of birds, scents from gardens, woods, and fields — or, rather, from the one great garden of the whole cultivated island in its yielding time — penetrate into the Cathedral, subdue its earthy odour, and preach the Resurrection and the Life. The cold stone tombs of centuries ago grow warm; and flecks of brightness dart into the sternest marble corners of the building, fluttering there like wings.

Comes Mr. Tope with his large keys, and yawningly unlocks and sets open. Come Mrs. Tope and attendant sweeping sprites. Come, in due time, organist and bellows-boy, peeping down from the red curtains in the loft, fearlessly flapping dust from books up at that remote elevation, and whisking it from stops and pedals. Come sundry rooks, from various quarters of the sky, back to the great tower; who may be presumed to enjoy vibration, and to know that bell and organ are going to give it them. Come a very small and straggling congregation indeed: chiefly from Minor Canon Corner and the Precincts. Come Mr. Crisparkle, fresh and bright; and his ministering brethren, not quite so fresh and bright. Come the Choir in a hurry (always in a hurry, and struggling into their nightgowns at the last moment, like children shirking bed), and comes John Jasper leading their line. Last of all comes Mr. Datchery into a stall, one of a choice empty collection very much at his service, and glancing about him for Her Royal Highness the Princess Puffer.

The service is pretty well advanced before Mr. Datchery can discern Her Royal Highness. But by that time he has made her out, in the shade. She is behind a pillar, carefully withdrawn from the Choir Master's view, but regards him with the closest attention. All unconscious of her presence, he chants and sings. She grins when he is most musically fervid, and — yes, Mr. Datchery sees her do it! — shakes her fist at him behind the pillar's friendly shelter.

Mr. Datchery looks again, to convince himself. Yes, again! As ugly and withered as one of the fantastic carvings on the under brackets of the stall seats, as malignant as the Evil One, as hard as the big brass eagle holding the sacred books upon his wings (and, according to the sculptor's representation of his ferocious attributes, not at all converted by them), she hugs herself in her lean arms, and then shakes both fists at the leader of the Choir.

And at that moment, outside the grated door of the Choir, having eluded the vigilance of Mr. Tope by shifty resources in which he is an adept, Deputy peeps, sharp-eyed, through the bars, and stares astounded from the threatener to the threatened.

The service comes to an end, and the servitors disperse to breakfast. Mr. Datchery accosts his last new acquaintance outside, when the Choir (as much in a hurry to get their bedgowns off, as they were but now to get them on) have scuffled away.

'Well, mistress. Good morning. You have seen him?'

'*I*'ve seen him, deary; *I*'ve seen him!'

'And you know him?'

'Know him! Better far than all the Reverend Parsons put together know him.'

Mrs. Tope's care has spread a very neat, clean breakfast ready for her lodger. Before sitting down to it, he opens his corner-cupboard door; takes his bit of chalk from its shelf; adds one thick line to the score, extending from the top of the cupboard door to the bottom; and then falls to with an appetite.

Excursions and Alarms

By what mysterious means Cloisterham has come by its population of hideous small boys is a matter that must always occupy the reflective mind. No family owns them; no one can remember their ever having been born. No one can recall a time when Cloisterham was ever without them: they have always been there, have always been hideous, have always been small. Fancy suggests that they are of more ancient provenance than the Cathedral itself, and were on hand to serve as models for the carved imps and demons that peep from under the seats of the Choir, to which monkish imaginings they bear an astonishing resemblance.

They are employed, on an irregular footing, at The Travellers' Twopenny Lodging, where, with horn lantern, it is their nightly duty to light the way to dusty bed. In the mornings (no part of their duties but offered as an additional attention), it is their custom to escort the parting traveller to the corner where the omnibus stops, with a hail of stones.

However, on this particular morning, which is seasonably warm and bright, the parting traveller (perhaps familiar with the inclinations of imps and demons), hastens on with such a look of rapt and filmy innocence that her followers soon drift away and she reaches the sanctuary of the omnibus with her retinue reduced to one. Even he appears to have lost interest, for he leans against a wall, pensively whistling through a huge gap in his teeth, until the arrival of Joe, the driver, when he vanishes with a suddenness that baffles the eye.

The traveller, her look of innocence unchanged, stows a dismal bundle under her feet and confides in her fellow passengers that he, the vanished one, was a dear little soul and she hopes he comes to no harm under the cruel wheels. Any further wishes for his welfare are deferred by the jolting start of the vehicle, which brings on a violence of coughing, from which she emerges, moistly and with difficulty, declaring that, poor her, poor her, she is dreffle bad, her lungs are in tatters and she hopes that the jinnelmin on the box won't stop till the Rellwy as she needs to get to London for her medicine. She receives no great sympathy, but settles back as if she has.

Her Royal Highness, the Princess Puffer, is well pleased with the result of her excursion; and, as she squints back at the gray cathedral tower she mutters:

'I knows yer now, poppet. Oh yes, I knows yer, deary,' and smiles, with something of the speculative affability of a python.

Then, bethinking herself of the dear little soul who had vanished, she glances back along the road for a sight of his mangled remains. But in this she is disappointed.

Once in London, where, as usual, the summer is unseasonably warm, and leaden, as if everybody has breathed out and nobody wants to breathe in, she proceeds, not to the dismal little court in which she lives, but to a shop nearby, where she is in the habit of purchasing the penny ink bottles from which she constructs her pipes.

Here, to the proprietor's evident surprise, she purchases a bottle with ink in it, a pen (with nib surreptitiously crossed as if it has taken precautions against the writing down of lies, and to which the proprietor does not feel obliged to draw attention), paper, wax and envelope. Then she hastens away, her mind so filled with her new possessions and the benefits that might flow from the use of them, that she scarcely notices what is before her, let alone what follows behind.

It is mid afternoon when she finally reaches her court, which, like many another so-called, is an unwholesome place, supporting worthless idlers, loafers, rubbish, and a superfluity of crawling, treacherous vermin. Jack Chinaman, in curious trousers and black silk tunic (obscurely gorgeous behind), is sitting outside his premises, enjoying the oppressive closeness of the weather. As he sits, he rocks himself to and fro, thereby revealing portions of a morose dragon that appears to have followed him all the way from China, and to be tapping him on the shoulder to beg a light for its long-extinguished breath.

He nods impassively as his fair rival crosses the court and enters her house. Impossible to tell if he wishes her well or ill. Impossible to tell if he wishes at all. Impossible to tell if the stifling air has, by malodorous association, caused him to waft himself back to China and that he is, in reality, sitting in a delicious little court in Pekin, and is honoured doorkeeper to a great Mandarin — or even the Mandarin himself — so that the hideous small boy who has just appeared magically before him, is, in reality, Aladdin of the marvellous Lamp. Consequently he, being the mere semblance of Jack Chinaman, might be nothing more than the pattern on a dirty plate.

'Er,' says the possibility of Aladdin. 'That Princess Puffer. Do she live in there?'

He jerks his thumb towards the doorway into which the woman has gone. Jack Chinaman nods impassively, and returns to Pekin; upon which the hideous small boy grins hideously and departs from the court with a dusty rapidity suggestive, to Jack Chinaman, of an unswept Flying Carpet.

From the court, the boy makes his way to the Railway Terminus, and, effortlessly eluding the vigilance of ticket clerks and guards, bestows himself inside a carriage where he sits with the satisfied air of one who, his worldly task having been done, is now going home in the confident expectation of receiving his wages.

It is night in the court, and sullen shadows crowd the doorways. Jack Chinaman has long since retired, leaving behind his head, it seems, swollen into a dirty yellow lantern that hangs outside his premises. The only other light comes from a window in the Princess Puffer's house where it gleams through a tattered curtain.

The lady, unnaturally awake, is seated at a table and is engaged upon a literary composition that appears to be affording her exquisite difficulty. Paper and ink lie upon the table while she inserts the end of her pen in her mouth and, for a moment, appears to be smoking it. Presently, in approved Authorial fashion, she casts thoughtfully about her, as if for some chance object to refresh her exhausted imagination. Inevitably her gaze falls upon her crazy shipwreck of a bedstead, which occupies the greater part of the room, even as it occupies the greater part of her life.

It is huge, tumbled and inexpressibly haunted; it is a bed on which a thousand Othellos might have strangled a thousand Desdemonas. However, she sees lying across it (in her mind's eye), not the tragic Moor, but another, who refreshes her imagination most potently. A look of frightful malevolence crosses her face and, with pen, ink and laborious words, she falls to with a will. Whether her energy proceeds from envy, hatred, a queer warped love, or greed, is not at all clear. Possibly each in turn takes a hand; for each time she falters a fresh impulse seems to seize her and guide the words that writhe on her lips down to her shaking pen.

At length, her task completed, she retires to the hearthstone, where, exchanging ink bottle for ink bottle (blackened, but not with ink), she makes shift to soothe her beating mind.

In a little while, coils of smoke gently suffuse her, and rise to make gray blossoms over her head, as if the flowers from which the burning drug had been extracted have mysteriously reconstituted themselves into phantom flowers, even as the foul, despairing room has begun to reconstitute itself in the woman's brain.

The grimy walls retreat, the stained ceiling floats high, and the candle, which had previously borne some resemblance to a dirty thumb, elongates itself into a tall white column, like the Monument, and crowned with fire. Even the bedstead, undeniable in its unseemly bulk, incorporates itself into the fabric of a mighty cathedral (St. Paul's is a mere thimble beside it!) of a grace and complexity far beyond the scope of human hands . . . though not, it would appear, of the human mind.

The woman, her heavy gray lips parted, looks on with some complacency at this sublime projection of her spirit, and begins to rock herself to and fro like an eager child. She smiles gleefully.

'Ah there you are, deary!' she mumbles. 'My sweet singer! Come, now, lay your head in my lap. What? All in white, are we? No matter, there's black enough within. And was it such a bad journey? It was good once, when first you came. The mixter, do you say, deary? Not the same? Oh deary-darling, not the mixter . . . not the mixter . . .'

She laughs teasingly, and then lapses into unintelligible mutterings as the drug begins to exert its full power. The rocking motion increases and a look of enormous contentment comes over the woman's face. It is curious that, while before the Choir Master excited her utmost hatred, now he is addressed with extravagant endearments as, in her fancy, he lies in his white surplice (exactly as she last saw him, leading the choir), with his head in her lap.

How often he has lain thus, both in fact as well as fancy, is beyond telling; and for how long he lies there, in fancy, is likewise beyond telling, as yesterday advances upon tomorrow and the poor candle sinks and dies.

The darkness that ensues is as much of the soul as of the atmosphere, for the power of the drug is waning and, like any other exalting of the spirit, is inclined to leave a gloom behind. Yet it is not quite spent. Unannounced, there has entered (from precisely where, the woman cannot determine; possibly the wall) an Apparition resembling an aged baby, inasmuch as it is a white-haired personage with a head several sizes too large.

This Apparition, after regarding her mistily for some moments, appears to remove a hat from inside its head and then to proceed, in a distinctly gossamer fashion, to the window, as if it is just passing through, and will, in a moment, fly on its way. The woman wipes her eyes on the back of her hand.

'So you are awake, then, mistress?' observes the Apparition.

'Who's there? I can't make ye out clearly. Who is it? Don't I know ye?'

'A friend.'

'Let me find my matches. Where are they gone to? Oh my poor fingers is as weak as leaves.'

'Why not draw back the curtain? It is broad day.'

Light comes abruptly into the room and the woman coughs convulsively, as if the light has got at her lungs.

'Now we can see each other, mistress.'

The woman, screwing up her eyes into frayed slits, makes out that her visitor is none other than the white-haired gentleman from Cloisterham. Instantly she is horribly frightened and suspects him of seeking to rob and murder her.

'How did yer git here?' she demands. 'How did yer know to git here? What do yer want? Did he tell yer?' She clasps her hands over her lap and looks down, as if the Choir Master is still there. 'Is it for a smoke, deary? Is that what you come for?' Hopefully she indicates the hearthstone, which is littered with evidence of her recent occupation; then, meeting with a decided negative, she begins to whine: 'I'm sick . . . I'm dreffly sick! Me lungs is all in holes! I can't hardly breathe, deary.'

Mr. Datchery refrains from confessing to a similar difficulty, for the air in the woman's room is peculiarly foul-smelling, and remains by the window with his hand still holding back the curtain, rather like Hamlet in the act of discovering Polonius.

'How did I get here?' he says innocently. 'Why, by train and on foot, mistress. No. I tell a lie. I took the omnibus from Cloisterham, and I indulged myself in a cab from the Terminus to here. And what do I want? Now what should an idle buffer like myself want with you, mistress?'

The woman, finding herself thus turned from questioner to questioned, is confused and resorts to a hideously flirtatious smile. Mr. Datchery acknowledges the receipt of it with a slight bow. He cannot help observing that the woman is probably not old. Although she is dreadfully wasted and yellowed, even to the whites of her eyes, there is still a grisly kind of youth lingering within her, like a child in a derelict house. It is possible that she is no more than two or three and thirty, and that opium has reversed the Psalmist's words to make of her yesterdays and watches in the night, each as a thousand years. He lets the curtain fall.

'I will tell you, mistress,' says Mr. Datchery, clasping his hands behind his back and strolling to the table with the hideously flirtatious smile in attendance on him, like a wasp. 'I will tell you what I want with you. I want a little information for the peace and contentment of my mind. I want a little knowledge for a curious hobby of mine. What hobby, you say?' (The woman had not uttered a word.) 'A good question, mistress. What indeed is a buffer like myself, getting through life on his means, to do?'

He pauses and picks up his hat, which is lying on the table, and appears to address the inside of it, and receive answers.

'Music? No ear. Painting in the way of water-colours? No eye. Literary occupation, in the way of Memoirs? No education for it.'

He returns the hat to the table and vigorously shakes out his head, as if the flirtatious smile has somehow got into his hair, with a view to stinging him.

'My hobby, mistress, is the study of human nature.'

He gazes blandly at the woman, as if she is a particularly interesting example of human nature; while she, feeling indistinctly that the epithet 'human' when applied to 'nature', confers a vaguely reprehensible air on the whole, feels herself to have been insulted and responds with a look of fathomless malevolence.

'Human nature, mistress, human nature,' says Mr. Datchery with an engaging smile. 'I love to sit and watch the world go by, and wonder what this man thinks, and that man does, and when some object of peculiar interest comes along I love to tease it out and discover all I can. Let me give you an example, mistress. I see a lady, plainly resident in the metropolis, come all the way to quiet Cloisterham. So I ask myself, what can have brought her here? Is it the country air? No. Is it the quaint old buildings? No. Is it the ancient Cathedral with its crypt, and windows and tombs? No. Why then has she come all the way to Cloisterham, with her little bundle and anxious eyes? Why? To find my neighbour, Mr. John Jasper, the Choir Master! For what purpose? It turns out that she is an old acquaintance of his and, in her very own words, knows him better than all the Reverend Parsons! Will you not agree, mistress, that this forms an object of peculiar interest that an idle buffer like myself cannot help but seek to tease out!'

Here Mr. Datchery gazes at the woman with such overpowering innocence, with an air of blandly guiltless inquiry, that it is several seconds before his possible intention sinks into her consciousness. When it does, she appears to go off into convulsions. Patiently, her visitor waits for her to recover.

'Come, now, mistress, I have been open with you,' says Mr. Datchery, rather exaggerating the case. 'Will you not be open with me? Mr. Jasper has, I imagine, been a frequent visitor here?'

He nods towards the hearthstone and the apparatus of smoking; upon which the woman goes into convulsions again.

'Does he come regularly?'

More convulsions.

'Does he talk? Does he ramble? Does he rave? In short, mistress, does he confide anything, when the drug has transported him, that might be, shall we say, of interest to a student of human nature?'

'Leave me be! Leave me be, deary! Oh I'm dreffle bad, I tells you. Oh my lungs is all wore out! I cough and cough and I shake and shake till I can't see nor think nor feel! Leave me be, deary!'

She glares at him through withered fingers with a dreadful mixture of fear and cunning; until Mr. Datchery puts his hands in his pockets and jingles some loose coins. At once she drops her hands and wipes them on her filthy dress with a compulsive· respectability, as if she has heard a doorbell ring. Mr. Datchery nods sympathetically.

'That's better, mistress,' he says. 'I think you will find it much better to be on a plain footing with me. Now will you oblige me by telling me when Mr. Jasper comes again? Will you send, or come yourself, to Staple Inn in Holborn? I take it that when he comes, he sleeps for some little while? He will not miss you?'

'Sleeps all night long, deary. Like a baby. Lies acrost the bed with his head there, and goes off like a baby. Sings, sometimes, sweet as Christmas. It's the mixter, deary. Jack Chinaman over the way ain't got the secret. You can tell by the screaming and shouting. It's a good mixter, deary, only the price is gone up dreffle high.'

Having discovered that she is to be neither murdered nor robbed, and that all that is required of her is a piece of betrayal that she might accomplish whenever it suits her, she waxes exceedingly confidential and goes so far as to propose that three shillings and sixpence changes hands on the spot. Mr. Datchery counts out the coins and lays them on the table.

'My name is Datchery, mistress. Dick Datchery. But you are to go to a Mr. Hiram Grewgious. Mr. Hiram Grewgious in Staple Inn. He will reward you further. You are to go to Mr. Grewgious just as soon as our mutual friend is asleep. Is that understood?'

The woman understands.

'Repeat it, mistress.'

The woman does so, and pledges herself so vigorously that Mr. Datchery cannot help having doubts.

'I hope that you will, mistress. I hope, very sincerely, that you will. And, as a student of human nature, I would advise you to think very carefully, very carefully indeed, before sending . . . *this.*'

To the woman's unspeakable terror, he picks up the envelope that contains her efforts of the night and holds it up to the window as if to read what is within. Or has he already read it? No, the seal is unbroken. All he can see is the address. Yet by the way he looks at her, and looks at it, he knows full well what it contains, knows the wild outpourings, the wild threats and the wild demands.

'Such a communication, mistress,' says Mr. Datchery quietly, 'to such a person to whom it is addressed, might well turn out to be in the nature of a Last Will and Testament. Think well, mistress, think well.'

With that, he returns the envelope to the table and departs, leaving the woman to weigh in the balance her hopes and desires against the precarious state of her mortality. She crouches in her chair and stares at the door through which her visitor has gone. What is to be done? Her life is not worth much; yet she clings to it with pitiful tenacity. What does it hold for her? Nothing but wretchedness between dreams. Would she not be better off murdered, if it should come to that? She shakes her head as if the thought has struck her that she might die in the midst of a bad dream.

At last the problem proves too much for her. She grunts, gives a decided jerk, and tumbles herself almost into the fireplace, as if she has been emptied out of an invisible scuttle. With shaking hands she seeks her customary solace; but either her agitation has impaired her skill, or the drug itself is powerless to reach the innermost core of her mind. The white-haired Apparition returns again and again; and, each time, as if successive films are being removed, he becomes a little clearer, a little harder, a little sharper, until he has an edge on him like a knife.

An Instrument of the Law

MR. DATCHERY, having descended the stairs, paused in the hallway and gazed speculatively at the rat-ridden doorkeeper, who, having emerged from his black hutch under the stairs, gazed speculatively back. These two speculations, which might roughly have been translated as (on Mr. Datchery's part) 'If I give him a shilling will he act honourably on it?' and (on the doorkeeper's part) 'Is he easy pickings for a shilling?' and the answer to both being a decided 'No', were concluded by the doorkeeper retiring to his hole and Mr. Datchery stepping out into the stale sunshine of the court.

Jack Chinaman, seated in his chair, nodded impassively, and two or three persons of a depressed, sea-faring aspect, apparently becalmed and in the doldrums, leaned up against doorways and idly puffed smoke. More speculation all round; following which, Mr. Datchery crossed the court and entered a house which he had earlier observed, which declared, on a fly-blown card exhibited in a window, that it possessed Commercial Rooms on Low Terms; although, from the hang-dog look of its door, and the crafty squint of its windows, Low Rooms on Commercial Terms might have been a more just description.

He remained inside for several minutes before walking briskly away, watched after dully by the becalmed seafarers, who puffed and puffed, as if trying to get up a sufficient head of steam to do likewise.

A little way beyond the court he turned into a small public-house where, declining the waiter's invitation to refreshment (and to that person's unspeakable wrath), he took out a pocket book and made long and careful notes before departing, unrefreshed, on his way. From then he passed through crowded dusty streets with an ease and familiarity altogether surprising in an idle buffer getting through life on his means. A man lurched out of an alley and knocked against him: a huge, ragged, violent man, whose fists were bunched, whose eyes were wild, whose breath was so foul with gin that a match might have exploded it.

'Sorry . . . sorry, your honour,' said this man, perceiving who it was he had knocked against, and retreating before Mr. Datchery's bland gaze. 'Didn't know it was you.'

Mr. Datchery smiled with evident pleasure, and walked on until at last he reached Holborn and turned in to Staple Inn. There, the heat of the afternoon had languished, as if it had collapsed in a heap. In the outer courtyard, a dirty judicial wig, lying on the stones in the shade of an exhausted tree, rose to its feet at his approach, wagged its tail at his approach, and then, giving up the hopeless pretence of being a dog, subsided and became judicial again. Ordinarily this animal — the property of the watchman and known, for sufficient reason, as Snap — was of a voracious, biting disposition; but in Vacation time lapsed into a fly-blown apathy, like the law itself, as if all unlawful appetites were but a source of dreamy speculation.

Mr. Datchery, bestowing the same bland smile on the dog as he had on the ragged man, passed through the archway into the second courtyard and entered under the portal of P.J.T. Briskly he ascended the stairs and knocked on the door of Mr. Grewgious's chambers. A gloomy voice bade him to come in.

'Why hullo, Dick!' cried Mr. Bazzard, forsaking his customary mood and rising from his seat with evident pleasure.

'Why hullo, Harry!' cried Mr. Datchery, forsaking *his* customary mood and, with equal pleasure extending his hand, which Bazzard shook warmly. 'Is he at home now?' He inclined his head towards the inner room.

'He'll not be back for an hour yet!' said Bazzard, with a cheerfulness that implied that Mr. Datchery was very welcome to partake of the respite afforded by the absence of his employer.

Mr. Datchery chuckled and, flinging his hat into a corner, very much with the air of throwing it over the moon, unbuttoned his surtout and settled himself in a chair. Mr. Bazzard produced a bottle of sherry and two glasses which he proceeded to fill; then, raising his own, proposed a toast.

'To The Thorn, Dick!'

'To The Thorn, Harry!' responded Mr. Datchery.

They drank.

'How does it go with you, Harry?' inquired Mr. Datchery, resting his glass on the edge of Bazzard's desk.

Mr. Bazzard smiled a peculiarly secretive smile, that suggested that IT went with him exceedingly well. He began to walk about the room, followed by Mr. Datchery's curious yet patient eyes.

'It's coming out, Dick,' he said at length. 'It's coming out!'

'What? Not The Thorn?' exclaimed Mr. Datchery, feeling compelled to take another sip of his sherry in order to digest the news.

'I assure you that it is!'

'The Thorn is coming out?' repeated Mr. Datchery wonderingly, and with yet another sip. 'The Thorn is really coming out on the Stage?'

At this point it became apparent that the subject of the conversation was not a sharp article of vegetation that had become embedded somewhere, but Bazzard's play, The Thorn of Anxiety.

'Well, not exactly on the Stage, Dick,' said Bazzard, with the merest hint of reproach. 'There is to be a Reading. Rooms just off Piccadilly. Some rather influential people have agreed to come. There's a Manager and a Man with Money. But best of all there's a lady who has promised to write an Article about The Thorn, for a Magazine, you know. I might say, Dick, that Things are Moving, at last! I shouldn't be surprised if as many as fifteen people don't turn up!'

The playwright said this with such simple and honest pride that Mr. Datchery could only clap his hands and declare:

'Why that's splendid, Harry, that's really splendid! In a way, it's even better than the Stage. With such an audience, with such a *chosen* audience, with such a *picked* audience, with such a *worthwhile* audience, every word will make its mark!'

'That's exactly what I think, Dick!' cried Bazzard, with the gloom that had threatened to overcome him when he had suspected his friend might not have thought fifteen to have been a sufficiently handsome turn-out evaporating, and a cheerfulness breaking out everywhere, excepting in his eyes which persisted in resembling ink-wells that had run dry.

When first Bazzard had come to London from Norfolk, those ink-wells had been full to brimming; but since then his midnight pen had dipped so often that they seemed quite used up. Bright with hope and the intimations of genius had the young Bazzard been; ready, even, in the spare time allowed him by his employer, to hold horses' heads outside theatres, as Shakespeare before him was reputed to have done. But alas! The holding of such horses' heads as came his way, led only to calloused fingers and a depressed public-house where he met with other geniuses, similarly with plays in their pockets and ink in their eyes.

It was there that he had struck up a friendship with Dick — Armitage then, but Datchery now — whose ambitions had also been fixed upon the Stage, but in the acting line. Indeed, Dick had actually appeared in the Provinces (over a number of declining years), and so was able to shed a kind of vicarious glory over the playwriting circle, in which he had been enrolled as a highly distinguished acquisition. Here it must be said that his fading from the theatrical scene had not been due to a deficiency of talent, but a deficiency of memory.

Dick Armitage then but Datchery now — was adept at assuming, down to the smallest detail, the very walk, look and accent of every character he was called upon to play. No one could do it better than Dick. He could have deceived his own mother, had his mother been conveniently placed in the stalls. But there was one fatal flaw. He could not remember his lines. It was not just a temporary lapse, but a blankness extending over the whole play. He could remember other people's; he had them off pat. It was only his own that eluded him. Every subterfuge had been resorted to in order to overcome this. In a Roman play his lines would be inscribed on scrolls; in a modern play, they would be written on his cuffs. In a comedy they would be posted up on the inside of a screen; in a tragedy they would be clutched in a murdered hand. But in the end it was of no use. It all entailed so much walking about, so much glancing at surprising objects and so much peering round unnecessary corners, that the action of the play was fatally undermined; so Dick — Armitage then but Datchery now — joined the company of playwrights in the depressed public-house off Drury Lane.

Mr. Bazzard, impressed by his ability, and moved by his want of a post, had recommended him to Mr Grewgious, who, with a respectful though shrewd appraisal of his talents, recommended him to the Detective Force, where his gifts for representing himself in a wide variety of parts had been turned to some advantage. His fatal flaw of memory had been overcome by the ingenious expedient of inscribing the name of the character he had assumed for the purpose of the investigation, on the inside of his hat. In the course of his detective work he had acquired several hats, to each of which he had been enabled to refer, for mental refreshment. Setting aside this one infirmity, Mr. Datchery — for so we must continue to call him to avoid confusion — was a most pertinacious officer and dedicated to his profession.

'And now, Dick, what of your news?' asked Bazzard, leaving, for a moment, The Thorn of Anxiety in order to inquire after his friend's concerns. 'How goes it in Cloisterham?'

'Gathering threads, Harry, gathering threads. You might say that matters are coming towards a Fifth Act.'

Bazzard nodded and picked up the discarded hat. He glanced into the lining.

'Datchery?' he said musingly.

'A poor thing, Harry, but mine own!'

'And who is this Datchery when he's at home?'

'A buffer, Dick, a buffer getting through life on his means. A King Lear who never had children. A Macbeth who never married. A — '

'An Othello without a Iago?' supplied Bazzard.

'No, Harry. Not an Othello, I think. No. Definitely not an Othello. Say, rather, a Mr. John Jasper without an Edwin Drood.'

Bazzard looked momentarily puzzled; then his brow cleared.

'I see what you mean,' he said. 'It is an interesting idea. I touched upon it, you recollect, in The Thorn.'

Generously Mr. Datchery refrained from saying that he recollected nothing of the kind; however, once brought in, The Thorn remained stuck fast in the conversation until Mr. Bazzard's employer returned. At once the friends re-assumed the parts in which Mr. Grewgious knew them best: Bazzard becoming gloomy and taciturn, and Mr. Datchery, buttoning up his surtout and holding firmly to his documentary hat, becoming the deft, quiet instrument of the law that went ingeniously into a case, rather like a corkscrew; and, when his grip was secure, opened it up.

'I trust I have not kept you waiting too long,' said Mr. Grewgious, whose sole concession to the summer seemed to be the display of a little more white cotton stocking at one end, and a little more neck at the other, as if the sun had made him sprout.

'No, you have not,' answered Bazzard sternly; whereupon Mr. Grewgious, feeling distinctly superfluous, retired into his room and beckoned Mr. Datchery to follow.

The instrument of the law obeyed, and, declining the lawyer's offer of a chair, stood before the fireplace in the upright, soldierly manner he assumed on these occasions.

'A little refreshment, Mr. Datchery?'

'Thank you, Mr. Grewgious. Mr. Bazzard has already entertained me.'

'Ah yes! I forgot. You are old friends,' said Mr. Grewgious, glancing a shade wistfully at his decanter of wine.

As this exchange (or something very like it) invariably took place, it was to be presumed that the lawyer found some difficulty in retaining the knowledge that Mr. Datchery had an existence, feelings and friendships unconnected with his present employment. It was as if, when the lawyer had secured his services (on a weekly footing) to keep a watch on John Jasper, to inquire into John Jasper, and to discover whatever secret there might lurk in the breast of John Jasper, he had done no more than to oblige Mr. Datchery's natural inclinations. The lawyer seated himself on an upright chair beside the fireplace and gazed expectantly at his visitor.

A pleasant interview

'You have something to tell me, Mr. — um — Datchery?'

Mr. Datchery produced his pocket book and, leafing through its pages, related to Mr. Grewgious the events in Cloisterham that had led up to his visit to the opium woman.

'Opium, you say?'

'Opium I said, Mr. Grewgious.'

'And you have made arrangements for me to be notified when the man should come again? Reliable arrangements?'

'I have made reliable arrangements, Mr. Grewgious.'

'And you think that the man might really betray himself while under the influence of the drug? Is that not, if you will pardon the expression, a little fanciful?'

'Not entirely, Mr. Grewgious. I have had some experience, and in my opinion — '

'Opinion, Mr. Datchery?'

'Not entirely, Mr. Grewgious. From the woman's interest, and the letter she had written, it would seem that the man has already betrayed himself.'

'Opinion, Mr. Datchery?'

'Not entirely, Mr. Grewgious. She was sufficiently alarmed when she realised that I had seen it for me to guess that it contained blackmail.'

'You did not read it, then?'

'It was already sealed.'

'You did not take it? You left it there?'

'I had some thoughts of taking it; but it would not have done. The woman, though sick and confused, was sufficiently cunning, I think, to have expressed herself in ways that only her correspondent would have understood. Nothing would have been gained, and much harm might have been done.'

'Harm?'

'She might have been too alarmed to proceed further. For, although I warned her (it was my duty) of the possible danger to herself of sending such a letter, I think she will send it. And I think that its effect upon our friend in Cloisterham will prove to be of interest. In my opinion — '

'Opinion, opinion! Is it not better to deal in facts? Are you not proceeding somewhat hazardously, Mr. Datchery?'

'Not entirely, Mr. Grewgious. I believe that the only answer to this affair must come from our friend himself. If he chooses to hold his tongue, we have no choice but to hold our hand. There is no other way, Mr. Grewgious, unless the dead return. It is a difficult business.'

'It is a sorry business, Mr. Datchery!' exclaimed the lawyer, with a sudden burst of anger that seemed to be directed against himself, for he struck his knee with his clenched fist. 'A dark, dreadful, wretched, sorry business! You have just come from this place, from this woman?'

He had himself just come from visiting his pretty ward, and the contrast struck him forcibly.

'I left her, sir, not two hours ago.'

Mr. Grewgious, perhaps realising that his anger might have been taken as being directed against his visitor, shook his head and passed his hand through his arid, sandy hair.

'A sorry business,' he repeated. 'I deeply regret, Mr. Datchery, that it should have taken you to so terrible a place. I would have shrunk from going there myself. And yet — and yet I ask you to go there. That is not fair, Mr. Datchery.'

'I have been in worse places, sir.'

'Degrees, Mr. Datchery, mere degrees! It must affect you. It must distress you! It must, if you will forgive my saying so, degrade you! And I —' He struck his knee again, with every sign of animosity, 'I am doing this to you! It is unpardonable!'

If the lawyer's outburst (prompted by the image of Rosa's innocent beauty that stayed obstinately in his mind) struck any chord in Mr. Datchery's breast, or awoke in him any sense of regret, it was not in the least apparent in his gentle shake of the head, his quiet smile and generous flourish of the hand, that had once been the ornament of the Provincial Stage.

'I thank you for your concern, sir,' he said. 'But I do assure you that there is nothing that I have come upon in the course of my Detective duties that has affected me half as much — nay, a quarter, a *tenth* as much as, say, Hamlet's fearful scene with his mother, or King Lear's howling in the storm, or Macbeth's aching despair! What can the woman I have visited this afternoon be beside these? These are tragedies, sir, that have indeed left their mark! These are tragedies, sir, that dwarf us; and in which, night after night, I have been privileged to take part, and in which, night after night, I have been struck dumb with terror and pity!'

He did not think it necessary to add that he had also been struck dumb on account of his failure to remember his lines, but concluded with sufficient fervour for Mr. Grewgious to agree that, after Mr. Datchery's lofty experiences, ordinary life must seem ordinary, poverty and squalor must lack distinction, and murder itself be a mere commonplace, committed by dull brutes, quite unable to call heaven and hell to account and bare their souls and raise the roof with words of anguish and remorse.

'You have an account of the money you have laid out, Mr. Datchery?' asked the lawyer, bringing the conversation round to pounds, shillings and pence, which was a subject on which he felt himself to be on firmer ground.

Mr. Datchery offered his pocket book for inspection. The lawyer waved it aside.

'Let Bazzard have it. He will recompense you.' Then, as if seeking to conclude the interview on a more amiable note, he said:

'I expect Bazzard has told you about his play? It is coming out, you know.'

Mr. Datchery confessed to having been already informed.

'Ah yes! I forget. You are old friends. But now you are here, Mr. Datchery, I would like to ask your advice on rather a delicate matter.'

Mr. Datchery inclined his head.

'This — um — coming out of Bazzard's play. This — this — er —'

'This Reading,' supplied Mr. Datchery.

'Thank you! This Reading. I understand it is to take place in rooms just off — er —'

'Piccadilly,' prompted Mr. Datchery, always ready with another's line.

'Exactly, sir. Off Piccadilly. I understand that there are to be a number of people, important people present. I don't recollect precisely how many —'

'Fifteen,' said Mr. Datchery.

'That's it. I remember now. Fifteen. Bazzard has asked me to come, and, of course, I am very proud. Between you and me, Mr. Datchery, I would have been bitterly disappointed if he had not mentioned it. But I would have understood. It is, after all, an affair chiefly for people connected with the Stage. Bazzard tells me that there is even to be a lady present who might — er —'

'Write an Article,' said Mr. Datchery, 'for a Magazine.'

'Exactly so. Now the delicate matter on which I would like your advice, is this. It would please me very much to take my ward and her friends to Bazzard's play.'

'Reading,' corrected Mr. Datchery.

'To Bazzard's Reading. Do you suppose that Bazzard would be offended if I was to purchase, say, half a dozen tickets? Do you suppose that he would think that I was — um — patronising him? I do not wish, under any circumstances, to offend Bazzard. I have the greatest respect for him. Indeed, I would rather not go at all than to cause him the slightest discomfort or embarrassment.'

He gazed earnestly at Mr. Datchery, who was able to assure him that the playwright was likely to feel a good deal more embarrassment from the sight of six empty places than six filled ones.

'Opinion, Mr. Datchery?'

'Not entirely, Mr. Grewgious, not entirely.'

'Thank you, thank you! You have quite set my mind at rest! You will — um — not be attending yourself?'

'I will be in Cloisterham, sir,' said Mr. Datchery regretfully.

'Of course, of course! I only mentioned it because I feared that my ward and her friends being present, might — er —'

'Might recognize me?' suggested Mr. Datchery.

'Exactly so. I had no other motive, sir. It was just that I felt that our own connection should be kept, as far as possible, between ourselves.'

Mr. Datchery bowed and departed, leaving the lawyer still seated in his chair. He stared at the closed door and gently rubbed at the side of his nose, as if to wear away any underlying angularity of the bone. His thoughts were still partly with Rosa, and with she of whom Rosa was an ever-present reminder; not that he needed any reminder, for death had by no means parted him from her. He smiled mournfully; that is, if a face as wooden as the lawyer's could ever be supposed to smile without doing itself an irreparable injury.

Then his thoughts reverted to the matter in hand, and he wondered how it was that he had been drawn into the dark business, and wondered if it had just been for *her* (of whom Rosa was a remembrance) that he had involved himself? Was it just for *her* that he was content to pay that respectable man who had just left him, to hound a fellow human being to his destruction? For no matter what that human being had done, no matter how wicked his acts, no matter how monstrous his attempt on Rosa (the lawyer's hands clenched over his knees), he was still a human being, with human thoughts and human feelings, for which, doubtless, He who made him might find justification.

'Opium,' murmured the lawyer. 'Doubtless the drug has blunted his sensibilities. And yet do we not all take it, in one form or another? Do I not take it when I say to myself that this man has sinned and must be brought to justice? Is not Justice itself a form of opium? Does it not blunt *my* sensibilities into supposing it to be the Will of God? And yet ... and yet ...?'

Thus Mr Grewgious continued to ponder, and to rub away at the side of his nose, and to come to no conclusion whatsoever, beyond the undoubted fact that he was an exceedingly Angular person, who was at his most awkward and angular with himself.

A Letter and a Lover

HER ROYAL HIGHNESS, the Princess Puffer, after severe cogitation, in the course of which her hopes had contended bravely with her fears, had decided that the tide of her affairs had indeed reached that degree of flooding that beckoned her on to fortune. Accordingly, she had carried her letter to the Post Office, from whence (after a week of further severe cogitation on the part of the clerks to decipher the address) it had been despatched to Cloisterham Cathedral. It arrived after the Choir Master had left, so the Reverend Septimus Crisparkle good-naturedly offered to deliver it to his lodgings.

Good nature there certainly was, both in the Minor Canon's obligingness and in the reason that had prompted it. Septimus hoped, he still hoped even after these many months, that he would be able to overcome the awkwardness he felt in the presence of Jasper sufficiently to discuss the matter that troubled both of them. Delighting, as he did, in fresh air, cold water and violent exercise to clear his morning head, nothing would have pleased him better than to clear the air between himself and the Choir Master.

Although he felt himself to be entirely justified in his continuing protection of Neville Landless, there was no doubt he was distressed when met by Jasper's look of sombre resentment. Many times he had made up his mind to speak out, and argue Neville's innocence; but each time Jasper's look had prevented him. It was as if every grain of love that Jasper had borne for his nephew had been changed into pure hatred against the only object he could find to blame. It was as if nothing less than the death of Neville would satisfy him for the loss of Edwin Drood.

As the Reverend Septimus passed under the gateway, he was accosted by Mr. Datchery, who, on this hot morning, had his door open and was watching the world go by. The Minor Canon, having some slight acquaintance with the gentleman, and rather liking his amiable interest in all things Cloisterhamish, was not at all averse from entering into conversation with him. Truth to tell that, although the Reverend Septimus really wanted to talk and clear the air between himself and Jasper, he was not at all averse from delaying the interview. Somehow that interview was rather like a rose-bush, inasmuch as the nearer he approached it, the more fraught did it seem with thorns.

However, on this occasion Mr. Datchery was not inclined to conversation. Indeed, when the Reverend Septimus remarked pleasantly that he was on his way to deliver a letter that had arrived at the Cathedral for the Choir Master, Mr. Datchery behaved very much like the Ghost in Hamlet. He started, like a guilty thing upon a fearful summons, recalled a pressing engagement, and hastened away, leaving the Reverend Septimus with the uncomfortable feeling that it had been he himself who had put the gentleman to flight.

Much puzzled, he ascended the postern stairs to Jasper's lodgings. To his relief (he was ashamed to admit), he found that Jasper was not at home. Mrs. Tope told him that Mr. Jasper had gone out a half hour since in the company of His Worship the Mayor. Rather than return later — which he well might have done — he left the letter in the care of Mrs. Tope and departed, feeling very much as if he had entered the ring and been knocked down, without ever having struck a blow. Mrs. Tope put the letter on the table in Mr. Jasper's room, to await his return.

Mr. Jasper was still with the Mayor. That worthy gentleman had called at the Gatehouse and invited the Choir Master to take the air with him. There was, it seemed, a trifling, yet curiously interesting idea that had occurred to Mr. Sapsea and to which he had given some thought. He had confided this with a peculiarly knowing smile, and had wondered if Mr. Jasper, being a person of musicality and taste, might care to express an opinion on it. Mr. Jasper had cared, and the air had been taken — or as much of it as was available between the Gatehouse and the auctioneer's residence. As they passed beneath the portals, Mr. Sapsea paused, turned back, and bent a long, appraising look at the Nuns' House, opposite.

'Fine edifice, sir. Fine example of ancient architecture. They knew how to build, sir. Dignity. And Charm.'

Mr. Jasper agreed, and the auctioneer, doubtless pursuing some internal connection proceeding from dignity and charm, transferred his gaze upward, to the wooden effigy of the previous Mr. Sapsea and remarked:

'Ah! My father, sir! The *first* Mr. Sapsea,' as if that departed parent had been the originator of the species and before him there had been nothing but trees.

Then, with a weighty nod towards the Nuns' House — as if the internal connection between it and the first Mr. Sapsea had been bolted into place — he conducted the Choir Master into his sitting-room, with the proposal that the warmth of port wine might be added to the warmth of the afternoon.

'We are comfortable, sir, we are comfortable,' said the auctioneer, when his guest was seated and supplied with refreshment. 'We are, I might say, well-provided with the good things of life. We are,' he said, with a wave of his hand, 'upon three floors with an extensive cellar and a garden behind. And we have' (with a further wave of his hand) 'considerable interests in the town. We are well situated, and, I might say, sought after, but —' (he drank) 'but we are mortal, sir. We are all mortal and we have our allotted span.'

Mr. Jasper knitted his dark brows courteously, as if the idea was quite a new one and demanded careful thought.

'Yes, we are all mortal, my dear Jasper, as you have tragic cause to know.'

Thus did Mr. Sapsea pay delicate tribute to his companion's abiding grief. Jasper's frown grew troubled and a look of dreadful misery came into his eyes.

'Indeed I have, Mr. Sapsea! It is always with me. And, more than anything else, it is the thought of — of that other one, in London, untroubled by grief or conscience, while my poor boy — is — is —'

'Enough!' cried the auctioneer, setting down his glass and raising a hand as if about to take an oath. 'We must, I venture to say that we *will,* sooner or later lay that villain by the heels. By the heels, sir, by the heels!'

Having delivered himself of this, he took up his glass again with an air of having settled the matter once and for all.

'But it was not entirely to your state, sir, that I referred. When I spoke of mortality' (drinking again) 'it was, rather, as a general idea, touching as much on myself as on another. We have, my dear Jasper, known each other for some time. We have, sir, become intimate. I have had the opportunity for observing you —' (here, a start on Mr. Jasper's part) — 'and you, sir, have had the opportunity of observing me.' (A relaxing on Mr. Jasper's part). 'You must have observed, my dear Jasper, since that auspicious day when first I showed you that little trifle that now graces Mrs. Sapsea's monument, that much water has flowed beneath the bridge.'

Here, Mr. Sapsea paused to make a gesture with his hands, suggestive of either a bridge or a benediction. Apparently it was a bridge as more port wine flowed into the glasses beneath it.

'Be fruitful and multiply,' invited the auctioneer, suddenly seeming to open up a new subject of conversation. 'If I might quote the Word of the Lord, my dear Jasper, be fruitful and multiply.'

Mr. Jasper, a trifle bewildered, nodded his acquiescence.

'My father,' said Mr. Sapsea, gesturing in the direction of the wooden effigy outside, 'the first Mr. Sapsea, *was* fruitful; and he *did* multiply.'

Mr. Sapsea modestly indicated himself as being the result of that multiplication, rather than anything in the arithmetical line.

'But Mrs. Sapsea — I refer to the second Mrs. Sapsea — although reverential and admiring — was weak. A failure of the liver. No issue, my dear Jasper. If I might quote again, Mrs. Sapsea was *not* fruitful; she did *not* multiply.'

Here Mr. Sapsea gravely shook his head, as if Mrs. Sapsea had been a singularly backward pupil.

'So I have given the matter thought, my dear Jasper, considerable thought; and if some suitable person should present herself — some person of taste, education and admiring manner — I would not look unfavourably upon a possible union. In a word, my dear Jasper, I have not cast from me the possibility of there being another Mrs. Sapsea. I trust, sir, that you, as a person of musicality and taste, do not consider this to be too hasty a decision?'

Mr. Jasper did not consider it at all too hasty, and went so far as to reiterate Mr. Sapsea's highly original expression concerning water flowing beneath a bridge in support of it.

'And have you,' he inquired at length, 'any person, any lady in view?'

Mr. Sapsea, in summery check trousers, summery fawn waistcoat and summery green frock coat, leaned back in his chair.

'I have,' he said, 'considered the matter carefully. Most carefully, my dear Jasper. I do not look for wealth, sir; although a competence would naturally be required. I do not look for the highest family in the land, sir; although, of course, there must be pedigree, English pedigree. I do not look for intellectual accomplishment; although there must be taste, reverence and appreciation. I look, sir, for nothing more than modesty, deportment and an ornament to my home. I look, my dear Jasper for fruitfulness and multiplication. I look for a mother, sir, to another Thomas Sapsea. And a Thomasina,' he added after a short pause. 'If posterity should demand it.'

It seemed, from the foregoing, highly improbable that the auctioneer did have anybody in particular in view, hence the Choir Master's surprise when Mr. Sapsea rose, paced the room, and returned to the subject of the Nuns' House.

'A fine edifice, sir. A cradle for fledglings about to fly forth and lay their eggs.'

Somewhat confused by this new turn to Mr. Sapsea's imagery, and the airy picture it presented of Miss Twinkleton's pupils, Mr. Jasper wondered if the auctioneer's heart had been enslaved by Miss Twinkleton herself.

But it was not upon Miss Twinkleton that the eye of the auctioneer had lighted, nor was it (Heaven forbid that so low a thought should, even for a moment, be entertained) upon her assistant, Mrs. Tisher. Soaring like an eagle, the Worshipful auctioneer had condescendingly inclined his beak towards the very fledglings in the nest; the fledglings who fluttered, frailly eager to fly the said nest and lay their eggs; the fledglings whose brains must have been so addled with Multiplication, and so wracked with Long Division, that they must have been breathless to turn it all to account.

Above the fledglings, then, did this eagle hover with beating wings, as if ready to put into instant effect the fable of the wren, and bear some tiny creature aloft into the Mayoral skies.

'MISS BUD!' said the auctioneer, coming to rest upon the very edge of his chair, as if it was a mountain peak. 'MISS ROSA BUD!' he repeated, with multiplication shining out of one eye and fruitfulness out of the other so brilliantly and unmistakably that Jasper would have liked to have taken them out and had them mounted, in brass.

'Ah! A child, you think?' went on Mr. Sapsea, apparently mistaking his guest's savagely incredulous look. 'Not so, my dear Jasper. A woman, sir; I assure you, a woman.'

He said this several times while attempting to cross his legs in various ways so that the checks on his summery trousers seemed to be multiplying themselves in Jasper's eyes. He did not seem to notice the extreme pallor that had come over Jasper's face, nor the trembling that afflicted his hands, so that the Choir Master tried to hide them, as best he could, down the sides of his chair.

'I impress this upon you, my dear Jasper, because, in your situation, it's a fact that might easily have escaped you. It is only natural for you to look upon her as a child. Though, as the world regards us, you are the younger man than I, in this one respect, sir, you are much my senior. By your very relationship with the young woman, by your very standing with regard to her and your late nephew, she must have seemed almost your daughter. A daughter, my dear sir. I repeat, your daughter.'

Mr. Sapsea, suddenly youthful Mr. Sapsea, leaned forward and gazed ardently at John Jasper as if, at any moment, he would kneel before him and cry: 'Father!' Jasper bowed his head.

'But consider, sir,' resumed the auctioneer. 'I beg of you to consider her plight. She is alone. She is, following the tragic loss of the young man who was to have shared her life, FORLORN. No prospect opens before her. Life holds out no welcoming hand. There is none to beckon, none to support, none to offer her those dear attentions which she has every right to expect. I repeat, sir, to expect!'

Mr. Sapsea painted this picture so feelingly that tears actually started to his eyes, before sinking back again, as if exhausted by the journey. The Choir Master maintained silence; such a silence!

'Yet she *is* a woman, sir. A woman. And we have no right, my dear Jasper, to deny her the happiness of being a BRIDE and a MOTHER!'

Mr. Sapsea refilled his own glass, which was empty, and attempted to refill the Choir Master's, which was full. He went on:

'Thus I lay it before you, my dear Jasper, not as any stammering boy, but as a person of some importance, a person unencumbered by mortgage, a person of wide interests in the town, and, I might say, a modest establishment in the country (a cottage, sir).' He paused to recollect the drift of his sentence. 'I lay it before you, sir, and I ask your opinion if, by making such an offer as I have mentioned, I am being overgenerous?'

He waited, as if to give his guest the opportunity of considering the possibility that the auctioneer was knocking himself down too cheaply.

'Come, my dear Jasper! Be open with me! Be frank! I will honour you all the more. All I seek is your opinion, sir; and, dare I say it? your blessing!'

'She — she —' said Jasper, in a low, terrible voice, '— the young lady has — has a guardian, Mr. Sapsea.'

'A lawyer! A dry-as-dust fellow in London! What can he know beyond his deed-boxes and Covenants? What can he know of that tender bud, that Rosebud, already opening towards the sun? No, my dear Jasper. Let her guardian look to her portion. Let you and I look to her heart! Speak for me, my good friend! Acquaint the young woman with my design! Offer her my — Why, what's the matter? What is it? Are you unwell?'

Jasper had risen to his feet. He was swaying and his brow had broken out into a profuse perspiration.

'Forgive me, Mr. Sapsea. It — it is the heat ... and, even as you talk of — of her, I cannot help thinking of — of my poor boy.'

'You must rest, sir. You must lie down.'

'No . . . no. I have . . . some medicine. I am subject, as you know, to — to fits of fainting. I will go, sir.'

'Let me walk with you.'

'No . . . no.'

'We must be careful, my dear Jasper. We must look after ourselves. We are not ordinary people, my dear Jasper. We would be missed.'

'You are very kind.' (Spoken so low as to be scarcely audible.)

'No less than you, my dear Jasper,' returned the auctioneer, pressing the Choir Master's icy hand with affectionate concern. 'No less kind than you. Speak for me, Jasper. Acquaint the young woman with my desire.'

'Acquaint the young woman with my desire!'

With face averted from the eager lover, Jasper all but fled away. With face averted from each passer-by, from each window, from each doorway, he hastened back to The Gatehouse. With face averted from his inquisitive neighbour, he opened his door with shaking hands, and stumbled up the postern stairs. Even within, even in privacy, he seemed to hide his face, as if from the possibility of a curious shadow.

The scene had been hateful to him, hateful beyond anything he could have imagined. (Yet there was worse to come.) Not only had the grossness and unseemliness of the man's proposals offended him, but the monstrous suggestion that he himself should further them had aroused in Jasper a wild anger and a frantic self-disgust. (But worse was to come.)

He entered his sitting-room and kept his eyes from where he knew a mirror to be. He shrank from his own scrutiny even more than from another's.

'Natural for you to look upon her as a child, etc . . . etc . . . By your very relationship, etc . . . etc . . . Your standing with your nephew etc . . . etc . . . Almost your daughter. Your daughter. I repeat, your daughter!'

Horrible idea! Yet in the world's eyes, in *her* eyes, might it not seem so? The auctioneer's words stung and tormented him. (Yet there was worse to come.)

His gaze which, until then, had been fixed upon the floor, shifted to the table. He saw the letter that Mrs. Tope had left for him. He took it up, examined it. The address was ill-written and ill-spelt. Doubtless it was from some choirboy, gone from Cloisterham and seeking a recommendation. He broke the seal and a stale fragrance escaped into the room. It was a fragrance that carried with it a haunting familiarity. He drew out the single sheet the envelope contained and unfolded it. Unconsciously he had retreated into the recess of his room, as if there had been a crowd of invisible watchers eager to look over his shoulder. (Such a man as John Jasper had become is never alone.)

'My beluvved frend,' he read with difficulty. 'I noe you now. I follered you and saw you singin in yor Kaffedrull, with all yor dear little souls around you. And I larfed till I was sick all down the side of the piller. I noe what you dun, poppet. I noe what you dun. But I woant say it on account of the goodness of my heart. As I sit riting to you I think how kind it would be if you was to show kindness of heart to me. My lungs is dreffle bad and I shake and tremble so as I can hardly rite. I need medicine and the price is gon up dreffly high. I hope you noe what I mean deary. I dreemed of you with yor hed in my lap and I did not noe to stroak it or put a skewer through it. I have some good mixter ready darling. Come and smoak and bring sum kindness of yor heart. Doant go to Jack Chinaman as you noe things would be worse.'

At the conclusion of reading this curious communication, Jasper uttered a moan. He crushed the letter in his hand and brought down his clenched fist on the grand piano, making a loud, jangling discord. The need to escape from his present wretchedness became overwhelming. Yet the only way he knew was by means of the drug (even though the worst of his wretchedness now proceeded from it). There came a knock at his door.

'Yes?'

'Are you all right, Mr Jasper? Is there anything wrong, sir?'

'No, no, Mrs. Tope. Why do you ask?'

'I heard the piano, sir. I thought you might have fallen.'

'It — it was nothing. Thank you for your concern, but it was nothing. I — I will be going out. I have to go out. I will not be back until tomorrow, Mrs. Tope.'

The good lady, perhaps not entirely reassured as to the Choir Master's state of health, departed; and Jasper hurried to his bedroom, where he packed his bag and searched to provide himself with whatever small articles of value he could find that he might sell. A watch, a shirt-pin, an amethyst fob, a pair of cuff-links and — and — He hesitated over one particular trinket; but finally decided and thrust it into his pocket. Whatever it cost, he must placate the woman. Whatever it cost, he must have her mixing of the drug. Whatever it cost, he must escape from the sense of huge horror and disgust that oppressed him. But there was worse to come!

In Thunder, Lightning and in Rain

It is a close, leaden evening with an early darkness that has forced up the street lamps into an anxious brightness. There is a general hurrying to vacate the streets; and St. Paul's Cathedral, unnaturally still, unnaturally black, stands up against the threatening sky like an enormous umbrella; but prematurely, for it is not yet raining.

Opinions are freely expressed that such an evening has not been seen before; as if it is quite a newcomer to a small but sociable circle of evenings, all of which have been in the habit of dropping in at the same time every night. It is an evening of unease, of disquiet and of anxiety; in particular, it is an evening of The Thorn of Anxiety, which is coming out in Greens Hotel, just off Piccadilly.

Greens is a traditional hotel; by which is meant that it has got into habits (mostly bad ones) and has not got out of them. It is a dismally discreet establishment, popularly supposed to have once been the favoured resort of foreign potentates, travelling under assumed names; and where the mutton chops still wear little white ruffs, fashionable in Queen Elizabeth's day, and register themselves on the Bill of Fare also under assumed names, generally in French.

There are touches of faded gold lingering about Greens: they glimmer along the lintels of doorways, they glint on the fearfully emaciated legs of its horrible chairs, and they hang, like trophies, upon the shoulders of the stuffed flunkeys who stare at you as if to say, 'In the old days, *you* would not have been allowed in here.' It is as if the tide of pomp that once beat upon Greens, had, when it went out, left these seaweedy fragments behind.

On the first floor of Greens, which is reached by means of a corkscrew staircase whose steps are so shallow that one walks and walks without ever seeming to rise, is a long, dismal room made available (at five guineas, refreshments extra) to Boards, Bodies and Committees, who have no long, dismal rooms of their own. Bazzard has bespoken this room; and, having been in some suspense that the threatening weather might keep people away, has been appearing and disappearing like a ghostly bloodstain, only white. Even now, when people have manifestly not been kept away, and are gossiping loudly by the hideous sideboard, Bazzard is still not at ease. He keeps staring anxiously at the door, at the windows, at the chimney-piece, as if he would dearly like to cut off all those avenues of possible escape.

He is everywhere; he is nowhere. He is deep in conversation with a short, stout person whose whiskers have run to seed; he is by the door, brooding fearfully. He is murmuring with a bereaved-looking female who represents the interests of the hotel and who has taken tickets; he is by the funereal window curtains, palely aloof. At one moment he appears at the end of the sideboard — on which reposes a modest number of bottles and an ambitious number of glasses — and tries to dismiss an excited fly that appears only to have come for the refreshments; at another he is back with the bereaved female and gesturing at the fly as if demanding to know if it has come in with a ticket.

In short he does everything rather than begin upon the Reading; and The Thorn of Anxiety (an ominously bulky volume), remains firmly under his arm. It is as if it has become so deeply embedded in him that to bring it out at all would cause Bazzard to bleed and to expose a wound that would, somehow, expose Bazzard the playwright once and for all as Bazzard, the melancholy clerk of Staple Inn.

But nobody minds as people generally prefer to talk than to listen. The Manager — a small-waisted, smoothly confidential person — talks smoothly and confidentially to the Man with Money, who is large-waisted, and wears heavy rings and a watch chain that looks like Newgate only gold, and keeps asking what actresses will be engaged, and keeps staring at a rather pretty, rather frayed young woman who does not appear to belong to anybody.

Three of Bazzard's playwrighting colleagues (among whom is the person with the overgrown whiskers), display, for the first time in their lives, an animated interest in each other's work, and none at all in Bazzard's; while Mr. Grewgious and his party, having been introduced to the Lady who is to write an Article for a Magazine, remain in attendance on her, as if magnetized by her black, metallic eyes, her black, metallic hair and her black, metallic beads.

This lady, whose name is Mrs. Chopper, is a widow whose husband — an exploring missionary — was eaten by an alligator, down to the last trouser button, in a remote and savage part of North America. There she remained, inconsolable, until befriended by the Snakebite Indians, a depressed and dwindling tribe, among whom she found the true, primitive Soul. She has brought along a sample of this Soul, preserved, so to speak, inside a mahogany-coloured, crafty-looking gentleman with a nose rather like a meat-hook.

'We have all lost something,' says Mrs. Chopper, shaking her beads. 'We are no longer close to the heart of things. We are no longer close to the buffalo; we are no longer close to the prairie; we are no longer close to the Totem Pole.'

Courteously Mr. Grewgious assents to this proposition, partly because it is an undeniable geographical fact, and partly because he does not wish to disagree with a lady who might well hold the fate of poor Bazzard's play in her hands.

Briefly Bazzard intrudes himself; and then, with a look of ghastly revelry, goes away without having said anything. Mr. Grewgious, who is nursing a guilty secret, watches after him and, observing The Thorn of Anxiety under his arm, reflects for the hundredth time, how dreadfully appropriate it is.

'We have lost,' says Mrs. Chopper, 'the language of the clouds, the language of the rain, the language of the thunder, the language of the waterfall, and the language of silence. We have too many words, and they suffocate the Primitive Soul.'

Here Miss Twinkleton bridles a little and leaves off presiding over Rosa and Lieutenant Tartar for long enough to protest that we have Poetry, which, far from suffocating the soul, has the object of freeing it. Many of her pupils (she mentions Miss Ferdinand in particular) write verses which actually express their souls; and, although artless and not to be compared with Mr. Wordsworth's, are quite charming. Surely Mrs. Chopper will not dispute that such effusions are to be encouraged and admired?

'Rosa, dear, did you not read Miss Ferdinand's poem about the honeysuckle and the bee?'

'Yes indeed, Miss Twinkleton,' says Rosa, withdrawing her gaze from Lieutenant Tartar for long enough to signify an appreciation of Miss Ferdinand's emerging genius.

Mr. Grewgious, briefly forgetting his guilty secret, takes pleasure in observing a certain shining in Rosa's eyes, and a certain mantling of her cheek. He meditates mistily on what pretty trifle he will scour the town for, to give to his ward when the time should come; for he deduces, from the aforesaid shining and mantling, that that time might not be far away. Then his brow darkens as he remembers a gold ring, with a rose of diamonds and rubies, a ring, taken long ago from a dead finger so that, one day, it might be placed upon a living one. It had vanished with the vanishing of Edwin Drood; and the lawyer finds himself becoming unfairly angry with the lost young man, as if Edwin Drood himself had been to blame.

'The Snakebite Indians,' says Mrs. Chopper majestically, having just demolished the whole of English Poetry, 'the Snakebite Indians have only one hundred and fifty seven words in their language.'

'One hundred and fifty eight,' says the mahogany gentleman, as if he has just added another.

'The Snakebite Indians,' continues Mrs. Chopper, after having gracefully acknowledged the correction, 'have no word for ticket–inspector; but they have five and twenty words for the sound of hail falling upon a wigwam. They have no word for area–railings, but they have seventeen words for the splashing of rain in a river. *That* is Poetry. *That* is not suffocating the Primitive Soul. You have only to be in the company of Jumping Crow,' (she prods the mahogany–coloured gentleman who jumps as if to illustrate his name) 'to comprehend the Primitive Soul, and to know what we have lost.'

The mahogany-coloured gentleman looks round with a singularly crafty smile, and Mr. Grewgious cannot help reflecting that the loss, when discovered, might turn out to be not unconnected with silver spoons.

The representative of the Snakebite Indians, the repository of the Primitive Soul, is tastefully attired in a black frock coat, fancy waistcoat, gray striped trousers and elastic-sided boots. His black hair appears to have been varnished, and his eyes to have been treated with the same preservative. They are, it must be admitted, rather unpleasant eyes, and when not fixed greedily on the bottles upon the sideboard, are peering rapaciously at Rosa or the rather pretty, rather frayed young woman who does not seem to belong to anybody. Curiously enough, he pays no attention to Helena Landless, who is, perhaps, the most beautiful woman in the room. It is as if he is afraid to meet her gaze; as if he senses in her something that does not wholeheartedly admire the Primitive Soul.

The Reverend Septimus Crisparkle, who forms the remainder of Mr. Grewgious's party amiably inquires if the late Mr. Chopper succeeded in introducing Christianity to the Snakebite Indians before his tragic loss; but it appeared that the alligator bolted down both Mr. Chopper and his satchel so promptly as to deprive the Snakebite Tribe of missionary and mission before they had received the benefit of either.

The Reverend Septimus, after expressing regret, moves on to more cheerful matters and inquires if Mrs. Chopper's interesting companion is married? Mrs. Chopper, with a glint in her black metallic eyes, and corresponding glints in all her black metallic beads, replies that the gentleman is a bachelor; for which there happens to be no word in the Snakebite tongue. Mrs. Chopper throws this in as an item of interest; but nobody is particularly surprised when they consider the frugal nature of the Snakebite vocabulary and the reckless prodigality with which what little there is, is lavished upon drops and drips.

'Was that not thunder?' says someone, as a distant rumbling briefly quietens the room, and is followed by a soft pattering of rain against the windows.

'Tell us,' says Mrs. Chopper, raising one large hand to her ear and placing the other firmly on the shoulder of her companion, in order to elevate the occasion, 'tell us what the rain is saying, my friend!'

The Snakebite gentleman listens cautiously, frowns, and then, after a great wag of his meat-hook, delivers himself of:

'Woach! Woach! Ha-ha! Hoch! Woach!' which everyone exclaims over, wonders at, and declares to be highly poetical.

The interpreter of the rain acknowledges the homage and then fixes the rather pretty, rather frayed young woman with so villainously ardent a gaze that she instantly takes fright and seeks refuge with the confidential Manager, who instantly (and confidentially) hands her over to the Man with Money, who exhibits signs of gratification, calls the young woman, 'My dear' and appears to be making an attempt to incorporate her in his watch-chain.

The Manager, now happily released from his task of watching the Man with Money, and making sure that he did not escape, flies about the room in an effort to get everyone seated so that the Reading might begin.

'If you would be so kind, madam! If you would be good enough, sir! Mr. Bazzard is ready! The Play! The Play!'

At last the audience is seated and puts on an expression of serious intelligence, as if it is about to undergo an intellectual trial of some severity from which it is determined to emerge with credit. The bereaved female departs quietly, as if it is all too much for her; and Bazzard watches her with some hostility. Mr. Grewgious fixes his attention on his knees.

His guilty secret is out. There is, beside him, an empty place, the ticket for which is still in his pocket. It is the result of a wretched misunderstanding. He had purchased six tickets and had naturally included himself among that number. It had not at all occurred to him that, when Bazzard had invited him, he was to be presented with his seat. He had felt it honour enough merely to be asked. Perhaps had he confessed to Bazzard, all might have been forgiven; but he had not confessed, and he feels, unhappily, that all will not be forgiven. He had hoped that Neville Landless might have been persuaded to take up the extra ticket; but that young man had pleaded study as an excuse. He had hoped that the extra chair might have been taken away; but it remained beside Mr. Grewgious, haunting him, nudging him, exposing him, so that its red plush seat seems to shriek aloud: 'I am one of MR. GREWGIOUS'S tickets that has not come! I am one of MR. GREWGIOUS'S friends who had something better to do!'

Bazzard, at his reading place, which is a kind of portable pulpit on castors, fixes his gaze irrevocably on the empty chair; and Mr. Grewgious trembles that he will inquire, like Macbeth:

'Which of you have done this?'

But Bazzard, in the last extremity of stage-fright, utters not a word. He is very pale and dreadful-looking, and resembles a man about to be hanged.

'The Thorn of Anxiety!' he croaks, at length; and thunder grumbles outside again, and a sudden lightning stares through a gap in the curtains and throws up the seat of the empty chair like a pool of blood.

Neville Landless who might, had matters been different, had *he* been different, have occupied that place, thinks of it with anger and bitterness. Thinks, with anger and bitterness, of the anxious look his sister had flashed upon him when it had been proposed that he accompany them. Thinks, with anger and bitterness, of the general relief when he had declined, as if his mere presence would have defiled Rosa, whom he loves. Thinks, as people do when left alone, that a thousand different things are to blame for making him the way he is, and not one of them is within himself.

The solitude of his room in Staple Inn oppresses him, and the increasing storm affects him strongly. He pushes aside his books and begins to pace the floor; and, with each grumble of thunder and each stare of lightning, he finds some new cause for resentment, and remembers that not one among his supposed friends had urged him to change his mind.

So he thinks and so he feels; for his is a nature that cannot endure the middle way. If he cannot be loved, he must be hated; if he cannot be warmly welcomed, he must be shrunk from with abhorrence and fear.

(And will find instances to prove it!) Although the kindness of Mr. Crisparkle and the deep love of his sister have always had some calming effect upon him, now that he has no companion but himself, and no adviser beyond the mounting storm, that calmness is blown to the winds.

Supposed friends. Although reason tells him that they *are* friends, and believe in him, something deeper than reason whispers that they still suspect him of the terrible crime of which he has been accused. Although reason tells him that they are united against his enemy and accuser, John Jasper, something deeper than reason whispers that they are united against *him*; for Jasper still haunts him, still hounds him, and not a hand is raised to strike him down.

'Mr. Jasper! Mr. Jasper!'

He stares through the window and down into the dark quadrangle, where the teeming rain makes the old stones run and run. A livid flash of lightning (which makes him livid to his fingertips), imprints on his inner eye the image of Jasper, standing under the withered fig tree. Then his eyes undazzle and the image fades, and there is no one standing down below. Thunder rolls round Staple Inn, rattling the windows and banging on the doors as if it would get in. Neville goes out upon the landing and peers down the black well of the stairs. Lightning bursts inside the house and wild shadows rush up the walls.

'Mr. Jasper! Mr. Jasper!'

He goes downstairs and pauses at each landing to whisper:

'Mr. Jasper! Mr. Jasper!'

There is a feeling within him, amounting to almost a certainty, that his enemy is close at hand. But where? He creeps outside, and the rain, beating down on his face, feels as warm as blood. He searches the doorways and then goes through the archway into the further quadrangle.

'Mr. Jasper! Mr. Jasper!'

Thunder growls and barks; and the dog Snap, from some hiding place, barks in reply, as if there is another, more tremendous Snap, hiding just over the rooftops, and having a tremendous time.

The heavy door that gives onto Holborn is shut; but there is a small barred window let into it, just sufficient to admit the upper half of a face. Through this opening Neville Landless stares out onto the dismal, rushing street, and wonders wretchedly how long it will be before his friends return.

Presently a hackney-cab draws up outside Staple Inn. Eagerly Neville waves and waits for his friends to emerge. But it is only a hideous small boy who gets out. This boy looks up and down the street, then at the heavy door, then at the face at the barred window. He approaches.

'I wants Lawyer Groojus,' he says.

'He's not in,' returns Neville, angry with disappointment.

'Yer lie,' says the hideous one. 'This is Staple Inn, ain't it?'

'Yes. But Mr. Grewgious is out for the evening.'

''E can't be. I got horders to fetch 'im.'

'What orders? Who from?'

'None of yer business. They're for Lawyer Groojus.'

'Then they'll have to wait.'

The hideous one, with the rain making false tears down his cheeks, screws up his face into a semblance of thought.

'Ain't I seed yer somewhere?'

'Possibly.'

'Ain't I seed yer in Cloisterham?'

'Possibly.'

'Then I 'ave seed yer, else yer'd say no. Are yer a friend of Lawyer Groojus?'

'Yes.'

'Then you'll 'ave to do. You come along wiv me and we'll ketch 'im while 'e's still at 'is hopium puffin'.'

'Who will we catch?'

'Jarsper, of course! Mister 'oly Jarsper!'

As the name is mentioned, the hideous one is gratified to see a wild, excited, glittering look come over the face at the window, a look that suggests that Mr. Jasper is well-known in that quarter, and that the desire to catch him is peculiarly strong. A moment later the door opens and Neville Landless comes out and climbs into the hackney-cab, which the hideous one has required to wait.

There follows a journey of about a quarter of an hour, proceeding, it seems, into the heart of the storm, for the thunder becomes tumultuous and the glaring lightning throws up the two faces inside the cab as plainly as if they had been drawn on paper. During this journey, the hideous one, in an effort to be companionable, confesses to being known as Deputy, and to be in the employment of the Travellers' Twopenny Lodging. However, at the moment, he has taken up temporary residence in a Commercial Room at a Low Rent, in Princess Puffer's court.

'Hopium puffer,' he elaborates, when Neville expresses puzzlement. ''Er what Mr Jarsper goes to.'

'Who arranged this?'

'A gennelmun what I knows. Name of Dick. I wants yer, Deputy, says Dick, to see and not be seen. I wants yer, when yer should see Mister Choir Master Jarsper come for 'is smoke, to go and fetch Lawyer Groojus from Staple Inn. And take a cab, Deputy; 'ere's money enough. For that's the way we'll ketch 'im, when 'e's pie-eyed wiv hopium, and not knowin' one word from another, nor one face from another, nor one day from another. We'll ketch 'im and 'e'll tell us what we needs to know. And won't that teach 'im fer 'istin' me off me feet; and won't that teach 'im for singin' wiv the angels when 'e ought to be screamin' down in 'ell!'

'And he is there now?'

Deputy, momentarily confused as to whether Neville means Princess Puffer's house or hell, decides that there is probably little difference, and nods his head.

'Then hurry, hurry!' cries Neville, letting down the window and thrusting out his head. 'Hurry, hurry!' he shouts to the cab driver, above the rattling of the wheels and the raging of the storm. 'For God's sake, man, hurry, before we are too late!'

So the cab rushes on through the storm, and Neville's heart rushes on ahead of it. Too late, too late. A lightning bolt strikes a chimney pot, and brings it crashing down, as if to halt the vehicle in its furious career. Too late, too late.

Where is Jasper now? Desperate, frantic man! The pieces of jewellery he had hoped to sell are still in his pocket, still clutched in his hand. In vain he had searched the darkest, filthiest parts of the town for some pawn-shop obscure enough for his purpose; but each time, when he had been on the point of entering, someone had turned to look at him, someone had stared curiously at him. And would remember.

At length he had abandoned the task and his thoughts turned only to the woman and the drug she prepared for him. An aching, overwhelming desire seized him, so that he would have submitted to anything she might have demanded. (Even to robbing the high altar of the Cathedral itself.) He dragged his hand from his pocket and stared down at the shining trinkets it contained. Would they be enough? (He would give them all to her, all, that is, except one.) Would she take them for what she had asked: 'kindness of heart'? She had her mixture ready for him; she had promised him that. He thought of the huge, evil-smelling bed, and of lying across it, and closing his eyes; and of the woman sitting beside him and murmuring:

'Here it is, my poppet. It's ready for you, deary-darling.'

When he reached the court, he was soaking wet, and a sudden glare of lightning illuminated him to all the watchful windows. The storm, fierce as it was, had scarcely entered his consciousness. He ran to the woman's house and stumbled inside. He mounted the stairs and tried her door. It was locked! He knocked. There was no answer; yet there was a light in the room. He knocked again, louder, and called out. Silence.

'Are you there? For God's sake, let me in!'

Nothing. A dread crept upon him that the woman was dead. He banged on the door with his fists.

'Let me in! Let me in!'

He pressed his ear to the panel; but could hear no sound from within. Shaking with terror and dismay, he went down the stairs and sought out the doorkeeper.

'Is she at home?'

The doorkeeper shrugged his shoulders. He had not seen her all day. She was either out, or asleep, either of which states amounted to the same thing; for when she was asleep, she *was* out, and one might knock and knock till Doomsday and never fetch her back.

Jasper staggered out into the court and glared about him, while the rain came down as if to wash him away. As he stood, swaying and caught by lightning, the Princess Puffer watched him through a hole in her tattered curtain. Neither dead, nor out, nor asleep, she had seen the Choir Master come, she had heard him mount the stairs, and had nodded as he had banged and shouted at her door. Not for worlds would she have let him in. In the interval between the sending of her letter and the present time, she had thought deeply. She had thought of Dick Datchery's warning, and life had become immeasurably precious and sweet. As she watched him through the hole in her curtain, she muttered:

'Go yer ways, deary, go yer ways. You'll not murder me. I'm wise, my poppet, I'm wise. Though it costs me pain and money to say it, you'll not sing to me again.'

She watched, and saw the lonely figure stumble across the court towards the dingy lantern that swung above Jack Chinaman's. She turned away; and it seemed that the rain had beaten through the glass, for her eyes and cheeks were wet.

'Has the honourable gentleman a pistol about him, or a knife, or a cord, or any other means of injuring his honourable self?' inquires Jack Chinaman, bowing courteously to his visitor. 'If it is so, will the honourable gentleman leave same upon humble table until departure?'

Jasper stares uncomprehendingly at a small painted table that is propped against the wall, just inside Jack Chinaman's door. A bludgeon and three or four knives lie upon it, and represent the amiable intentions of certain sleepers above. One knife in particular catches Jasper's attention. It is a Lascar weapon with a broad, serpentine blade. He stares at it intently.

'Permit me to inquire again. Has the honourable gentleman a knife?'

'No. I have no knife.'

But he has; for as he climbs the narrow staircase, he carries with him the image of the serpentine blade. It will not leave his thoughts. It is with him in the tattered silken room into which he is conducted, and where a woman (supposedly Jill Chinaman) nods and smiles and begins to prepare his pipe. It is with him when he lies across a heavy, soiled divan, about which, to afford some privacy, have been hung various ancient, fringed shawls. It is with him when he draws in the powerful smoke, and the fringes of the shawls seem to close, like deep lashes, behind which a hugely watchful eye gleams down upon him. It forms, as it were, a black snake down the middle of his sight. He grows restless and alarmed.

'The mixture,' he mumbles, struggling to reach the huge eye. 'It is wrong! I cannot begin!'

'Soon, soon,' promises the woman, turning aside the man's reaching hand. 'Draw deep. Puff, puff. It will begin ... very soon ... very soon.'

But it does not begin; and he hears himself beginning to shout and scream; and he remembers the warning he had had, that if he was to go to Jack Chinaman's, it would be worse. The hugely watchful eye with its fringed lid, floats before him and the black snake writhes across it.

What is he screaming, shouting now? Incomprehensible, incomprehensible! The woman lays a restraining hand upon his breast. Savagely he throws it off, staggers to his feet and flings down money.

'Why you not stay? Have beautiful dreams very soon.'

He shakes his head violently, as if to rid himself of that watchful eye and that serpentine blade; and rushes out of the hateful room and down the hateful stairs. How long has he been there? Ten hours, or ten minutes? He cannot tell; for what is time but what can be accomplished in it? Is it morning yet? Jack Chinaman smiles, opens the front door and shows the night.

Jasper gives a shriek of terror, as if the dingy yellow light of the lamp outside has revealed that the watchful eye is out there, in the teeming night. He stands, swaying in the narrow hallway, and, to steady himself (or so it seems) he rests his hand upon the painted table and dislodges the weapons that still lie upon it. They fall with a clatter and Jack Chinaman stoops to pick them up. Jasper pushes wildly past him and goes out into the darkness and rain.

If he had hoped that what he had seen had been a phantom of his mind, and would be dispelled by the rain and night air, he is wretchedly misled. If he had hoped that, by hurrying away, with clenched fists (and frantic glarings behind), he would escape, he is again misled; for he carries them with him, the watcher and the knife.

They attend him as he hastens from the court and plunges into the maze of narrow black streets that surround it. They attend him (the knife now

Hunted – or hunter?

before, and the watcher behind) as he strides along echoing alleys, turns precipitous corners and stumbles down precipitous steps. A furious excitement seizes him as he becomes aware of the journey upon which he has embarked. (He, or one very like him, has taken this journey before.)

He increases his pace till he is almost running, as he travels on and on through the storm, pausing, when the lightning glares, to look back at his pursuer, the watcher from the court. Then, in those sudden moments, pursuer and pursued, hunter and hunted, stand stock-still and stare at each other, as if the livid flash that has revealed each to the other has shocked them into streaming stone.

The storm is now at its very height: the lightning glares with unbelievable ferocity, the thunder crashes and the rain rages down, making black foaming rivers where it will. How much further must the travellers go; how much more of the journey remains? Not very much, not very much. Is it down this dark, narrow passage that can only lead to some rat-infested dock? Yes! First the hunted, then the hunter (or has he been merely the follower?) vanish from sight and are seen no more.

In Greens Hotel, the Thorn of Anxiety is out at last. Bazzard has finished and the audience, relieved of the necessity of looking seriously intelligent, nods and smiles and applauds in a self-congratulatory way, as if it feels that it has come through its trial of intellectual severity with flying colours. There have been a great many characters in Bazzard's play, but as they all spoke in the same strangled tones, and stared from the pulpit in the same wild fashion, nobody can be absolutely certain as to what has happened; still less, why. But it is over. That much is certain as the book has been shut.

Bazzard bows and the confidential Manager rushes from seat to seat inquiring if the play has been admired; and if it has been admired, would the admirer put his or her (favourable) opinion into writing and send it to the Manager, as letters carry great weight.

It is over and eyes turn hopefully towards the bottles on the sideboard; but before a move can be made, there is an interruption. A scream! It is a shrill, wild, despairing scream, that fills the room with its anguish! It is a scream as if half a soul has been torn from its body!

Helena Landless sits, staring at the empty place. What is it? What has she seen there? Her friends gather round, smelling salts are brought, for she is nearly fainting. She points to the empty place.

'Neville! Neville!'

She covers her face with her hands to hide the ghastly phantom she has seen, sitting in the empty chair. It was her brother; and there had been blood pouring from his breast!

A Communication from the Tomb

WHILE the storm still rages over London, glaring down alleys, flashing upon the oily, heaving river, cannonading the clustering vessels thereon, and whitening the five hundred church steeples so that they stand up all over the town like ghastly prison spikes, Cloisterham dozes and the massy tower of its Cathedral gazes somnolently towards the distant flashes in the sky like Lot's salty wife, with an eye of stony censure.

There is peace everywhere in Cloisterham: there is peace in the Deanery, where the Dean, Mrs. Dean and Miss Dean lie secure in the knowledge that Matthew, Mark, Luke and John are at their bed-posts; there is peace by the Gatehouse, where Mr. and Mrs. Tope lie side by side, secure in the knowledge that they are a respectable couple, and Mr. Tope puffs out his lips as he dreams of being high with visitors; there is peace in The Nuns' House, where Mrs. Tisher, the permanent garrison, lies wrapped in innumerable mysterious fragments, secure in the knowledge that all is prepared for the return of the pupils and Miss Twinkleton will be pleased. There is peace in the streets and in the odd quaint corners, and in the tall arched darknesses of the cathedral; there is peace everywhere, except in the one place where it might most reasonably have been expected: the churchyard. There, a mournful dusty figure, illuminated by a mournful dusty moon, trudges from tomb to tomb, like some convivial spectre, drunkenly seeking the grave from which it has emerged.

It is Durdles, Durdles bereft of Deputy, his guardian imp (who has been inexplicably spirited away), and with none to stone him home; so he walks and falls, and gets up and walks again, and most mysteriously is back where he began. God knows what time it is, but Durdles, with the chill of near sobriety coming upon him, feels it to be the very witching time of night; and various gloomy shrieks and dreadful tilting of monuments confirms him in the suspicion that he is in dire need of the steadying influence of refreshment. So he sits himself down upon a pale sarcophagus (work of his very own hands) and gazes speculatively about him.

Now Durdles has, in the course of his stony labours, deposited in certain tombs and monuments, certain bottles containing exalting spirits, as if he had been an Egyptian leaving libations for the dead. To these bottles, whose existence is a profound secret known only to Durdles and the silent inhabitants of the tombs (and for which reason he always keeps the keys of his work), Durdles has recourse at various lonely and shiversome times of the night.

His eye, sweeping the quiet confines of the churchyard, lights (or, rather, darkens, as there is not much of an illuminating nature behind it) upon a particular monument that, by reason of its proximity, presents no difficulty in finding again when he should get up. It is the monument of Mrs. Sapsea, the reverential wife, and is connected in Durdles's mind with a bottle, three quarters filled, which he had left there when he had completed his work. It is a small, dignified Villa, with no windows, a Greek portico, and a green front door. There is something rather homely about it, suggesting the reverential wife patiently awaiting the homecoming of her spouse to share her immense evening and night.

Durdles nods sagely and begins to search, first his person and then his dinner bundle, for the key. He cannot find it, so he searches again, this time laying out all his possessions beside him; which loss of ballast causes him to feel distinctly insubstantial and airy, so that he is inclined to sway in the breeze. He still cannot find the key. It has vanished as if it had never been; so Durdles, irrevocably locked out from his bottle, sits upon a low monument, rather like a sorely tried Patience, scowling heavily at grief.

At last he rises, and, clutching his hammer for support (as if it was a staff with an invisible extension to the ground) approaches the edifice that contains the remains of Mrs. Sapsea and the remains of his bottle. He reaches the green front door and halts. He finds it, upon close and meticulous inspection, to be so very like the front door of a house, only lower, that he knocks upon it, first with his knuckles, then with his hammer, and finally with his boot; and, receiving no answer, shouts abusively:

'Let me in! Let me in, you feeble old baggage!'

Upon which, and without any warning, the door opens and the deceased wife of Mr. Sapsea, in a long white gown and with a bandage round her chin, presents herself to Durdles's astonished gaze and humbly begs pardon for having kept him waiting but she had been taking a nap.

Now it might be supposed that Mrs. Sapsea, having been dead for upwards of a year, would have presented a somewhat decayed and bony an appearance; and, had she opened her jaws to speak, most likely the bottom one would have dropped off, bandage or no; and, therefore, the pale apparition confronting Durdles is, in all likelihood, a fermented product of his liver and brain. And yet she is very real, and very sad, and very depressed, and even goes so far as to apologise for that weakness of her constitution that led to her demise; which Durdles, with a gallant wave of his hammer, brushes aside.

'Oh, Mr. Durdles,' says she, in a voice that tends to howl, 'I forsook him too soon! I might have served him longer; but I failed. Tell me, oh tell me, how *is* my saintly Tom Jackass now?'

Durdles, conceiving that the reverential wife must be referring to the Worshipful Mr. Sapsea, assures her that all is well with the auctioneer and that his worldly state has improved; and then goes on to throw in a few items of recent occurrence in the neighbourhood that he thinks might be of interest to one long removed, when the lady halts him by wagging her forefinger in a way that reminds him most forcibly that she had once been a schoolmistress by the name of Brobity, which he has quite forgotten until this moment.

'I have,' says she reproachfully, 'a bone to pick with you, Mr. Durdles.'

'Very likely, ma'am,' says Durdles, feeling at a slight disadvantage when he considers how well she must have been situated to get into practice.

'I have been intruded upon, Mr. Durdles.'

'Worms, ma'am?' suggests Durdles, discreetly.

'I have been trespassed upon, Mr. Durdles.'

'Dry-rot, ma'am, from the poor wood of the coffin?'

The deceased lady shakes her head, and, rather coquettishly, tucks a stray roguish curl, that looks remarkably like a worm, back under her cap.

'By Another, Mr. Durdles.'

'Old 'un, crumbled away down below, ma'am?'

Again the shake of the head, again the curly, roguish worm. Then, in tones that tremble with girlish naughtiness, she murmurs:

'By a young 'un, Mr. Durdles, by a YOUNG 'UN! Oh what would Mr. Sapsea say! Oh let me with a blush retire!'

And retire she does; and shuts the door in Durdles's face, with his bottle still inside the monument. So Durdles, chilled by his unearthly encounter, takes the turf for his mattress and a headstone for his pillow, and tries to sleep it off.

Morning, when at last it comes, finds him ghastly (and likewise he the morning) as he rises, to the fright of passers by, from a grassy grave and glares about him. Some remnants of his vision still remain, but are rapidly becoming confused with previous visions, all of them of a ghostly nature. He casts a probing look at the monument of Mrs. Sapsea, and another at his hammer, and another at the sky, as if, somewhere between them all, lies the answer to a singularly troublesome mystery. At length, with a last unsteady look at the monument, he makes off to his yard where he unjustly berates his journeyman, and searches yet again for the vanished key.

XXVIII

Mr. Datchery Pays a Call

THE guardian imp, unaware that his dereliction of duty had encouraged the grave to ope and the sheeted dead come forth, presented himself at the churchyard railings at noon; and, observing his charge wandering solemnly within, attracted his attention by means of a shrill whistle and a well-aimed stone.

'Yer owes me!' he yelled.

'I don't owe you,' returned Durdles, slowly rubbing the back of his head. 'You wasn't here.'

''Ow could I be 'ere,' demanded the imp reasonably, 'when I wos up there?'

He jerked his head and rolled his eyes in a manner suggestive of having put several girdles round the earth and being still giddy from the exertion.

'I was out all night,' said Durdles, with a hostile look towards Mrs. Sapsea's monument. 'So I can't owe you.'

'Right-o,' said the child, after considering the argument and finding it sound. 'I'll ketch yer out tonight, then.'

He turned his back upon the wanderer and, leaning against the railings, awaited the arrival of his friend and employer, Dick Datchery. Presently that gentleman arrived, with a lightness of step, and a brightness of eye, buttons and boots indicative of being prepared for the receipt of good news. However, after a few moments of discreet conversation, it was to be observed that the brightness departed, first from his eyes, then from his buttons, and finally from his boots, as if following the course of his sinking hopes, right down to their ultimate extinction.

Faithfully, and with appropriate gestures and distortions of his features, Deputy recounted how he had seen Jasper enter the house of Her Royal Highness, the Princess Puffer; how he had waited for two or three minutes, and had then gone, as swiftly as an arrow, to Staple Inn, where, to his indignation, Lawyer Grewgious was not to be found. So instead he had fetched away one Neville Landless, who had claimed to be a friend of the absent lawyer.

'Did I do right, Dick?'

'You did right, Deputy.'

But alas! by the time they had got back to the court, (again with the same feathered speed), the bird had flown. Even as he and Mr. Landless had mounted the stairs inside the Princess Puffer's house, the doorkeeper had shouted up at them that it weren't no use as the lady was either sleeping or dead, for a previous gentleman (answering pretty exactly to the description of the Choir Master), has tried the same not long before, and had banged and shouted and kicked at her door, and then gone away like a madman!

'And you took that fellow's word for it?' demanded Mr. Datchery irritably, and staring down at his boots.

'Yer lie!' returned Deputy, highly indignant that he should be suspected of belief in any shape or form. 'We went up and listened at 'er door; and we looked through the 'ole; and we tried the 'andle; and we banged a bit; and it weren't no use, like 'e said.'

'So you went away? You never waited in case our friend returned?'

'Yer lie again. I goes straight back into me Commershul Room and never leaves me winder till it wos light.'

'What is he doing that for?'

'Oo?'

'Mr. Durdles, over there.'

Durdles, who had been drawn back to the churchyard as if by a magnetic force, was engaged upon administering sharp knocks upon Mrs. Sapsea's door, and sharp taps to her walls, and, standing back, casting sharp frowns over the whole of her, as if challenging her to strike back.

'Whyncher arst 'im yerself,' said Deputy, with a coolness of manner that provoked a strong desire in his companion to pull his ear.

Mr. Datchery compressed his lips and returned to the disappointing events of the night.

'And Mr. Neville? What of him?'

Deputy leered contemptuously. ''Im? 'E didn't last long. Not wiv all that weather. It weren't minutes afore I seed 'im 'urry off out of the 'owling rain like 'e wos being washed away.'

'And Mr. Jasper?'

'Never seed 'im all night long. 'E never come back.'

'He's doing it again.'

'Oo?'

'Mr. Durdles.'

Deputy shrugged his shoulders; and observing that his friend's mind was on other things, hazarded:

'Yer owes me.'

This time the universal creditor met with success. Mr. Datchery absently parted with a shilling before returning to his lodgings, with his hat under his arm and his head bowed, as if under the weight of too much hair.

He opened his cupboard door and stared long and thoughtfully at the roughly chalked marks within. The old tavern way of keeping a score, illegible to all but the scorer, seemed to please him no longer; and he frowned as if it were scarcely legible even to him. He shut the cupboard door and shook his head.

'But this is not the way of it! It is not as if I have been playing for double or quits! The score still stands.'

He sank into a chair and, still holding his hat, stared into it thoughtfully.

'Like a madman!' he murmured, recollecting his informant's words as if he would salvage something from them that he might turn to advantage. 'He went away like a madman. Yes, that I can understand. Yet why did he not return and try again? Perhaps he did return, and saw the boy, and Landless, and took fright? Was that it? Yet in such a state, where did he go? How did he pass so dreadful a night? And now? How is it with him now?'

He reflected on these questions with increasing interest, until at length he stood up and inquired of his hat:

'How is it with my neighbour now? No way of knowing but to ask. And why not? Might not an idle buffer, with nothing to occupy him but an amiable concern for those about him, call upon his neighbour in order to see for himself how things are with him now? I think indeed that he might.'

Mr. Datchery, with the blandest of smiles, left his room and went, by way of the upper stair, to his neighbour's door. As he drew near, he heard sounds of a piano being played within. He paused to listen. The music was calm and ordered; and Mr. Datchery, who knew little of the science, supposed that there might be something fugue-ish about it. He found himself admiring the skill whereby the two hands, playing independently, combined to produce so harmonious a result.

He knocked and the music ceased, leaving the listener with the uncomfortable sensation of being left suspended. After a moment, the Choir Master spoke:

'Is that you, Mrs. Tope?'

'No, sir. It is your neighbour, Datchery.'

The door opened and Mr. Jasper, shrouded in a dressing-gown of a blue, so many fathoms deep that his face and hands looked like the face and hands of a man drowned, courteously greeted his caller.

'Has my playing disturbed you, sir?'

'By no means, by no means!'

Mr. Datchery observes that Jasper's eyes, though shadowed as if from loss of sleep, are singularly bright and steady. (It would seem that things are well with him.)

'I trust,' says Mr. Datchery, indicating several folio volumes lying on the piano, 'that I am not intruding upon your work, sir?'

Mr. Jasper, lacing his fingers as if he is about to construct something ecclesiastical in the way of a church and steeple, assures Mr. Datchery that he had been playing for his own pleasure. A gold ring on one of his fingers glitters sharply.

'Will you not come in, sir, and take a glass of wine?'

Mr. Datchery is much obliged; comes in, admires the room, admires the furnishings, admires the unfinished portrait of the pretty girl that hangs over the chimney-piece (all of which he has seen before but not in so favourable a light), and seats himself upon the very edge of a chair to one side of the fireplace. He balances his hat on his knees and looks round amiably for something else to admire. Mr. Jasper pours out two glasses of wine, bestows one upon his visitor (who admires it) and seats himself on the other side of the fireplace, where he is much subdued in shadow.

Mr. Jasper raises his glass and a stray beam of light, reflected off some polished surface, catches it so that it blazes redly. Although the room is sombre, there are, nevertheless, various strayings of light that catch, from time to time, on such reflecting articles as wine-glasses, Mr. Datchery's buttons, Mr. Jasper's ring, and Mr. Datchery's boots. Mr. Datchery, having sipped his wine, repeats his concern that he has intruded upon the Choir Master's work.

'Not in the least, sir. I assure you that I had no intention of beginning upon it until tomorrow. There is another full week before Miss Twinkleton's pupils return from their holidays.'

'Miss Twinkleton?' says Mr. Datchery, with all his buttons twinkling in speechless imitation. 'What an odd name.'

'Do you think so, sir? I never thought it so. She is the principal at The Nuns' House, you know. I give music lessons to the young ladies.'

'Oh yes, of course! How foolish of me. I have often seen your pupils, sir, walking in the town. And delightful creatures they are, to be sure! So gay and spring-like that they make the heart of a buffer like myself turn somersaults. I envy you, Mr. Jasper, for it is always said that pupils are inclined to lose their hearts to their master!'

Light flashes in Jasper's glass as, involuntarily, he glances up to the portrait over the chimney-piece before disclaiming any sovereignty over the hearts in question; then the light is extinguished, only to burst out upon Mr. Datchery's boots. Mr. Datchery eases himself back an inch or two into his seat and consults his hat. He appears to be overcome by a sudden embarrassment.

'You must forgive me, Mr. Jasper, if I appear to be blundering in where I should not; but if I offend you, pray only consider it to be a harmless old buffer claiming the privilege of being a neighbour, sir.'

'Offend me, sir?'

'I hope not! I sincerely hope not! But I really called, Mr. Jasper, to ask you if all is well with you?'

'I don't understand you, Mr. Datchery.' (A glitter of the gold ring.) 'Why should you think all is not well with me?'

'I happened to see you depart yesterday, sir, and you looked to be in some distress. I was concerned, Mr. Jasper, and I inquired of Mrs. Tope if she knew of any cause. She told me, sir, that all she knew was that she had left a letter for you. I do hope, sir, that it did not contain bad news?'

'No, no! Nothing of the kind!' exclaims Jasper angrily. 'I fear that — that Mrs. Tope has too lively an imagination. The letter was of no consequence. She should not have mentioned it. I am sorry that her thoughtlessness should have caused you any concern, Mr. Datchery.'

'I am sure she meant well, Mr. Jasper. We both thought only of your welfare.'

'Yes, of course, you are quite right,' says Jasper, his anger departing. 'Mrs. Tope is an exceedingly good soul; and I am grateful to you, sir. It is just that, living as I do, entirely on my own, I find it a little surprising to discover myself to be of interest to others.'

Mr. Datchery agrees that it must be surprising; but surely it must be comforting, too, for are we all not of one family? Mr. Jasper nods; and Mr. Datchery, by way of excusing his own curiosity over the letter, remarks:

'I had feared, my dear Jasper, that the letter had contained some news of that poor young man, and that he had been discovered under tragic circumstances.'

If Mr. Datchery had intended his remark to placate the Choir Master, its effect is strikingly to the contrary. Jasper starts forward, and everything about him expresses a dreadful bewilderment.

'You mean — you mean my nephew, sir? You mean my poor boy?'

'I did indeed, sir.'

'Of course! What else? I was only surprised to find that you know about my — my loss.'

'Common knowledge, my dear Mr. Jasper,' says Mr. Datchery wryly. 'And common concern. One family, one family.' Then he goes on to repeat his fears that the letter had concerned Edwin Drood.

'Would to God that it had, Mr. Datchery!' cries Jasper, leaping to his feet and beginning to pace the room. 'All these months of knowing nothing, nothing for certain! If only it could be known what has become of my poor boy since that terrible night!'

'Then it is not absolutely certain that he is dead?'

'Oh yes. It is certain,' says Jasper, pausing to gaze forlornly out of the narrow, deeply set window. 'I know it. I believe that I knew it, in my heart of hearts, that very night. I believe that I knew it at the very moment when the breath left my poor boy's body. Can you believe in such a thing as that, Mr. Datchery?'

Mr. Datchery can believe in it, and goes so far as to adduce instances of which he has heard, in which something of the kind has taken place; of the deaths of twins being mysteriously communicated so that one, in England, maybe, leaps up in the middle of the night and cries: 'My brother in China is dead!' So why should it not be so between an uncle and a nephew? Oh yes, Mr. Datchery finds no difficulty in believing that such an uncle might know, to the very last heartbeat, when his nephew ceased to be.

Jasper remains gazing out of the window; and Mr. Datchery, who can only see his back, which is in profound shadow, has the odd idea that it is really his front, and that Jasper is leaning backwards and watching him. Then the Choir Master steps back and says:

'Here is Mr. Crisparkle. I believe he is coming to call. It must be on some Cathedral business.'

'Then I will leave you, sir,' says Mr. Datchery; but as he takes some time in doing so, Mr. Crisparkle is already at the door.

The Minor Canon is white of face and looks bleak and suddenly old. His eyes are gloomy and filled with grief. As he stands in the doorway it is dreadfully apparent that there is very little sparkle remaining to the Reverend Crisparkle now.

'You are unwell, my friend!' cries Jasper, extending his hand.

Unconsciously, it would seem, Septimus shrinks from it; but then, making something of an effort, he takes it in his own and shakes it.

'No, Jasper. I am well enough. I came to tell you — I thought it my duty to tell you that — that the unfortunate young man is dead.'

Following these words, there is a stillness in the room. A stray beam of light blazes fiercely on Jasper's ring. Mr. Datchery, standing to one side, waits for the violent outburst of feeling that must follow. But, curiously, he is disappointed. Jasper, although giving every appearance of shock, remains in command of himself. In a low, strained voice he asks:

'How? How is he dead? A seizure? An accident? Or — or did he take his own life?'

'No, thank God! not that! He was murdered, Jasper.'

Again Mr. Datchery awaits the outburst; and is again curiously disappointed.

'How murdered? Where? Is anyone taken, or suspected of it?'

'It was during the night. I was staying in Staple Inn with an old school-fellow. We had all been out for the evening. When we returned it was quite late; and he was gone. We thought that he had gone on one of his long walks through the town, and had taken shelter from the storm. But then, at about six o'clock this morning, Mr. Grewgious received a message that the body of a young man had been found near the river, and that there were papers on him — letters I believe, mentioning Mr. Grewgious's name. Although we feared at once that it must be poor Neville, we went with the messenger to make sure.'

Mr. Datchery, who, until now, had supposed the murdered man to have been Edwin Drood, who had been the subject of their recent conversation, is bewildered to learn of his error; and his thoughts, temporarily, are thrown into the utmost confusion.

'It was him, Jasper. It was poor Neville.'

Septimus falters and rubs his eyes with thumb and forefinger, as if he would wipe away for ever the sight they had rested upon, in a foul, dirty room, and on a foul, dirty table.

'It was a strange thing, Jasper, but his sister Helena had known that it had happened, had known it many hours before. But I believe it is often so with twins.'

Here indeed the Choir Master does start, and violently, too; but Mr. Datchery puts it down to his being startled by the coincidence of their having talked of such a matter only minutes before hearing of it.

'He had been stabbed to the heart. The Police Inspector was of the opinion that it was the work of a Lascar seaman, as he had recovered the weapon which turned out to be of a type carried by such men. But there is little hope the man will ever be caught, as he might be on his way to China by now.'

'So it was robbery? He was struck down and robbed?'

'No. He was not robbed. The Inspector thought that the murderer must have been disturbed and run off immediately after committing the crime. All Neville's possessions were still in his pockets. Everything was there. And in addition, Jasper, there was something that I wish with all my heart had not been there.'

'What was that, Mr. Crisparkle?'

'A ring. A gold ring with a rose of rubies and diamonds. It was a ring that Mr. Grewgious instantly recognized as being the very one he had given to your nephew, not long before he disappeared. It was a ring, Jasper, of such meaning and importance to your nephew, that Neville Landless could only have come by it by some violent act. I tell you this, Jasper, although it makes me wretched to do so, because you have a right to know. Neville's possession of this ring forms the strongest evidence in support of your own suspicions that it was he who murdered Edwin Drood. I was mistaken in him, and I ask your pardon for having opposed you for so long.'

The Choir Master bowed his head, so that Mr. Datchery, peer as he might, could not make out what expression Jasper was seeking to hide.

Mr. Crisparkle Pays Two Calls

MR. CRISPARKLE, his hard duty done, returned to the ancient peace and the ancient sunshine of Minor Canon Corner where the latticed windows seemed to gleam down upon him with a tenderly reproachful air for being so low in his spirits; and the closely confiding ivy whispered (it always whispered whether there was a breeze or no) that the Minor Canon looked exceedingly pale, which was a bad thing in ivy; and that it showed one the folly of not being rooted in one spot (like ivy) and wandering about and having nothing old to cling to, which, in the case of ivy, would have meant collapsing in a dusty heap. Even Mrs. Crisparkle seemed affected by the surroundings, for there was, in her affectionate greeting, a faint, but unmistakable air of reproach.

When her Sept had first returned from London that morning, and had looked so terrible, and had told her about Neville Landless (omitting only those grim details of procedure attendant upon 'Found Dead') she had, of course, been deeply frightened and shocked. But it had been more on her son's account than pity for the murdered youth. 'My Sept! My Sept!' she had cried out at intervals as he had told her, as if to say: 'That you should have seen such things! That such dreadful happenings should have fallen in your way!'

Then she had gone to her herb-closet for a glass of Constantia, as it was dreadfully plain that her Sept needed support. She had been a long time in fetching it — or so it had seemed to the Reverend Septimus; and when she had come back, it had seemed (to the Reverend Septimus), that the glaze upon the china shepherdess was a little cracked, and the delicate colours a little changed for the garish, as if she had been taken from a cabinet and brought into the harsh light of day.

But she was herself again, and not to be argued with, and firmly decided on all things; so that when he told her of his intention of calling upon Jasper, she had nodded and said:

'Of course, my dear. That is exactly what you ought to do. You must call upon dear Mr. Jasper,' as if there had never been the slightest doubt of it in either of their minds.

Now, when he came back, after having performed that painful duty, and recounted the performance of it to the china shepherdess, and she sat and knitted at a tremendous rate, he could not help feeling that there was a gentle reproach in her every nod, as if what had happened never would have happened if he hadn't gone out. It was as if he was a boy again, and had come back with grazed knees after all previous warnings, so that the nods and sighs seemed to be applied like salves, that smarted as much as they healed.

'I suppose,' he said at length, 'that his sister will be returning to Miss Twinkleton's, Ma.'

'It would be for the best, Sept.'

'I suppose it would not be suitable for her to stay with us, Ma.'

'It would not be suitable, Sept. You are quite right, dear.'

'I suppose, Ma, that I ought to inform Mr. Honeythunder? After all, he was their guardian.'

'It would be considerate, Sept.'

'I shall write to him directly . . . although it is difficult to put such a matter into a letter. At least, I would find it difficult.'

'I know you would, dear. And if you'll forgive my saying so, Sept, you do not write a very good letter. You are always too roundabout, and not at all like your usual self.'

'Then I had better call upon him, Ma.'

'Of course you must, Sept. You must call upon him tomorrow.'

So the Reverend Septimus, thus confirmed in his feelings, obtained leave from the Dean and travelled to London on the following day. He disliked the idea of calling on Mr. Luke Honeythunder quite as much as he had disliked the idea of calling on John Jasper, but there was no help for it. It was as if he was undergoing a penance for some mysterious, unacknowledged guilt.

The London offices of The Haven of Philanthropy were in full swing. There was a great deal of coming and going and a strong impression that what came was full and what went was empty. Although The Haven covered much the same ground as Charity, it seemed to do so in the opposite direction; while Charity proverbially began at home before venturing forth and abroad, The Haven began forth and abroad, and brought the spoils back home.

It was in expectation of this that, when Mr. Crisparkle applied to a black-suited individual for audience with Mr. Honeythunder, he was accommodated almost directly. Mr. Honeythunder, who was sitting with his committee, being told (by the black-suited individual) only that a reverend person wished to see him, naturally supposed that here was a migratory philanthropist bringing him in rich gifts, which could only redound to his, Luke Honeythunder's, credit.

Naturally, therefore, he was considerably displeased to be confronted by Mr. Crisparkle, and made no bones about it, and cast away, with an angry gesture, the black-suited individual who had betrayed him, as if he had been bread upon the waters that he hoped would not come back to him even after ever so many days.

'Might I speak with you in private, sir?' requested Mr. Crisparkle, after Mr. Honeythunder had coarsely demanded to know what the devil he wanted; and then, before Mr. Crisparkle could answer, had gone on to inform his committee that here was a person, employed in one of our cathedrals, who had grievously disappointed him.

'No you may not speak with me in private, sir!' shouted Mr. Honeythunder, recollecting that their last meeting had not ended in his personal triumph, and being determined to avenge that defeat. 'You find me among Brothers, sir. There is nothing you can say to me that cannot be said in front of my Brothers!'

He indicated, with a sweeping motion of his large hand, four or five astringent-looking Brothers among whom there appeared to have been slipped in a Sister; but as she was rather a masculine lady, with a leaf of gray hair that kept falling and being pushed back, as if in the grip of a hopeless autumn, she passed for a Brother without dissent.

'We are not *private*' (he made the word sound like a dastardly action) 'here, Mr. Crisparkle. We do not go about our business in a *private* way. We are *public*,' (he made the word sound like a burst of sunshine) 'sir. We are a Brotherhood, we are a Union! We scorn the private. We despise the private; and, sooner or later, we will root the private out of the land!'

He paused as if for a burst of cheering and was rewarded with several 'Hear, hears!' and a vigorous nodding of heads, in the course of which the autumnal leaf repeatedly fell and was repeatedly pushed back.

It was an uplifting sight, and the Reverend Septimus, as he gazed at the astringent brethren, each of whom resembled Mr. Honeythunder so closely that, had he vanished in a puff of smoke, his place might have been taken without any sense of change, reflected that they might very well carry all before them and achieve their stated aim; and it would, on the whole, be a sad thing when the private vanished from the land and each man was another man's master and never his own, and when even Charity itself was taken away from the private heart and was made into a Public Matter, so that one man might never help another, save by public debate and consent.

'So there is not the slightest use,' bellowed Mr. Honeythunder, thrusting forward his large, inflammatory face, 'in your coming here to browbeat me, sir! We are united! We are Brothers, sir! We stand, All for One!'

'Aye, and all for none,' thought the Reverend Septimus, whose Christian forbearance was being stretched so far that he contemplated not so much browbeating, as nose-beating, and eye-beating, and fleshy stomach-beating the worthy Brother and his dismal Brethren. However, he said quietly:

'I came, sir, with no other purpose than to acquaint you with an event of which I think it is your right to know. Your late ward, Neville Landless, is dead.'

Upon hearing this, a certain amount of wind was knocked out of the Philanthropist's over-filled sails. He leaned back in his chair, frowned, and then, recollecting that he was a public person, and his committee was attendant on his every word, exclaimed:

'Dead? You come here and tell me that he is dead?' as if to impress upon all present that the young man had never shown the slightest sign of having been in that condition when he, Luke Honeythunder, had had the charge of him, but no sooner had he passed into the reprehensible hands of the person who stood before the Brethren, than there he was, dead. 'How is he dead? Why is he dead?'

'He was murdered, Mr. Honeythunder.'

A moment of shock, of fear even, as this most private of crimes (for murder, even if committed before a multitude, is a monstrously private act) laid its chill finger upon this most public of men. Then he became blusterous again, demanded to know who had committed the crime, and, when told that the murderer had fled unseen, loudly informed the Brethren that there had been grave suspicions against the young man himself, so his loss was not to be deplored.

'Is that all you have to say, sir?' asked Septimus, guiltily refraining from confirming these suspicions. 'Have you no word of pity or compassion for his sister?'

'No, sir. I have no such word for his sister. When I washed my hands of that pair, I washed them clean.'

He held out his large hands, perspiring palms uppermost, and the Brethren dutifully looked at them; and lo! they were, figuratively speaking, clean.

'I leave such words for you, Mr. Crisparkle,' went on the Philanthropist; and added with coarse contempt, 'No doubt the stipend you continue to receive will amply recompense you for any trouble in that direction.'

Septimus flushed angrily.

'No doubt it will, Mr. Honeythunder.'

'I take it, then, that is all? You have no further demands on my time? Then good day to you, Mr. Crisparkle. My respects to your mother.'

'I think she will be sufficiently recompensed by your absence, Mr. Honeythunder!' said the Minor Canon, with a degree of indignation that caused the autumn leaf to fall and hang untended.

He left the philanthropic presence and departed from The Haven, above whose stony portals was engraved:

'Come all ye who labour and are heavy laden,' to which might have been added: 'Preferably with oxen, and with cattle, and with vineyards, and with Deeds and Reversionary Interests, and, in short, with anything readily convertible into Cash.'

As he walked, he strove to thrust from his mind all thoughts of the bullying philanthropist and his narrow, dismal Brethren, and the narrow, dismal state into which they sought to bring their fellow men. Two tasks had he accomplished; but there was a third at hand. Although it was a task to which he went willingly, and with a rapid step, it was yet the hardest of all. He went to Staple Inn, where Helena Landless sat in her brother's room, cold and motionless with grief.

In spite of the urgings and pleadings of Rosa, and Miss Twinkleton, and Lieutenant Tartar for her to leave Staple Inn for Southampton Street, she sat where Neville had sat, and stared where Neville had stared, and clasped and unclasped her hands as if Neville's hands lay between them. Her dark beauty seemed now only painted upon her, for there was such a gray pallor beneath it; and her eyes, when she raised them, lay drowned in tears.

Mr. Grewgious alone neither urged nor pleaded with her; but sat, when he was in her presence, with all his angularity upon him, and with a face of wood. When Neville's possessions had been brought back, and given to her, and she had blindly fingered through them, it had been he who had seen the ring. It had been he who had demanded to know how Neville had come by it; it had been he whose voice and look had accused. She had raised her eyes and stared, it seemed, deep into the lawyer's heart. Then she had whispered:

'Neville, Neville, Neville! Oh my poor unhappy Neville!' and the lawyer had bowed his head in acquiescence.

Naturally he had spared her everything he could of the grim necessities following her brother's death; but otherwise it was as if there was a barrier between them. He felt himself accused for having, even for a moment (though it was longer than that) accusation in his heart.

Of all those who tried to comfort her, including, be it said, Bazzard, who, with speechless sympathy, brought her a book, it was to Mr. Crisparkle that she was most inclined to open her heart. Only then, when he was with her, did she cease clasping and unclasping her hands, and clasp his, so tightly that she left red marks.

'He did not do it, he did not do it, Mr. Crisparkle!' she pleaded, fixing her eyes upon him so desperately and so fiercely that, even had he wanted to, he could not have looked away. 'I *know* he did not do it!'

'How can you know such a thing? How can any of us know what is hidden in another's heart?' murmured Septimus, very gently; for it seemed to him that, were he to agree with her for her peace of mind, she would know instantly that he was deceiving her and would despise him for it.

(Yet why was it, though he credited her with the power of looking into *his* heart, he denied her the same power of looking into her brother's?)

'You ask me that? You ask me how I know that, when I knew the very instant that he died? (For I felt that half my soul had died!) Do you not suppose that I would have known if he had had so terrible a secret? For I swear to you that, whatever was bad in him, was bad in me, and would have found its echo.'

'And what was good?'

'He had much more of that than I!' she cried, with a wild look, as if he was standing in the room. 'He had all that openness and honesty of feeling that I have learned to hide. He was a free spirit, and I am in chains. I cannot even weep and tear my hair with grief, as he might have done; but I must sit with a dead heart, and with dead eyes. It would have been a thousand times better if I had died and he had lived!'

'A thousand times better . . . for whom?' murmured Septimus; but this she did not answer, and, instead, went on praising her murdered brother for those very qualities that, had he been still living, she would have censured in him.

Then, quite suddenly, as if with one breath that had long been pent up within her, she cried bitterly:

'Landless! Landless! Landless! Oh how well we were named! We are Landless; we are homeless! We are wanderers on the face of the earth!'

'Your home is here, dear Helena,' said Septimus; and hoped, with all his good heart, that this kind deception (for deception it was, as she spoke the truth) would not be uncovered by the girl's anxiously seeking eyes.

'You are right,' she said. 'My home is here.'

When he left her, she was still sitting where Neville had sat, and staring where Neville had stared, and clasping and unclasping her hands about those of a ghost.

He spoke with her friends, who had engaged a servant from Furnival's Hotel to look after her; and he was grateful for the presence of his old friend, Lieutenant Tartar, who, although some seven years his junior, seemed, with his sailorly ways and his sailorly neatness, to be so much more able than he. Surely such a splendid fellow, who must have gone aloft in raging tempest and howling storm and thought nothing of it, who must have commanded in fierce battles and never turned a hair, and who must have navigated between fearsome rocks and dreadful whirlpools and brought his vessel safely into harbour without a scratch upon her – surely such a splendid fellow as Septimus hoped his friend to be, might be trusted with the safety of a girl?

Then there was Miss Twinkleton, excellent Miss Twinkleton, skilled in Geography and Mathematics, wise in History, well-versed in German and Latin, and familiar with Measles and every other sickness attendant on young girls; surely such a paragon as Miss Twinkleton could be trusted with the care of one young girl?

And Rosa, what of she? Who better than Rosa to comfort her dearest friend? Who better than Rosa to understand the griefs and fears of one of her own age and sex? Surely Rosa above all might be trusted to devote herself to the care of Helena while Septimus was away?

Thus carefully, thus seriously did Mr. Crisparkle undertake the duty of guardianship, without a thought that the memory of himself might also have some sustaining power. Unlike Helena's previous guardian, who had all faith in himself and none in the rest of the world, the Reverend Septimus had great faith in others but very little in himself.

'You may set your mind at rest, reverend sir,' said Mr. Grewgious, when the Minor Canon called upon him before returning to Cloisterham; and expressed some concern for Miss Landless. 'She is in good hands. I take it that it is your wish that she should return to Cloisterham with Miss Twinkleton?'

Such was Mr. Crisparkle's wish; but only, of course, if it was Miss Landless's wish too.

'Under the circumstances, reverend sir, it is your wish that carries the day.'

The Reverend Septimus, feeling himself to have been gently reprimanded for displaying an unguardianly indecision, lowered his head.

'You are returning, reverend sir, directly to Cloisterham?'

'I am, Mr. Grewgious.'

'Then would you oblige me, reverend sir, by conveying a message to a — a client of mine who is residing in that city?'

'Certainly, Mr. Grewgious. If you will tell me his name and where I might find him, I will convey your message as soon as I arrive.'

'His name is Datchery; and I believe he is residing with a family by the name of Tope.'

'I know the gentleman, Mr. Grewgious.'

'Excellent. I would be obliged if you would tell him that the matter on which I engaged — that is to say, the matter on which he engaged *me*, to — um — to — er — to act for him, is nearing its completion. I would be obliged if you would instruct, that is to say, if you would ask him to call upon me at his earliest convenience.'

'I will indeed, Mr. Grewgious.'

With that, Mr. Crisparkle left Staple Inn; but not without casting a thoughtful glance upon Mr. Bazzard, as if wondering whether he, too, might not be enrolled on the list of those already charged with the supervision of Helena Landless. So the Minor Canon completed his third hard task; but with no feeling of completion whatsoever.

An Enchanted Residence

THOSE entrusted with the care of Helena Landless fulfilled their duty with that kindly tyranny so often displayed by good people whose hearts are in the right place but at the wrong time; who urge forgetting when the greatest need is to remember, who try, by wonderful means, to take one out of oneself when the dearest, the most precious thing is within, and every instinct cries out: 'Let me stay a-while!'; as if unaware that grief is a wound like any other, and is best treated where the knife went in.

Lieutenant Tartar, performing prodigies of horticulture on his garden in the air, persuaded it to bloom outside Helena's very window; and, wherever it showed the least sign of resistance, sternly executed the rebels and arranged their heads in a silver bowl upon her table as if to show them where their allegiance lay. Miss Twinkleton encouraged reading and brought a volume for the purpose, of History in which monks and monarchs fell upon each other with bell, book and battle-axe, for causes so remote as to be viewed with perfect tranquillity; and the servant girl, a native of Ireland, was continually fetching cordials from across the street, and, when they remained untasted (as they generally did) loyally and with many a 'God save us!' drank them down herself, as if she would raise her mistress's spirits by proxy.

Although Neville's murder and Neville's guilt were talked about, no word of either was ever mentioned in Helena's presence, as if her grief would go away if only she could be kept in ignorance of its cause. Thus there was an air of conspiracy that operated as much against the sufferer as on her behalf; and because of it, Rosa, who most of all might have comforted her friend, found herself the least able to do so. Had she talked openly and freely of Neville, all barriers might have been overcome; but, as it was, she could not help feeling herself to be partly to blame. She could not help feeling that, by unwittingly and unwillingly having aroused Neville's heart, she had brought about the tragedy. She felt that Helena must always be thinking of this, and must always be hating her; so she shrank from that very closeness that might have comforted them both.

Poor Rosa! She could not help thinking also of Eddy — lost Eddy — whose life had been so closely linked with hers, and whose death had come as a consequence of it. Poor Rosa! In the quietness of the night she could not help thinking herself to be an accursed creature, doomed to bring misfortune upon all who were close to her. In the quietness of the night she re-lived every look, every word, every action that (in the quietness of the night) turned her innocence into guilt till she felt that she was unfit ever to be loved. In the quietness of the night, John Jasper stood before her and accused her of harbouring only vanity in her heart; for was not he a victim, too? He would creep into her room and stand at the end of her bed, glaring down upon her till she summoned up enough strength to cry out; and Miss Twinkleton would come hastening from next door and tell her that everything was all right and she had only had a bad dream; and would sit beside her while she cried and cried for the sin of being human. In the quietness of the night . . .

Daylight however brought relief, chiefly in the shape of an early call from Lieutenant Tartar with the latest news from Staple Inn. He could not have been more conscientious had he been reporting aboard the Admiral's flag-ship, nor could he have been more smartly attired. If there was a fault in him, it was only that his knock upon the front door came a little earlier every morning; but even so, Mrs. Billickins was unable to deny that Miss Bud and Miss Twinkleton had been up this past hour and were expecting him.

Only a week in London remained as Rosa was to return to Cloisterham with Helena and Miss Twinkleton. Only a week remained, which seemed far too short a time for Rosa to satisfy that ardent desire for knowledge about the River Thames, between Temple Stairs and Queenhithe, that had unaccountably sprung up in her.

She went twice upon the river, with Lieutenant Tartar and his man at the oars, and Miss Twinkleton beside her, pointing out the various objects of historical interest. On the second occasion they visited the lieutenant's yacht, which lay in a small, secluded dock which rather resembled a large packing-case filled with water.

It was the most perfect yacht imaginable; and several sailorly old men, sitting in the doorways of warehouses and puffing blackened pipes, plainly thought so too, as they gazed at it with drowsy admiration. It was painted mostly white, and when a small boy, who pretended to be fishing, threw a stone at it, Rosa felt so indignant that she could have thrown *him* at it — if he would not have scratched the paintwork even more.

'Be careful now, Miss Bud, be careful . . . and you, too, Miss Twinkleton!' cried Lieutenant Tartar as he assisted them aboard; and Mr. Lobely, bringing up the rear, said smilingly:

'Easy as you go, ladies. Easy as you go.'

'What if,' thought Rosa of a sudden, as her foot touched the deck and she felt it breathe and sway beneath her, and she experienced that feeling of being detached from the land (even though it loomed all about her), with its attendant sensations of unimagined freedom, 'what if that rope that holds us fast should part and we should float away? What if,' she thought, as she glanced from sunburnt Lieutenant Tartar, to sunburnt Mr. Lobely, and to a man who sat, bare legs over the side, and stitching at a sail, 'what if they should turn out to be pirates, hoist the black flag and sail us all a thousand miles to sea?'

The more she looked at Mr. Lobely and the sailmaker, the more piratical they appeared to be; and the more she looked at Lieutenant Tartar, the more she thought that a cutlass and a large gold earring might have suited him very well. The very furnishings on the deck — small brassbound chests and cupboards — seemed quite likely, now she studied them carefully, to be concealing cannons ready to poke forth and take their prize.

The lawlessness of such an enterprise did not in the least distress her, as it had been so fleeting a notion that it had departed almost as soon as it had entered her head.

They went forward and saw where Mr. Lobely and the sailmaker had their quarters, and where the cooking was done. They went below ('Please be careful, Miss Bud . . . and you, too, Miss Twinkleton!') and were shown a charming little state-room and two diminutive cabins with mahogany bunks and cheerful cotton quilts. It was no longer a pirate vessel, but a cottage, a cottage of such neatness, cleanliness and convenience as to render it the most desirable residence in the world. It was an enchanted cottage, a magically voyaging cottage, so constituted that, on one day one might open the door and step out upon China; and on another (after suitable passes with sextant and compass) behold! there would be Egypt, conjured up out of the sea, with all its Cheopses, Sphinxes and Pyramids.

Then this notion too was dispelled when she heard Lieutenant Tartar, who had been explaining some point of navigation to Miss Twinkleton, say that, although the vessel was by no means large enough for ocean-going, she might sail quite comfortably as far as Calais or Boulogne. Miss Twinkleton, who had spent several pleasant summers in a pension in Boulogne, was at once reminded of them; but, being in the academic state of her existence, connected them with the study of the French language (in which Miss Ferdinand was peculiarly backward considering that she had a cousin who lived in Paris) declared that Boulogne was a delightful town and that she had often thought of taking a party of pupils there, so that they might gain proficiency in the language.

'Rosa, dear, do you not think that a stay in Boulogne would do Miss Ferdinand the world of good?'

Rosa, who had not been thinking of the French language, instantly connected in her mind Miss Ferdinand and Lieutenant Tartar's yacht, and Miss Ferdinand and Lieutenant Tartar; and made haste to dispel *that* notion at once.

'Where will you keep your ship, Lieutenant Tartar, when you leave London?' she asked, thinking of some quiet English harbour, far from the perils of Boulogne. (Thus far had her imaginings shrunk from China and the Sphinx.)

'I was thinking of somewhere near Portsmouth, Miss Bud. I have friends there who are still in the service. Do you know Portsmouth?'

Rosa did not know it. (In fact she knew very little beyond the confines of

Cloisterham); but she had read about it and had formed the opinion that it must be one of the prettiest places in England.

Lieutenant Tartar warmly agreed (which would have been much to the astonishment of Portsmouth had it heard) and offered to take Miss Bud and Miss Twinkleton to see the town just as soon as arrangements might be made. He gave the impression that that very afternoon would not put him out in the least. But of course it was impossible as they were to return to Cloisterham on the following day; so the visit to Portsmouth was put off, with a sigh of disappointment, until the Christmas recess.

They left the yacht ('Let me help you, Miss Bud . . . and you, too, Miss Twinkleton!') and there once more were the tall warehouses, looming all round them like gaolers round the bed of a prisoner, as he awakens from a dream. There were the sailorly old men, puffing and dozing in the doorways; and there was the fishing boy.

The "Rosa Bud"

Rosa, when she stepped onto the dockside and felt the sternness of the land once more beneath her, experienced in reverse those earlier sensations of freedom. She looked back at the vessel and wondered if she would ever see it again.

'When I bought her,' said Lieutenant Tartar, gazing fixedly at the prow, 'she was called "The Lady Amelia". Would you mind, Miss Bud — and please say if you would, and I would not take it at all amiss — would you mind if I renamed her, "The Rosa Bud"?'

'I — I would be honoured, Lieutenant Tartar!' cried Rosa, glancing in confusion to Miss Twinkleton, whose two states of existence exhibited alarming signs of colliding. 'But would it not be unlucky . . . I mean, changing a name?'

'No more for a ship than for a woman!' laughed Lieutenant Tartar. 'And ships, as you know, are always spoken of as "she". We sailors, Miss Bud, are sentimental folk, and superstitious, too. Is that not so, Lobely? We think it the luckiest thing in the world to change the name of a ship. Is that not so, Lobely? The name will be painted on this very day. You will attend to it, Lobely? And now Miss Twinkleton,' (casting his eye over the vessel) 'do you not agree, ma'am, that there is no prettier, no more charming craft afloat than "The Rosa Bud"?'

Miss Twinkleton, mindful of her charge, agreed cautiously; but at the same time, and by means of determined stares at the vessel, let it be clearly understood that she was agreeing to the compliment being bestowed upon the vessel and not upon her pupil, who, by reason of a certain misty lightness apparent to Miss Twinkleton, might also be deemed to be afloat.

They returned to Staple Inn; and it was exceedingly hard for Rosa to bring herself back to the unhappiness of her friend. The room looked so bare and sullen, and utterly dead. Helena, just as she had been left, sat staring out of the window, clasping and unclasping her hands. Her trunk, in readiness for the return to Cloisterham, lay in the middle of the floor, and the servant girl was staring at it with cordial dismay.

'She wants me to unpack it, miss! And me only just havin' managed the straps!'

'Why, Helena, why?' cried Rosa. 'It will be much better when you are away from here!'

Rosa appealed to her friends to plead with Helena; but Helena only shook her head and repeated:

'I must stay.'

Miss Twinkleton urged upon her the impropriety of a young person living alone in Staple Inn.

'What of Neville, Miss Twinkleton? Was not he a young person, alone?'

'My dear — my dear! I meant a young woman!'

'Oh yes, of course! It would not be proper. I forgot. You see, I am a stranger,' said Helena, calmly; and looked at those who wished her well as if all were strangers.

'But Mr. Crisparkle will be so distressed, Helena,' said Rosa; and wished with all her heart that, for her friend's sake, the Minor Canon had a vessel at his command, as she could imagine nothing more likely to persuade a heart from its grief.

'Mr. Crisparkle,' said Helena, 'will be all the better without me. And Miss Twinkleton! I understand your concern, ma'am, and do indeed honour it. But there is no need. I will attend to it directly. You will see.'

She went from the room, leaving her friends to wonder what it was they would see. She was gone for no more than a few minutes; and when she returned, there was a cry of astonishment, and even of fear. It was not Helena who came into the room. It was Neville, murdered Neville!

She had cut off her hair and put on Neville's clothes, so that the resemblance, which had always been striking, was now uncanny. She was Neville. Her very look was Neville's look, and the wildness of nature, so much under control in Helena, now shone forth as if she was wearing her brother's eyes. Then the fire in them died down as she turned to Miss Twinkleton.

'You see, Miss Twinkleton, there is no impropriety now! When I — we were children, and were trying to escape from great cruelty, I dressed as a boy, and passed as one. So why should I not do so now . . . to escape? Surely there is nothing strange in my doing so?'

'But there is, there is!' cried Miss Twinkleton, alarmed and distressed by matters she did not fully understand.

'Why is it strange, Miss Twinkleton?'

'Because you are Helena, my dear. Because you are Helena.'

'No, Miss Twinkleton. I am Neville. I am Neville.'

An Awkward Interview

MR. GREWGIOUS, dry, lawful, angular, methodical, unmarried, unlikely-ever-to-be-married Mr. Grewgious sat in an upright chair beside his fireplace with his angular hands placed firmly upon his angular knees, as if to restrain them.

Matters had been settled — not entirely to everyone's satisfaction, but then they never are for some nagging doubt must always remain; but they had been settled nonetheless. The departure from the Billickins had taken place and Miss Twinkleton's little party had been seen off at the Railway Terminus with sufficient baskets of fruit, bundles of periodicals, wavings of hands, scarves and handkerchiefs to have done justice to an expedition to the North Pole.

Now they were gone; Staple Inn and Southampton Street knew them no more. Mr. Grewgious gazed steadfastly into thin air; then, momentarily releasing a knee, took out his watch, consulted it and made methodical calculations to determine how far upon their journey the travellers might be. Apparently satisfied, as if his watch and the train were in close communication and any calamity to one would be infallibly reflected in the face of the other, he replaced it. Matters were undoubtedly settled.

Beside him, on a small round table, lay the pretty gold ring with its rose of rubies and diamonds. He gazed at it and clasped his knees more tightly than ever. He watched it, as if he was some singularly perverse alchemist, waiting for gold to turn into lead. Not unreasonably the ring remained unchanged ... yet one would have thought that some shadowing, some tarnishing would have fallen across it. One would have thought that, having once been taken from a dead finger, and now from a murdered man, it would have displayed some spotting of death. He, Hiram Grewgious, certainly felt shadowed, and not a little tarnished, as he gazed at the ring which had once been evidence of love and was now evidence of murder.

Yes — matters were settled, although not entirely to everyone's satisfaction.

There came a knock on his door.

'Yes?'

Bazzard's gloomy head appeared. Poor Bazzard, whose personal triumph had been utterly overcast by the crime! Poor Bazzard, who had been aching to enlarge on every detail of his success; who had been yearning to fill every ear with the optimistic remarks of the Manager who had promised that a highly Complimentary Article was about to appear and that it was an impossibility for The Thorn of Anxiety not to take the town by storm; poor Bazzard with all this bottled up inside him, was condemned to utter no more than:

'Mr. Datchery is here.'

'Then show him in, Bazzard.'

'I was going to,' said Bazzard, and departed with the air of one who has been asked to post a letter on his way to drowning himself.

Mr. Grewgious waited; and, by the way in which he gripped his knees, it was apparent that Bazzard's announcement had not materially added to his peace of mind. Mr. Datchery came in and stood before the lawyer in the soldierly attitude he always felt to be appropriate.

'Will you take some refreshment, Mr. — um — Datchery?'

'Thank you, Mr. Grewgious, but Mr. Bazzard has already — '

'Has he indeed! Very well, then, very well!' (Mr. Datchery frowned a little at this departure from the lawyer's usual greeting.) 'Pray tell me, Mr. Datchery, are you in good health?'

Mr. Datchery, his puzzlement increasing, glanced at the lawyer's wooden face as if for enlightenment; and finding none, frowned more deeply as if he was making a careful inventory of his organs and limbs before committing himself as to their condition.

'I believe I am in good health, Mr. Grewgious.'

'I am glad to hear it. And your lodgings, and Mrs. Tope's cooking are no doubt to your satisfaction?'

Again the glance, again the frown, as if considering Mrs. Tope's skills in every particular before venturing on their praise.

'They are sufficient for my needs, Mr. Grewgious. The lady is agreeable and the linen is clean.'

'I am glad to hear it. It must be quite delightful in the old town at this time of the year. It must be highly agreeable to stroll in the Cathedral Close and investigate the antiquities. Do you not find it so, Mr. Datchery?'

'I cannot say that I have noticed, Mr. Grewgious. But I suppose the quaint old place might appeal to some.'

'I am glad to hear it. You must have made many friends in Cloisterham, Mr. Datchery. I trust that they have given you pleasant evenings?'

'I have made acquaintances, sir,' returned Mr. Datchery, baffled by the lawyer's drift but sensing that it had direction and not altogether liking it. 'I have passed the time of day with the Reverend Crisparkle, who is certainly an amiable person.'

'Ah yes. The Reverend Crisparkle. It was he, was it not, who conveyed my message for you to call upon me?'

'It was indeed, sir.'

'That was six days ago, Mr. Datchery, was is not?'

Mr. Datchery consulted his pocket book, and it was to be observed that his face was grown a little redder, and his hair, by contrast, several shades the whiter. He reached the place in his book from which he was able to confirm the lawyer's statement.

'I am glad to hear it. I am glad that we agree on that, Mr. Datchery. So now perhaps you will set my mind at rest concerning a little problem that has been troubling me. You have not been unwell; your lodgings, though sufficient for your needs, are not so delightful as to have captivated you to the exclusion of all else; the town holds no extraordinary attraction for you; and no warm friendship has arisen that might have swayed you. Yet it has taken *six days*, Mr. Datchery, for you to answer a summons that, as you may recollect, contained the expression, 'at your earliest convenience'. Why, sir, did you feel yourself to be justified in attaching as much emphasis to *convenience* as to *earliest*? Why did you not come at once?' As the lawyer put his question, he glanced again at the ring. 'Matters are settled, you know.'

Mr. Datchery following the direction of the lawyer's eyes, said quietly: 'I take it, sir, that that is the article that was found upon Neville Landless?'

'So you know of it, then?'

'I was present when Mr. Crisparkle called on Mr. Jasper with the news. He spoke of the ring and the significance attached to it.'

'Then you must have known, even before you received my summons, that the matter was settled! If you will forgive my saying so, that rather increases my puzzlement than diminishes it! Why, sir, knowing that nothing further was to be accomplished, did you continue in Cloisterham at so many pounds, shillings and pence per week?'

It was evident that the lawyer was angry and that the causes were probably many and various, and that Mr. Datchery's apparent rebelliousness was only a small part of them; nevertheless that small part drew itself stiffly to attention and proceeded to address a place about a foot above Mr. Grewgious's head, as if there was another Mr. Grewgious, wiser and more just, in attendance there.

'Mr. Grewgious! When first you opened this matter to me, and made me acquainted with the circumstances so far as you knew them, you did so because your suspicions had been aroused. By communicating your suspicions to a person of my profession, you offered him a scent.'

'That is so, Mr. Datchery. I do not deny it. But now —' (another glance at the ring) — 'matters are settled.'

'I took that scent, Mr. Grewgious,' continued Mr. Datchery to the wiser Mr. Grewgious, 'and it has been with me ever since. There has not been a moment when I have lost it; and there has not been a moment when I have been led to believe that it might be a false scent.'

'A man may be mistaken, Mr. Datchery. Even a man of your profession.'

'That is possible, sir,' said Mr. Datchery, with the air of one agreeing that, under certain circumstances, two and two might make five but that he personally had never come across them.

'Then why did you not come?'

'There was, Mr. Grewgious, in the course of my interview with Mr. Jasper, an oddity, a curiosity that gave me cause for some thought.'

'How so?'

'There was a strong feeling — I received a strong impression that our friend had some prior knowledge of the crime.'

'Of Drood?'

'Of Landless.'

The lawyer removed his hands from his knees and placed them on the arms of his chair. He leaned forward.

'Can you be certain?'

'No, Mr. Grewgious. I cannot be *certain.*'

The lawyer leaned back and glanced again at the ring.

'Then it is not evidence in support of a crime. But I take it that there is more?'

Mr. Datchery consulted his pocket book.

'Our friend was in London on the day that Landless was murdered.'

'A man may be in London when he pleases. It is not evidence in support of a crime.'

'At about ten o'clock on that night, our friend was observed, by the watcher I had employed, to visit the court where the opium woman lives.'

'A man may do as he pleases with his health and time; and provided what he does entails no injury to another, it cannot be evidence in support of a crime.'

'My watcher, observing our friend to enter the woman's house, went at once to Staple Inn, as had been arranged. He inquired for you, sir, but finding that you were out, came away with the only person having any connection with you. He returned to the court with Neville Landless.'

The lawyer drew in his breath sharply.

'And our friend?'

'Had gone.'

Mr. Grewgious seemed to crumple a little. He shook his head.

'No evidence, Mr. Datchery. No evidence.'

'Yet suspicion, sir. And a little too strong for a false scent.'

'Possibly, possibly. Your watcher saw nothing more?'

'He saw Landless hurry out of the court, as if, my watcher said, he was being washed away.'

'No more than that?'

'His view from his window could not command all of the court.'

'No more can ours, Mr. Datchery. There is still no evidence in support of a crime. Nor, Mr. Datchery, if you will forgive my saying so, is there sufficient evidence in support of your six days' delay. Why did you not call upon me before?'

'I waited for the young people to return to Cloisterham as I supposed that they would be frequently with you after the tragedy. I thought it wisest to obey your instructions, sir, and keep our association as private as possible.'

Mr. Grewgious, who felt very much inclined to burst out with: 'Why did you not tell me this at once?' shook his head and passed a hand through his hair.

'Very well, Mr. Datchery; and what have you accomplished in those six days, at so many pounds, shillings and pence by the week?'

'I have, Mr. Grewgious,' said Mr. Datchery, permitting himself the faintest of smiles, 'made warm friendships, as you suspected, sir. Our friend and the Worshipful Mayor have been my guests to dinner (at so many pounds, shillings and pence) and I have been theirs. I have, as you also suspected, strolled in the Cathedral Close and investigated the antiquities there. I have been fortunate enough to have been conducted over the place by the Cathedral Stone-mason, one Durdles, who has shown me his remarkable skills. It seems that it is possible, by the judicious tapping of his hammer, to discover the whereabouts of monks and bishops long dead and crumbled away. In the course of his tappings among the old walls and tombs and monuments, Durdles has made many remarkable discoveries; and, I think, is likely to make many more.'

'What manner of discoveries?'

'Among other things, a lost key,' said Mr. Datchery, suppressing the affair of Mrs. Sapsea's ghost, which Durdles had confided to Deputy, and Deputy to him. In the present context he did not feel that Mrs. Sapsea's ghost and its interesting communication constituted evidence in support of anything except Durdles's drunken condition.

'And this key is evidence?'

'As much as the ring.'

'Ah! But the ring has been found! The key, you say, is lost.'

'But will be found. Mr. Grewgious. It will be found.'

'And then?'

'And then the matter will be settled, sir.'

'Very well, Mr. Datchery. You are, I take it, returning directly to Cloisterham?'

Mr. Datchery hesitated for a moment, and then nodded.

'Then I would be obliged sir,' said the lawyer, pursuing his habit of ending his interviews with Mr. Datchery affably, 'I would be greatly obliged if you would spare the time to tell Bazzard how very much I admired his play. I don't think he believes me. But I really did admire it, Mr. Datchery. I could not have attempted such a work myself even to save my life. Not that that is much of a recommendation,' he added with a smile.

When Mr. Datchery had gone from the room, the lawyer returned once more to gazing at the ring; and his hands imperceptibly returned to gripping his knees. His look was once more the look of a perverse alchemist seeking to change gold to lead. The ring had always seemed to him to be a symbol of the ultimate happiness of Rosa, so that without it, that happiness would be clouded. The ring troubled him in the strangest way. Although he approved of Lieutenant Tartar almost as much as did Rosa herself, he could not see anything beyond the ring. Untarnished itself, it tarnished everything else. He knew this to be foolish and superstitious in him, but superstition dies harder than reason, even in the wisest of us. There are ghosts.

The Play's the Thing!

THERE was a healthful glow in Mr. Datchery's cheeks following his interview with Mr. Grewgious, as if that inquisition had served merely to promote his circulation. His step was light, his head was high and there was an air about him of never having faltered under fire. Entering the outer office he conveyed, in accordance with the lawyer's wishes, Mr. Grewgious's high regard for Bazzard's play.

'Oh yes, I know he admires it,' said the author, accepting the tribute rather off-handedly. 'Everyone did, you know.'

There was, if anything, a mild dissatisfaction in Bazzard's voice, as if universal admiration had been a veiled criticism, an implied disregard. Unhappily Bazzard possessed the true artist's temperament which decrees that no praise, however lavish, can be adequate for the cherished child of his brain. To have been told that it was good would have implied that it was not excellent; to have been told that it was excellent would have implied that it fell short of the superb; to have been told that it was the equal of Hamlet would have implied that the teller thought more highly of King Lear, and that Hamlet was a botched piece, unworthy of a cultured person's consideration.

'There was a good deal of clapping, of course, and Bravos, and that sort of thing, but really, Dick, I doubt if one in a hundred really understood it.'

Mr. Datchery, making a rapid calculation on the basis of an audience of fifteen divided by a hundred, and arriving at an inconvenient fraction, duly commiserated.

'Not that one could have expected complete understanding at a first hearing!' Bazzard hastened to say, for he did not wish his friend to think that he had read to fools. 'One couldn't have counted on that. But they were engrossed, Dick. One could see that they *felt* it. All things considered, one could say that it went marvellously, extraordinarily well. I don't think that's putting it too high. Calmly speaking, I think one could say that it was a triumph. The effect of the thunderstorm, flashing and banging outside was really tremendous. The elements, you know, always help. And then that scream, right at the end. Wonderful!'

'There was a scream? I don't recall your having a scream at the end, Harry?'

'Oh no. It wasn't in the play. It was Miss Landless. She screamed out quite suddenly. The effect, one might say, was chilling. Do you know, I think I will write it in? It would be a fine stroke, a real coup de theatre. First the curtain, then the storm of applause, and then the scream. That would be a touch to send people home with, eh?'

'Miss Landless? That would be Neville Landless's sister, would it not?'

'Yes, yes. There was an empty chair, you know. I don't know how it came to be there. Perhaps somebody was ill at the last minute? Anyway, Miss Landless thought she saw her brother sitting in it, bleeding all over. It was quite like Macbeth. I can't imagine how there came to be an empty chair. It was the only one, of course.'

'She is a twin, is she not? She was her brother's twin?'

'Yes. Astonishing resemblance. Only yesterday she cut her hair and put on his clothes, and the effect was quite ghostly. It might have been him. Miss Bud was quite frightened. Do you think the empty chair could have been intended for the lady who took the tickets and she felt uncomfortable about sitting down with the guests?'

'One supposes then that Miss Landless might actually have seen her brother's image at the very moment that he died. With twins, you know, such things can happen.'

'Can they? How odd. But now you mention it, I believe I have heard something of the kind. Do you know, Dick, I think I will go back to Greens Hotel and ask about that chair. One has a right to know.'

Mr. Datchery agreed, and, after offering further congratulations, left the author continuing to brood upon the empty chair and upon the spectral presence that had occupied it; until at last he managed to derive some crumbs of comfort from the happy thought that a man, on the point of expiring, had bethought himself of Bazzard's play, even though he had arrived late and without a ticket.

Mr. Datchery, still thinking of Miss Landless and the astonishing resemblance she bore to her brother, left Staple Inn and walked down Chancery Lane. From there he threaded his way through a maze of side streets until he reached the neighbourhood of Drury Lane. It was a neighbourhood where life, as represented by a poor player (by a great many poor players in fact) strutted his brief hour upon the stage. It was a neighbourhood of actors who, at that moment, were not acting, of poets who, at that moment, were blank of verse, and of thin, haunting managers who, at that moment, were without anything to manage. It was a neighbourhood of many corners, on each of which a dismal public-house seemed to have broken out, like a sore patch; and in which, by grace of the honourable democracy of the profession, the famous and the obscure rubbed shoulders; but nothing came off.

Mr. Datchery passed them by with a reminiscent smile and turned into a narrow court where he occupied a pair of rooms on the first floor of a depressed-looking house. This house lay under the dominion of one Mrs. MacSiddons, a mountainous female always to be observed in a fiercely plaid gown, reputed by some to have been the original garment worn by the original Lady Macbeth on the occasion of Duncan's entry under her battlements. In her youth she had been on the stage herself and consequently was not to be deceived.

'I am not to be deceived,' she was wont to say, when begged by some impecunious Thespian for a trifling extension of credit or a crust of bread. 'I 'ave been in the profession myself so I knows a piece of hacting when I sees one.'

She was not to be deceived by tears, pleadings or dismal lamentations; she had not even been deceived by a broken leg (occasioned by an anguished inhabitant leaving by way of his window rather than face her upon the stairs); and above all she had never been deceived by Mr. MacSiddons, who, after having attempted that supernatural task over many years, had at last expired, rather unconvincingly, Mrs. MacSiddons thought.

It was her custom, whenever she heard anyone approach the front door, to issue forth in a rush and knock her servant girl aside. However, on this occasion, finding that her visitor was Dick Datchery, her ferocity subsided and out of the strong came forth sweetness. Dick Datchery, since he had relinquished the stage, was favoured in her sight above all other mortals in her house. She doted upon him, kept his room spotlessly clean and regularly brushed his collection of hats.

'Oh! Oh! Are you come 'ome at last, Dick?' she panted, shutting the door and leaning against it, with her hands pressed to her bosom to subdue its palpitations.

'I happened to be in London, ma'am,' said Mr. Datchery, with the air of one favoured above his deserts. 'So I took it into my head to look in upon you.'

'Ah, Dick, you're always welcome 'ere, as you must know! You in there!' she shouted suddenly. 'You're not deceivin' me for a minute! Not for a minute, do you 'ear?'

A low moan, proceeding, it seemed, from under the floorboards, gave notice that the would-be deceiver had heard. Mrs. MacSiddons smiled plaintively.

'You got no idea, Dick, you reely can't 'ave any idea what it's like with a 'ole 'ouseful of 'em tryin' to pull the wool over my eyes! And sich bad performers, too! Why, Dick, as we both knows, they wouldn't 'ave lasted five minutes in the old days!'

It was a fiction to which Mrs. MacSiddons subscribed that the old days represented a standard of artistic excellence to which the present generation could not hope to aspire.

Then, with a further warning, addressed, apparently, to the house at large, Mrs. MacSiddons accompanied the favoured one to his rooms on the first floor.

'I'll bring up some tea, Dick, and some cake, and we can talk.'

She departed and left the favourite in his domain. Mr. Datchery, like most people whose triumphs have been ephemeral, liked to collect things that reminded him visibly of those golden moments that, otherwise, would not have left a rack behind.

Chiefly they took the form of playbills, framed and arranged in sequence, that charted his rise in the profession, from small print at the bottom, to honourable situations half way up. There were items from provincial newspapers in which his name appeared (and was underlined); and, in particular, there was a glowing account of his performance as the drunken Porter in Macbeth, which had been the very peak of his career. His usual wanderings about the stage in pursuit of concealed lines had so accorded with the tottery state of the character, that he had been cheered to the rafters, night after night; and for the rest of that season he had been the lion of the company and the toast of provincial beauties among whom he had been known as, 'that wonderful, wonderful Mr. Porter!'

His gaze lingered on it (it always did) and he smiled. Then he passed on to 'Last Appearance this Season', and finally, 'Positively Last Appearance on Any Stage'; after which the playbills ended and his second profession began. Strange indeed was this collection: there was a short length of rope, a knife, a curiously shaped bottle, a pair of spectacles with a broken lens, an iron bar and a letter that had been torn into fragments and carefully pieced together. These articles, and others of a similarly miscellaneous nature, were displayed in flat boxes, and represented golden moments (though perhaps not quite so golden to some) of a more recent date.

There was no doubt that Mr. Datchery, in his second profession, had made quite a habit of success; so much so that the very idea of failure was apt to rob him of sleep. Thus when Mr. Grewgious had put it to him that the Cloisterham affair was settled and his task to be abandoned, he had been quite distressed.

Curious, bland, yet deeply various gentleman, ready, in his first profession, to weep for Hecuba; yet in his second (where Hecubas were two a penny though not so named) passing by dry-eyed. Possibly it was because he had failed in his first profession that his devotion to his second was so complete. He was very like a convert to a new faith, who walks in the ways of the Lord with such assiduity as to obliterate His footsteps entirely. Once taking a scent, be it never so foul and corrupt, be it never so injurious to life and limb, be it never so contrary to a thousand pleaded wishes, Mr. Datchery pursued it as if it was the headiest of perfumes and he its most abject slave.

Mrs. MacSiddons, preceded by the servant girl (unreliably reported to be her step-daughter on account of her frequently appearing to confuse the girl with steps), came in with the tea-things and found the favoured one in contemplation of his playbills.

'Well, Dick,' said she, supervising the laying of the cloth and then ushering out the girl with a friendly motion of her foot, 'when are we goin' to 'ave somethin' new to 'ang up?' She glanced meaningfully towards the miscellaneous items as if to draw her favourite from dwelling on matters that might have led him in the ways of deception. 'And what will it be, Dick? A bludgeon? A meat-chopper, or a 'orrible spike?'

'I rather fancy it will be a key, ma'am. Or maybe a key and a ring.'

'A ring, Dick? What manner of ring?'

'A gold ring, with a rose of rubies and diamonds.'

'That'll be 'andsome! But you'll 'ave to put it on veller, else it won't show. I'll look through me old articles and see what I can find.'

'Perhaps the key will be sufficient, ma'am,' said Mr. Datchery, apparently unwilling to involve his protectress in close needlework on his behalf. 'We will not put the ring on the wall.'

'Just as you wish, Dick, just as you wish,' sighed the Undeceivable, glancing, in a veiled fashion, at her hugely dimpled hand where tributes from the late Mr. MacSiddons lay buried in portly fingers that had become, through passage of years, soft cemeteries of rings. 'A wall ain't reely the place for joolry.'

Thoughtfully she pressed each of her fingers in turn, as if it had crossed her mind that Dick might have had such a destination in view for

Mr. Datchery's past and Mr. Datchery's present

the trinket, and that one day Dick would be translated from the first floor front to those spacious regions below, where she reigned in single splendour, with none but the little servant girl to fill the widow's cruse.

If indeed the fair lady harboured such a hope, it cannot be said that Mr. Datchery had ever given her encouragement, unless unfailing courtesy and unfailing rent be tokens of more than ordinary esteem. So was it possible then that the Undeceivable had at last fallen victim to that arch-deceiver of us all? Had she deceived herself?

'Tell us about 'im, Dick, the one you're out to catch,' said Mrs. MacSiddons, referring to Mr. Datchery's quarry in Cloisterham, of whom she had previously been apprised; for Mr. Datchery liked to unfold his mind when he was at home. (Perhaps it was on account of these musings, by their very nature, confidential, that the widow had been given cause to hope?)

'Well, he's a gentleman, as I told you, ma'am. A musical gentleman with a fine voice who sings in church and leads the choir.'

'You'll catch 'im, Dick! And then 'e'll sing another tune! Tell us the crime!' Mrs. MacSiddons leaned forward mountainously and munched cake, so that her chins, which she wore in rows, like necklaces, trembled with excitement. 'Murder, you said?'

'Murder most foul, as in the best it is!'

'Ah Dick, Dick!' exclaimed Mrs. MacSiddons, wagging a fat forefinger as she dimly apprehended the lofty accents of a play. 'You'd 'ave made mincemeat of 'em all!'

'In the old days, ma'am!'

'The old days, Dick!' sighed Mrs. MacSiddons, making a snapping gesture with her fingers which had reference to her own time upon the stage, which had been in the popular line, with dogs. 'Blood, was there, Dick?'

'In as much as it is thicker than water, ma'am.'

'A relative!'

'An uncle.'

'Of an age, Dick?'

'Maybe seven and twenty, but he looks older.'

'And a gentleman. That makes a change, Dick. There's a refinement in it you can't deny. Like Emlit, is 'e? Speakin' of uncles, I mean.'

'I wouldn't say that, ma'am. To tell the truth, I wouldn't care to say what he is.'

'Never mind, Dick, you'll catch 'im! The key now, and the ring. Tell about 'em, Dick!'

'Ah, the key! There's the rub! The ring proves nothing, or at best, a lie. But the key, ma'am, the key!'

'And do you 'ave it, Dick?'

Mr. Datchery shook his head sadly.

'Never mind! You'll find it, Dick! You'll find it!'

'Not I, ma'am, not I. Were I to find it, it would mean no more than the ring. He must find it himself.'

'Then you'll make 'im, Dick!'

'Ah but how, ma'am? How is he to be made to betray himself?'

'Whisper in 'is ear! Put pison in 'is dreams! You knows a 'undred ways to catch 'im!'

'Yet why should he betray himself now that the ring has acquitted him?' murmured Mr. Datchery, apparently discounting his patroness's sage advice. 'Why should he, of his own accord, awaken suspicion when he has already put it to sleep? For what reason should he disturb the dead, ma'am?'

Mrs. MacSiddons shook her head and smiled roguishly.

'You know, Dick, don't you! I can see it in your eyes, I can see it in your smile! You already knows a way, Dick! You wants me to guess, and I won't! You wants to 'ave your joke with me, Dick! Tell us, Dick, 'as the idea just come to you, or did you know it all along?'

'Little by little, ma'am. I knew a little when I came; and the rest soon followed.'

'Will you give me a 'int, Dick?'

Mr. Datchery laughed.

'I will give you a hint, ma'am,' he said, rising to his feet and clapping his hat upon his head. 'And you may puzzle it out! My hint is this. The play's the thing! The play's the thing!'

He took his departure and Mrs. MacSiddons, with cake in her hand, and cake in her mouth, and cake dropping down on her lap, munched and munched and frowned and smiled.

XXXIII

Enter a Porter

MISS TWINKLETON'S pupils, refreshed from family excursions to German watering-places, Alpine hotels and various depressing towns in France, have returned to the rigours of academic life noticeably improved (they tell each other), in height, complexion and form. They have arrived after the manner of migratory birds, in a seasonable flock; and the romantically inclined youth of Cloisterham, who (like the Cathedral rooks, have not migrated anywhere, and never do), have congregated outside The Nuns' House to express rapturous approval by means of chirping whistles and declarations, in chalk, upon the wall.

The boxes and trunks are duly unloaded from the bespoken carriages and are distributed by Miss Twinkleton's porter and his boy; and presently the austere chambers of The Nuns' House are wondrous with flying bonnets, ribbons, sashes and gowns. It is as if the visions that the original inhabitants had long ago fasted and prayed for, have at last been granted in the surprising shape of straw cherubs, taffeta angels, and clouds of muslin grace.

Gifts are exchanged: inscribed paper bags smelling of peppermint, vanilla, cinnamon and cloves, and fastened with coloured string; and soon the passages and stairs of The Nuns' House are whisperous with little fluted brown-paper cups, upon which Mrs. Tisher treads and straightway thinks on her cabinet of remedies, as if she expects sickness in the night.

Nor is she misled. One or two of the weaker vessels do succumb, and there is much traffic of ghostly handmaidens bearing candles, basins and towels, and Mrs. Tisher herself, mistress of mysteries, carrying goblets brimming with potions. For the rest, however, it is a time for eager confidences whispered from pillow to pillow, and having much to do with dark-eyed waiters, brigandish policemen and god-like mountain-guides, to whom, in the fierce flashing of a foreign eye, Miss Twinkleton's pupils have surrendered a secret portion of their English hearts.

In the fullness of time, no doubt, these visions will fade; but in the emptiness of it (which comes at the end) they will return, altered, but not as men would be. *Their* hair will not be thin and white, *their* limbs will not be weak, *their* breath will not be tedious; rather will they be yet more dashing and lively, for dreams grow young even as the dreamers grow old. And will those humble waiters, those weary policemen, those toiling Alpine guides, when they have grown fat and have fat wives, in their Swiss hotels, their German watering-places and their depressing towns in France, will they dream of wild-eyed, slender English nymphs who flashed through their summer long ago? Most probably they will; for we all plant regrets and lovingly tend them until they give out a perfume sweeter than roses.

Great rumours are afoot. Mrs. Tisher is to be married again (which she is not); Miss Twinkleton has dyed her hair (which she most certainly has not); and an Indian Princess is to arrive tomorrow, on an elephant, for the new term. But above all these matters, the murder of Neville Landless takes pride of place. Pale, slaughtered youth! Wept over, talked over, gossiped over, and one might almost say, picked over until his bones are clean. Much is made of Rosebud, whose situation, having been deprived by death of two prospective lovers, is as interesting as it is piteous; but little now, and less in the days that follow, is made of Helena Landless, whose misfortune is as strange as she is herself. Never has there been such an odd young woman, with her chopped-off hair and her brooding, solitary ways. Great sympathy is extended to Mr. Crisparkle, who tries to do his best and gets his head bitten off whenever he calls. The poor man is at his wit's end to know what to do.

It is rumoured (on the authority of a maidservant who appears to be gifted with second sight by way of compensation for a notorious lack of the first in the matter of seeing dust) that Miss Landless has an elderly admirer, living in Cloisterham under an assumed name, and that she has assignations with him in the back of the Lumps of Delight shop every afternoon.

It is rumoured (on the same authority) that this admirer has followed Miss Landless from Ceylon, and is immensely rich and, when Miss Twinkleton gives the word, will bestow great largesse on the school, in the form of ruby rings. It is rumoured that the gentleman has already bespoken the Cathedral for his nuptials, and has arranged the music with Mr. Jasper and the Dean.

These interesting conjectures appear to receive some confirmation when, one morning, Miss Landless is sent for in the middle of History, as a gentleman has called. The gentleman, satisfactorily ancient and with a large head of white hair, has, contrary to all precedent, been closeted alone with Miss Landless in Miss Twinkleton's private parlour, for ages and ages and ages. The possessor of second sight (wonderfully sharpened by application to a keyhole) has been able to confirm that Miss Landless sat in a chair with her hands clasped, while the elderly admirer walked to and fro. He had been distinctly heard to refer to the forthcoming nuptials by mentioning the Cathedral, Mr. Jasper and a ring. More than this the visionary has been unable to determine as the interview was terminated by Miss Twinkleton going in and Miss Landless coming out, trembling all over and with her eyes like coals on fire. Nevertheless it is highly probable that, at this very moment, the elderly admirer is pleading with Miss Twinkleton to grant the school a half-holiday.

Thus rumour, with just sufficient flavouring of truth to make it palatable, holds sway, and prayers are offered up for the softening of Miss Twinkleton's heart; and, strange to relate, had but the visionary re-applied her eye to the key-hole, she might have detected symptoms of that softening taking place, and so gained a better opinion of the power of prayer.

These symptoms, against which Miss Twinkleton struggles in vain, take the form of a fluttering of the hands, suggestive of invisible embroidery, and a misting of the eyes, suggestive of invisible spectacles. She sits in a low quilted chair, placed between the terrestrial and celestial globes, as if she is, quite literally, suspended between heaven and earth and is awaiting a summons from one or the other, but is not at all sure which.

Her visitor, the elderly admirer, sits in another low quilted chair, some distance away and with his hat upon his knees. He also exhibits interesting symptoms, suggestive of invisible spectacles and something absorbing in his hat.

'Although I am naturally curious, Mr. — er — Datchery,' says Miss Twinkleton, the fluttering of her hands extending itself into her voice, 'to know what it is you have been talking about with Miss Landless, I will not ask you. Mr. Crisparkle has told me that you are acquainted with Mr. Grewgious, so I must conclude that it concerns some business of his.'

'Quite correct, ma'am,' returns Mr. Datchery, warmly addressing the inside of his hat.

'You have known Mr. Grewgious for some time?' inquires Miss Twinkleton, leaving off her embroidery as she speaks and then returning to it with renewed industry.

'Three or four years, ma'am,' Mr. Datchery informs his hat . . . He casts a brief look upward, appears to be considering a smile, and then decides against it.

'A very agreeable gentleman,' says Miss Twinkleton, apparently including the two globes in the conversation; 'though quiet, of course, and a little settled in his ways. But then one supposes that gentlemen often are who have remained unmarried. You are staying with the Topes, you say? A respectable couple; always most polite. And the Cathedral so near. A little oppressive, don't you think? But venerable. King John in parts, I am told. And the misericords, you know. Sometimes one wonders about the early clergy. We are very old here, you know; I mean the building. Nuns. Poor souls! Yet the atmosphere is beneficial, as I always explain to parents. Have you visited our theatre? Of course it is quite small and humble, but at Christmas . . . Not to be compared with — with the metropolis, of course, or — or even . . . But nevertheless . . .'

'Ah! The theatre!' says Mr. Datchery, as Miss Twinkleton falters and inclines her head towards the celestial globe as if she has received some communication. 'The theatre!' repeats Mr Datchery; when Mrs. Tisher, after knocking softly and coughing feebly, comes in and says that she fears Miss Ferdinand has taken a chill.

'That cannot be!' says Miss Twinkleton, embroidering fiercely. 'There must be some mistake! You had better look again, Mrs. Tisher,' she says, apparently under the impression that what Miss Ferdinand has taken did not belong to her.

Mrs. Tisher, confused and feeling obscurely guilty, retires and develops an unreasonable grievance against Miss Ferdinand, which will shortly be expressed in finding fault with her (not difficult) and complaining about the state of her hair.

'You were speaking of the theatre, Mr. Datchery,' says Miss Twinkleton, arriving, it would seem, at a knotty point in her embroidery which requires some frowning and biting of the lower lip. 'Are you — have you been a great admirer of the play?'

Mr. Datchery, after giving the matter grave consideration, admits to a deep admiration. Miss Twinkleton nods.

'I, too! I, too!' she says; and then, with an oddly playful, and wholly astonishing gesture, raps the celestial globe with her knuckles, thereby causing the constellations to jump and forsake their wonted stations. 'Knock, knock, knock,' she proclaims. 'Who's there i' the name of Beelzebub?'

Mr. Datchery, for the moment nonplussed, declines to answer.

'Here's a farmer,' suggests Miss Twinkleton.

'Who hanged himself in th'expectation of plenty!' exclaims Mr. Datchery, as memory returns and he hears once more the fatal knocking on Macbeth's grim door. 'Come in time!' he invites, putting down his hat and rising to his feet. 'Have napkins enow about you; here you'll sweat for it!'

'Knock, knock,' interposes Miss Twinkleton, applying now to the terrestrial globe. 'Who's there i' the other devil's name?'

To which Mr. Datchery, gently staggering and flailing his arms, to the acute danger of certain china ornaments on the chimney-piece, responds, 'Faith, here's an equivocator that could swear in both the scales against either scale; who committed treason enough for God's sake, yet could not equivocate to heaven.'

He pauses, perhaps from old loss of memory, or perhaps from a superabundance of it. There is very little of triumph re-lived about him as he stands, with bowed head and hands hanging limply by his sides. He is the very image of one who has failed to equivocate to heaven.

'Oh come in, equivocator,' prompts Miss Twinkleton gently, her hand still resting on the terrestrial globe; and, as the equivocator raises his head, she says: 'I thought it was you. And then I knew it was you.'

'And I knew at once,' says Mr. Datchery. 'For you, at least, have not changed.'

'In fifteen years?'

'Is it fifteen years since —'

'— Since that season in the Wells? Since that season when you were wonderful Mr. Porter, and you gave us all such joy? It is fifteen years.'

'Is it fifteen years since we used to meet in The Pantiles and —'

'— and drive in that little coach to Eridge and dine at The Crest and Gun? It is fifteen years. Dear Mr. Porter — or was it not Armitage then?'

'Armitage then, but Datchery now. And were you not Miss Augusta then?'

'And Miss Augusta now.'

Mr. Datchery smiles wistfully; and then, with a grandly florid gesture that always brought the house down, says:

'I pray you remember the porter.'

'I always have,' says Miss Twinkleton. 'I always have remembered him.'

They both fall silent and gaze at each other: he conscious of his white hairs, his lined brow and his portly build, and she of the prim lines about her mouth, the wrinkling of her neck and that certain hardness that has overcome her curls, as if Time had been the Medusa's head and turned them into stone.

'You have not changed,' says he.

'Nor you,' says she. 'Very much.'

Then, this first shock over, he resumes his seat and she rises, and offers sherry in a glass about the size of a thimble; and they fall to, and talk of old times with a practised ease, and he learns how once she thought him proud and aloof, and she learns how he once thought her likewise proud and aloof; and they laugh, and somehow there is something grisly about it, as if they were a pair of corpses talking about the sportings of their ghosts.

'And have you never left Cloisterham?' he asks. 'I remember you said that you wanted to live in Tunbridge Wells.'

'That was fifteen years ago,' says she; and counters with, 'And did you never leave your rooms in Drury Lane? For you too, as I remember, expressed a wish to live in Tunbridge Wells.'

'Fifteen years ago.'

'And now you are no longer on the stage?'

'All the world's a stage, Miss Twinkleton.'

'Then what part do you play now?'

'The slippered pantaloon, I fear.'

Miss Twinkleton laughs and gently chides him; and so they go on, each, from time to time, making some veiled and glancing reference, like a child cautiously skirting a slumbering beast, and poking at it to see if it is still alive.

At last Mr. Datchery rises to take his departure, and Miss Twinkleton accompanies him to the front door; and as she walks thoughtfully back, Mrs. Tisher catches her and tells her that Miss Ferdinand has done up her hair like a bird's nest; and Miss Twinkleton looks at her and, for the moment, wonders who Miss Ferdinand is.

Mr. Datchery also, when he leaves The Nuns' House (though he has accomplished the purpose for which he called) finds, for a little while, the world to be a strange, unreal place, in which present events move like phantoms over an old grave. Then he goes back to The Gatehouse and the phantoms assume dread proportions and crowd upon him sombrely. He stands for a while under the archway and stares up and down the street. Then he walks a little way and looks up at the Choir Master's window; then returns to where he was before. Presently, and with a satisfied nod, he walks off and looks for Deputy, with whom he converses long and deep.

Mr. Brobity's Snuff-Box

ALTHOUGH Spring is widely held to be the season most propitious to love, it cannot be said that Autumn lags far behind. Indeed, the leaf may be observed to flutter even more wantonly when it is about to fall than when first it peeped forth, shy and green.

Mr. Sapsea, having made repeated applications to his friend, John Jasper, to intercede for him with Miss Bud, has been, since the return of Miss Twinkleton's pupils, in a high flutter of spirits. He is grown quite boyish; and is to be seen, at certain times of the day, standing in his doorway with thumbs hooked in the arm-holes of a wonder of a canary satin waistcoat, and bending an ardent gaze upon the gables of The Nuns' House.

Immediately above him, the effigy of his parent, with hammer upraised, seems to be inviting one last bid for the magnificent article at present before the public; and drawing attention to the numerous improvements (in the way of youthful boots and polished hair) that have been put in at great expense. All is in readiness for that dear young person for whom the auctioneer's heart, confined within his canary waistcoat, eagerly throbs.

New curtains have been hung in the principal bedroom, to delight the young person's eye; an elegant sewing cabinet has been purchased (at the sale of a noble lady's property) to fill the young person's leisure hours; and a heavy silver chain (from the same sale) has been prepared for the young person to wear round her slender waist so that she might jingle delightfully with the household keys. Nor is this all. A cradle (reputed to have been occupied by the infant Charles I and resembling a coffin on rockers) has been placed in what had been the first Mrs. Sapsea's little parlour for the reception of that tiny Thomas (or Thomasina) with whom the auctioneer hopes to be blessed; and for whose dear sake an oval portrait of the departed Mrs. Sapsea has been removed from its silver frame in order to make way for a likeness of its very own mother.

Thus Mr. Sapsea, well-kept, much sought after, and standing in his own grounds, waits under the hammer, so to speak, with the air of one who has been 'going' for quite long enough, and expects, at any moment, the final 'gone'!

'My dear Jasper!' says he, catching, at last, that gentleman in the act of coming out of The Nuns' House. 'My dear friend! Please come inside and take a glass of wine. Come, sir, I will not take no for an answer. I insist!'

Mr. Jasper smiles, frowns, declares himself honoured, but, unfortunately, he has much work to do as Miss Twinkleton has informed him of several new pupils for whom he must prepare.

'Come, sir! An hour will not deprive the young ladies!'

Mr. Jasper is desolated, but fears that even an hour, at the present time, would be an hour he could ill afford. He begs to be excused.

'But this is not friendly of you, my dear Jasper; and were you anyone else I would take it amiss. But I understand. The young ladies must be attended to. I will not come between you and the young ladies.' (A roguish smile.) 'So, if you will allow me, I will walk with you to your lodgings.' Before Jasper can reply, the auctioneer links arms with him, and perforce they stroll away together. The Choir Master is, as always, sombrely dressed, and he cuts an odd figure beside his exuberant companion. He calls to mind one of those grim confessors that attended on the triumphs of the gaudy old emperors to remind them of mortality. However, at the present time, he serves only to remind the auctioneer of the dear young person on whom his heart is set.

As they walk, they talk; which is to say that Mr. Sapsea talks, chiefly of civic matters and improvements to the town. As yet no mention is made of Jasper's visit to The Nuns' House (in the course of which Mr. Sapsea feels that his friend must have spoken of him to Miss Bud) as it is a matter of some delicacy, and the auctioneer is nothing if not a delicate man. From time to time he steals a glance at his silent friend; but Jasper's steady expression gives him no help, and the auctioneer begins to feel mildly impatient with his friend.

Although over the months he has become deeply attached to Jasper, there have been times — as there are always times between friends — when the Choir Master has undoubtedly irritated him; and he has been apt to dwell — as are we all — on the faults of his friend. It is true that, since the death of that scoundrel Landless and the discovery that he had almost certainly made away with Edwin Drood, Jasper's gloomy, unsettled mood has undergone an improvement. He has even declared that now he has come to accept the certainty of his nephew's death, he is able to look back more justly and with a calmer mind. He has even admitted that his nephew's carelessness of manner might well have provoked young Landless to his murderous assault. To which Mr. Sapsea, responding from the Bench, as it were, pronounced that, if carelessness of manner be accounted a justification for homicide, then the world would be a good deal emptier than it is; and that young Landless, by getting himself killed, had done the country a service by saving the expense of having him hanged.

One might have supposed that Jasper would have warmed to the Worshipful opinion; but he only shook his head as if he grieved not only for

Edwin Drood, but for his murderer, too. Mr. Sapsea cannot help regarding this meekness of Jasper's to be a fault; a fault on the right side, but a fault nonetheless. Consequently he is inclined to look down on Jasper, as we are all inclined to look down on people who, we suspect, are morally better than we are, as if they are still children in a hard, clever world.

At length the friends reach The Gatehouse, and Mr. Datchery, sitting with his door open, gives them 'Good Morning!' to which Mr. Sapsea, who wants to keep Jasper to himself, responds brusquely. Together they go up the postern stairs; and it is in vain for the Choir Master to remind Mr. Sapsea that he has work to do, for he can see that nothing short of shutting his door in the Worshipful face, will detach him. Together, then, they enter Jasper's rooms and, passing briefly through a dusty beam of sunlight, resemble an ogre-ish canary bird, arm in arm with an ogre-ish black dragonfly.

Mr. Sapsea seats himself by the chimney-piece and Jasper, after offering wine, settles down at the grand piano.

'You will forgive me, sir, if, at least, I do a little work?'

'By all means, my dear Jasper! You know how music delights me. And we must never forget the young ladies. Shall we drink a toast?' He raises his glass and twinkles across the brim. 'To the young ladies of The Nuns' House!' He drinks off his wine in the old manner, gallantly and at a gulp, so that Jasper is forced to rise and replenish his glass before settling down once more at the piano. He begins to play, quietly and evenly, pausing every now and then to make indications for fingering on the sheet of music before him. Mr. Sapsea crosses his legs and beats time on the arm of his chair.

'Ah music!' he sighs. 'The food of love, sir, don't you think? One might say that it is the very roast beef of the heart!'

He glances hopefully at the Choir Master, who, however, appears to be absorbed in the movements of his hands over the keyboard.

'Another toast!' says Mr. Sapsea suddenly. 'Come, sir, another toast! I give you, my dear Jasper, one lady in particular in The Nuns' House! I give you, Miss Rosa Bud!'

Jasper, somewhat taken aback, plays a wrong note, a very wrong note.

'That was an odd sound,' says Mr. Sapsea with interest. 'It was quite strange.'

'It was out of tune, that was all. The lower notes require re-tuning,' says Jasper rather quickly.

He begins to play again, when Mr. Sapsea reminds him that they have not drunk their last toast. They do so; and Jasper attends to his companion's glass and resumes his playing. Mr. Sapsea listens and cannot help admiring how skilfully Jasper manages to avoid the odd-sounding lower notes.

'Is it a love song, my dear Jasper?'[1]

'No. It is a minuet.'

'It sounds very like a love song, if I may say so. There is quite a suggestion of wedding bells chiming. Are you sure it is not a love song?'

Although Jasper repeats his denial, the auctioneer smiles knowingly, and feels that he has sufficiently prepared the ground. He rises.

'You are leaving, Mr. Sapsea?'

'No, no. It is just that there is a small matter on which I would like your opinion. As you know, my dear friend, I have always had the highest regard for your taste.'

He removes from his coat pocket a quantity of jeweller's wool from which he extracts a small silver box, horribly disfigured by small coloured stones, that seem to have broken out all over it, like boils.

'Indian work, I fancy,' says Mr. Sapsea, holding it up to eye-level.

The Choir Master, turning on his piano stool, sees no reason to doubt it.

'Examine it, sir, pray examine it.'

Jasper takes it and examines it. He offers to return it but Mr. Sapsea has retired out of range.

'It is a snuff-box, sir. In fact it is, or rather, it was the property of the late Mr. Brobity. You are aware, of course, that the first Mrs. Sapsea (I mean, of course, the late Mrs. Sapsea) was orginally a Miss Brobity and consequently Mr. Brobity was my own father-in-law.'

Jasper indicates that, although he has been aware of it, it is a fact that does not stale with repetition.

'This box, my dear Jasper, was given by Mrs. Brobity to Mr. Brobity on their nuptial day. A love-gift, sir. On Mr. Brobity's decease (Mrs. Brobity having previously expired following the production of a daughter, Ethelinda) the article passed into the possession of his issue. That issue, my dear Jasper, became the first Mrs. Sapsea (for so I must think of her), who bestowed it upon the husband of her choice. Thus it has descended, from loving hand to loving hand; and thus it demands to continue on its rosy way. Open it, my friend, open it!'

Jasper does so and finds within, to his surprise, a lock of faded gingerish hair. Mr. Sapsea, with an impatient clucking, darts forward and removes the intrusive lock with thumb and forefinger and tucks it into his waistcoat pocket.

'The inscription, sir. Pray read the inscription on the inside of the lid.'

He stations himself behind the Choir Master and bends over him as he reads.

'Rosa Sapsea. Wife to Thomas, Mayor of Cloisterham. May the Candle of Love never be Snuffed Out.'

'You will notice,' says Mr. Sapsea complacently, 'the play upon words. Snuff-box, you know. And snuffers, for candles, of course. It came to me quite suddenly and required only a little thought to phrase it neatly. And now, sir, pray give me your opinion.'

Jasper shuts the snuff-box with a snap and returns it to the auctioneer. He fixes upon him a steady, unflinching gaze so that Mr. Sapsea retreats a little.

'It cannot be, Mr. Sapsea. It cannot be.'

'It cannot be, sir?' repeats Mr. Sapsea blankly. 'I do not quite understand you. It is already engraved.'

'I do not mean the snuff-box, Mr. Sapsea. I mean that Miss Rosa Bud cannot be your wife.'

'Miss Rosa Bud cannot be my wife?' again repeats Mr. Sapsea, as if there is some other construction to be put upon the words that he has not quite grasped. 'I simply do not understand. Pray make yourself clear, my dear Jasper. Pray do not beat about the bush.'

'I cannot be clearer than I have been, Mr. Sapsea. I cannot be plainer than to say to you that what you have proposed is impossible. Miss Bud cannot, shall not be your wife. Please do not ask me to say more, as it would be painful to both of us.'

Mr. Sapsea retires to his chair, sits in it, stands up, begins to pace the room, crossing and recrossing the dusty beam of sunlight which he angrily gestures aside. At length he halts and stares incredulously at the seated Choir Master, as if that sombre person had suddenly declared the world to be flat.

'Miss Bud shall not be my wife? But this is nonsense, sir, this is madness! Shall not be my wife? I understood that the matter was as good as settled. I had informed you of my intention, and I had considered that to be sufficient. Shall not be my wife, you say! And why shall she not? What reason is there? Is she not unmarried? Does she not have a modest portion? Does she not desire what every young person desires, the hand and heart of a superior man?'

Having delivered himself of this powerful argument, the Worshipful auctioneer recommences his pacing, while the Choir Master silently looks on. He halts again and strikes his brow, as if to draw thunder from it.

'You say that what *I* have proposed is impossible. Well, sir, I say to you that what *you* have proposed is impossible. Are you aware, sir, that I have made preparations? Are you aware that I have made purchases and gone to considerable expense? Are you aware that there is expectation among the tradesmen of the town? Are you aware of — of *this*?' He holds out Mr. Brobity's snuff-box in a trembling hand. 'It is engraved, sir, it is en-*graved*. Do you suppose that these are matters that can be lightly set aside?'

Thus Mr. Sapsea, in the fullness of his anger and the extremity of his disbelief, stalks and rages, while the Choir Master, more than ever the grim confessor, quietly watches his gaudy emperor, without, it would seem, one spark of pity for that wretched man.

At last, however, the unhappy auctioneer masters his feelings. Possibly he has been brought to realise the absurdity of his hopes, possibly not. All he can really think of is to extricate himself from the situation with dignity.

'Very well, my dear Jasper,' he says, with a tolerable assumption of resignation. 'I understand. There is no need for you to feel distressed on my behalf, sir.' As Jasper has not looked to be in the least distressed, it may be taken that the auctioneer's remark is intended as a preventative. 'I am a sensible enough man to realise that some unforeseen impediment has been found to the match. No! I do not wish to know what it is. I do not wish to know if it is because some newly discovered stain upon the young lady's birth has been brought to your attention, or because of some regrettable misfortune in her family that must preclude her forever from becoming the second Mrs. Sapsea. I accept, sir, that something of the kind has happened, and I respect your delicacy in refraining from making it common knowledge. I assure you, my dear Jasper, that no word of it will ever pass my lips.'

He places his finger upon his lips by way of illustration, and Jasper nods. It is noticeable that, throughout the foregoing, the relative situations of the two men have changed, and Jasper is now in the ascendant. His very silence

has so imposed itself on the auctioneer that the unfortunate man now feels
that he ought to offer some sort of apology.

'If — if I might have appeared a trifle agitated, my dear Jasper,' he says,
brushing aside the sunbeam again, 'it was only because I was, quite
naturally, put out. I have, after all, made preparations. I refer, principally,
to Mr. Brobity's snuff-box. A valuable article, sir, and of great sentimental
importance. In fact, it places me in rather an awkward situation. An
exceedingly awkward situation . . .'

He falters and Jasper rises from his stool and goes over to the window.
'The metal, you understand,' explains the auctioneer, 'having been
engraved twice before, is now rather thin.'

The Choir Master stares impassively out of the window and down into
the street below. Mr. Sapsea fancies he sees a faint smile on Jasper's lips, and
draws encouragement from it.

'I fear,' he goes on hopefully, 'that a third erasure would be too much.'

Mr. Sapsea fancies that Jasper has nodded.

'I am, perhaps, a little to blame in being premature. But it is done. The
name is there. Nevertheless, my dear friend, I can draw some comfort from
the fact that it is not an uncommon name. Surely it is possible that, among
Miss Twinkleton's young ladies there — there is —'

Mr. Sapsea fancies that Jasper has stiffened slightly, as if he is about to
turn and offer his heartfelt assistance in finding what the auctioneer now
seeks.

'— another young lady who bears the same name?'

Jasper does indeed turn. But not to offer his assistance. His face is as gray
as the face of a corpse, and his eyes are starting from his head! He points to
the window and, with a terrible cry, falls to the floor like one struck dead!

The Murdered Man

He had seen the murdered man! He had seen him in the street, looking up at the window. There could have been no mistake. Jasper knew Neville Landless as well as if he had created him. Every last detail had been clear: his angry eyes, his dark complexion, the set of his shoulders, the tilt of his head. He had seen the murdered man!

'Mrs. Tope! Mrs. Tope!'

Mr. Sapsea was shouting, shouting at the top of his voice. 'Mrs. Tope! Come quickly, ma'am!'

The auctioneer had rushed to the door. He had opened it — accursed man! Someone was mounting the stairs! Shut the door! No matter, no matter. It was only Mrs. Tope. Mrs. Tope, hastening, wondering, fearful, all aghast.

'What is it, sir?'

(He has seen the murdered man.)

'Mr. Jasper here. He has had a fit, a seizure.'

'Poor gentleman! He's all awry. Lift his head, sir, and let me lay a cushion under it.'

'Good God, he is cold! He is like ice! Where is his medicine?'

'I'll call Mr. Tope. Mr. Tope, Mr. Tope!'

Who was that on the stairs? A heavy tread. Shut the door, shut the door! No matter, it was his neighbour, that white-haired fellow, Datchery. Mr. Datchery, kind, concerned, curious, bending low.

'What's this? I heard the shouting. I came to see if I could be of assistance. What has happened to him?'

(He had seen the murdered man.)

'He was by the window. He cried out, and fell.'

'Loosen his collar, untie his cravat. Let him have air. Will you open the window, your Honour?'

(Not the window! Keep away from the window! Keep away from the murdered man!)

'If you will help me, Mrs. Tope, and you, honoured sir, we can lift him and lay him on the couch. See! I think a little colour is coming back. Perhaps some brandy, Mrs. Tope? He will be better by and by. I have seen things like it before. The room is close, oppressive. It must have been the heat. Yes, yes, he is recovering. A little more air is the thing. Come, your Honour, you take one arm and I will take the other. We will walk him to the window.'

(Not the window! Not the murdered man!)

'There now, there now, my dear Mr. Jasper! Lean outside and breathe deeply, sir. You were overcome by the heat. It is over now.'

It was over; there was no one in the street below. (And yet he *had* seen the murdered man.)

'Thank you, thank you, you have all been kind,' muttered Jasper, clutching the window-sill for support. 'I am better now. But I must lie down. Please, if you would leave me . . . I will try to sleep. Please.'

They glanced among themselves, nodded and left him. When they were gone, he shut the window and locked the door. He lay down on his bed and gazed blindly at the ceiling. After a little while he rose, went again to the window and, overcoming a strong repugnance (would that he could have overcome that stronger repugnance when he sought to look into his heart!) looked down into the street.

People were passing, but there was no sign of the murdered man. Yet he had been there. He had not been in the garments in which Jasper had last seen him, nor had there been a hideous wound in his breast. (Even the risen Christ had displayed His wounds!) He had been wearing the pale gray coat and soft-brimmed hat he had worn on that night when Ned had vanished for ever. (That in itself was curious, although Jasper did not, at the time, guess at its significance.)

He retreated from the window and seated himself at the piano, where he remained, with bowed head and hands clasped over his knees. He wondered if he would be able to play, or whether his hands would so shake and tremble that they would strike those ugly, muffled notes from which he shrank? He raised his hands and, to his surprise, they were quite steady. He began to play, and his fingers performed the music quite independently of the pressure and agitation within his breast; even as his voice, when he led the anthems, would fill the Cathedral with a sweetness of which he himself had no part.

He played for several minutes and the physical activity had some effect of calming him. Presently he ceased, stood up and went to unlock his door. He opened it, went out upon the landing and began to descend the stairs.

At the bottom, just within the doorway, stood the murdered man! Jasper uttered a low, harsh moan; and the figure nodded and went away.

If any communication of looks had passed between them, no comprehension of it remained with Jasper. He felt only the deepest, most unutterable horror. He leaned against the wall until the feeling of sickness subsided; and then went outside.

'Ah! You have recovered, I see!'

'Thank you, thank you, Mr. Datchery. I am quite well now, sir! Quite well.'

'It is a fine afternoon, sir. Allow me to recommend a stroll.'

'Yes, yes. Again, thank you, sir.'

He began to walk rapidly and aimlessly through the streets; that is, if it is possible to walk aimlessly and have no concealed purpose. Although he knew the crooked little town well, knew every byway, every corner, every house, door and projecting gable; although he knew, from childhood, every beckoning vista of green and brown countryside that gave relief from brick and stone, somehow he found himself in places that were utterly strange to him, found himself in streets he had never seen in his life before, found himself standing upon corners that might have been corners in China or on the moon. Although the day was warm and bright, and many people were about, he passed none he knew and retained no memory of a single face.

It could not have been much past four o'clock when he had left his lodgings, yet it was dark when he returned; and, to his bewilderment, he discovered that he was wearing his surplice. He must have attended the Evening Service and come away without disrobing. Of this, too, he had no recollection.

He mounted the stairs with the terrible conviction that the murdered man would be waiting for him. But there was no one. Mrs. Tope had lighted his lamp and, when she heard him enter, came to lay his meal.

'You are looking much better now, Mr. Jasper. You have quite a colour!'

He thanked her and, subduing the anxiety in his voice, inquired:

'Did I not see you at the service, Mrs. Tope?'

He wanted to discover if he had behaved at all oddly, if he had said or shouted anything. But Mrs. Tope had not been there. (Yet surely she would have heard by now?)

That night he rested not at all. A hundred times he rose from his bed and crept into the room where the piano was, expecting to see the murdered man sitting there. A hundred times he went to the window and stared down into the moonlit street; and a hundred times he went out upon the landing, and, holding up his lamp so that the banisters made a shaking prison, peered down the darkened stairs.

On each of these occasions dreadful shades confronted him, stray beams of moonlight assumed the likeness of a pale figure, and countless creakings in the ancient house gave warning of somebody behind him, or standing just upon the other side of the door. But there was nothing; only the expectation and the dread.

When he rose in the morning, Mrs. Tope, laying his breakfast, remarked on how refreshed he looked.

'If I might mention it, Mr. Jasper, you are looking quite a new man.' And then, somewhat contradictorily, 'Quite your old self again, sir.'

(She said this, yet he was not aware of having slept for an instant!)

Mr. Tope, unlocking the Cathedral doors to let out the nightly ghosts and let in the morning sun, so that the powers of light and the powers of darkness met in mid-air, in a jostling congregation of dust, declared himself happy to see Mr. Jasper so bright and early and in such radiant good health.

(Yet there was a sickness within him to which he was frightened to give a name!)

After the service the Dean himself was gracious enough to let it be known that the Choir Master had been in excellent voice, quite the best he had heard, heavenly, he might almost have said: which, coming from the Dean (who might have been supposed to have had some preferential experience in that line) was a tribute not to be lightly set aside.

Yet as the words of the Morning Prayer had been intoned: WHEN THE WICKED MAN TURNETH AWAY . . . the great door had moved and Jasper had seen, standing in a broad scimitar of sunlight, the murdered man! He returned to The Gatehouse.

'My good friend! Forgive me, I did not see you coming so quickly! I just stepped outside. I trust I have not hurt you?'

'No, no. It was my own fault, Mr. Datchery. I — I was lost in thought, sir.'

'Ah! Lost in thought!' (Laying a hand on Jasper's sleeve and detaining him.) 'An interesting expression, that. We all use it; but what do we mean by it? Lost in thought.' (He frowned and shook his head.) 'We may be in a great place, like London, and find our way from broad streets to little courts and even through narrow winding alleys, without faltering once; yet we say we are lost in thought, as if there is a mighty, pathless forest inside our heads. Bounded in a nutshell, as we say, bounded in a nutshell, sir! But I am detaining you. Forgive me. You must pardon an old buffer for a harmless habit of philosophising.'

He released the Choir Master and went back into his own lodgings, leaving Jasper, irresolute, in the pathway. Jasper had, of course, been lying. He had not been lost in thought; he had seen the murdered man, passing through the gateway, and had hurried, half intending to accost him, when his neighbour had stepped out and the gray clad figure had vanished.

Four times now he had seen the figure, always in the light, always clear. He knew it was no product of an opium dream. He had not touched the drug since the night of the storm. Indeed he had come to shrink from it, as he had come to shrink from many things (hiding them and pushing them away, like unopened letters). It might have been said that he moved among his thoughts with the same fantastic care and delicacy with which his fingers moved over the keys: not this note! — not that note! Here — here is the harmony! In consequence of this, there had arisen a feeling that, if only he could continue to walk, looking neither to the right nor to the left, he would infallibly come to some mysterious prosperity.

Latterly this feeling had grown so strong that it had replaced entirely his craving for the visions of the drug. Even his love for Rosa, that had once consumed him to the point of madness, had been tempered, so that, although he still desired her, he felt that she, like much else, could wait until the coming of that prosperous time of which he was so certain.

Lost in thought, the old gentleman had said, and had made some chance references that had briefly troubled him. But Jasper could be no more lost in thought than a man can be lost in a tunnel when already he sees a light at the end of it!

He left the gateway and began to walk, with long, rapid strides, through the streets of the town. There was a mounting excitement within him of which, as yet, he dared not guess the cause. He was pursuing both a ghost and a reality; he was searching for the murdered man.

It had come to him that, until now, until yesterday when he had looked out of the window and had first seen the figure that had so terrified him, he had been imprisoned in a dark and hideous dream. It had come to him that he was at last awakening, and that all his inexplicable fears had only been phantoms conjured up by the drug. The man he was searching for had never been murdered, save in his horrible dream. *Nothing had ever happened.*

His pace grew faster and more eager; and the inhabitants of Cloisterham were treated to the spectacle of the cathedral's Lay Precentor skipping between carriages and alighting, with flying coat-tails, upon pavements and dancing off down streets like a large, highly delighted crow. They were treated to the spectacle of that sombre gentleman laughing to himself and appearing to pursue his own shadow; and when greeted, declaring that it was quite a remarkably fine day; and when asked if something agreeable had happened, answering that:

'No! No! Nothing has happened! Nothing at all has happened!' as if that nothing was everything, everything that was good.

'Good afternoon, Mr. Jasper. How odd it is to see you here, sir!'

Delicious, almond-sweet odours engulfed him as he stepped inside the Lumps-of-Delight Shop, where he had not set foot for many a year.

Miss Ferdinand, Miss Blush and Miss Giggles gaped to see their grave music master intrude upon their sugary retreat, and felt obscurely guilty, as they always did.

'Odd? Is it so odd, Miss Ferdinand? Why do you say that?'

'I don't know really,' said Miss Ferdinand, which was her habitual reply to everything, from What is the Capital of India, to How many times will Seven go into One Hundred and Thirty-four?

'I promise I will not tell Miss Twinkleton,' said Jasper; and the young ladies breathed a unanimous sigh of relief.

Visits to The Lumps-of-Delight Shop were not encouraged, as the Lumps were considered to be antagonistic to young ladies' figures, and might better have been called, not Lumps-of-Delight, but Lumps-of-de-Heavy. But, wonder of wonders, the music master purchased for each of the young ladies so large a bag of the forbidden sweets that he might have been empowered by the Sultan of Turkey (whose tastes were well-known to run to size) to provide for that discerning monarch three portly English maidens, in time for Christmas next. He laughed, and, as he departed, they wondered audibly what on earth could have happened to that sombre man?

Nothing had happened, nothing. Neither this, nor that, nor even — the other.

Yet what was it — this *other* — that caused him to pause and frown and shake his head? What was this *other* that caused his eyes to cloud and some colour to leave his cheeks? What was it that caused his heart to beat so dreadfully when he returned to his lodgings late that night?

He seated himself at the piano and, late though it was, he began to play.

'If nothing happened,' he whispered, 'then *that* never happened. That, too, was a dream.'

He watched his fingers intently and observed, with some shadows of uneasiness, that they still avoided certain notes.

'If nothing happened, then *that* never happened!' he repeated.

He grasped his left hand with his right and forced his fingers to strike upon the notes they shrank from — there! there!

The notes were still muffled and ugly. Again and again he struck them; but made no improvement in the sound.

He lifted the lid and thrust his hand inside. There came a weird glimmering of sounds as his fingers brushed across the strings. He breathed deeply and withdrew his hand. He was holding a large, heavy key.

He stared at it uncomprehendingly; then, slipping it into his pocket, he lighted a lantern from his lamp and turned down the flame till it was no more than a worm of light.

'A dream, a dream,' he whispered; and, leaving his room, went down the stairs and out into the street.

He looked searchingly towards his neighbour's lodgings; but all was quiet. He looked up. There was a quarter moon and many stars. He would hardly need the lantern.

'A dream, all was a dream,' he repeated. 'Nothing has happened.' He hastened to the churchyard and slipped within that dark sea of sleep. He moved among the tombs, and the yellow worm he carried brought brief life to the pale monuments, the brooding angels and the quiet urns.

At last he stood before the discreet villa in which Mrs. Sapsea lay at rest. He stared at the door, upon which his own shadow seemed to be knocking for admittance. He started. Had something stirred just beyond the corner of his eye? No, no. All was quiet.

He placed the lantern on the ground and took the key from his pocket. He stared at it, and the fancy struck him that it was, in reality, the key to heaven and not, as he had once supposed, the key to hell. For all had been a dream, and nothing had happened. He inserted the key in the lock and turned it.

'So,' he whispered, 'so it is with all of us. That which we most fear, we ought most to love. That which we shrink from, we ought to embrace. That which we hide away in shame, we ought to sing aloud.'

A wind passed across the churchyard, animating the grass and fallen leaves and stirring various floral tributes. (Was that someone whispering among Durdles's stony work? No, no. All was quiet.)

He pushed on the door. It would not move; and, for a moment, a great happiness filled him. (Nothing had happened; even the key had been a dream!) Then he remembered that the door opened outwards. (How was it that he remembered such a thing?)

He pulled; and a darkness yawned before him. He lifted up the lantern and went inside the tomb. The odour within was hideous, like a huge, poisoned sneeze. It was as if he stood within a Lumps-of-Horror Shop, a Lumps-of-Disgust Shop, a Lumps-of-Corruption Shop, so that he could scarcely breathe and the ground seemed to heave beneath his feet.

Dimly the lantern revealed the coffin of the reverential wife lying upon a stone shelf with Durdles's bottle beside her, as if she was enjoying a long sleep after a brief conviviality.

He brought the lantern lower, until its light fell upon a patch of whiteness

The image of a youth

on the ground. A curious patch of whiteness, of a length, say, six feet; and of a breadth, say, two. It might have been a sheet left carelessly behind; it might have been a shroud, abandoned in some secret resurrection.

Yet he who held the lantern knew that it was none of these. It was a pit of quicklime; and, as the lantern descended closer, it could be seen that the gases had swollen within it and forced up a counterfeit image of what it had consumed.

There, upon the ground, lay the whitened image of a youth. His white eyes were starting from their crumbly sockets; his white mouth was gaping and within it, his teeth (still unconsumed), gleamed like beads. But worst of all, round his white neck was the knot of the white scarf (once black) with which he had been strangled! The burning quicklime, like the burning mind above it, had thrust up the knowledge of the crime! The ghastly effigy, that crumbled at a touch, was Edwin Drood!

Everything had happened! EVERYTHING!

Jasper uttered one wild, dreadful scream of despair; then dark figures rushed suddenly in upon him and seized him by the arms. A voice that he knew, and yet knew not, a voice that was somehow close with affection, yet remote with judgement, a voice that was hollow within the monument, yet filled up all his head, uttered:

'John Jasper, I arrest you for the murder of Edwin Drood.'

He had dreamed nothing. The nightmare had always been the truth.

Mr. Crisparkle
Pays Another Call

MORNING comes to drowsy old Cloisterham, bright, cheerful and with a pleasing retinue of country scents; on which Cloisterham opens its windows, steps out of its doors, and generally congratulates itself on yet another fine day — which Cloisterham is inclined to regard as being no more than its due. There is a contented feeling in Cloisterham (not to say, a hope, — for what is the pleasure in being blessed unless someone else is cursed?) that it is probably raining in Canterbury, pouring in Dover, thundering in London, and dismal in Deal; while upon ancient Cloisterham the sun always shines.

Until a whisper goes round. It is a strange, dismayed whisper that seems to have arisen out of nothing, as if it has always been going on but has required a certain silence in order to be heard.

The whisper goes round that all is not as it should be with Cloisterham, that something disagreeable has happened, of which it is best not to speak in front of the young. It would seem that the morning itself has heard this whisper (most likely from the censorious old Cathedral tower), for it quickly clouds over to a white-gray, like dirty plaster-work, as if it has been advised (by the tower) to deny Cloisterham the blessing of sunshine.

The whisper goes round that something has happened in the churchyard, that a portion has been roped off and two persons, of grimly constabular aspect, have been busy in a certain monument, with spades, a hand-cart, and several lengths of stained green sheet.

The whisper goes round that something has happened to the Lay Precentor, and that his voice is absent from the choir, which, consequently, wanders leaderless in the holy vaulted air; that the Dean is deeply troubled and that the Mayor has fainted twice. The whisper goes round that the Lay Precentor is not to be found in his lodgings, where two more persons of grimly constabular aspect are searching, while Mrs. Tope looks on aghast.

The whisper goes round that there are to be no more music lessons in The Nuns' House, where speculation is intense that Mr. Jasper has been murdered by the choir, buried in the churchyard and dug up by the Dean; while Miss Twinkleton, sitting forlornly in her parlour, wishes, perhaps, that it was so, as she strives to shield her charges from knowledge of the real darkness of the world.

Mrs. Tisher knocks inaudibly on her door and enters on a cough.

'Is it your wish, Miss Twinkleton, that Mr. Crisparkle should see you first?'

'I think it would be best, Tisher. I think we must speak with him first.'

We? Who then is with her on this morning? Mr. Datchery. Mrs. Tisher coughs again and departs; and Miss Twinkleton bestows a melancholy smile upon the door. Mr. Datchery walks uncomfortably about the room, as if in search of a concealed speech that will somehow get him off the stage.

Mr. Datchery, who has been at The Nuns' House for some time, does not at all look to be a man who has succeeded in his appointed task and who has recently enjoyed a triumph. In fact, he seems rather diminished, and his white hair to have gone a little dingy and gray. Nor is his attire as immaculate as usual; there are traces of mud on his boots and on the bottoms of his trousers.

'I am sure,' he says, 'that she will soon recover.'

Miss Twinkleton examines her fingers before replying:

'Oh yes. I am sure she will.'

Mr. Datchery nods in some relief. He cannot help feeling that he has played the part of the porter of hell-gate all too proficiently, and has opened the door a little too wide.

The subject of their remarks, and their thoughts (and, in Mr. Datchery's case, guilt) is Helena Landless, who is desperately ill. She had collapsed when she had been told of the arrest of John Jasper, as if the recollection of the part she had played in driving the murderer to betray himself had suddenly overwhelmed her with an unbearable horror. Since that time she has remained, icy cold and scarcely breathing, responding to nothing, save, from time to time, a dreadful shadow that seems to pass before her eyes.

Mrs. Tisher, returning to Miss Landless's room, finds matters, if anything, a little worse. Helena's dark beauty has faded to a yellowish tinge, and her black hair, spreading across her pillow, seems drowned. Despairingly she watches Mrs. Tisher come in and go to the window where the doctor is standing; then the shadow crosses her eyes. Rosa, who sits beside her, gently strokes her brow and murmurs:

'It is over now. It is all over, my darling.'

The doctor, a lean, clever, glaring-looking man, glances at Rosa sharply, comes to the bed-side, lays a finger on his patient's thin wrist, studies her faintly moving bosom and mutters: 'Tcha!', with a mild irritation that suggests that it is not all over, miss, and I do not in the least approve of your meddling with my patient's brow, as the patient is my property to do with as I choose.

There is a knock on the door. Mrs. Tisher goes to answer it, followed, as before, by Helena's despairing eyes. It is a servant. Some murmured words pass, and Mrs. Tisher departs. Rosa holds Helena's hand.

'Oh you are so cold, so cold!' she exclaims involuntarily.

The doctor, who has retired to the window, comes quickly back, lays two fingers on his patient's temple, delivers himself of another, 'Tcha!' (as if wondering if there can be any limit to the impertinent ignorance of the unqualified) and retires again. He is a formidable man, a scientist to his finger-tips, beyond which well-scrubbed articles he admits to the existence of absolutely nothing. He is President of the Cloisterham Literary and Scientific Society, which he regards as being a rival institution to the Cathedral: the Cathedral having its Dean and Chapter, and the Literary and Scientific having, so to speak, its Dean and Volume.

A pattering of footsteps once more rouses Helena to her anguished look, which, on the return of Mrs. Tisher, is shadowed over more darkly than ever. Mrs. Tisher confers with the doctor and elicits from him several more 'Tchas!' and a final 'Hm!' remarkably expressive of exasperation. Rosa looks inquiringly at Mrs. Tisher, who nods; and presently, although it seems long, there comes a quick, firm step in the passage (which produces a sudden quickening in Helena), and Mr. Crisparkle enters the room.

Some news of the monstrous happening in the churchyard had already reached Minor Canon Corner. At first the Minor Canon and the china shepherdess had refused to believe it; then at last they did believe it, and had stared at each other appalled; and it had only been with the greatest difficulty that Septimus had left his mother to come to The Nuns' House in response to Miss Twinkleton's summons.

'Would it not be better, Sept, to wait until she recovers? There is little you can do, dear.'

'But it is my place to go to her, Ma.'

'But the doctor is with her, Sept. She is not alone, dear,' said Mrs. Crisparkle, implying, rather plaintively, that *she* would be alone, and with no one to talk to about what had happened in the night.

'I would never forgive myself, Ma, if something terrible was to happen.'

'But something terrible *has* happened, Sept.'

'I must do my duty, Ma.'

'Yes, my Sept. I suppose you must, dear.'

Now, as he enters the room and looks at the bed, it would seem that his worst fears are realised, and his good-natured face is overcast with dread. Although the cause of Helena's collapse has been explained to him by Mr. Datchery, and although he has been warned, by Miss Twinkleton, of her present state, the sight of her shadowy face on the pillow drives tears to his eyes. It seems to him that Helena is at the very point of death. He kneels by the bed and takes her hand in both of his.

'Dearest Helena! Dearest, dearest Helena, why did you do it? Why did you bring this on yourself?'

'Neville . . . Neville,' she whispers. 'It was Neville. It was he who haunted Jasper, just as Jasper haunted him. It was Neville . . . Neville.'

She closes her eyes and Rosa whispers that this is the first time Helena has spoken and it must be Mr. Crisparkle's presence that has wrought the change; upon which Septimus feels several large and undeniable tears run down his cheeks. He makes as if to brush them away, but any motion of his hand away from the one he holds is answered by a fierce seizing of his fingers. So he bows his head and the tears fall freely.

The doctor, who has been regarding the scene with angry contempt (not because of the feelings displayed, but because he considers the Minor Canon to be a representative of the rival institution who has no business to be where he is), goes to the bedside and takes possession of his patient's disengaged wrist. He screws up his face into a scientific scowl as he feels the thread–like pulse and decides that there is absolutely no improvement that can be attributed to the ecclesiastical intrusion. He says, 'Pah!' rather severely, implying that he knows perfectly well what is wrong, where it is wrong, and why it is wrong; and that if anybody present mentions anything as unscientific as a troubled soul, he will take great pleasure in knocking him down. He returns to the window and gazes out upon the gray morning and wishes he had brought an umbrella as it is beginning to rain.

'I must go!' moans Helena, her eyes opening enormously and a look of terror coming into them. 'I must go now! Anywhere . . . a journey. I must go before . . . it happens. I must not be found. Please, please, I must hide . . . I must go!'

Septimus presses her hand as tightly as he dares. He cannot imagine in what fearful regions the girl's mind is wandering, whether she is recollecting some misery of her childhood, or whether it is something here and now, that he cannot see. He prays with all his might to have some influence and draw her away from her terrors. He does not know what he would do if Helena should die. The very thought freezes his blood. And yet . . . what will he do if she lives? There's another thought that affects him deeply. He knows, in his heart of hearts, that he loves her. He smiles faintly and shakes his head, as if aware that there are too many obstacles between him and the girl for anything to come of it.

He lifts his eyes, and meets Rosa's. She nods. Had she read his thoughts? Was she agreeing that nothing could come of it? Did she know, as he knew (or thought he knew) that there was something lacking within him, without which any love he might offer Helena would be a hollow mockery?

'Let me go! Let me go!' mutters Helena, suddenly restless and grasping Septimus's hand so that her nails dig into his flesh. 'It is beginning . . . it is beginning!'

A perspiration has broken out on her brow, which Rosa wipes away; and a strange film comes over her frightened eyes. Septimus, as he watches her, is suddenly reminded, not of her brother who would seem to have possessed her, but of John Jasper!

Why of Jasper? What can there be in her that was in the murderer too? What can she and the wicked man have in common? The Minor Canon is bewildered and sorely afraid, until he sees, on a table by her bed, a bottle of laudanum. At once he guesses that it is only the drug that is affecting her, even as it affected Jasper.

He feels a tremendous sense of relief as Helena's eyes close, her clenched fingers relax, and she drifts away into sleep. Again he looks across the bed at Rosa; and again Rosa nods. His eyes return to the sleeper, and he cannot help contrasting her fierce dark beauty with the delicate complexion and almost childish prettiness of her friend. He cannot help reflecting that, contrary to all appearance, it is Rosa who is the stronger; it is Rosa who will weather the storm, for when the wind blows, Rosa will bend, while Helena is like to break.

However, this latter thought does not unduly dismay the Reverend Septimus Crisparkle as he leaves the room and leaves The Nuns' House. His own broad shoulders, he hopes, will be sufficient to stand between Helena and that wind when it blows.

Mr. Datchery Bestows a Ring

THE sun, which had earlier abandoned Cloisterham (doubtless to shine unjustly on Canterbury, Dover, London and Deal), seemed to have retired for good; and the dirty sky added injury to insult by depositing rain upon Cloisterham – not in an uproarious shower, but in a thin, grizzling drizzle.

However, it was a mood that suited Mr. Datchery well enough as he took leave of his many friends in Cloisterham and discovered (as we often do) that it was a great pity he was leaving as he had been on the point of being invited to dinner, that a party was being got up to which he most certainly would have been asked, and that, not half an hour earlier, he had been the subject of the warmest discussion as to whether he would care to make up a table for whist.

Mr. Datchery smiled ruefully. He knew well enough that, among his many friends, there was only one who was at all sorry to see him go; that there was only one who had not turned a little away from him when his purpose in the town became known; that there was only one who had accompanied him to the omnibus stop and stood in the rain with him until the vehicle arrived; that there was only one, who, (after a passage of coins), had shaken him by the hand and said:

'Sorry ye're goin', Dick. It won't be the same no more.'

It was Deputy; a glum, bereft Deputy, with no more secrets to share, and with nothing more to look forward to in life but the steady stoning of Durdles. Yet not entirely so; there was still a certain event to which Deputy looked forward, a certain event which occupied his childish mind, a certain event that lent a little zest to the dull, flat time that must precede it.

'You'll be comin' back, Dick, fer the 'angin'?'

'If it comes to that.'

'Course it will! It's only natcheral. 'E done it so they'll 'ave to 'ang 'im.

And serve 'im right. That'll teach 'im to go 'istin' me off me feet! Now they'll be 'istin' 'im!'

And Deputy, with his head cocked at a grotesque angle, performed a jerking little dance, highly suggestive of the event to which he had alluded.

In reflective mood, Mr. Datchery journeyed to London where the rain seemed to have followed him (or the sun to have fled his presence); in reflective mood he went to Staple Inn, where the dog Snap, mistrusting the size of his boots, snarled and avoided him; in reflective mood he stood before the portals of P.J.T. and, as Mr. Grewgious was wont to do, unconsciously sought to attach words to the letters.

'Perhaps Jasper Too', he murmured at length; and went inside.

His friend, Bazzard, was away in Norfolk, and his place taken by a youth on loan from a firm downstairs. Mr. Datchery was not sorry as his continuingly reflective mood would not have inclined him to humour the playwright. After a few moments he was admitted to Mr. Grewgious's room. The lawyer rose to greet him.

'Am I to offer you refreshment, Mr. — er — Datchery?'

Mr. Datchery nodded and was rewarded with a glass of sherry.

'Are we to drink a toast, Mr. Datchery?'

Again Mr. Datchery nodded.

'Then confusion to our enemy!' cried Mr. Grewgious, raising his glass. 'Frustrate his knavish tricks!'

The lawyer drank, and Mr. Datchery courteously sipped.

'And now sir, if you will be seated, I would like to hear precisely how our enemy has been confused, and the degree to which his tricks have been frustrated.'

They sat; and the lawyer, leaning forward with his hands on his knees, listened keenly while Mr. Datchery, with frequent reference to his pocket book, related the circumstances of John Jasper's arrest.

'A remarkable achievement, Mr. Datchery,' said the lawyer, when he had heard all. 'You are to be congratulated, sir. I *do* congratulate you. You must be very pleased.'

Mr. Datchery, to whom nodding seemed to have become a habit, did so again.

'I take it, Mr. Datchery, that your slight gloom, if I may call it such, is due to a lack of sleep?'

Yet another nod.

'Otherwise I should have expected you to be sporting a flower and a smile, sir. I should have expected a jauntiness in your step. But I understand that lack of sleep can indeed depress a man. I hope, sir, I hope with all my heart, that you sleep well tonight. I hope that we both sleep well tonight. Do you think it possible that we will, Mr. Datchery?'

Mr. Datchery seemed to have used up all his nods, and the weariness on his face deepened.

'Come, sir, let us look upon the bright side. A monster has been uncovered and brought to justice. Is that not a cause for rejoicing? No? Then let us try again. A young man, cruelly murdered, has been avenged. Is that not a good thing? No? Then let us try yet again. Another young man, also dead, has been cleared of suspicion of a terrible crime. Is it not a good thing that his sister must be grateful for it? Ah! You nod. I am thankful Mr. Datchery, that there is something to satisfy you. I am thankful, sir, that the task I set you has not been entirely without reward. I refer, of course, to reward in the mental sense. The other, as you know, is available to you as soon as you present your account.'

'Thank you, Mr. Grewgious.'

'So — all is in hand. You are certain of the witnesses?'

'I am certain.'

'And the evidence?'

'Is strong.'

'Could not a clever lawyer attach other meanings?'

'I do not think so.'

'Opinion, Mr. Datchery?'

Mr. Datchery smiled and took another sip of his sherry.

'And Miss Landless? It must have been a great strain upon her. She is well looked after?'

'She is in excellent hands. None could be kinder than Mr. Crisparkle; and your ward, Miss Bud, never leaves her side. And Miss Twinkleton — '

' — A doctor. Has she a doctor?'

'Indeed she has. But, as it says in the play, sir, "More needs she the divine than the physician." If she is to recover completely, it will be because of the reverend gentleman.'

'You are a shrewd fellow, Mr. Datchery. Come, sir, allow me to refill your glass.'

The lawyer rose, and then, striking his forehead with the palm of his hand, as if some brilliant notion had suddenly flashed upon him, cried:

'But what are we thinking of? That excellent fellow Tartar must be told! Yes indeed! We must send for Tartar. He would never forgive us!'

Mr. Grewgious poked his head out of his door and gave instructions to the youth on loan (who was somewhat haughty to find himself used as a messenger when he was an articled clerk) to summon Lieutenant Tartar on a matter of great importance.

Lieutenant Tartar arrived in a panting condition, with a trowel still in his hand from tending his airy garden. His bronzed face was pale with alarm, for he fully believed that some disaster had overtaken Rosa. However, Mr. Grewgious's expression and the offered glass of sherry at once undeceived him, and he was required to seat himself while Mr. Datchery was invited to repeat the story of his great success.

Patiently Mr. Datchery complied while Mr. Grewgious paced the room; and, as each sharp suspicion, each damning piece of evidence was touched upon, the lawyer halted, and, raising a finger at Lieutenant Tartar, said: 'Item!' as if Lieutenant Tartar was an inattentive pupil who, later, was to undergo a rigorous examination on the subject in hand.

'So you see, my dear Tartar,' said Mr. Grewgious, when the story had been fully told, 'everything is now, as you would say in your profession, plain sailing.'

'So it would appear, sir. And Mr. Datchery here has navigated it most skilfully. Mr. Datchery, sir, I trust that Miss Bud is quite well? She has not been affected or deeply distressed? And Miss Landless too, of course?'

Mr. Datchery assured the Lieutenant that Rosa was quite well. He did not touch deeply upon Miss Landless as he judged that she stood, as it were, only in the suburbs of the young man's concern.

'Plain sailing; yes, plain sailing,' repeated Mr. Grewgious, apparently lost in a sudden abstraction and gazing at Lieutenant Tartar with such fixity that the young man, with his glass in one hand and his trowel in the other, felt quite awkward; and Mr. Datchery, who had brought the good news, felt excluded and dismissed.

'Forgive me!' said Mr. Grewgious, coming to himself and passing his hand through his thin, sandy hair. 'It was a small matter that occurred to me. It was something that — that has been on my mind.'

He went to his desk and unlocked the secret drawer; and even to the onlookers there was something acutely angular in his attitude, as if, at any moment, he was going to shut himself up and put himself away in a box.

'Mr. Datchery!'

'Sir?'

'I have been told, Mr. Datchery,' said the lawyer, clasping his hands together, 'that is, Mr. Bazzard has told me that you have — um — quite a collection of articles representing your — um — triumphs. I would like, if I may, to add to that collection. I would be obliged, sir, if you would accept this. It — it is not of very great value. There is no cause for you to feel reluctant. Pray take it, Mr. Datchery. Pray oblige me and accept it.'

He held out the gold ring, with its rose of rubies and diamonds. As he did so he glanced at Lieutenant Tartar; and, for an instant, the lawyer looked almost ashamed.

Mr. Datchery hesitated for a moment; and then, with an inclination of his head, accepted the gift and took his departure. Long after he had gone, and after Lieutenant Tartar had gone (eagerly to Cloisterham by the very first train), Mr. Grewgious sat in his chair, with his hands on his knees, and staring at the door. His face was, as always, like a face carved out of wood.

'Now it is done,' he whispered. 'At last it is out of my hand. She — she could never have worn it. It was defiled. So he has it . . . that good man. Yet I meant well by him. I meant so well that I sent him out with his burden like a scapegoat into the wilderness.'

Mr. Datchery's wilderness was his lodgings off Drury Lane. Although it had been late when he arrived, he had been welcomed by Mrs. MacSiddons with an enthusiasm quite bruising to the servant girl who had been hurled aside in a transport of delight.

'Why Dick!' cried the good lady. 'You're back to stay! I can see it in your face! There's a fire laid and I'll fetch you supper right away! I can hardly wait, Dick, to hear you tell of how it went! What's that, miss, what's that you're snivelling? Now don't you try to deceive me with yer lumps on yer head and pains in yer back! I've been in the profession so I knows hacting when I sees it! Oh Dick, what a life it's been without you!'

She led the way upstairs and soon the fire was blazing, supper was on the table and he sat in his chair while Mrs. MacSiddons sat hugely opposite and plied him with questions and wine.

'So you caught 'im, Dick, you caught 'im in the end!'

'He caught himself, ma'am.'

'Tell us, Dick, tell us how it was done! Was there a struggle, was there screams, was there blood?'

'There was a little struggle, but not much. He was in no state to offer resistance. He came, as we say, quietly.'

'No more than he should! But before! How did you bring it about?'

'Rather like Hamlet, ma'am. He was frighted with false fire.'

'Oh the wicked deception of you, Dick! Was there a ghost?'

'In a manner of speaking. There was the twin sister of a murdered man, and she wore her brother's clothes. She changed into them in my lodgings and stood under his window so that he thought — '

'He thought that he was goin' mad? That's capital, Dick! That's better than any play!'

Mr. Datchery glanced towards his playbills, and gently shook his head.

'The play's the thing, ma'am, the play's the thing.'

'Give me real life!' said Mrs. MacSiddons, absently helping herself to a mutton chop. 'You and me's been in the profession, Dick, and, though it was better in our day, it's still deception; and I won't, on any account, be deceived! Have you got the key, Dick, to 'ang on the wall?'

'Not yet, ma'am. It must be shown in evidence.'

'They won't keep it, Dick, will they?'

'No, ma'am.'

'I s'pose we'll 'ave to wait till he's 'anged.'

Mr. Datchery nodded; and then, in order to bring a little cheer to the occasion, said:

'But I have the ring, ma'am. You remember the ring? It was given to me today. Here, here is the ring, ma'am.'

'Oh Dick, it's pretty! Oh Dick, it's real 'andsome!' cried Mrs. MacSiddons as Mr. Datchery displayed the trinket. 'I got some veller that'll show it up nice . . . and a gold frame.'

'Keep it, ma'am,' said Mr. Datchery abruptly. 'Keep it for yourself.'

Mrs. MacSiddons, astonished into opening her mouth and displaying therein what appeared to be a worked-out mine of mutton chop, cried: 'Oh Dick! Oh Dick!' with such dreadful joy that Mr. Datchery was quite aghast when he realised the possible interpretation of his gift.

'Pray think nothing of it, ma'am! It is only a gift, no more!'

'Oh Dick! Oh Dick!'

'A trifle, ma'am! I assure you, only a trifle!'

'Oh Dick! Oh Dick!'

'It means nothing to me, ma'am! I have other rings,' said Mr. Datchery distractedly; and, rising from the table, went to a cupboard in which he kept remembrances of his past career.

'Here, here is another!'

He held out a huge, ornate ring, mighty with coloured glass. It was a ring that would not have deceived a child; and yet, from the back of the gallery might have been worth a king's ransom.

'Oh Dick! But this one's real!'

It *was* real, and there was no deceiving the good lady, who, soon after, departed with more 'Oh Dicks!' and was heard thumping and thundering in regions below as, presumably, she surveyed her domain in happy anticipation of its being shared.

Mr. Datchery sighed and gazed forlornly at his playbills. As always, his eyes lingered longest upon the framed reminder of his greatest triumph.

'Knock, knock,' he whispered. 'Never at quiet. What are you? But this place is too cold for hell. I'll devil-porter it no further.'

What part then? he wondered, as he looked along the line. A ruined prince? An injured general? A tyrant? A philosopher in a wood? He shook his head. None of these. Rather would he play a buffer, a harmless buffer getting through life on his means.

Thus Mr. Datchery, in his comfortable lodgings, continued to make unfavourable comparisons between the Stage and Life, between dreaming and waking; even as another, in his lodging (which was by no means comfortable), continued to make comparisons between *his* dreaming, which had been nightmarish, and *his* waking, which had been worse.

A Humorous Occasion

THE crime of the Lay Precentor did not go unremarked in the world at large; and the world at large became aware of Cloisterham much in the way that a man might become aware of some hitherto unnoticed internal organ — only when it is stricken by disease.

The Lay Precentor (the world at large hastily informed itself precisely what a Lay Precentor was) having been committed for trial, lay in gaol in the Assize town and awaited his fate. Certain meagre comforts, in the way of books and a change of linen were conveyed to him, but otherwise he was as a man cut off, a man already dead. Although, in the eyes of the law a man is deemed innocent until proven guilty, the world at large dismissed this as a legal fiction and, as always, took the opposite view. Should the man have been proven innocent to the satisfaction of God and all the lawyers, the world at large would have taken it merely as a tribute to the mendacity of the accused. So the Lay Precentor lay in gaol; but his crime, like a blameless citizen, walked wide and free.

It walked in many places, and cast shadows curiously unlike itself. It walked in public-houses, in drawing-rooms, and it stood upon street corners with a gossipy, button-holing air; it scrawled and scratched itself across legal documents, it printed itself in newspapers, it found its way (in the shape of appreciative coins) into Mr. Tope's pocket when he showed visitors where the Lay Precentor had sat in the Choir, and pointed out the monument in which the crime had been concealed; and it occupied, teasingly, the professional interest of a long-faced gentleman who lived above a harness-maker's in Clerkenwell, did a little cobbling on the side and had small gray eyes with an expression that was said to be singularly sweet.

It entered, with grave face and upon gaitered legs, into the very palace of the Bishop, in the person of the Dean; and there it cast a curious shadow indeed.

The Bishop, a perilously doddering dignitary, had somehow got it into his theology-battered head that a throat had been cut on the Cathedral's high altar and, therefore, Desecration raised its interesting head; and nothing the Dean could say would entirely disabuse him of the idea.

'Not upon the altar then? You are certain, Dean? Well, well, I suppose we must be thankful. So it was the nave. I do not think the nave will present us with quite the same problem. If I might make use of a Christian image, Dean, I rather fancy that the nave will turn out to be quite a different kettle of fish. Gorringe must look into it. The nave. Had it been the porch, of course, it would have been another matter again. I think we might have been quite safe if only the porch had been concerned. I am not sure, but I think so. Gorringe shall look into it.'

Gorringe was the Bishop's chaplain, and a mighty man on canon law. The Bishop kept Gorringe by him, and was inclined to put him on, like a pair of spectacles, when any obscure problem of Procedure required looking into. Consequently Gorringe, a lean and hungry cleric, was heartily disliked.

Patiently, and inch by inch, for the Bishop fought him every step of the way, the Dean managed to shift the crime outside the holy edifice itself; and the Bishop rather sadly nodded his head.

'I suppose,' he said, 'we must be thankful, Dean. And I suppose also that it is fortunate that the — um — person was a *Lay* Precentor. Had he been clergy we might have been confronted with quite a task. Yes indeed, clergy would have raised quite peculiar problems. I must ask Gorringe to look into it.'

Then the Bishop wandered away, in mind if not in body, leaving the Dean with the feeling that the Bishop rather expected him to advise the Chapter to hold its hand in the way of murder until Gorringe had looked into it.

If there was no stain on the fabric spiritual, the same could not have been claimed on behalf of the fabric temporal, on which spots had fallen from which the cleansing power of all Neptune's ocean might well have retired in defeat. The tomb of Mrs. Sapsea had been most hideously defiled; and when the Worshipful Husband had recovered (as if he ever really would) from the shock of the Lay Precentor's crime, when he had overcome (as if he ever really could) from the revulsion he had felt on discovering that he had nursed a viper in his bosom, he was left with a sense of outrage that buzzed in his head like a hive of bees.

A fallen giant, who, as the poet tells us, suffers as much in mortal pangs as does the beetle we tread upon, he sat in his dull sitting-room, pondering (for thinking scarcely expressed the marble pace of his meditations) the frightful affront, and absently drinking port wine. Came Durdles, with hammer, rule and dinner bundle, to stand before him, swaying slightly.

Durdles eyed the decanter of port as if unable to speak until moistened. Accordingly the auctioneer, disinclined to rise himself, gestured Durdles towards a glass and chair. Durdles sat and, thereafter, the decanter passed between them much as the solitary eye and tooth might have passed among those ancient dames upon whom Perseus called, so that each might take a turn at sight and speech; for he who had the decanter uttered, and he who had it not, lapsed into a wordless fog.

'I will not hide it from you, Durdles, but the blow has struck deep.'

The decanter passed and Durdles uttered.

'No more'n eighteen inches,' he said, marking it off on his rule; for he was under the impression that the excavation in the tomb had been referred to, and not that deeper one in the auctioneer's pride. 'If Durdles bricks over it will come out as good as new.'

The decanter passed.

'Oh Durdles, Durdles! Everything is shaken to its foundations!'

The decanter passed.

'The foundations, Mr. Sapsea, is sound enough. Durdles saw to that. It will come out at two course of bricks, Mr. Sapsea. Durdles will put it in hand.'

The decanter passed.

'The monster! The scoundrel! Oh how cunningly he knew where to strike me down! Not in my life, Durdles! My life, I might say, is invulnerable. My life, Durdles, is strong. My life, I might say in all modesty, is a monument. My life is mighty; but my dead, Durdles, my dead is weak. He has struck at my dead. He has ravished my dead. He has disturbed the reverential slumbers.'

The decanter passed.

'There won't be no disturbing, Mr. Sapsea. Durdles will put a sheet over the coffin and she won't know a thing.'

The decanter passed, and lo! it was empty; so the Worshipful auctioneer rose uncertainly to his feet and, mindful that he represented in his stately person all established forms and time-hallowed customs, all civic dignity and respectable family life, delivered himself of this final summing up:

'Durdles,' he said. 'Hanging is too good for him.'

However, the Mayor of Cloisterham's opinion was not universally held; in particular it was not held by Deputy, who regarded the individual's merits as being quite sufficient for the occasion; and in general it was not held by the long-faced gentleman with the sweet little gray eyes (which rather resembled two bits of old marzipan) who lived above the harness-maker's and who was busied with a contraption of straps and buckles of his own concocting, bewildering to behold. *He* was of the opinion that hanging was the right of every true-born Englishman and was an edifying spectacle that no man, woman or child ought to be denied. What was more, were this right ever to be taken away, it was well-known (and had been proved to several people's satisfaction) that the streets would be running with blood, that no man's property would be safe and that the whole fabric of society would be rent in twain, like the veil of the temple. It was well-known that, were this right to be taken away, there would be nothing at all to discourage every true-born Englishman from giving way to his natural inclination towards murder, robbery and rapine. It was well-known that society (which might appear to the ignorant as being a rather select Club of limited membership, devoted to the heaping of honours on its own committee) had to be protected at all costs.

It was in pursuance of this lofty purpose that there appeared in the streets of the Assize town, one gray October morning, two ancient gentlemen dressed in a quaint and bygone fashion; two ancient gentlemen with wigs that were too big for them (or heads that were too small) upon dried-up little legs, with dried-up little faces (and, most likely, dried-up little hearts) and bearing little posies of dried-up herbs and flowers. They tottered in procession, with retinue of red-nosed hirelings, and not a soul among the crowding onlookers ventured to laugh.

Yet were they not the very stuff of comedy — these two ancient gentlemen with their shuffling ushers and greasy clerks? Would they not have brought the house down at Drury Lane if put upon the boards? Would they have deceived, for a single instant, any audience of sensible men and women into supposing that they were anything other than a pair of dusty old clowns?

And would not any child, seeing them stagger up the steps of the Court-house, with fat Sheriff and his Officers (oh Robin Hood and Little John, where are your arrows now!) suppose it all to be a fine Pantomime and that, at any moment, a lady in tights and spangles would appear, wave her magic wand and bring Robin safe back home?

Yet no one ventured to laugh; not even when it was solemnly proclaimed that Her Majesty's Judges were Sitting, when it had been all too plain that they had been scarcely able to stand. For this was real and in cold earnest; it was no play upon a stage. There would be no lady in tights and spangles (unless she was put up in the dock) to make all well again; for we in our grown-up wisdom, have dispensed with that magical essence, with that hope, with that dream, and have retained but an empty suit of clothes.

Yet no one ventured to laugh; perhaps because, in our heart of hearts, we know we ought to weep when we see what we have done, when we see how we have used illusion and make-believe to hide and suffocate the truth, instead of, as the poets do, used it to show us what we really are.

In the fullness of time, for there was much business to be got through and the ancient gentlemen were very slow and hard of hearing and frequently forgot their lines, the Lay Precentor was brought from his cell and exhibited, and his crime put upon him like a Black Coronation. He stood in the dock with a ghastly pallor, while the circumstances were related and witnesses called.

Durdles was put up, took the oath apparently on his dinner-bundle, from which he had declined to be parted, and explained how the accused had obtained knowledge of quicklime and access to the key of the monument. A shabby old barrister (who, together with a sharp young solicitor had managed to inveigle himself into appearing for the defence) attempted to discredit the witness by asking him the date of his birth; but made a poor impression when, requested by Durdles, he had been unable to recall his own.

Miss Rosa Bud was put up, gave evidence as to possible motive for the crime; was not cross-questioned as the shabby old barrister was reminded of his daughter and did not wish to appear ungallant before the jury.

Mr. Grewgious was put up; and then Mr. Datchery and then several persons of grimly constabular aspect, who gave evidence concerning teeth,

Durdles gives evidence

pieces of thigh bone, several buttons (identified by a tailor as belonging to a garment worn by Edwin Drood), and a singularly damning fragment of black scarf that had escaped the action of the lime.

'Are we to conclude, then,' demanded the shabby old barrister, when his turn came to address the jury, 'are we seriously to conclude, from the evidence presented to this court, that my client is guilty?'

The question did not remain long unanswered. The jury retired, deliberated, and returned. It was their verdict that, beyond all reasonable doubt, John Jasper was guilty of the murder of Edwin Drood; whereupon the shabby old barrister and the smart young solicitor threw up their hands (and the case) in disgust.

The judge, after congratulating the jury on their perspicacity, declared that he had never, in all his long career on the Bench, come upon so vile a crime and so vile a criminal; and that there was no punishment he could inflict (he gave the impression that there *were* punishments but he was no longer empowered to inflict them) that would fully express the disgust all right-minded persons must feel for one, who, while sheltering under the very cloak of the holy church, had sinned so monstrously against God and man.

Having delivered himself of this (with some difficulty and confusion) he put upon his head a square of black cloth (which he had purchased only the week before from a Robe and Wig-maker in Chancery Lane for two shillings and sixpence) and required that John Jasper be taken from hence to a place of execution and there hanged by the neck until he was dead.

'And may God have mercy on your soul,' he added, almost as an afterthought. And *still* nobody laughed.

When the Hurlyburly's Done

THE condemned man was quiet and respectable, and made an exceedingly good impression on those set to watch over him. He never cursed, or swore, or attempted to deface his cell. He was always clean and careful in his habits and sometimes, in the evenings, he sang. Consequently the watchers treated him with courtesy and consideration; and were peculiarly attentive to make no mention of anything in his presence that might have brought his mind to bear upon the prospect that, inevitably, lay before him.

The barber who came to shave him was studious not to refer, in actual words, to such an article as a *neck.* A man who brought him a parcel of books of an improving nature (left by an Anonymous Sympathiser) and had difficulty in unfastening it, would sooner have bitten off his tongue than uttered the word: *'Knot.'* And Rope! Rope was a word unthought-of, a word that was no part of any language known to man; and had it appeared, in letters of fire, upon the wall of the cell, it would have taken a Daniel to decipher it. (Yet it must have been there, day after day, and night after night.)

Nor were times spoken of that lay, of neccessity, beyond the condemned man's reach. There was no Christmas, no November, even; and, by and by, no tomorrow night. Yet all was still cheerfulness, as if nothing much of any consequence was going to happen; and would their amiable friend like anything in particular to eat and drink; and would he, by way of pleasant company to pass away the time, care to see a priest?

'A priest?' said he, looking up in some surprise, that made the watchers think all the better of him (and of themselves) for entering into the spirit of things so well. 'A priest?' he repeated, as if it was a remarkably fine idea that had only just occurred to him. 'Yes, yes. I believe I would. But — but here's a problem.'

'What is it, sir? Pray tell us what it is?' urged the watchers, with affectionate concern. 'Problems are for us, sir. That is what we are here for. Do not let anything distress you.'

'But I do not wish to put you to any trouble.'

'Trouble? Trouble? Ha–ha! What an idea! What trouble can you give *us*, sir!'

'I do not wish to give offence to the gentleman who usually attends.'

(Oh the kindness! Oh the thoughtfulness! But he won't mind a bit!)

'It is just that I would like — if it is at all possible — to see a clergyman from Cloisterham. I would like to see — that is, if he himself has no objection to making the visit — I would like to see the Reverend Septimus Crisparkle.'

Whatever objections the Reverend Crisparkle might have had, remained unspoken as Mrs. Crisparkle, shocked and distressed by the idea, made haste to put forward her own.

'It is not your place to go, Sept,' said she, staring rather fiercely at her son. 'It is for the prison chaplain, dear!'

'Yes, Ma. You are right. It is for the prison chaplain,' said Septimus, agreeing with his mother somewhat mechanically, as if the haunted look in his eyes (which corresponded with a haunted feeling in his heart), was concerned with something quite different.

'There, Miss Landless! He says so himself!' said Mrs. Crisparkle, turning to Helena, who, much recovered, was at Minor Canon Corner for the Sunday afternoon.

Helena nodded; and Mrs. Crisparkle, taking this for assent to her own proposition, continued:

'So it is not your duty to go, Sept.'

'No, Ma. It is not my duty.'

'There, Miss Landless! Did you hear? He says so himself!'

Again Mrs. Crisparkle applied to Helena, and again Helena nodded; and again it was not entirely to Mrs. Crisparkle's satisfaction.

In fact it might be said that Helena Landless herself was not entirely to the good lady's satisfaction. It was not that Mrs. Crisparkle at all disliked Helena; indeed, she thought her very lovely (in a dark, un–English way) and was truly sorry for her tragic situation; it was just that she could not help feeling her to be too young, too wild (with her cropped hair and disturbing eyes) and with too much of the mysterious East about her for the comfort of Minor Canon Corner.

Here it must be admitted that the neat, precise, pretty old lady had an unconquerable distrust of the East. Even the East referred to as being the provenance of the Three Wise Men and the Christmas Star, she thought of, for the sake of inward peace, as being situated somewhere in the vicinity of Margate, and the inn, stable and manger as being of sturdy English manufacture. Consequently she was unhappy and bewildered, was the china shepherdess; (to whom, of course, the very shepherds who had watched in the fields were china shepherds, with china sheep, and worshipping a china Babe.)

'It is not as if he was a friend, Sept,' she went on, to her troubled son.

'No, Ma. You are right. He was never a friend.'

'There, Miss Landless! Sept says himself that he was never a friend. Oh, Sept! It was very wrong of him to ask! He had no right to ask you, dear.'

'No, Ma. He had no right.'

'Oh Miss Landless! You must tell him that he should not go! It will upset him dreadfully. I know it will.'

Again she turned to the dark, silent girl; and again she received no more than a grave nod in response. 'She is heartless!' thought the china shepherdess bitterly. 'She wants him to go! She wants him to suffer!'

In a way, the good lady was right. Helena, seeing all too clearly the wretchedness of the Minor Canon, did indeed wish him to overcome it by enduring it to the end; but she was far from heartless. Her heart was breaking as she saw the anguish reflected in Septimus's face; and, though she wanted desperately to lend him support, she could think of no way of doing so without adding to the general distress.

'I must go now, Ma,' said Septimus at length. 'You know that I must go, Ma.'

'I don't know anything of the kind! Really I don't, Sept!'

'I will be back tomorrow, Ma.'

'Oh Sept! My Sept!'

'Helena, dear Helena, will you stay with my mother until I come back?'

A last grave nod from the girl, a last look from the Minor Canon; and then he left the parlour, left the house and left Minor Canon Corner to comfort the condemned man in his last night upon earth, and to go with him, even to the very scaffold.

He walked to the Assize town. Though it was all of nine miles, he walked, avoiding, where he could, the easy road, and choosing, in preference, the roughest way. He strode, across heavy fields and down the stoniest and narrowest of lanes, so that the hawthorn hedges, after he had passed by, seemed spangled, not with berries but with the Minor Canon's blood.

He chose the roughest, harshest way, not because it was the shortest, but because he felt the need of some outward pain to distract him from the leaden apprehension that clutched at his soul. Had there been a raging torrent at hand, he would have swum it; had there been a fire, he would have walked through it.

'Oh give me the uncomplaining animals,' he muttered, as he strode through the darkening day, 'that go to their deaths without philosophising!'

He feared what the man would say to him; he feared how the man would look at him; and he feared, even to contemplate, what the man must be thinking now. He had, in the course of his duties, attended the dying before; but not like this. There had never been such a dreadful certainty of the very hour, the very minute, *known to both of them,* so that there could not be even the fraillest thread of hope to be offered and gratefully clutched at.

He reached the Assize town in the gloom of evening and saw, with a shudder, that the scaffold was already prepared outside the gaol. How like a stage it was!

He inquired for the condemned man, and explained that he had been sent for.

'Oh yes, sir! You are expected. No need to be distressed, sir. You will find him in wonderful spirits. Really quite like you and me! If you will follow me, sir. This way . . . along this passage and down the steps.'

His guide was a short, gray-haired man with a pleasant, unremarkable face that somehow conveyed the odd impression of being quite a good likeness of somebody or other. He talked rapidly and amiably as they walked through the stony, murmurous prison.

'He had a pain, the other day, sir, in his back. We had a doctor, of course, who prescribed physic, which, we are happy to say, did a little good; but of course, it takes time. The doctor was of the opinion that he needed to be taken out of himself.'

The Minor Canon glanced uneasily at his guide; but saw no ghost of an ironic smile. No gallows humour had been intended.

'Ah! Here we are, sir!'

They had come to a heavily barred door with a small barred window placed so high that the guide had to stand upon tiptoe to look within.

'As I said, sir, you will find him in good spirits . . . only he has one or two odd habits that you mustn't mind. We don't mention them, you understand; we don't like to. He has rather a queer way of looking at you every now and then. He draws one eyebrow right down and the other goes up as if it was ready to fly off. Don't be alarmed by it, sir; he don't mean anything by it. And sometimes he mixes up words. But I'm sure an educated gentleman like yourself will soon get the sense of it. My colleague or myself will peep in from time to time, to see if you require anything. But there is refreshment within. There is a bottle or two, sir . . . if you in-dulge. And why not, sir? As we say, bad for the liver but good for the head!'

With an apologetic shake of his head, he inserted a key in the lock, turned it and drew back the bolt. He knocked on the stout panel.

'In come,' came the voice of John Jasper.

'There! You see?' murmured the guide. 'He really meant to say, "Come in". But you'll soon get the hang of it, sir.'

He opened the door. The cell, no more than eight feet long by six feet wide, was lighted by a single oil-lamp suspended from the ceiling. It was heavily barred, like everything else, so that the flame within was an ingenious representation of the prisoner himself. There was a small window that presumably gave out onto a yard; a plain table, two chairs and a stone bench on which there was a mattress. The prisoner's books were neatly piled on the floor with the exception of the one he had been engaged in reading, which lay upon the table.

'The gentleman from Cloisterham is come, sir,' said the guide; and John Jasper rose from his chair to greet the Minor Canon.

'It is exceedingly good of you, Mr. Crisparkle. I appreciate your kindness.'

He extended his hand, which Septimus would have taken, had not Jasper moved his to one side as if there had been another, phantom hand that took precedence over the Minor Canon's. Bewildered, Septimus glanced back to the door, and was reassured by a nod from the guide, who then shut the door upon them and was heard to bolt it, doubtless apologetically.

When he turned back, he was startled, though he had been prepared for it, by the look on Jasper's face. One eye was bulging incredulously, while the other had quite disappeared under the heavily drawn down brow. Then the curious expression vanished, and the Reverend Septimus saw that John Jasper was excessively pale, with a yellowish transparency about him, due partly, perhaps, to the yellow light cast by the lamp.

'We have not met for some time, Mr. Crisparkle; and we have for not longer even talked,' said Jasper, frowning slightly as if he suspected he had misplaced some words but could not quite determine where.

He gestured the Reverend Septimus to a chair and resumed his own. The Minor Canon seated himself and wondered, rather emptily, what he should say. He had, during his long and painful walk, attempted to find forgiveness in his heart for John Jasper's crime, forgiveness for the deceit of the man, forgiveness for his pretence, and forgiveness for the monstrous way he had sought to throw suspicion on another. He had attempted to find within himself that calm radiance that a man of his calling ought to have had, that would reach out and comfort the distressed soul. But as he sat opposite the condemned man, he could feel nothing, absolutely nothing; and was consequently bitterly ashamed of the shallowness of his own feelings.

He glanced down at the book that lay on the table between them, and saw, with a slight pang of guilt, that it was the Book of Common Prayer. His sense of guilt arose because he realised that he had come away from Cloisterham without any book of his own. Jasper, observing his visitor's look, pushed the book towards him; or, rather, towards a phantom visitor by his side. The Reverend Septimus took and examined it as if he had never laid eyes on such a volume before. It had once been the property, he noted from a gilt inscription on the cover, of a clergyman in Crewkerne, who would have been much astonished had he known its present whereabouts.

'I was reading,' said Jasper, taking back the book and opening it, 'the Morning Prayer. When the —' he began, when a church clock, somewhere in the town, started to strike. At once Jasper looked up from the book with the same extraordinary, quizzical expression he had displayed before, as if he was a wonderfully critical clockmaker listening for a fault in the chime. At the same time his lips moved with amazing rapidity and when the clock had finished on its seventh stroke, he remarked:

'Forty six thousand eight hundred, I think.'

He returned to the book.

'It says here, "When the wicked man turneth away from his wickedness".'

'"That he hath committed",' interposed the Minor Canon softly, '"and doeth that which is lawful and right" —'

'Yes, yes!' exclaimed Jasper a trifle impatiently, '"He shall live his soul a-safe!" I know! I know! But it is about the wicked man. You and I, my dear Crisparkle, must think about him. We must do what we can for him.' Again the grotesquely quizzical look. 'Forty six thousand, six hundred and ninety.'

There came a knock on the door and the Reverend Septimus, looking to the little window, saw his guide's head pop up, like a frog from a pond. A moment later, the bolt was drawn and the guide entered, carrying a tray with two bottles of claret and two glasses.

"Forty six thousand eight hundred"

'I said there was refreshment, sir; if you would be so kind as to help our gentleman when he wishes. Bad for the liver but good for the head, as we say.'

'We must do what we can for the wicked man,' repeated the Minor Canon, unconsciously suiting his action to the words by pouring out wine after the guide had departed.

'Thank you, Crisparkle. That is kind of you. I spill it, you know. That is why they take it away. I believe, also, that they fear I might break a glass and cut myself.'

'The wicked man. What of him?'

Jasper, who had been conveying his glass into his ear, it seemed, set it down and his strange look became almost ferocious.

'Ah! The rubble tris, Cristerparkle, the trouble is that he has *not* turned away from his wickedness. Not away! I have done what I can; but I am at my wit's end! I do not know what to do! Really! I want know to do what! Oh my friend, I have tried! But the wretched fellow, the wretched fellow!'

He took up his glass and Septimus gently guided it to his lips. Jasper drank, and went on:

'He has always been the same, even when we were children. He used to tell me of the wild and terrible things he wanted to do. I said nothing, because he was a child, and I hoped it would pass. But it never did; and the more I tried to turn away from him, to show him my disgust, the more frightful became the things he talked about. Yet he was talented, so talented! He had a better voice than mine, and was far more musical. He might have done great things, composed great anthems to the glory of God. But no! He had only eyes for the demons that were carved under the seats of the Choir. Wretched fellow! But what could I do with him? I tried. I never stopped trying. I went with him, even, to those places of infamy that he delighted in; those fearful smoking dens, and worse. He laughed in my face. I warned him that I would speak with the Dean about him; that I would see that he was dismissed from the Cathedral. But of course, he knew that I wouldn't. Forty five thousand eight hundred and fifty two!'

Jasper paused on this last, inexplicable announcement; and the Reverend Septimus took the opportunity of pouring out more wine and guiding the glass once more to Jasper's lips. Then he listened, with increasing bewilderment and anguish, as the divided man went on:

'Hoped I had, Parklecris, really hoped that someone might bring him to his senses. I thought Rosa might, dear, lovely Rosa. But he spoke of her in such terms, expressed such wild desires that I was forced to clap my hands to my ears! He said he loved her. Love? What was love to him? I remembered how he had talked of it when we were children. Oh it was monstrous! I warned him that she was destined for another, for my nephew, Ned. I told him that she would spit on him if she knew an inkling of what he had said. I told him that Ned would thrash him with a whip. I told him all this; and his only answer was, "Then Kill Ned!" He planned it weeks and weeks before he did it; and nothing I could say would make him change his mind. Wretched fellow! Wretched, wretched fellow!

'Poor Ned came back from walking with Neville Landless late that night; and he talked a little wildly of Rosa, and showed the ring. We drank, perhaps too much, and I proposed a walk outside in the wild wind, to clear our heads. He took advantage of it. He had always intended to use the monument, and had the key with him all the time. He waited until we were quite near to the place; for why not get Ned to walk to his own grave? I could do nothing. He had strangled my poor boy with a black scarf, even as I watched. So quick! Scarcely a struggle, scarcely a gasp. Dead. I shrank from him in horror. This, this he had come to! Murder! I would never speak to him again! For answer, he wrote in my diary that Neville had done it, that Neville must be punished. And he hunted Neville down.'

'Yet why, why did you not speak to someone of — of him?' whispered

Septimus, terrified by the thought of the agony the man must have endured.

'How could I?' cried Jasper fiercely, striking, not the table, but the air beside it. 'How could I when, every time he swore to me that, if I held my tongue he would repent? And is it not said that he who converts a sinner shall save a soul? So what could I do? Even at the trial I said nothing; for he promised that, if I did not betray him, he would repent. I tried, I tried so hard to save that soul! But it is damned. He has not turned away from his wickedness. I know it. He has told me. So what is to be done? What is to be done with him now? How can we help him? What can we do for him, my friend?'

Jasper wept in despair; and, raising his glass, thrust forward his lips and poured the wine upon his shoulder. Septimus gently wiped away the liquid and refilled the glass. His eyes fell upon the opened book.

' "To the Lord our God belong mercies and forgivenesses" . . .'

'I know, I know, and the Kingdom of Heaven is at hand,' said Jasper, with an aching weariness. 'Forty two thousand, two hundred and fifty. Shall I tell you what he says of the Kingdom of Heaven? Hearsay, hearsay, always hearsay; but never, never *theresay*. What can be done, then, with a wretched fellow like that?'

'I will read to you; and to him,' murmured the Minor Canon. 'I will talk to you; and to him. We will succeed; you and I.'

'But there is so little time, so little time! I am frightened to go with him, you know. I am frightened that even *then* he will not turn away.'

'I will go with him,' whispered the Minor Canon. 'We will go together. I promise you that.'

'Oh the wretched fellow!' sighed Jasper. 'What a singer he might have been! Listen!'

And Jasper began to sing, not an anthem, but an old tavern song, with a great many farewells and adieus, and damsels dark on Friday nights, and turtle doves carved upon breasts to signify that the singer died of love.

When the Battle's Lost
and Won!

THE night has passed and the arrival of glorious morn is signalled by a generalised grayness that creeps over the prison, as if it has aged, frightfully. The walls are gray, the heavy, studded door is gray, and the smoke that drifts up from unseen chimneys makes long gray smudges upon the gray sky. In all this grayness there is but one blot of black, as if the morning has forgotten it; as if it is some oblong pit into which the morning pours and pours, and vanishes. It is however nothing more remarkable than several yards of thick black cloth that have been draped about the lower portion of the scaffold.

In the cell, the little window that gives out upon the yard has also gone gray, and consequently the flame inside the barred lamp presents a starved and ghastly appearance. Nor do the two men, who still sit at the table, opposite one another, display in their weary faces any of that rapturous heraldry popularly reputed to accompany the rising of the sun.

Two empty bottles on the floor, and two more on the table, together with a plate of cake-crumbs, suggest that they have made a night of it; and, in consequence, both now stand in need of an early night. (For one it will be early indeed.)

They talk little now, and chiefly in commonplaces. Although they are not, in any way that is generally understood, friends, they are most profoundly acquainted, so that their commonplaces carry great weight.

Comes the barber, with razors, towels and bowl and smooth-faced boy to learn the trade, who gazes at the two men and wonders which it is who should be the object of peculiar interest. Presently the cell is steamy and agreeable with the smell of soap. The barber remarks that he thinks the day will turn out fine, but does not specify at what o'clock. Begs Mr. Jasper to unscrew his face a little as he does not wish to cut him.

'Five thousand, four hundred,' says Jasper, as a half hour strikes.

Comes breakfast, brought by the watchers who carry napkins, like waiters, and bow the barber out. Remark on how smart and fresh the gentlemen look. 'Considering!' they add, as they pick up the empty bottles with a laugh.

'Bad for the liver, but good for the head, as we say!'

They stand by the door, as if waiting for more toast to be ordered.

'There is quite a nip in the air,' says one; while the other begs mildly to disagree and points out that, if one wraps up warm, one hardly notices.

'I really think, sir, that if one is to go outside, one would quite enjoy it. If one wears a coat and gloves, one might find it a pleasant stroll. I do not think there is anying that could possibly inconvenience one.'

'Three thousand six hundred,' says Jasper, bulging an incredulous eye.

Comes a dull sound from outside, as of someone stamping on wooden boards, and a murmuring of many voices, and a shuffling of many feet. The two watchers look bland and unconcerned, as if (if one puts one's mind to it and enters into the spirit of things), one can hear nothing that need cause one the slightest alarm.

'A glass of brandy, sir? If one is to go outside, one might well take a little brandy first.'

Come footsteps in the passage outside and, briefly, a strange face peers through the window in the door. It is a face that, though glimpsed but for an instant, impresses by the singularly sweet expression in its small gray eyes.

'A gentleman from London, sir. No concern of yours, we assure you.'

'One thousand, eight hundred.'

'More brandy, sir? You spilled a little before. A hat, sir? No. It is not really so cold as that. Your cravat, sir? We cannot imagine what has become of it. But no matter. If, sir, you button up your coat, it will not be noticed.'

More footsteps, and a party of solemn dignitaries arrives. They wait.

'Well, now, sir, I think we may say that we have passed the time pleasantly. I'm sure my friend will join with me in wishing you the very best. There is really, sir, nothing to worry about, nothing at all. Oh! That is very kind of you, sir, very kind indeed! Your cuff-links . . . and — and your watch?'

'Let me see it for a moment! Ah! Six hundred!'

Jasper, with the Minor Canon at his side, steps out of his cell and the waiting party closes round him, to escort him along the stony passage and into the morning air. As he no longer has a watch, he is forced to reckon, by the ticking of his heart, how many seconds remain.

How many now? What? A mere four hundred? How can all those thousands have gone by? That fellow in front of me has bunions by the way he walks! Poor Crisparkle! He looks quite worn out. He must go to bed early. I'm sure the Dean will excuse him.

Ah! It is quite a fine day after all! But they were right. There *is* a nip in the air. It strikes through to the bone.

'A hundred and fifty.'

What a crowd, what a crowd! And so many women and children! That little one there will surely be crushed to death! And who is that? Isn't that a face I know?

'The steps, John Jasper. Shall I help you up the steps, my friend?'

'Thank you, Crisparkle. That is kind of you. I do seem to stumble a little.'

Good God! Such shouting, such cheering! It deafens me! That face now. The one I knew. Where is it?

He glares about him, his strange grimace more pronounced than ever; he glares about him, anywhere but at the dreadful object to which he must come.

'A hundred, is it? No, no! Ninety! No, no! I have lost count! It is sixty, sixty! No, no! Even as I think, it is going! How long, how long?'

Again he stares frantically for that face he knew; and, not finding it, returns to his desperate calculations that, in the end, have gone awry.

A hand touches him upon the shoulder. He turns and stares into a pair of small gray eyes, whose expression is singularly sweet.

'Come, friend,' says this person, quietly. 'Let me help you on with it.'

And, in a moment, Jasper finds himself fitted very neatly with a complicated harness of buckles and straps.

'My own invention,' says the person, with an undeniable pride. 'It won't chafe, you see. It won't cause no inconvenience at all.'

And he buckles the straps about Jasper's arms and legs.

'Jasper! John Jasper!' cries out Septimus. 'He has turned away! I know he has turned away!'

'Now you won't bite, friend,' says the person with sweet eyes, fumbling in his pocket and drawing out a black bag. 'You won't bite when I slips it on? There's no call to bite me, for it's nothing, really, nothing at all.'

'His soul shall be saved alive!' shouts Septimus, his voice straining to be heard above the roaring of the crowd as they see the last preparations.

'Here, friend, just this bag over your head.'

'Hide thy face from my sins, and blot out mine iniquities,' says John Jasper, as the world shuts its eyes.

'Here, friend, this is it.'

There is a dreadful moment, inside the musty darkness, when Jasper's mind quakes with horror and he thinks that what is happening cannot possibly happen; and, like a child, he believes with all his heart that, at any instant, a lady in spangles and tights will come, and wave a wand, and set him free. Then his mind clears, and he sees the wicked man on the scaffold beside him; and the wicked man turns, not away, but towards him, and weeps. Three . . . two . . . one.

Towards Another Christmas

SHORTLY after nine o'clock on the same Monday morning, Mr. Bazzard, clutching to his bosom a very large brown paper parcel that attracted the vociferous admiration of the dog Snap, entered Staple Inn. His face, when visible above the parcel, and when not directed discouragingly towards the dog Snap, was seen to be stamped with that aching melancholy associated equally with authors and mothers, following the production of a child. He had just returned from a visit to Norfolk where, at last, he had summoned up his courage and mentioned, in passing (loitering might better have expressed it) his artistic triumph. It had been greeted with vile ignorance and a surly demand to know if there was any money in it.

'Man doth not live by bread alone,' Bazzard had quoted; upon which Bazzard Senior had basely leaped to the conclusion that there had been no money in it and, therefore, it was, financially speaking, worthless; and, under pain of parental displeasure, Bazzard was not to do it again.

Following this remonstrance, Bazzard Senior had requested his son to convey his compliments to Mr. Grewgious, together with a turkey of gigantic size. This article, this monstrous, bloated fowl, wrapped in brown paper, was, to Bazzard, a fearful insult. It was as if his father was presenting it to Mr. Grewgious in compensation for what he, Bazzard, had done. Consequently the dead bird with its wrung neck represented, to Bazzard, the blind contempt of a blind world.

He entered his employer's chamber and was surprised to learn, from the woman who cleaned, that the lawyer had overslept and had only just awakened.

'It is really after nine, then, Bazzard?' inquired the head of Mr. Grewgious, putting in an exceedingly tousled and bewildered appearance round the door.

'Yes. It is.'

'Good heavens! I thought my watch must have been wrong! Nine o'clock —'

'Ten minutes past. I am sorry that I am late.'

'Oh no! Not at all, Bazzard! Please do not think that I meant to reproach you! But I can hardly believe that it is already — *already* after nine!'

'Well, it is.'

The head vanished and, after a moderate interval during which Mr. Bazzard wondered idly why the lawyer should have appeared so pleased with himself to have overslept, the whole of Mr. Grewgious emerged, attired for the day, glad to see Bazzard back, glad that his family was well, and highly delighted to receive the deceased fowl.

'We shall have it tonight!' he declared, rubbing his hands together in an anticipatory fashion. 'If it can be prepared in time, we shall dine off it tonight! I hope you will join us, Bazzard? There will be Miss Rosa, Lieutenant Tartar and myself. There is some claret I have been saving that I think will be very suitable. I hope, Bazzard, that you have no other engagement for tonight?'

Bazzard, having no other engagement, agreed to haunt the festive board with his gloomy presence; while Mr. Grewgious returned to the extraordinary occurrence of his having overslept, which he had not done for years. Indeed, he kept returning to it at intervals throughout the day, and shaking his head, as if it was a matter of total astonishment to him that, on this morning of all mornings, the bustle of the day should have failed to awaken him; that, on this morning of all mornings, he should have been asleep when the City clocks struck eight, and remained asleep for a whole hour afterwards, so that a certain nameless event that had taken place outside the prison in the Assize town at eight o'clock (and the twenty minutes during which the body had been suspended thereafter) was now in the past.

It was over; and he had slept through it. There was no doubt that the lawyer was light-hearted; and equally, there was no doubt that his light-heartedness concealed a vague, gnawing sense of shame. It was shame for no particular reason, unless it was because he had not stood, with bowed head, when the fatal hour had struck.

Nonetheless the light-heartedness was well-sustained, and, when the time came, enlivened the little party that gathered in his chambers for dinner that night.

'For this, we must give thanks to Mr. Bazzard's father!' he exclaimed, as the defunct bird, magically transformed by the agency of a discreet fairy from Furnival's, emerged in steaming glory from the concealment of a large, plated dome.

'Thanks to Mr. Bazzard's father!' cried Lieutenant Tartar, raising his glass.

'And thanks to Mr. Bazzard!' added Rosa, her eyes shining in the candlelight more brightly, it seemed, than the candles themselves.

Rosa was in London, and staying in Furnival's Inn, at the suggestion of her guardian, as a certain matter had come to such a pass that its resolution could not conveniently be effected at Miss Twinkleton's, in Cloisterham. Or so the lawyer felt; and so did Rosa, and so did Lieutenant Tartar, without the slightest hesitation.

This decisiveness on the part of the sailor filled the angular old lawyer with admiration. He himself was always wracked with doubt. But then, he reflected, he had never had men under his command (save Bazzard, who seemed to command *him*); had never been exposed to storm and tempest (save once, long ago, when he had foundered and gone down without a word); and still had such a dread of water that he could not, even now, look upon a river without thinking of a young woman, drowned.

"All happiness and prosperity!"

'Would you oblige me by carving, dear sir?' Mr. Grewgious asked; and Lieutenant Tartar, feeling that his whole career was at stake, that rocks loomed and grapeshot was in the air, firmly took the implements and dismasted the fowl with consummate skill.

Smilingly the lawyer watched; and was filled with further admiration for the sailor's practicality. Those firm hands, thought Mr. Grewgious, have already made a garden in the air; how much more lovely a garden will they make upon the land!

Two dusty bottles of claret, brought up from the cellar of P.J.T. stood upon the table. Their presence marked the resolution of that certain matter that had brought Rosa to London; for they were the last of the very wine in which Rosa's birth had been toasted — 'not so very long ago,' whispered the lawyer to himself.

'Mr. Bazzard!' said the lawyer. 'I am going to let you in to a secret. I am going to make you party to a matter of the greatest importance. This dinner, Bazzard, this dinner to which your father has so handsomely contributed, is by way of being an Occasion. A great occasion, perhaps the greatest I shall ever see. I have to tell you, Bazzard, that Lieutenant Tartar has asked Miss Rosa to marry him; and, furthermore, I have to tell you that his offer has been accepted! There, now, Bazzard, is that not a fine piece of news? Is that not something to which you and I should raise our glasses? Is that not something to which you and I should drink with full hearts?'

Poor Bazzard! When his employer had mentioned a great occasion, he had inevitably thought that a reference was being made to his play. However, he swallowed down his disappointment, and, raising his glass, said, with a tolerable impersonation of pleasure:

'To Miss Rosa and Lieutenant Tartar! All happiness and prosperity!'

The toast was drunk, and then Lieutenant Tartar proposed:

'Mr. Grewgious and Mr. Bazzard!'

Then Rosa proposed:

'The sailors of England, and one in particular!'

Then Lieutenant Tartar proposed:

'The young women of England, and one in particular!'

Then Mr. Grewgious proposed that they should do justice to Mr. Bazzard's gift, before it grew cold; which they did, and then proceeded to nuts, which kept going off like an ambush, while the wine spread an agreeably fanciful glow over the little table and the little party.

The old lawyer, his angularity much softened, kept gazing at his pretty ward, and marvelling, for the hundredth time, how grown-up she had become; and marvelling how she, the innocent cause of tragedy, had emerged from its shadow as fair and bright as the countryside itself emerged from the darkness of storm.

The innocent cause! Yet not really the cause, which lay, partly, in the folly of trying to unite destinies without reference to hearts. The lawyer shivered a little, as if a ghost had suddenly entered and breathed upon his back. Was it perhaps the ghost of Edwin Drood, returning to witness the betrothal of Rosa? The lawyer did not think so. Was it, then, the ghost of Neville Landless, returning to Staple Inn? The lawyer did not think so. He knew, in his heart of hearts, who it was who had joined the feast. He saw, between the shadows, between the looks, between the little silences, the dark eyes of John Jasper, gazing on the scene with a muffled sadness and regret.

'I wish,' Rosa was saying, 'that Helena could have been with us!'

'My dear,' said the lawyer, dismissing the ghost with a shake of his head, 'I understand she is not recovered sufficiently.'

'But Crisparkle must be with her,' said Lieutenant Tartar. 'I can think of nobody better than him!'

'It was you who saved his life!' said Rosa, implying pretty definitely that, she, most certainly, *could* think of somebody better.

'He makes more of it than I do!' said the sailor with a smile. 'I think he might have saved himself, you know! He really is a wonderful fellow. Another man, having nearly been drowned, would never have gone near the water again. But he! He went straight back and learned to swim!'

'Did not you teach him?' asked Rosa, unwilling to yield a jot of her lover's glory.

The sailor laughed.

'Yes, I taught him. But the credit, you know, must always be his. After all, I was an insignificant junior, while he was a hero of the school. It takes much, I think, for someone full grown to learn from a child!'

But Rosa would not have it, and maintained her lover's excellence until the nuts, the wine, the talk and the candles gave out. Then all ended in departures and the room was left to the glimmering shadows cast by the dying fire. Strange shadows, sometimes like reaching hands that brushed across the empty bottles on the table.

'Come,' they seemed to whisper, 'let us drink the ghost of the wine.' And the bottles smiled in the firelight, even as other bottles had seemed to smile in the starved, wasted light of a barred lamp.

The barred lamp, with its starved prisoner within, stayed curiously and obstinately in the Minor Canon's memory as he returned to Cloisterham, this time by way of the omnibus. Its image remained with him even more strongly than did the hideous images of the morning. It swung and gleamed in the darkness of his thoughts with such clarity that his inner eye became dazzled by looking at it, and he would have closed it, if he could, to give some relief. But he could not evade it, and it was before him even as he approached Minor Canon Corner, where the ivy rustled warningly, as if it suspected him of hostile intent.

Mrs. Crisparkle, who had been apprised by Helena (who had never ceased looking out of the window) of her son's coming, had hastened to provide a large draught of Constantia; but even she, when she greeted him, felt that all the remedies in her cabinet would be insufficient to restore a spirit so deeply sunk. She felt, with a sudden clutch of fear, that perhaps there was no remedy, that her Sept, her good, kind, cheerful Sept, had been injured beyond redress. (Yet in her heart of hearts she knew there *was* a remedy, only to her it was a remedy worse than the disease.)

'Sept! Oh Sept!' she cried. 'How ill you look, my dear! You must go to bed directly! You are quite worn out! Miss Landless, must he not go to bed at once?'

Helena looked at him gravely.

'Was it,' she murmured, 'was it very hard for you?'

'I think it was harder for . . . him.'

'Oh do not talk of such things now!' cried the china shepherdess. 'You must not! Tell him, Miss Landless, that he must not talk of such things! He must put them out of his mind! He must sleep and forget! Is that not so, Miss Landless?'

'I cannot tell, ma'am,' said the girl quietly; and the china shepherdess's eyes filled with china tears, that made them sparkle prettily, like a child's. She was half afraid of the girl, whose strange power, she sensed, had driven her son from the quiet contentment of the Cathedral Close to the very end of the world. And to what purpose, to what purpose?

'He was a wicked man,' murmured Septimus, rubbing his eyes with thumb and forefinger as if to dispel some image within. 'Yet he turned away from his wickedness.'

'I do not want to hear about it!' wept Mrs. Crisparkle. 'Please, Miss Landless, tell him that he must stop!'

'Your mother is right,' said Helena. 'Please do not distress her any more.'

'Helena, dearest Helena,' said Septimus, with a quick glance towards his mother as if to make sure that she was comfortably settled and in no danger of falling to the ground. 'Dearest Helena, can you find it in your heart to marry a humble Minor Canon?'

'Sept! Oh Sept!' wailed the china shepherdess. 'Miss Landless, he does not know what he is saying! Miss Landless, tell him to stop!'

'I must tell you to stop, sir,' said Helena, her dark eyes glowing and shining with tears. 'Your mother bids me.'

'Can you find it in your heart, dearest Helena,' pursued the humble Minor Canon, regardless of the order to cease, 'to marry one who has long loved you, but has long been afraid to declare it?'

'Miss Landless! He must rest! He is tired! Do not let him go on!'

'Your mother bids me to tell you that you are tired, sir.'

'Can you find it in your heart, dearest, dearest Helena, to return that love?'

'Miss Landless, Miss Landless, he is unwell! You must tell him so!'

'Your mother bids me tell you, sir, that you are unwell. And in answer to your question, sir, I am sick with the same complaint. I am, dear Septimus, quite sick with love for you!'

*   *   *

The foregoing events, having taken place around the middle of October, it follows that, by December they were not considered worthy of remark; and even the chief protagonists were themselves so occupied with new coats, new hats, new trousers, new gowns, new veils, new shoes and, in Lieutenant Tartar's case, a new house, that the course of events that had conducted them to their present situation had become something of the stuff that dreams are made on; with, however, the proviso that revels, far from being ended, were about to begin.

The Pantomime is announced; the Waxworks returned (presumably in compensation for the loss of Miss Twinkleton's young ladies who are gone on their holidays) and mistletoe and holly abound in Cloisterham in a regrettably Pagan fashion.

Mr. Sapsea has got over his horrible disappointment and has discovered that Miss Ferdinand's first name is Rosanna (for which 'Rosa' might well be taken as a shortened form) and entertains sanguine hopes of that lively maiden's becoming the recipient of Mr. Brobity's snuff-box and, consequently, the Mayoral hand. Possibly in the New Year.

Durdles, in celebratory mood, has thrice seen the ghost of the Choir Master, dancing a jig under the Cathedral porch (and has been taken up for it); and Deputy is mysteriously in Christmas funds.

Even the Topes are in good spirits; for Mrs. Tope has let her lodgings again; an event which had been quite beyond her hopes. She has let it to Mr. Datchery; for Mr. Datchery, by devious means, desperate falsehoods and frantic ingenuities, has succeeded in withdrawing, first his belongings and then (in the smallest of small hours) himself from Mrs. MacSiddons's establishment by way of the window, leaving behind for the consolation of the deceived one, his handsome collection of hats.

Of all professions, that of the actor exerts the strongest hold on its practitioners. No matter how far the Stage might lie behind them, there is always an audience in the heart. Sooner would a leopard change his spots, an elephant forget his trunk, than an actor quite give up acting and forgo the relish of a part.

Of all the parts that Mr. Datchery has played — tyrants, princes, soldiers, porters — that of an idle buffer getting through life on his means, appeals to him most strongly at the present time. In fact, so strongly does it appeal, that the man has quite become the part, and, with certain minor adjustments, the part has become the man. These adjustments are chiefly concerned with the idle buffer's means, which, it turns out, are not quite up to his getting through life comfortably on them. So, with the very greatest delicacy, and with the utmost refinement (in which nothing in the nature of a salary is actually mentioned out loud) Mr. Datchery has been persuaded to undertake lessons in the Drama to the young ladies of Miss Twinkleton's school; and has been included in the Prospectus for the New Year.

In consequence of this arrangement, it has of course been necessary for Mr. Datchery to take tea with Miss Twinkleton on more than one occasion. But whether these visits are at all connected with a fresh crop of chalked marks that have appeared on the inside of his cupboard door, is purely conjectural; as must be any connection between the preponderance of mistletoe and Mr. Datchery's returning from The Nuns' House with a broad smile and remarking, chalk in hand, that:

'I think I am entitled to a moderate stroke.'

Then, Mrs. Tope's care having spread a very agreeable supper, he shuts the cupboard door and falls to with an appetite.

About the Author

Leon Garfield was born in Brighton, England, in 1921 and was educated there. His brief art studies were interrupted by the outbreak of World War II, when he joined the army and served in the medical corps for five years. After the war he worked as a biochemist until his success as an author enabled him to write full-time. He is the winner of many awards, including the Boys' Club of America Junior Book Award, the 1967 Manchester Guardian Award for Children's Fiction, the Arts Council Prize of 1969, the 1966–68 Best Book for Older Children, and the 1971 Carnegie Medal for *The God Beneath the Sea*. Among his many books are *Jack Holborn, Black Jack, The Confidence Man,* and *John Diamond*.